D1739869

LINES OF FLIGHT

Lines of Flight is a rich, many-layered portrait of Rita Finnerty, a young Australian artist living and working in France. Through an exploration of her various relationships, past and present, the novel traces the symbiotic evolution of her personal and artistic lives.

Concerned with personal location and expression, *Lines of Flight* is a vivid, poetic account of the ambiguity of the female situation. Conscious of the difficulty of language, that women are defined by default against the male position, it is a novel about moving away from self-obsession and concern with identity.

Marion Campbell is a writer of great versatility and originality. With sympathy, humour and language that is both vital and precise, she has produced a first novel which is a highly sophisticated *tour de force*.

Cover photograph (Solar Salt Ponds) *by Richard Woldendorp.*

Born in Sydney in 1948 Marion Campbell attended the Universities of New South Wales, Western Australia and Provence, France. She has published essays and short fiction in journals and anthologies, and in 1988, a second novel, *Not Being Miriam* (FACP) which won the Western Australian Literary Week Award for Fiction. More recently she has written for the theatre: *Dr Memory in the Dream Home* (in collaboration with composer, Stuart Davies Slate) and *Adriadne's Understudies* (in collaboration with director, Noelle Janaczewska). She is currently short-listed for the Canada-Australia Literary Award.

She teaches in the English and Comparative Literature programme at Murdoch University.

LINES OF FLIGHT

LINES OF FLIGHT

a novel

MARION CAMPBELL

FREMANTLE ARTS CENTRE PRESS

First published 1985 by
FREMANTLE ARTS CENTRE PRESS
193 South Terrace (PO Box 320), South Fremantle
Western Australia, 6162.

Reprinted 1992.

Copyright © Marion Campbell, 1985.

This book is copyright. Apart from any fair dealing for the purpose of
private study, research, criticism or review, as permitted under the
Copyright Act, no part may be reproduced by any process without written
permission. Enquiries should be made to the publisher.

Consultant Editor B. R. Coffey.
Designed by Susan-Eve Barrow Ellvey.
Production Manager Helen Idle.

Distributed in the USA and Canada by International Specialized Book
Services, Inc., 5602 N.E. Hassalo Street, Portland, Oregon 97213-3640, USA.

Typeset in 11/11 Garamond by City Typesetters and printed on 90gsm
Offset by Lamb Print, Perth, Western Australia.

National Library of Australia
Cataloguing-in-publication data

Campbell, Marion, 1948 — .
Lines of Flight.

ISBN 1 86368 0217.

I. Title.

A823.3

For
Fred Campbell
(1915-1952)

and for Roma

ACKNOWLEDGEMENTS

The author gratefully acknowledges the assistance of the Literature Board of the Australia Council during 1979 when she was the recipient of a New Writer's Grant.

Earlier versions of parts of this novel first appeared in *Decade: a selection of contemporary Western Australian short fiction* (edited by B. R. Coffey, Fremantle Arts Centre Press, 1982) as "Ramshackle" and in *Westerly* as "Peepshow" and "Celeste".

Publication of *Lines of Flight* was assisted by the Literature Board of the Australia Council, the Australian Federal Government's Arts funding and advisory body.

Fremantle Arts Centre Press receives financial assistance from the Western Australian Department for the Arts.

CONTENTS

I

CUMULO-NIMBUS

That orange. Chiaroscuro of the pitted skin. Oblique smudge of shadow and then a fainter reflection in the desk. Could be any time.

Of course you could do something with it, find some conjunction to situate it by. Pluck a line from the sleeve of some surrealist conjuror like: *Le ciel est bleu comme une orange* and frame after frame, juggle the alternatives. Seriously though. You could eliminate the perfectly satisfactory sphere of the orange on the desk, its attendant smudge and vertical ghost, and just present that suave link: *blue like an orange,* equating the blue sphere with the orange one, the colour with its complement, the yin with the yang or whatever. Pirouette out of contingency, kilojoules and francs per kilo. That's abstraction for you.

You certainly wouldn't paint its pitted skin. Why should it be a split, your leaving. We can call it a completion, a rounding off. I can round it off, swallow the idea of a sphere if you like, Laurence. Fill my head, fill it with the plump presence of this little globe, leave room for nothing else. That would be a worthy exercise? Not this endless tumbling out of sleep, this falling through a whole decade. There should be no more dreams, right? No more messy emotions. The orange is on the desk. Your train is leaving for Marseille at 16.50 and then there is the one for Paris. I can have the orange for breakfast.

My skull is pith, cerebrum contoured segments all tucked in snugly, convolutions containing the juice. Hold it, hold it, trying,

3

I'm trying but . . . head is cleaving, hemispheres pulling apart, cleft soon, no, that's a bad sign, the fragile membranes mustn't tear . . . and now, it's coming, coming again, that split showing the intimacy of it from the wrinkled pip right through the juicy plump tearing the pith the pitted skin and now this drop quivering in my palm . . . and you can take it in, simply that: the idea of the acid sting and then quietly prepare your palette. Not for the sensational smack the eater gets. There is simply some relation to be established between the smarting orange and the possibility of blue. *The sky is blue like an orange,* or something like that. The sky is not polarized, will not snap. There is no whip-crack with the lightning jag. No drama. Of course you are right. It's simply a matter of *calm sight not vision,* even I know that. You put your back to the sky: it's too busy with other clues. In your storm painting, the future fruit emerges from that filigree division. And there it is: blue like an orange. You affirm the idea of wholeness.

Here are the bits of broken peel, the pale withered pips on the desk. The sky is undifferentiated, grey, sun dissolved in the wash. Could be any time. Laurence could have left by now. Slipped out. Decided it's better that way. *No more dramas.*

Stripped bare already. Slight Ajax dust lifting from the sink with the draught. She has dismantled it. The whole portable decor: hangings, curtains, rugs, drawings all gone. There is no bequest. As bleached out as a Carmelite's cell this. Maybe the violets; but they have darkened and folded. No sound, nothing from the studio either. It's no longer that anyhow. A hiatus, a designified space, reverted to the *trois pièces* Sérisier will advertise at the Office de Tourisme.

She must be at the station already. The Rue Van Loo Boulangerie has a mid-afternoon look, those shadows . . . Aix has washed, breakfasted, caught buses and trains, read papers, made money, consulted, evicted, kept appointments, poured bronzes at the Beaux Arts, bought flowers, cruised in cafés, lunched, siestaed, digested and now is back buying, selling, consulting again. I didn't wake up, she didn't wake me. Yes, blundering farewells should be avoided. We have gone through it all too many times.

That one I am leaving for you, she said.

And before I got out the Oh Laurence, she moved in deftly, her expert tongue emitting the quick succession of syllables, never tripping, never caught.

There is a possibility of a joint exhibition with Claude Wahl, so I won   want to include a lot of this.

And she leaves me this gold landscape, the one she calls the Inscape.

Pompous, posturing, precious, Denise calls her. No.

It is inscape with its minimal happenings, virtually effaced, the insect activity caught, fossilized below the surface.

Refusal of the rhetoric of expression.

Such a sparse calligraphy articulating the great spaces. Even the colour has only a tenuous hold, its denial leaving just this faint rhythm of ethereal breath. Thing of beauty constructed through elimination. At the interface between Zen quietus and nihilism. As if the sum total of human endeavour, all the struggles, all the querying through the centuries, were exactly equivalent to this: a rock face scarred with the indecipherable, gilded only by this wisp of a mirage, its own ironic emanation.

No, you see, I want to put all that behind me now, she said. Move on to other things. I'll be able to work in Claude's studio. He lets me be. He's not invasive.

Then that's what I've been. Invasive. Noise. Brute breath. Gesticulating personality. But I didn't tell her I got the nuance: only the hotness rushing to my face.

And you, Rita? You will carry on here, I suppose? Ah, society will reward you, Mademoiselle Finnerty. You tread the right paths.

Didn't say I got the jab intended and rattled off the automatic rosary, said I didn't know any more oh yes, the Beaux Arts with its easy praise for strong standing nudes and lyrical expressionism had been a survival kit but was all sham now, thought I was ready for some new departures.

Then her lips made a funnel, her nostrils dilated as she nursed the bony thrust of her knees in her hands. The rippling, almost continuous cylinder of her silver bracelets: *Ah, mais REE-TAH* if you only would. You talent has always been more robust than mine.

Knew what that meant. That my work is readable to the whole world. The rips, jerks, opening fruits and staccato rhythms are all readable through basic drives of course. But hers can only be accommodated by more evolved spirits. By slow acquaintance with her work, a Happy Few will develop the faculties to receive it. Anyhow, I said nothing. Was able to get up and walk to the table, find something there to comment upon: You haven't packed these, Laurence. Of course she hasn't packed them, stupid. Note books, acrylic sketches, her open photograph album. The snap-shot taken when they first arrived in Australia.

Her father's fine Parisian bones half eroded in the glare. Laurence all limbs, flat-chested still. The same intent gaze on the camera, same oval eyes, the tapering of the lid towards the tuck in the corner, the darks of the pupils continued by the irises and the flash of the iridescent whites.

You were so alike, you and your father.

Yes we are alike, she said, musing, not very committed. She was watching the long cylinder of ash on my cigarette. It was just caught in my hand. There was a faint whiff of ammonia in the air. My throat was closing in its pulp. I coughed though, converted it to a laugh: You will get back your bond, I said. Got away quick, the stairs trembling the phantom images.

Now I can plant foot after foot between them. I did not fall then, will not fall now. Will get dressed, quick. Get to the station. She mightn't have left yet, always very cautious about time. My turbulent bed. Pull the cover over it all. The collapsed clothes from yesterday still in their vertical order on my boots, as if magically eluded. Shove them in the wardrobe. My blur in the mirror. Apply some kohl, give it eyes. *Yes, we are alike,* she can say that. Present tense. Back there in Australia, the great house by the river they rented. Tudor touch as an afterthought at the gables, the spired tower, shingled roof. European deciduous trees sifting the light, dappling the lawns.

But Rita, I hate it, she said. It's vulgar.

And when she saw mine: Knew you wouldn't live in one of their mock castles.

As if I had the choice.

Not like Arlie. Arlie said: S'pose your mum could have it brick veneered, you know, when she . . . gets the money?

6

The front door is pressed back into the shadows away from the garden. Dull white of animal fat, the fibro-cement exterior. Moulded into it, the great meat slab of the painted verandah. The wide overhang of the roof bends its shadows around it all, darkening the complicated play of passing cloud and reflected leaf venetian blind-folded at the windows. The red cement tongue of path, extending the verandah, is suddenly arrested at the letter-box. The roof heaps up its tile-upon-tile, variegated green to the big blue. The lawn is luxury. There is a name for it. *Superfine.* It subtly rashes legs afterwards like the lingering irritation of riverwater. The banksia's roughness against the superfine skin between the legs. Gnarled but strong rooted, it balances again and again away from its history of disequilibrium. The four legs lowered from the tree tilt the feet horizonwards. Knees blind-nudge the suburban street unfurling apron lawn upon apron lawn. Drop to a soft thud on this lawn. She must have said something to provoke it:

I'll show you his picture if you like.

They used to say: *The carpet is mushroom wall-to-wall.*

The carpet is mushroom coloured superfine and mushrooms are the carpet colour digestible, as oysters the sea as they slip away, the deep sea smell, the big wet organism contained in the neat membrane. The *chiffonier* is pruned back by the frame of the door, but as you advance, turrets arise in inextricably complex postscripts to the first impression.

Pillars wind around their own axes, mirrors catch glimpses of tree ramifications, syncopated butterfly flights, other accidents. Her pale, pale unblinking eyes and the paler stubble, wheaten, of the lashes. Pushing, recoiling, gesturing, recesses and bulges. The key is in one of the recesses, on the cool marble part, below the tier of mini-drawers. It jerks into the teeth of the lock. The door on the right pulls away. Sheer sonic veil behind: the crackling static of summer insects. The carpet is uniform wall-to-wall, but it has embossed mounds. They imprint textured welts on your knees and shins. The shoe-box is split on the side. Spills its slippery load as it is withdrawn. Photographs. In many the image has retreated into the sepia fog.

Families arranged in precarious little pyramids around garden benches, smarting at the camera-sun. Light enlarges noses astoundingly. Bellies of the children on a brighter plane too. The larger photographs curl around the other ones. Grandma's dynasties of cats. The Mullewa Tom. The Bunbury Cheshire. Tabbies on floral laps on striped deck-chairs, light-dappled. There he is on the deck of a ship. Shirt blossoming over the belt. Same benign camera-sun squint. The other photographs shuffle him away.

The leg in profile is poised above the other one on what must have been a prop of some kind. A few wiry hairs protrude above the horizon of the thigh. This was taken in gym. The neck is thickly muscular. There is a rush of blood, burns cheeks to a scorch. Carpet imprints floraflora binding me here. The back is arched with great ribspan to where the face nestles, fostered by its curve. The leg must have been lowered after the photograph, the towel unslung from the neck, stretched to slow whipcrack in the air and then saw-tense between the flexed back biceps as he laughs in the steamed up bathroom: Mon! *Could you fetch my pants?* Little beads condense and slow trickle down the mirror. Is buttock-heavy, calf-heavy, chest-tense, eyes puffed as if the face were foot-lit. Strokes the overnight beard, engines droning already, heavy bellied plane. That photograph catches the touch of fatigue, faces of the others darkened too, skeins of cloud rip past, heading for the big one, the big one metal belly buffeted in the flux of the canyons of it turbulence *turbulence* you learn that word at the age of three and cumulo *cumulo-nimbus* as the seas receive their human confetti man and man's machine with cloudburst pulverized come on come on collect your speedy particles ah no full fathom five this just a slight silt absorbed like communion wafer to the flat lapping seatongue and then the slow ooze osmosis. The journalists blunder past the window with the sealed face, their fingers are at the photographs: *Sorry Madam*, we've got a job to do. Headlines, yellow clippings unfurl.

Hey! Rita!

The voice cuts hemisphere from hemisphere. Wire through a plump cheese.

What are you doing there?

She is standing in the distended triangle of light at the kitchen door, in the crazy whirlpools of illuminated dust. Elsie knows more. She was five when it happened. The hem of her skirt is awry above the band-aided shins, the eyes are narrowing their glint, face looks contorted in pain or betrayal.

Ah just showing Arlie the fatcotoes the kkkcat photos.

Words come out all grated.

Should have cleared throat. She starts towards us but meditatively lunges at the apple wedged between thumb and forefinger. Dishclatter. Fridge closed. She knows the pull too. But she would never display the relics in the cardboard sarcophagus.

Brain revulsing. Summon up a catalogue voice.

Ah yes. Yes. Yes. This is the dog on the farm I told you about. Zozo. Kelpie. Good sheep dog. You were bitten alive by mosquitoes under those peppermint trees. The yellow eager eyes, the spurt of the tongue, and through the mean anatomy of the gums, the dust-puffed horizon.

Mmm, she says. *Mmm.*

The photographs slip one behind the other. Not as obedient as cards. The box is reloaded, its side gaping wide open now. The key droops, back in the lock.

Peepshow. Show you my father's body. And yours, blood still pounding in his ears, still with beard growth overnight, yours the unshowable. Showers behind drawn curtains, closed doors. Can't see Arlie's face, still lowered, hair-curtained. And now she tosses the hair back. A little saliva beads, balloons at the corner of the lip. A word inflated, sucked back. She knows now. She knows. It's locked up, nut-tight in the neat little skull. And now, now out it comes.

Yeah . . . in a five second yawn. Hate her furiously for the drawl of it.

She can still get up, walk easily down the entrance hall over the mushroom carpet and out through the door. She knows. She can even let the flywire door flap back, crush the superfine with foot after foot. Follow her to a pile of blue metal, weed infested, left on the edge of the block from the building . . . She kneels. The nylon dress foams around the dusty ankles. She plays limply with the blue metal, streams it through her fingers. She has it. Turning metal to liquid. Sibyl is closed. No oracles today.

But that wasn't really like him at all. And he didn't pose for it. It was just taken.

Oh. Really.

The voice changes register on the 'y', descends the scale, the metal dribbles from the parted fingers, her hair slides, hers not wiry, massive, parts like waterveil around the swan neck. The downy swan neck.

Well. What was he really like. This father of yours?

This father. As if there were . . . There is a series. Learn the *coquetterie* of orphans slipping from daddylap to daddylap.

He was a clown.

Ha. A clown. How can you know . . .

I know. I know when I am a witch the siren airqueen and leap from the jumbled pile of jarrah behind the shed and shout
I am Zora born of lightning fed on firefrost and frisky nights.
I know.

I don't know. That photograph was taken in a gym. He . . .

Who tells you. Your mother?

She has a father with workshop and carpentry set, wood shavings, grows watermelons, makes the toast for Saturday's breakfast, passes the butter for sweetcorn, calls her Bubs, drives the family in a long and polished car, comes in from work, tie barely relaxed, silk tassles of the dressing gown girdle dangling from under the morning newspaper, leaves the shaving dregs, foam and whisker splinter on the basin sides, calls out from mouthful of food as the front door slams: *I'm off bye Mum, bye Bubs, be good,* horn toot, blown kisses.

No clown. No upside-down acrobat. No shoe-box father that. She knows.

Along the loops of river, blue and a billion pricks of light, through the first stragglings of city, smell of cabbage, hospital, smell of hops, brewery, then the sudden office towers. The school bus pulls up at the final stop. Dark glasses of citymen are glinting together in the sun. Throat parched, you can see those fountains breaking through the seat panels of the bus. The press of bodies to the exit. Crumpled grey of the uniform in front adheres to those legs. The dress no longer obeys the geometry of cut, marries the volume of body; drawn in between the thighs, its creases are caught SMACK to their sweat. The slack flap of the panama hat truncates the view to this and this is all of Cathy I can see. The most battered hat has prestige. This one has been taken through an acclerated ageing process: sat upon, left out in the rain, flung about. The fingers of gloves too must be nibbled, monticules of fluff must cast their many tiny shadows. The creases behind her knees are reddened. The black sketched in there. From next to the driver's seat you can hear the wires singing in the heat. The city is heated to blanching point: a vague linear etching, the rectangular blocks, the cubes, their edges corroded by heat ripple rising in the whiter sky. Then there is the shock of the pavement echoing the glare.

Only a few of them come this far. Most live in the elevated suburbs flanking the river to the north, weeping willow suburbs. Lazy roads where no real traffic comes, only the odd purr of the resident car. Silent Sundays. The noises of the swamps though, the ragged bush, they talk about them sometimes. Claim to glory.

Spend a day with Rita. The quick-sand and the platform up the stringy-barked gum: the *swamploft*. The name thought up when the challenge came was unquestionably adopted.

Ah, but of course you haven't been to the sky-loft yet . . .

You mean the SWAMPloft don't you?

Have a painting: people, all Egyptian frontal profile, bare-footed. There is a short-cut to drawing feet: proud, high instep, only the big toe showing, the foot always parallel to the base-line of the drawing, always left to right. This a a family walk.

Hatted shoeless dad walks hatted shoeless mum walking of course one child male and one child female. But the colours: yellow road, puddles green and the great clouds busy with birds. The orange sun burns a hole. The bus conductress takes one corner and it slides from my hand:

That's a fine painting, love.

She looks over to Shelley behind: Her daddy will be pleased with that, won't he?

The metal floor-grip glitters on the edge of the bus-step.

Sliding into that lapse again: if I don't look now just keep on skipping pepper pepper pep it up between the sharp slap-slaps of the rope, that car purring behind me will stop, the door will swing open and open the big face the eyes heaven blue the voice deep musical laughing will come to claim me and I'll be buoyed up by those great arms above that manicured lawn, those moulded kerbs and the hedged tennis courts. He is dark now. He is laughing still and a shell dangles on a pendant from the neck:

I drifted for weeks, months, years, I don't know, on the tip of the wing and then . . . one day, the waters seemed strangely warm, shallow and there was white sand. I just walked ashore. I'll take you back to the island.

Yes, I hope he will, I say.

Shelley's voice rings out:

Rita doesn't have a father. He's dead! He's dead!

The conductress puts her arm around me, slips the painting back into my hand, closes my fingers around it:

Ah, never mind pet . . . I'll bet you have a lovely mum to show it to.

Mrs Halliday is 'olive-skinned'. Sets us exercises to perform with pen, dip-pen, only the exercise book we are using on the desk, and in silence. And then she surveys the class, reads, manicures a nail, sitting on the great desk at the front, cocks one tiny foot, dangles her stiletto-heeled shoe from the big toe, turns the foot through the scope of her gaze . . . same operation with the other foot:

Write me a story which you will call *The Thunderstorm*. You are in a room with windows set high in the wall, so that the sky is all you see.

Her auburn hair bristles and glints with pins where it twists high in the French roll. The horn-rimmed glasses are lowered on the nose. The eyes are on my desk now, seeing my red hands, the dog-eared exercise book.

Just write, Rita, stop dreaming.

I couldn't sleep tonight. There was just the blue light coming in from under the door. Ace stopped snoring so that all I could hear was the slow trickle down the urinals. Outside there was a sudden rush of wind. The square of sky in the window was still the same pitch black. But then there was a long hoo-hoo and that wind started whooping around, sounds of branches thrashing, like witches' brooms. I was thinking of that nursery rhyme:

> *Old woman, old woman, old woman, quoth I*
> *Oh wither oh wither oh wither so high?*
>
> *To sweep the cobwebs from the sky . . .*

and the cell seemed warmer, damper, and it was good to be with that wind. Then we were travelling through the wind. The prison was adrift and we were buoyed upwards with it and then the stone, wind-bitten, became like sponge and we were drawn up and up and up. There was a sudden vacuum. We were being drawn up into the eye of the storm-cloud. Our sponge walls, unfolding around us, were soaking up the rain teeming in there. We were all shouting:

We are where the thunder will be.

We looked at our bodies and laughed to see that we had become like sponges. We WERE the prison walls and then someone started singing:

14

*We are the spongey fruit sowing seeds in the storm
and, somehow everyone began to laugh. We took in the
sweet rain-water and yet how we flew! There are two
thousand of us I was thinking, most of us are strangers
but we are laughing and our laughter is thunder. Our
bodies were really beginning to speed. The wardens had
been tossed up with us, I suddenly realized, and their
huge bunches of keys made the whole sky jangle. Like
random molecules, we sometimes collided but the impact
was sponge to sponge. The air was cracking and crackling
around us, now and then, a sudden jag of lightning would
catch a cheek-bone, a glint of laughter in an eye. Someone
said:*

Now I get you . . . voler: *to steal and to fly!
And again we all laughed:
Thieves in flight!,
Aviators all of us!,
Riding high on a cum . . .*

The word won't come. Cum . . . cumula . . . cumulo. Stratus, yes
cirro-stratus . . . cumulo . . . There is geography book in my desk.
Halliday is gazing out of the window. Tennis is going on, dull
whack-and-thud, whack and thud of the ball behind the pruned
hedges and cyclone fences. Lift the lid of the desk. One inch
should be enough. And the text book is open on the cloud page.
Miraculously. And there it is: CUMULO-NIMBUS . . . and
another good word to use: OZONE.

> *ulo-nimbus. Then there was that
noise of keys again and I fell and was throttled back on
my mattress. But when I looked over at them, the
sleeping mounds of their mouths were just slightly
puckered at the corner. The pure smell of ozone is still in
the air, balmy now even in this cell and I know that in
the morning I will be laughing in the bulldog faces of the
wardens. That we all*

Rita! What WERE you doing under your desk-lid?

She swings her legs down from her desk. The bottle of ink flies
off mine as my hand shoots across it. A great circle of it now, still
spreading its boundaries over the scrubbed floor boards. Ink on

15

the grey school dress. She is prising open the lid of my desk with the very tips of her finger-nails. They are lacquered wine-red.

So-oh . . . Rita needs a geography text to write about a thunderstorm!

She consults the gazes of the others. All pens must be suspended now: there is no more scratching. She is using the silence she has created. Their eyes are boring into my back.

Don't you have a memory for what you have seen with your own eyes?

Let us see what you do with your geography, Rita . . . Ah!

Her voice is lowered. The fine arch of the eyebrow: it pushes up little puckers of skin.

So you see yourself straight away in a prison, do you?

The tongue cracks around the words again. She is beautiful: that reddish light in the dark brown eyes. Seen photographs of Maria Callas. She is like that in her miniature way. There are isolated giggles behind, suppressed, bursting out again . . . chain-reacting now. Her stare silences them.

Go wash yourself, girl. You are ALL ink!

The corridors are hung with school bags and gym tunics grey, grey, panamas, wax-yellow and cream. The mirror shows a round pink face and the lips have taken the ink like wood-grain. On the basin there is only a slimy vestige of soap pressed into the corrugated part of the enamel. The blunt, black-edged nails claw it out. Cheeks are fiercely burning and they still burn through the cold slaps of the water. Take the uniform off, must soak it, the ink welling up now to the rim of the basin, more and more clouds of it being released, the enamel already blue-black with it, strange purply reds breaking away from the blacks. Wringing it out now but the ink won't stop coming. These goose-fleshed thighs taking me back. The raised pores reddy black. And the gym tunic doesn't cover their dark stain. Take time, take time. There must be recess soon. The uniform is on my hook dripping dark onto the corridor floor. Slowly, slowly . . . But here is the door and I am knocking.

Come in. Rita Aviator!

There is a chorus of laughter. They are laughing more and more,

She makes an exaggerated show of licking her index finger to turn the last page of the composition.

*... and I know that in the morning I will be laughing in the
bulldog faces of the wardens.*

Someone growls like a dog. Shelley maybe.

Well, Rita, I don't think *cumulo-nimbus* saved the
composition.

The laughter drains away to silence cut by the bell.

At assemblies, always this same blending of hair: pale sand, gold sand with the dull, the chestnut, the honey, the squirrel red, the foxy red, the odd red-black and the very rare blue-black punctuating it all. They are filing their glossy heads past now. The composition books are piling up on Halliday's desk. Arlie's hair is back to its regulation symmetry again, with the pale parting between the bunches, caught perfectly in the blue nylon butterfly bows: silky, pure silk and there is silky blond down on her golden tennis player's calves. The silky film of saliva stretches . . . breaks, the smile indents and parts the lips: She knows of course, she already knows and shows the others too with her mystery smile that she can give peep-show of prison-cell and flourish from her magician's hat Rita-plummeting-aviator, then Rita-drowned-in-cumulo-cloud-of-ink.

Arlie mouths her words with darkness too and her slowness adds to it. She also knows about puberty: *And then my mother said, Well dear, you're a woman now.*

The others are grouped on the lawn and the satellite clusters are already forming too, around their sub-leaders, casting their dense shadows. They tug at the tiny teeth of grass as she crochets, crochets the network of words around them. She has a mystery library of books too: *There is a fatty deposit and that mound is the Mount of Venus . . . Pubic hair: there is down at first, a soft down, becoming gradually coarser. The real wiry fuzz comes later . . . Ovaries, vagina,* she says, *uterus, vagina, labia majora, labia minora* they nod and sway as they pluck more furiously at the

18

blades of grass. From time to time they raise their faces, nervy rabbits . . . At a cue from the magician, they sniff the air she breathes for a clue to the mystery she deals out in little doses and they are grateful for it, each recess. From time to time too, they swing their heads away to watch the hop-scotch going on behind them: some with tenaciously flat chests hop and skip on spindly stork legs resisting the puberty talk of Arlie and Co., the serious games of Shelley and her Gang.

But Shelley calls herself a *Warrior* and so she is for everyone, the moment war is declared . . . on Laurence for instance standing there. At sport her hands clap around the air, never the ball. She is not uncoordinated, nor particularly unmuscular — that wouldn't matter so much. She is not there on the field where they are, her teeth are never gritted with the effort, her body is never tensed with that animal vigilance, her attention never riveted on the ball as ball: she follows its flight casually, with dreamy bemusement. And so it does matter when she walks away with a laugh and a shrug, having *let the team down.*

Oh, they whine, can't Laurence be reserve next time Miss Buckley?

Well, says Laurence, fixing them with those dark eyes — it seems as if she can contract the irises at will to intensify that kniving thrust, that black defiance —

In *Fronce,* we do not take these games so *sayrayursley.*

Oh-oh.

Shelley's blue eyes retaliate with their icy glitter.

Bert thees eez nert Fronce, thees eez PERTH, Australia, latitude thirty-two degrees south, longitude one hundred and fifteen degrees east . . . Perhaps you didn't realize? Laurence?

And the eyes shift their crystals to tear a snatch of giggles from the others.

Shelley and her Gang have their den: a hollow in the grass, between the hibiscus bushes, where the roles are dealt out:

This is Espionage . . . Ronny, you are the *Envoy* to our connection at Base II and you others are the *Avant-garde,* on *Reconnaissance* to the enemy stronghold.

She points to the great retaining wall around the sports field. They must run to their desks afterwards, to consult their dictionaries, but for the moment, they nod, too, in knowing consent. And each time it is Laurence Santey or else Esther Wong who is target. When they come across Esther, the signal is *somesings wong calling Base I somesings wong . . .*

Shelley is versing them one more time before they leave the hide-out on their mission:

Now you know the pass-word, don't you, for re-entering Base I?

But Laurence has sauntered right up to them. She doesn't seem to know the importance of this grassy hollow. The hibiscus here are like all the others . . .

What is it that you are doing? She is blinking in the sun.

What is it *that* we are doing? . . . the echo runs around the group: laughter.

Unit 22x, says Shelley, the Enemy has walked straight into the *Ambush*. Proceed with *Interrogation*. Dinah produces a note-book from her pocket, licks the end of her pencil, ready to take it all down. Lou swallows, blushes:

Tell us why you have come to this country. We know you haven't given us the real reason. Full identity, please. Address.

It seems to amuse Laurence or is she sneering? The light hovers around the profile. She always answers their questions but each time differently. This time it is:

Father: oceanographer, working up north to harness the motor-force of the tides. Mother: beauty consultant with Esthée Lauder.

Oh, don't give us that. *We* know it's a cover-up job. Just like the word 'masseuse', 'beauty consultant' must hide a *multitude of sins*. I know because Mum and Dad were joking about that the other night.

It's the first time I've seen a *warrior* resort to quoting his *mum* and *dad*.

Laurence laughs. She gives that shrug with the backward toss of hair and walks away with:

Anyhow if it makes your game interesting to think that, why not?

Her skin is translucent, stretched fine and tight over bone-thrust: nose ridge, over-hang of brow, sharp jag of jaw away from the neck. The eyes swerve their gaze as she moves away from here. The head is held strangely still as the tiny ankles — how does she walk without snapping at such a fragile fulcrum? — take her down the slope. That tug of her gaze as she walks, I walk. The gang is shrunk to dolly size behind us now, almost merged in with the hibiscus shade. The mass of hair curves away from the jaw: it has been *styled,* whereas ours is lopped. It flashes its metallic blues, its travelling reds. Now there is an aura, red haze of it in the sun. Our legs dangle against the rough limestone of the embankment. Her feet reach so much lower than mine. It is suddenly extraordinary that I am here with her, that there is this silence, away from them, that they should remain so miniature, in obedience to perspective.

Rita, why do you hang around them, watching their games, as if you want to be in it all?

I could ask her why she bothers to answer their questions. Her lips are sharply edged but the mouth is soft, closes slowly its cushion-on-cushion . . . opens again:

And yet . . . you let them laugh at you. Maybe you think that you should be like them with their potato faces, their copper-plate writing, their nice little thunderstorms with toy puffs of cloud and zig-zags of lightning.

Tongue kicks back in its pink cave, can feel only the corrugated pinkness of it and no words coming . . . as if the hand that makes the ink bottle fly through the classroom were begging for an audience, asking for it all: Halliday's finger-nails edging into the desk, *Rita-Aviator* and the bulldog growls . . . tongue curling up as tidy as a cat in the pink cave of a mouth, closing in on its space, shutting out the words, dreaming the dream of a cave, of a shell, stuck stiff and mute only the tides and tides of her talk so far away . . . you let yourself be Mrs Halliday's toy, her very favourite toy. They are right in a way, when they call you *teacher's pet.* She needs you for her games. You're in the same game . . . just like those prisoners and wardens in your story. She won't let you be, she won't leave you alone as long as you sit trembling there, like a cornered mouse. I don't understand why you act so ashamed, it's as if you are, you really are . . . you don't even speak up for yourself. They laugh, they are out to get you because they are jealous, I suppose, but they don't understand why. But it's only when you do something stupid that they think they can move in on you. And when it's safe, when Halliday invites them . . . And then you come back all hunched up, like a cripple. You let them cripple you, it's strange. Just because you are trying too hard to be like them.

21

You're so serious about it all. I don't know. I've never let that sort of thing get to me. Never been in one school for very long. So these gangs with their stupid games, I don't take any notice. But I suppose I'm older than all of you . . .

All of you. All of you. Far away electric buzz. The groups break up their circles. They are trooping up towards the classroom block. And now they will be saying: *Rita-and-Laurence,* Rita-and-Laurence . . .

Most of them inter-urban commuters, the train an evening reflex: no one sees them off. *Dutiful daughters* — irresistible instinct to type-cast, cosiness of the air-tight category, shut out the anxiety of contradictions: within its curly brackets, the great set of all people, and then, nestling within, subset within subset within . . . ad infinitum . . . infinitely trapped, as handy as a Russian doll — they are clamping their polycopied sheets into their files, and of course he would provide the right-wing professorial figure . . . or is it the solicitor: diplomat glasses, sheer navy socks moulding the ankles to where the pleated spine of trouser-leg begins — *Mais Monsieur est toujours impeccable,* boasts his maid — crossed precisely under the pleated copy of the *Figaro.* Someone behind the *Marseillaise,* but most of the workers take the bus. And anyhow, it's too early. Slick luxury train this is, with its observation tank sealed off: not for probing.

Laurence *you* send me back to the very blank where it all begins . . . and yet nothing moves in to take up the space already vacated.

Suppose you feel something else: a concentric numbness welling, rippling out, misting up the thick glass walls of your airy aquarium, closing you in your own time.

I thought it wouldn't be this but wild vertigo, intoxication of turning on my own axis in freed space. In a long greedy scrutiny of space from that pinnacle, I would see that crazy queue of arbitrarily fused selves, oh yes, from moments past recede, I would pluralize and scatter on horizons ebbing into horizons that composite persona which you, your eyes, your words, your space, your time concertina into *personality*. The mock determinism in the definitions you and all the rest of them offer.

> *Ah, but you have always been an image-monger conning up your audience. People only exist for you in so far as they ripple with the impact of your words, the pebbles you throw out to shock and to perpetuate your own drama . . .*

Gestures congeal, moments heap up, the sentence cannot any longer be completed, be resolved even by the caprice of grammar, even the fictitious solution of past-participle, full-stop, etc... the hiatus is is is and somehow that hyphen, your gaze, is weakening, can't bridge it anymore... breath no longer follows in the wake of breath... beyond reach already: the astonishing simplicity of the train. No apparent tractor device and, somewhere in its neatly moulded body, your five neat cartons of belongings with their maniacally knotted string and your crated canvases will glide discreetly with the rest, almost imperceptibly away and still the face refracted by the glass is is ... as if inscribed in filigree far below the skin, as ever, tight and precise as a drum: sealed in its own time. The eyes swing through their ninety degree arc ... do they aim their flash? An offered face: a mollusc for the forking. No. Yours, in its glassy shell, can send its missiles now. But it took time for you to compose it, it wasn't always so complete. It always emerged slowly from its settled mould on waking... hair like the defeat of grass after some savage withdrawal, distinct as a Dürer.

> *You are binding me to another element.*

Go on. Go on. Name it then. Or am I so unspeakable? So unspeakably *earth* or something? You claim the air as medium, a calm translucent surround: hard to contest. Something in someone else's world of essences you can't contest anyhow. And I can be beguiled by it: play the air if you must and have me be earth, vigour, lust, pragmatic thrust, you name it. You began to smell like air, Laurence, and when I draw you, clouds dissolve the brow, soften and pillow the pressure of lip-on-lip, the breasts too, they pale away . . .

> *Reach away from sense coarseners.*

My refinements issue from the *cultivation of guilt*. The kind of dumb guilt of Perceval, sullenly aware as he crosses that first stone bridge, of Mother, behind in a crumpled heap, a tiny collapse at the end of the world to be explored: he doesn't look back. What it becomes in his head is necessary. The unformulated guilt to catalyse the quest . . . for what? A formula perhaps . . .

Stop those ritual slaughters inside.

Your formulae, Laurence. I didn't, don't know what you mean. Okay. Cast me as an abatteur then. Go ahead. The axe is hovering above the jury, effortlessly upheld by my svelte dreamstalker, the Birdwoman, and then, for she's a dancer too, the blade takes off . . . and, tangent to its orbit, she pole-vaults over them, leaving them floundering for a name for the crime . . . How's that for a *slaughter?* Did I get the right picture? Did I, Laurence?

Each dream, each fantasy, each word to free myself from your words, theirs, enacts a mini-slaughter. In your words, since we argue in your vocabulary, ride your metaphors in tandem, each word marks out a sacrifice. Not something missing. But something willed missing, given up. Okay, let's make it that *sacred abattoir* then. Thing, world, you, your gestures, your words, are gone so that I can be and say it: *I can be, could have been, would dream myself here.* No, of course, it's all a game. But you are dead serious, it's you who are serious, Laurence, listen to you:

> *These lonely performances of yours . . . you juggle up*
> *your anecdotes, induce impossible love. Searching out the*
> *sacred has nothing to do with your ludic brand of*
> *onanism: you stake it out, your sacred space, just so you*
> *can get your kicks transgressing imaginary boundaries . . .*

. . . boundaries, limits, boundaries . . . that glass: the face is already blurring as it glides down the rails. It jerked just as comically from its inertia as all the rest. Our faces back to their original two dimensions. As always. Every time there is a split from friend or lover. And the same nagging question: *Who will cut along the dotted lines now?* The paper doll screams from its prison page: *Cut me out! Give me a text! Superimpose me there!* Magically, to be my own ventriloquist at the right time and not become *his her their* rendition. And even then, *your his her their* ears play tricks on us and the ventriloquist's dummy is back on some borrowed daddylap, defined and humbled by love for the maker — *in the beginning was the word* — so ready to be the courtier, act out the definition and, each time, as a believer: *This* is my authentic self. *So you have come to Europe to find yourself,* they say. Ha.

Your egosystem.
No room for anyone else.
Too choked on you you you.

Perhaps. I ask for my *mode of growth.* Or do I? Your usual sustained metaphors aping logic. And I had to adopt them to make room, to *give.* But there was a limit. So I sought out the fiestas, the clowns, the dope-artists, the ham-actors and the real actors — dispersing myself, you said, just to get away for one sweet moment from that bloody *self* you would have me obsessed with . . .

You want to betray me. You do. I can see it on your face when you come in. To distance yourself, you ironize with other people. You have left me before I ever left you. You produce against me too . . .

I produce away from her. She is drawn away gone. It's so simple. She is gone so that she can be, so that I can be and yet . . . No way to free the throat of the vertical shriek it's nursing. She can't receive it.

Inscribe it somewhere, let is emerge or cancel it out, call fiction what follows now, an irresistibly self-generating text, that down-hill slide . . . of course I'm not that slash of pink upon the rails, bared lip and limb and . . .

Go on, do it again in slow-motion.
Die your little deaths in little mirrors.

. . . but how to pack away that gravity-giddied god and not find the plummeting diver's mouth in dream even . . .

I have worked at eradicating all that in me. The received anecdotes. You cling to your fatherless childhood as if it were some kind of sovereignty. Darkness in the midst of the day. Ah but you will always have people hooked for a while. Dark voice. Dark imagery. Get rid of the mystery, get rid of the drama. Make happiness a value. Or else you'll just keep drifting in and out of other people's lives: chance social collisions . . . let slip a formula here, create your effect, insinuate an enigmatic signal to keep them going. Petite allumeuse! *Find your myth, get rosy for a while on their crass group eroticism, their neurotic need to celebrate boredom, donate a witticism for their ping-pong surface exchanges, and then, you'll always slip away, unchanged and leaving them wondering, but the flush will fade and your mouth will begin to set in a cynical mould . . . they will have you in the end. Your drawings and paintings are starting to show it. The easy gesture of the 'personality' you let them abbreviate for you. The same old bent-nail motif, the same self-crucifixion, the same self-germination in the cracks and folds, same cry from below the surface:*

Coming, ready or not!

But always with the same hide-and-seek ambiguity: Now you see me, now you don't but see me come all the same baby . . .

Machine désirante. Their words. Ever shunted from desire to desire? Perhaps there never is any real dialogue anyway. And Jean, then, what was it with him? There was never this clash of words, this jamming of metaphors. Jean Le Dantec: the silences he established. It wasn't as if we didn't go through the whole round of puns when his friends were there, he wanted that, the company maintaining the game, coupling us as we were never really coupled: he'd serve, I'd move up ready to volley from the net, *wham slam* what a couple, *very* nifty, the way he'd let the ball dribble onto the racket, scoop it up casually, loop it through the air and *pow*: where did I get that backhand? But it was a sad kind of truce. The scarred look would return to his mouth: world weary at thirty. And that fear of being alone together. Because he knew it could never be what he wanted. He wanted me to say: *Yes I am you you you, welcome, welcome to the space where you can be. Your reality, not mine.* He achieved that in a way, that sickness, that sickening fear of what became of what I said in his head, increasing his otherness, bringing on that tense rebellion in his body. It was his problem. He disabled me with his problem. *Please, please, please say what you mean,* he'd beg. *I don't feel I know you any better after all these months. Sorry, Rita, but I've got no use for enigmas.*

Say what I mean? How can he assess that? How can I say what I mean anyhow, when as soon as the words are out, they become what *he* means?

He takes out another Gitane. It's near closing time in the café: the white light of the bare bulb multiplies in mirrors. Beyond, there is the kitchen: the zinc surfaces give no clues. No answers from the barman's face either. Sealed in its fatigue. And Jean is still waiting for *what I mean.* Here is our cognac: we stare into that as if it could be the medium. And now he's said it, begged for what I mean, my tongue is a dumb bell, still, dull in its mute dome. TONGUE TONGUE TONGUE . . . His eyes hold mine: is this a final interrogation? Is this the last chance I am given to find that space where we might meet? And all that is in my head is the dead echo of it: TONGUE TONGUE TONGUE while we maintain this terminal separation across the table. If words could make a space to hold one time . . .

Take that empty kitchen

clean surfaced we are
no food outside ourselves
maintaining this and yet
retreating
what tinkling chain
to throw to you what name to give
what lies between our boundaries
unendingly

> the tap drips on
> the sink spills out
> its mirrors
> droplets multiply

we have not lived here it's clear

SHUNTED

to another room our serial mouths yawn out
their *Bejahung*
balloon again the collapsed geometry of sheets

28

suddenly outside

the tree is not upstretched for you
perhaps does not peg out that sheet of sky
but as my hand contours the slopes it never knows
it grows: I say the tree is simply there
as bones are in the body

WHITE

LIES

for dawn the sky soothed out its skin *for quietus*
you might have said but as I heard
it shrilled its wires arched
became a sculpture taut from pole-to-pole POLE-
VAULTING into sea's own pattern
just to show that everything
is always something else unhinged

but still we sit in our drum-tight skins
eyes down our separate glasses
glide straight beyond the razor slip
between the drink-edge and the lip
where all the colour pulses

That pulsating colour always beyond, always that same barrier of
glass, doctor, daddy, why? The glass between me and the garden
snaring the profligate yellow of the wattle tree in its ice: pushed
my hand through quite casually towards the end of this endless
adolescence and then, just as absent-mindedly, sawed, gently at
first, soon in panting earnest at that little wrist standing out so
surprisingly separate . . .

Later, on a solitary honeymoon, booking into the hotel as Mrs R.
Fini to wait for the end in all seriousness: no watch to monitor it
by, just the pulse at the wrist pushing out the lapse of time . . .
minutes, hours . . . It became boring of course . . .

But now that the glassy observation carriage has slipped away, can't resume where I was before. Must have a lapse of time to improvise, extract what's latent. Porous. That's it. Need to be promiscuously porous. She has left: there is no colour, neutral, sexless, beige. Station really ochre of course and yet drained to such a pallor. Pale ochre and cream. A cream you can't feel your way into. Day unformed. Look at this dark sleeve standing out from it: no chance of blending in. The great chalky face of the station clock: 16.55 and such an awful distance from sleep. The station master must wonder . . .

The normal taxis are waiting. Now will walk along that little back street running absolutely parallel to the railway line in the opposite direction from Marseille towards that tunnel, past the stationer's shop, past the Persian carpet shop, past the back entrance to that supermarket, up those stairs, between the irises early spring, poppies later . . . There are none now. Each step is a retreat from what is anticipated. Only anticipate the past anyhow.

The air has stolen the contours of things

think it, try my tongue on it, feel the lie . . . feel it, feel it . . .

Watch the corpse invent a lapse of time

. . . walking . . . puts only this: foot after foot into my gaze. Delayed sensation of something lived. Smack, smack, smack of pavement tracks up, up and what I receive: the impact of déjà-vu, but from such an elevation. The air dulls the pointillism of faces, can't focus on them, can't focus on the embankment, up the steps, trace the shadows in pitted stone, the patina of railings, people, more and more of them about now, but living it on the commitment level of a T.V. viewer in front of a test pattern, unfocused at that, *unfocused at that,* find some comfort in an encapsulating analogy, Laurence could. Struggle to keep all the planes of sensation together. Shiver. The scurrying locus of the shiver. Little droplets on this coat-sleeve. The sky is whitening, the lopped stumps of plane trees that thrust their swollen knobby outgrowths into it — the annual amputation — come spring, they spike it with new vigour and Van Gogh lives on, swish of traffic circling around the Rotonde and the great glass façade of the Office de Tourisme divides it into panels and swinging glass doors, odd flaw in the glass where it knots and bubbles out, refracting maliciously snatches of it all: trees, traffic, crowd, beige, predominantly beige rain-coated, the cubistic canopy of umbrellas already, this coat stretched, dwarfed, concertina'd, diminished to an emphatic line as it goes from panel to panel of the glass façade. Sky is a huge glare again and such a long exposure home, the steps run downwards to the *passage souterrain* and the roar of the traffic is already distant, dulled SSSSS

Ssssalut Ritaaaa!

The blur of faces is mouthless, not one owning the echo *ah-ah-ah-ah* resounding through the underground crossing but there he is, breaking through: hair frizzing into its fans on either side of the jagged parting, the smile jangling the broken lines of his face, flicking the shadows around the beak nose, light swimming in the black eyes: Antoine.

Putain Rita ... depuis le temps qu'on s'est vu! Eh qu'est-ce que tu deviens? His voice runs at machine-gun delivery sentence into sentence with the throaty rattle fuzzing the ra-ta-ta, ra-ta-ta.

You on your way home? *Mais tiens ...* I was heading for the Théâtre du Centre, you still live alongside?

He's all angles as he gesticulates, the elbows threatening to break through the frayed sleeves. The jacket is under-sized: the buttons strain with the busyness of the knobbly torso.

But I tell you, nothing's happening here. *Absolument QUEdalle.* Nothing, nothing at all . . *Je commence à*

31

m'emmerder sérieusement. And you?

Is it just put there to make me feel at home in the monologue?

But Antoine, why in the hell did you come back so soon then? Things don't change so quickly here, you know. I mean, you said exactly the same before you left.

But my dear Rita, for the dole! You have to register at one place and, oh, you know, my wife was getting demoralized by it all . . . You know, you knew I have a wife . . . and a kid. Well I finally had to make some sort of gesture for the kid. *Pour le gosse, tu sais!*

He gives a great open, mock-heroic swoop of the arms.

Come on, Antoine: *the* wife and *the* kid can be handy alibis, can't they?

He gives a complicitous chuckle: Yes, but Rita, I can tell you, things are really moving in Paris. *Ça bouge, ça bouge vraiment en ce moment, on fait des choses* . . . Ah, Rita, we were putting this play together, this black guy, brilliant . . . *absolument mais ab-so-lu-ment gé-ni-al* . . . he's worked alongside Growtowski, you know? Yes, well . . . Next time you come up, you'll have to meet him . . .

But what about the production: Is it . . .

Oh . . . you know, always the same old problem: bread. No bread for anything. We were into street theatre too, oh, political stuff but sort of local . . . but then they blew it in Chile with the C.I.A. crushing Allende and all that . . . Well it all seemed so laughable: what we were doing just seemed a mild little bourgeois exercise. It lost energy, we went our different ways. Oh, but we will get it together again one of these days. Look, you should come up and join us: we could do with a mask designer . . . eh? *Mais je te jure,* Rita!

There is something in the febrility, the insect activity of the eyes, alighting with transient avidity on this, on that, then this again, my hand as I speak, the sign SUMA on the shop, the pot-holes in the pavement, the scavenger cat, and always, it's the inward gaze as he talks to himself. No intrusion and yet . . . In the light the eyes aren't totally black: there are strange amber flecks in the darkness . . . Why, why not? Ask him up for a drink.

Antoine, *tu veux pas monter prendre un pot chez moi . . . et on pourra parler de tout ça . . .*

The words came glibly enough. He can do without my offering him some jaded provincial form of Bohemia and . . . for what? A little warmth, to postpone for a moment the mirrored door unhingeing from the wardrobe, meeting my eyes: the bed is fixed opposite the mirror — by whose design? — and we combine in sleep; give me a bed within the bed within your frame . . . Words combine always beyond the mystery guests welcomed in the mirror, of the Van Eyke, no, it's not Antoine I'm trapping there of course, *c'est un copain, c'est tout,* we can speak together, swap our narcissistic monologues and drink to that exchange, part again without anything being threatened, bet anyhow that he's a slipper man at heart, a *pantoufflard* when it comes to the crunch and yet, now he comes with me as if it's the most natural thing in world, up these stairs, many of the little hexagonal terracotta tiles dislodged centuries ago, up to the first landing, exactly because I am the farthest possible from his home ground: a *déracinée,* to whom he never has to speak again if he likes, through the yellow door swinging unevenly on its hinges too, the frame not perpendicular to floor, the floor not parallel to ceiling — many nights spent puzzling just where the geometry went wrong — revealing my little nest now, it looks so offered to the reader, he reads it, his eyes are reading the room as choice: *so this is where you have shacked up,* reading the jaundiced wall-paper with its vestigial maiden's bouquets, they read the triptych and the studied casual way it has been pinned there, with one panel dislocated from the base-line of the others . . . and now his eyes are ferreting the little bed, so narrow beneath the *Self-Portrait with Pomegranate,* reading of course like the delirium of a nicely nested virgin and I let his avid eyes swoop crawl flicker-lick all over it . . . over to the mantelpiece now, last night's slack camembert, last meal with Laurence, sitting plump and squat on the marble along with the crumbs of broken bread, half a litre of Côtes de Provence, I can pour him some of that, and then the books, spine after spine: Rilke, Mallarmé, Artaud. Ponge, Sollers . . . He extracts the Denis Roche, fanning the pages out under his thumb:

Mais Rita . . . tu ne lis pas cette merde? Surely you're not conned by this bullshit? A university stooge like this?

What's coming is the sort of soliloquy I know:

. . . an anti-prophet, one of these anti-heroes of anti-culture lounging for the reporters, doctoral students, critics and camera men in the forcibly dishevelled luxury of inherited

33

apartments, bored as Faustus with the gastronomy of western culture, reciting Valéry strictly on the bidet for the public, playing games with words and metre that only academics can understand, just to ensure the next tour in the provinces, to be able to star as pouting enfant terrible *at the most prestigious seminars and, perhaps, one day, take up a chair in creative writing . . .*

But Antoine simply smiles as he pursues his inventory; he absent-mindedly takes this glass I hand him, his eyes still scanning the room alight casually on Laurence's canvas, graze it, are tempted to prise my back-the-front stack away from the wall, flit over the spines of the books again:

Ah. *Mais là j'suis tout à fait avec toi.* Artaud, that's a man who took real risks.

His eyes back on my studio drawings say it clearly enough:

Where's the risk in this? You produce the goods for your Beaux Arts *diploma, depositing them, punctilious as a battery hen, for your professor's approval, palpitate and cluck for the bland caress at your wing-stump . . .*

He swills the wine in his glass, squints at the black nudes through the rosy, wobbling liquid.

Our backs are against the mantelpiece now. Silence marked out only by the sipping of the wine, sour from overnight exposure, the odd putt-putt of a moped down the road and Mme Sérisier downstairs on the phone:

Eh oui, ma belle . . . Bon, alors . . . MA FOI . . . Oui, une soupe aux poiraux, je lui dirais 'Ça suffit pas non?' Mais que veux-tu? Une fille comma ça, faudrait lui donner une bonne fessée . . . MA FOI . . .

The dampness is creeping in now between the French windows, as they say anywhere but here. The old lace is darkening against the sky and the sheer plane of ochre leaning away up to the right: Denise's window where she'll stand and bellow along to Joplin at the stars in her fanciful version of the American, Southern Comfort scream and sob of white female blues not for Laurence . . .

Antoine's teeth are so perfect, white, as the lips part and those eyes, are they still reading it all, following mine along the jagged caprice of cracks in the wall, losing their way in the leafless tangle around that attic window . . .

Mais Rita, tu as l'air si crispée! Décontracte-toi bon sang . . . Why are you so pent up? Eh? Relax a bit. You know, in that coat . . . Isn't that the song: *Lovely Rita Meter Maid?* You do look just a little like a military man! Do you always keep yourself locked up in that carapace?

Ah, there you've got it wrong: this is a Flyer's coat, the real thing, R.A.F., she quips as the double-breast unfolds, the label is displayed, he edges her me swinging coatless in the wardrobe mirror towards the bed, she doesn't, hasn't protested, after all, it is the only thing to sit on apart from two spartan upright chairs and here they are: our thighs aligned, his so wiry, mine with their softer spread, a centimetre gap maintained between them. He leaps for the bottle. He empties all of it along with the sediment into the glass nested in these crab-red hands.

The bottle is on the floor, there is no gap between our thighs, there is a hand at the nape of my neck, pushing away the weight of my hair, pouring the warmth in ...
    Mais Antoine enfin ... What do you ...
    The dark hand, veins standing out, separate coarse hairs, travels, slips, between my legs; this crab-hand goes for it, guides it back home — like some errant animal, lost its way — onto his lap.
    Je t'en pris ... Please Antoine ... Isn't it poss ...
    He guides my head into focus: his eyes, lips, glistening ...
    You've got me wrong ...
    Ah, Rita ... Don't give me the barricade of words now! What are you trying to prove *my lovely maid?* Can't you drop the defences and be yourself for once? *Hein? Hein?*
    I *am* being myself! *Merde!* And in any case ... *You* reminded me that you have a wife, that you have a child ...
    Oh! Come on, Rita! I didn't think you'd slip into that. Don't give me that *cinéma américain,* please. In any case, my marriage isn't like that. You know perfectly well. I have always insisted ...
    What? What have you always ...
    That we remain open as a couple ...
    Why do you talk about *my* wife then, why bother to get married ... Why do you ... I mean, what sort of 'open couple' is it if you have to leap to the defence with 'I have always insisted'?
    Can't you think for one moment past possession? Of course it's a commitment ... And an anchorage too, for us both, if you like ...

Wine, the numbing laziness spreading. His eyes are just a blank lizard stare now. There is a tangle of hair and fluff caught under the leg of the chair. Our dual breathing ... Such a fatigued old battle finally. What can be brought up in Cartesian evidence to against this hand, that hand, the tug of torso-to-torso ... We lurch on the edge of the stupidly narrow bed, I grip the spread, stand, am being pulled down again, Rita, Rita, Rita, he is murmuring ...

Antoine, je t'aime bien, tu dois le savoir... I just don't want to get involved that way, that's all. I don't want to be some sort of ... episode in the margins of your marriage.

Oh là là là ... NOW she says it: *in the margins of my marriage,* eh? She's not bad at rhetoric, this girl! So, you want me to divorce, do you? Before I can put a friendly hand on your shoulder? Maybe you should know, Rita, that your little body plays tricks on you: perhaps you left my hand on your neck a little too long? And the way you leapt up just then didn't look all that convincing to me. Timing, Rita. Timing is one of the most important things in acting ...

Antoine! I don't feel in the mood for that kind of sarcasm ... Would you go now?

His brow puckers. Mock surprise.

We really are pent up, aren't we? I do apologize for any errors in tone! See you again, lovely Rita, when you're in a better mood ...*Ssssalut p'tite chatte!*

A slow motion bow fit for the court of Louis XIV and the svelte figure negotiates an exit between the mantelpiece and the desk. The yellow door obliterates him.

There is still the nudge of those pointed buttocks left in the bedcover: perfect imprint. The feet neatly trip down the stairs, fainter, fading and now the jerk-click-thud of the great front door, the footfall dies away on the street ... This Duralex glass remains, smeared, with the dark sediment, inside this nest of fingers and the index strokes up and down, soothing, channelling its caress up and down in the grooves of the glass. As the glass rotates, the spines between the grooves catch stars of light from under the door. The walls tilt downwards, closing in towards the floor, but the room is all in height, geared to have you gaze at that ceiling with its plaster moulding of entwined leaf and flower around the light-bulb dangle, the textural accidents where it has shed its paint, the stains, the yellowing, the nicotine yellowness, more stains, the dark oil splutter growing its culture of dust where the chicken flambéed too furiously, catching the wall paper, obliterating the bouquets, curling it, bringing Mme Sérisier bellowing up the stairs — she had proudly indicated that cut-off corner established by the washable contact paper and the camp-cooker as the *'coin cuisine'!*... Space filling with all the silts from cooking, painting, eating, smoking, washing . . .

But it is inside-outside. It gapes wide on the sky too: open to cicada, cricket, a swallow mistakes it for an alcove of the garden, knocks its beak against the glass, finds an issue, is gone. Spring nights soon: there'll be the bigness, buoyancy of night outside... Can take out my inks, unwind the old umbilicus, big bellied mother-night, take off, be nude again between white sheets and let it flow back again, back from the pen, seismograph of an origin that somehow might happen here. I can stay on between the chorus of the frogs and the syncopated bursts of coughing from old Sérisier down below. The bankruptcy of virile song can leave a space in which perhaps... But always at one remove. The window gapes. The mirror smears and swings the stars. Or this parade of men and chance. *Explore the space you already know,* Laurence said. Her attention riveted on a small square of sky, a clear male brow. Of course I am the open one, I sing, the generous one, I call for admirers, yes I say, come, and let them in to shifting chambers where each will find what he deserves and every time an exquisite irritation carves — dunes beyond the first encounter — another space where I can love that space at one remove . . .

Timing, Antoine said, timing. Did he know, had I told him about Jean? Jean's perfumed body, his heavy grace. He knew about timing, the actor schooled by the Comédie Française, his expert archery of word and gesture not really acquired, simply coaxed into perfection. Or at least, so he'd have them acknowledge the thoroughbred in him. Oh, the largesse of the Count, as they call him. They all troop up to his place to eat and admire his panache as he sets down before them the *civet de lapin. Mais t'es un cuiston vraiment génial, mon vieux,* they say and then, as he goes out, regret how his style has become fatigued these days and bitch on together and win with a wink, a trick of the tongue, the wine he has poured, a promise of the role already promised to Jean and the director dabs red lips with the serviette and compliments the chef as he returns with more wine, more bread, cheeses.

And yet he still attends all their first nights, a parody of the image they have of him, the Disinherited Count from Brittany: head erect, nostril flared complementing aquiline curve of nose and then the lazy, hooded stare of the amber eyes, always aware of the mirrors recording him in this role as if it were enough to be the travestied avatar — and very much taken to flesh — of Villiers de l'Isle Adam, for instance, because as he says, *I only begin to exist under their gaze.* You see me, they see me and therefore I am . . . for the duration of the lie . . .

Break out, break through the mirrors. Leave the actors to their timing. Be with real people, on the street. The door breaks through. The eyes of straggling shoppers are set on things out of focus. They do not record. This cone of breath smokes, frays in the air. Cold, cold, schluck-schluck, the sole of my boot come loose, a backward tongue lapping the pavement, down the Rue du Onze Novembre, past the morgue, past the Câlissons D'Aix factory, sugared almonds, the fairy industry of the town, past the mechanic's workshop where . . . he is as usual: same red-checked shirt, blue worker's pants, face dark red splitting on the set of broken teeth, leaning against the entrance, Gitane, a yellow pendant from the lower lip, the lip ejects it, the canvas shoe squashes the butt but he doesn't lower his gaze. I squash my butt too in front of SUMA SUPER MARCHÉ.

The doors are closed soon. Silence. All is gloss. Most housewives of course are more efficient than this, dinner long since planned and prepared, aroma of it greeting the *chef de famille* as he alights from the wrought-iron cage of the lift. But there are still a few who have scurried out for some odd item . . .

. . . Take a trolley: the little wheels glide us past the great array of cheeses: provençal pepper and herb-covered goat's cheese — one franc, fifty, Corsican — *mais ça sent le bouc* — all tumbling in their random hillocks at the foot of the mountainous slabs of gruyère, emmental, *Bonsoir Madame,* says the nice creamy face of the *fromagière,* blonded hair showing just a centimetre of greying black at the roots, *Bonsoir Madame,* and the trolley whirrs on past the *harengs sauce piquante* past the piled up cans of *cassoulet* and here is the *charcuterie* already: *saucisses, jambons, pâté en croûte* . . . ten, fifteen francs to spend and then the hundred franc bill for Sérisier's rent . . . *saucisses de Strasbourg* . . .

Little Gérard with his fine straight nose, teeth not quite bucked but catching the lower lip, chestnut eyes with black lashes curling astonishingly, making him look constantly surprised, his rapid nervous delivery of sentences in tight little spurts, wrists outgrowing the sleeves and those long fingered hands: *Rita, but you really must meet Raymond, he's the most amazing guy, you know, just the way he can carry anything off with a bit of chic . . . he vamps up as hors d'oeuvres some cocktail sausages with a dash* of Meaux mustard and everyone approves, *just something about him, the guy's really got style, you know . . . you should see the way he's decorated his apartment . . . far out . . . Rita he's really saved me . . . I realize now just how lost I was,* **PAUMÉ** complètement paumé *. . . he can coin a phrase that puts it all into place. What was it he said?* une carence d'autorité *. . . that I've got to work these things out and Rita . . . ah but you'll just have to come and meet this guy: he's a what do you call it, a psycho-critic, you know, you can talk about books and art and stuff with him, he looks at the way the structure of the personality shows up in language, image and all that, you know . . .* and here is a little packet of Strasbourg sausages . . . the production line must be amazing: endless tube of pale pink emulsified meat, as homogenized as bland as a cherub's cheek, sliding through some vacuum machine into the long column of red skin and then there must be some kind of twisting device to divide the infinite sausage, another to slap them side to side, pushing out the air, shrinking the plastic pack around, so snug around these neat little jobs: toy phallic food of a ludic psycho-critic. In the trolley is the plastic litre of *Grand Margnat,* three francs fifty, green lentils, two francs forty, pale food of denial that one flavours over hours with this and that; will try it, have a holiday from the rich animal fat, eat it as floury air food for Laurence, her palate so discerning that the faintest taste becomes a wealth and now . . . hand is on the little round-contoured block of mini-sausages; for fun, against the lentils, will dine on that, and so very cheap, somehow the pack is so graspable, it is graspable, the hand is slipping into this pocket not into the trolley, I have done it *I have done it* and as I reach for the milk, suddenly the left hand is the only one available, trolley glides its reflection over the mock-marble vinyl tiles the gloss the gloss of it, smiling, again at the *fromagière,* this is the treacherous smile now, there is no stitching in that pocket, bottomless . . . hand must suspend the sausages against the leg and sausages strung on air, approaching the check-out desk now . . *This, my dear is the real thing,* she quips, genuine R.A.F., a flyer's coat Rita Rita Aviator. This right sleeve is joined now to the pocket, fingers married to the little pink stubbies dangling in the void . . . **MADEMOISELLE** *venez par ici, s'il vous plaît . . .* and what is the moustached giant in the dark blue suit doing here now? Up there the little office with its glass walls is . . . its door is open: he has descended from his elevated aquarium to invite me to another cash-desk and yet, why this privilege? At the one I have chosen there is no great queue. Now with the left hand, must do some tricky steering of the trolley, the wheels have a will of their own, how to pay for the wine, milk, lentils with this left hand? The purse won't obey, stud will not give way under thumb . . . does it look feasible to keep one hand casually pocketed while struggling with the other one to unload the goods from the trolley and pay up? MADEMOISELLE, *voulez-vous bien retirer votre main de votre poche?* Hand from pocket, he wants the hand from the pocket . . . the words making another fish-bowl around me . . . no a gossamer globe rather and what a relief in the take-off up up up going up, people heaping up behind me, *ces mères de familles, je sais voler, on m'appelle voleur* . . . the coat is separating me, darkness severs from the gloss of it all and I was wrong, they are so red, not pink, so nude, on the cash-desk, the *saucisses de Strasbourg 'VENEZ PAR ICI MADEMOISELLE'.* When you buy you are *Madame,* when you steal you are *Mademoiselle* up up we go together, dark dark blue with the dark dark blue to the glassy observation booth where, why . . . yes, of course, he has seen it all.

BONG, Mademoiselle, he says *bong* like a good marseillais, *vous ne savez donc pas que cela s'appelle voler, nong?*

It's called theft, theft, theft, you know but he is not aware of the pun or else he is very subtle: *voler* is to fly, is to steal . . . No, but this is a fish bowl I am in still: My words bubble out in silence and yet it's strange how he is shouting now:

Vous n'avez évidemment pas le sens de la propriété!

No respect for what is not yours . . . but then WHO is SUMA? Some gracious lady of the heights? Again no words come out.

This time! he is saying, you will get away with it for just a fine, but *ATTENTIONG,* Mademoiselle, next time it will be straight to the *PRÉFÉCTURE DE POLICE . . . dix mille frrrunG, Mademoiselle!* Mouth gapes: ten thousand francs, I will never be able to say anything . . . *dix mille frrrunG toute de suite ou je téléphone à la préfecture!* The hairy finger, flesh cushioned around the great silver ring, *argent massif,* with its oblong black stone, it's poised now, theatrically suspended over the dial of the telephone: ten thousand old francs were what he was talking about, this note is what he wants, it is a one hundred franc bill still here in the little change purse, crumpled like thieves' money. He spreads out its wrinkles in slow motion, as a teacher does,

intercepting a note between pupils . . .
Go and collect the goods you have deigned to pay us for!
Down the steps, back to the glossy acreage of vinyl tiles.

The little clump of worthy shoppers has heaped up even more, immobile, eternal, and an eternity it is taking to place the wine, milk, and lentils in the two dimensional, still resisting the third dimension, crisp paper bag; aperture still not wide enough, it will rip, take it, this is my bundle, give them my back for their eyes to bore: *Ladies, this is the back of a thief,* out through the glass doors . . . Half a month's rent gone on Raymond's mini-sausages and we shall eat lentils. This coat, this chance buy in Portobello Road, drizzle bringing its fatal weight down now: *a flyer's coat,* you must have been joking and the door on the room with its toy bolt will not hold either . . .

Boulevard Sextius, of course not, Antoine, I don't live here, no, I live in Armistice Street, Rue du Onze Novembre, you know, the street that elbows off from Sextius, not on Sextius and I didn't come away with the Strasbourg sausages. Of course, here it is a political act to steal, yet I get the point: systematized, it will push inflation to its limits, burst the capitalist balloon and bring them crashing down ... Oh yes, for the moment they're reckoning on it, there's a five per cent margin built into the price-tag to allow for the shoplifters and still safeguard the profits but they could soon be disarmed . . . Just look at the beautiful choreography of the rebel supermarket trolleys in that film, what was it? *Tout va bien,* multiply that by the hundred odd thousand supermarkets and what do we have, baby? Yes you do it *pour contester, démarche révolutionnaire,* for a laugh also, *pour rigoler* and simply because you don't have the bread to feed these gargantuan monsters: MONOPRIX PRIXUNIC CASINO . . . but then, SUMA is a tricky individual, haven't seen any chain-reacting SUMA phenomenon in these towns as there is with the others. Oh, I know, it's also a matter of honour to steal: But you didn't PAY for it did you? . . . Are you joking? Lifted it, of course, *mais qu'est-ce que tu penses? je l'ai fauché.* No, really, it's not just a case of giving Big Papa of Authority a voice and a face, coming into some rapport of intimacy with him, seeing the oblong black stone on the hairy finger dial the number to bring the little daughter back home: ha! Gravity giddied god all right, swooping down to show the nicotine stains on his teeth, deliver the oracle into the sonorous conch of her ear, and then release a cloud of garlic over the prodigal child . . .

He's still there at the doorway of the black garage, a new Gitane stuck to the lower lip, that's all. From now on, will have to go down Sextius on the other side, away from him, away from SUMA.

What a cell: vertiginous Gothic of heaped penumbra, denser shadows scuttle through the whole volume as the door gives way. The wardrobe mirror wobbles the wall-paper bouquets, and that face below the waves is fish-numb, lips swollen, poised apart, glazed eyes. Walt Disney Ophelia. The dampness in here, green reaches pooling darkness. The walls in the cabinet de toilette are growing their moss. Pink and rust of the ochre tiles through the little window. That is the roof of the morgue. Sometimes in this narrow street, the hearse gets caught taking the corner into the Rue Van Loo: extraordinary manoeuvres are necessary to let the dead pass through . . .

The ancient woman mutters her anger from the basement flat, the disease is growing in her mouth, filling her space, sometimes takes an excursion into the street as she spits through the bars of the half submerged window and everywhere DÉFENSE DE CRACHER formulates it, gives official status to the national bronchitis, and yet she has a joke for the stooping shape that pauses to take her shopping list: he still chuckles as the *boulangerie* door flaps behind him.

The lentils slide like beach pebbles out of the plastic into the water. And what is there to add: no bay leaf, no good old bacon bone. Let them simply soak in the still water. Thin membrane of the aluminium top peels away so easily from the plastic Margnat bottle. Nothing has happened, just got cold that's all, all that's needed is a good dose of mamma warmth, get toasted against the central heating radiator and red without and red within watch you pop your luscious seeds pomegranate . . . Gauche surrealism, really Finnerty, something even regressively fin-de-siècle about its lyricized eroticism, *that,* you're joking, is that its title: *Self-Portrait with Pomegranate?* The metamorphosis of the pomegranate figures clearly enough from the timorous pink of the ripening fruit to the expulsion of the glistening seeds, six states serially exhibited and multiplied by the three piece mirror. And the *Jeune Fille à sa Toilette* motif is only gently parodied, if that, as she gives her back and her red hair to the mirror, apparently tackling the imagined effrontery of the viewer's gaze. Oh dark stranger, save this maiden from her short-circuited fertility. Texture, I must say, is ably handled, the bolder impasto being reserved for the multiple image of the pomegranate, the girl's face simply stained . . .

But Hérodiade is still within the wintry snake sheath of that skin, dreaming of opulent gardens and the sun beyond is such a cruel scythe, it will reap the fruit, but caressed within the inner lands of ice, of glass and glacial mirrors, its abstract blades will do no harm . . . Yet now the burns of ice and sun are fierce, are one, the glaciers will melt, she shudders between the poles: the horror, sweet horror of virginity:

> *J'aime l'horreur d'être vièrge et je veux*
> *Vivre parmi l'effroi que me font mes cheveux*

and a glance is all it takes, as easy as the pop song:

> *Just one look, that's all it took, yeah*
> *Just one look*

for the splitting of the tutti frutti heroine when the Saint's head is brought in on a platter, golden, it makes a solar halo, so symbol severed from the body takes flight and, divided by its abstract orbit, purely abstract mind you, daddy can she dance — her daddy is gone too you see, warrior he is, in a high landscape bristling with blades, raising his trumpets to the erectile pines — and so she dances, one breast, the other, this thigh, that, nudging the perfect sheath of dress . . . Oh no, she doesn't move, it's all in the annals of the mind, you see, Antoine, but the blank page divides, says Mallarmé, around its deepened pleats, ineffably cleft by the saintly song, into its fragments of candour and the music is heard welling welling, not yet that high piping but Hérodiade, despite the di di diamonds of her name is as sombre and as red as a pomegranate unfolding its teeming fertility, her seed is sown in his silent song *aboli bibelot d'inanité sonore* she is . . . Leave me alone with this head, she says, aaaah bolii *ah beau lys,* the saint as man abolished, abstracted by the bowl from which she flings his head, his necrophilic gaze pillows her between the pleats, the belly beneath the textual mesh becomes — she hums a music contradictory to the intellect — we all know of course that intellect is Phoebus, solar, male, and virile flight alone is saintly yet . . . The rhythm, man, the rhythm of the drives we get from mother night, it's heard now through her jungles, insistently it pounds and pipes and her name is sown below the respectable words in the text, opening them up for ever *eh eh éros héro* and *dia* not of diamonds anymore but *dia* for that separation where same is not its mirrored same, for that endless inner cleft and *roses,* roses all the way, she unfolds her read interior, splitting infinitely now, she becomes the body of the text and poetry will never be the same again and our well tended semantic fields are sown with mines, this is an anarchist, says Sartre, but his bomb is a book, yet Mallarmé watches the milky Rhône flow on through Avignon while painter friends and future poets die like flies in the Paris Commune: this is a regrettable disturbance to the inner vision of the Book, politics an anecdote to be packed away, dispatched with a letter on a train; death stalks the famished streets of Paris and poems germinate in Provence . . . Oh yes, Antoine, this is the man I have reached some highs with, yes yes you put it the right way: *Lovely Rita Meter Maid* made by metre not by men, never quite making it out of the margins, locked in the mock military carapace, strip that off and you find she invents another retreat: No you can't come in she purrs alluringly from behind the barricade of borrowed words . . . MADEMOISELLE RITA ARE YOU THERE?

Mademoiselle Rita! On vous demande au téléphone, Mademoiselle Rita! The stairwell is resounding with the gravel voice and the *Oui Monsieur, j'arrive,* comes out a barely audible croak. Quick quick rinse away the purple stain of wine on lips, strange child this Hérodiade with her private fiestas: stupid solemnity of it all really and FLUCK, too much toothpaste quirts out of the tube. *Mademoiselle REEETAH!* The waves of his voice break on the edge of another octave: Sérisier is becoming exasperated. No. Eight-thirty, can't be Laurence, she could hardly be past Lyon and Jean . . . Impossible, doesn't even have the number. Sérisier's face is straining upwards, his eye pouches foot-lit like a stagey Degas, the whole face a meaty contortion between the foreshadowed flights of stairs, must try a series sometime, call it The Landlord or *Le Propriétaire* or Lines of Flight, yes the uneasy tenancy of the organic in domestic rectilinearity. *Mademoiselle Rita, c'est un monsieur, il a l'accent parisien, Mademoiselle.* Simply Mademoiselle Rita not Finnerty

	Finnerty	fine air
		fine art
Rita	Finnerty	ra-ta-ta-ta Rita *finie*
		rites of inertia for tin divinity
		fin inert
		can't swim
		away

All those times spent scrawling the permutations and combinations of it, never unlocking the inscrutable syllables of the absurdly inherited name. Dropped from the fine air my father did, but sprinkled the sea with these pixie syllables to tinkle tinkle on . . . infinitely.

Good old Sérisier in a more jaundicing light now, the crew cut crop bristling yellow, smile clenching the pale eyes in the delta webbing of creases, the sun-spotted parchment of skin on the hands cupping the ear and mouthpiece of the receiver. Ceremony of it: he offers me the voice of a man, passing me the treasury of little black holes as one transforms in passing the pepper shaker, for instance, in the trance of desire. He tiptoes over the mirror surface of the parquet, slips between the panels of the double door, doesn't know the rent is blown on a pack of mini-strasburgers . . . *Allô allô . . . Ah, c'est toi, Rita?*

That caressive muffled voice . . . Jean's coming out of sleep. Secure the mouthpiece of the receiver with the other hand as well, keep cool, keep cool, he must be asking for something from me but now my razor-sharp *Oui, c'est moi* has cut the silence. Clinical clarity of it: fit for that heart surgeon anyhow.

But how dddid you know I was here, Jean?

There was no sense in asking that.

Ah bébé, he is saying. *Bébé,* yes of course, that's what his siesta and stage life has diminished it to. Lids shuttering the amber light of those eyes as he moves wordlessly towards me and then: *Bébé.* His sleep or the amber stillness of the whisky he has been staring into has produced this diminutive deposit: Rita reduced to *bébé* at the bottom of the glass and attainable before she drains away through the black holes of the receiver and here we go again, breathing out our silence along this line from Paris to Aix-en-Provence *no tinkling chain to throw to you no name to give what lies between our boundaries unendingly* and groping out of the entanglement of blankets and sheets, his warm flesh has vague faunesque memory of something graspable and gone so grasp the receiver . . .: *ah bébé.* The original Rita-*oiseau* dropped in primary colours from the bald Australian sky just like the parrot in the blue cloudless void of the Sidney Nolan. Put the birdie in a golden cage, let it paint and speak the barred world and *Look, Jean-Marie, did you ever see anything like it, and when it talks Bernard, never heard anything like it either, this little rousse australienne with its mixture of Belleville slang and Racinian French.*

Non non, ma p'tite Rita, it's not my telepathic powers, they've atrophied since you left, you know. Ran into your old *copine* Christine Ricardou the other day. She gave me your number. Who's old gravel-voice who answered the phone? Got yourself a new protector *hein?* Is it because you're still so *mal-armée* against the advances of actors?

Ha ha Jean, that was my landlord. Still the same compulsive Parisian need to pun . . .

Comment? What was that?

Oh nothing, nothing. I don't understand, Jean. That's all. After all this time.

After all this time I thought you might see things a bit more in perspective . . . Even thought I might be able to treat myself to a little excursion down south one of these days . . .

Yes, of course. Should see things obediently remote like the background of a Florentine Renaissance painting. Blued and kept at bay. Never let the past intrude on the action poised in the charmed foreground. And would you keep me here, acquiescent to your gaze, your voice, the rhythm of past curves never threatening the evidence of the isosceles triangle. Never let those other voices butt in on the visible harmonics of your surface rhetoric. Frame me, freeze me in your lines of flight o lord.

So I am the one who sees things . . . warped?

O là là! Take it easy. Still the same little hedgehog is our Rita, I see. All prickly defences.

> *Bristling hemisphere of toothpicks I am, still coquettishly bearing my browned cocktail onions and sweaty cubes of cheddar after the party. Take it, take my tainted load. If you can brave the prickly defences, that is. Tell him. Tell him now but calmly, mellifluously as he would do it, that it's no use going on.* Moi voleuse de saucisses.

No, no. Sorry Jean. It's good to hear your voice. It's just . . .

> *No better as a shish kebab. Self-portrait as shish kebab. Skewer shaped like a pen or brush.*
> *Silent motor turning my meat and vegetable load. My singed meats. One day I'll act it out too,* Monsieur le Comédien.

It's just what, ma grande taciturne?

> *Always my or our Rita. First I'm little, then I'm big . . . Ladies and Gentlemen, let me present the prototypical inflatable woman. Guaranteed obedience to perspective. Place advance order now.*

It's just that I don't know whether it's any use reactivating things after all this time . . . I mean . . . what makes you ring, Jean?

Surely, *ma chérie*, it doesn't need all that justification. Christine mentioned that Laurence was coming back up to Paris and that, if you'll forgive me, my dear Rita, reminded me of you. I did feel a little more for you than you gave me credit for and I wondered if you were still so angry, so . . . mutinous? But I gather time hasn't helped as far as you're concerned . . .

Mutinous? I was hardly what you could call mutinous with you Jean. That's just it. I didn't know where I was any longer, what I wanted. Began to despise myself for being so totally pliant, so . . . I had to salvage something of myself after you . . .

> *Far from mutinous with you Jean. That was a fine slip as you would say anyhow, as if you saw me as the rebel crew and you the lordly captain. Let your fingers idle over me, nude to your parted peignoir while you toy with some other bait, of course a work call, an actress in your new show, the* Fraise

musclées *or something, something more delectable on the other end of the telephone line. Bet you're making some other captive* odalisque *just that little bit insecure now as you make this call. Ah yes. Put down my brush, grapple for the turps rag and a change of clothes while you rattle your car keys, forget my classes at the* Beaux Arts, *that bronze I was about to pour, my man is manifest and rearing to go at his appointed hour. And Rita, he says, those tights are really impossible, haven't you got something more suitable? ... Last night you were so aggressive at dinner; what was all that crap about* scopowhatever *in the theatre? ...*

After what? After I *what*, Rita, what was that? It seems to me that it was *you* who shot through without any explanation. I've never been able to fathom what that final tantrum was about. And the number of times I rang only to be told by that bulldog bitch of a concièrge of yours that Mademoiselle was indisposed or working and not to be disturbed or not there . . .

Simply hang up now and reinforce the Hystérique *identikit he's pieced together. Mellifluous and resonant, he thinks he's got the whole simmering female soma on call with that voice, maybe he has, up and down France, callous jauntiness of it, anyhow, it's for Laurence he's ringing. Get round the red one, inscrutable, taciturn and mutinous and now it's* impenetrable *he's saying. Impenetrable, yes because when it comes to that, you haven't been able to empty her of all her contents, two cursory words of tenderness and then you ramrod sperm-spurt shudder heavily collapse, perhaps there was something else inside after all, something that resisted, makes her find her own way home to* Ménilmontant . . .

I ran, yes I did run, Jean. I couldn't explain.
Say it, say it now then. Do me the favour of at least explaining, Rita.
I think at best I was some quaint fey child for you. Something a little exotic from the Antipodes. Occasionally I could summon up some wit and that was all right for a while. Or I was a rather pitiable *paumée* for you, a would-be painter doing some kind of finishing-school time in Paris. And I felt . . . My little store of self-belief was being constantly ransacked by your ironies. I had to

get away to salvage something. I couldn't explain. I had no voice left.

Well, at least you seem to have found it now ... your voice. And perhaps I'd better leave off here before ... What was it? Before I ransack your store of self-belief again? Ah, Rita.

You're doing it again. Quote me in slow-motion to reveal the little melodramas you think I'm addicted to. Like Laurence. Perhaps they could harmonize their classical ironies.

Would you like Laurence's address, Jean?

What happened, Rita? You know, ha ha, we called you the Siamese twins? I thought you two were going to exhibit together down there.

Oh? No, no. I'm not ready for that. Laurence has decided to do hers in Paris, that's all. Look, I'm sure she'd be glad to see you. You can contact her at Claude Wahl's studio or chez Danièle, Château de Vincennes.

And you? You won't have it that it's for you I rang, Rita ...

Look Jean, I will write. Find it hard to talk like this. I'm sorry. Perhaps we can get together this summer ...

Ah, but that is a long time *ma chérie* ...

His voice is not committed, trailing off into silence already with the muffled stream of formulae *allez, salut ma belle Rita, à bientôt j'espère quand-même, hein? Je t'embrasse* ... click.

Siamese twins eh ha ha. Hyphenated identity broken down, snapped on the hiatus the French brings to it: Rita-et-Laurence. The red one tried, tasted, reinvestigated. Still too dark, let's try the other one now. But Laurence will know how to deal with him, not so easily taken in. Anyhow, she has Maurice, her nice industrious lawyer friend. Outwardly a bit bland, a bit boring even, like the lentils. But to the knowing palate! *I knew instinctively Rita, that behind all those neutral bourgeois-Mr-Anybody statements, there was a real depth. Doesn't waste himself in a flashy display.*

Now he is gone. That's finished. Antoine swivels on his heels, leaves the dumb door to be stared at. And now the receiver like a stupid dog's bone in my hand. Black holes we sift ourselves through ... *And who shot through, hein?* Slipped out even that first night from under your sleep-heavy body, your interior still hung with her tapestries, *Rita, I'm sorry, I'm still not over Chantal, I'll get there, give me time,* and her prints of strangely British horses mounted on their red watered silk, into the coiled pantyhose before the sun came. No no, *Monsieur Mallarmé,* no lusty cymbals clashing, no giddy split gobbling the perspectives of the early morning Auteuil streets, bumper-to-bumper the frosted cars to disappearance point suck into her and out, out not as waves push out again no, not that, left behind those alabaster hips, the concave belly, suddenly pre-nubile as an Edvard Munch against his heavy maturity, now sore where she was numb, numbed his drunken agitation to sleep did she, silent buffer to the distant bang-bang: what has this heaving mass, the hills and precipices of it to do with me, working away so industriously, quite touching really, and yet it doesn't touch, lapping up the mileage, on it strives, changing gears, the remote insistence of it, walled in she is, never quaking at the prod, the prod repeated and steadfast, she watched from her battlements, her head a sentinel perched on high . . . IMPENETRABLE she is indeed: I did not ask this stranger here to dine, the drawbridge will not be lowered . . . And to think she used to wince at the literature of love-as-war: now watch her live the metaphor! Besieged and now a sordid refugee but disembodied and the kohl-blotted eyes meet their ghosts in the glass of the Metro doors, swing away until it is his golden body left behind with dreams of *Gummipuppen,* Barbie Dolls and WHO shot through, *hein, hein?*

Did the same to him, that machismo caricature, wouldn't negotiate with the real voice and now it trails its wake, little parcels of energy exploding, tracking through the network of telephone lines and nerves. Some voices seem to have a certain pitch with you, a certain resonance that seems to work retroactively with you, eh, Rita. Hmm, very interesting. And tell me, is it enough to bring you to a pitch of pleasure? Hmmm? Some kind of ecstasy enabled by his absence. That's right, the disembodied residue of the male, the voice, and even that, at such a distance, drained back into the dot-dot-dots morse-coding in your flesh. And yes, was that you talking of oral fetishism or is it aural? So this is the way we might come is it? Symbiotic union reached for you, but after the event of course, is a tongue at one end of France and an ear at the other. No furious battle of limbs is necessary then, is it? Tell you what: why don't you buy yourself a recording, store him on cassette, play him to the rotations of the sculpture you've dreamt up . . . or better still, dream up the resonance for surely, the memory of aural hallucination is an even better solution for a girl like you . . . hmmm?

Sérisier looks solicitous.

Bonsoir Monsieur.

He looks perplexed rather. Replace the receiver. The wrong way.

Ça va, Mademoiselle? He wants the story.

Mais oui Monsieur, merci.

Bonsoir, Mademoiselle Rita.

Here again on this narrow plank of a bed. Groping for sleep. Always as solution. Suspend all the carping particles in the stagnant waters of it, tepid, tepid, slipping into it again, anyhow should be allowed this indulgence . . .

Laurence, you have a way of planning a day for your friends. Will tell her that one day. Pillow with its perfect moulding all the same . . .

Surely not lost again in another library and all the books are summed up so succinctly here on the catalogue cards, Antoine: it is Antoine I am explaining it to, and here they are spine-to-spine, but no: they are all encased in a strange cardboard housing, boxed. He extracts one. No, it isn't Antoine at all, someone else; his eyes have a marble gaze and he is explaining it all to me:

The boxes are all empty, Mademoiselle. We got rid of the books to simplify things for the reader of the future, you see and ... (he extracts a white card) all that is left is this. It records the residual impact on the collective imagination. (A nictitating membrane slides across his gaze — is he winking at me?) Imagination is but the faculty, of course, to abbreviate experience (same wink) *resonantly*.

Great conical shafts of light are cast from the eyes, more like glazed jelly now, sweeping the shelved corridors. I see that he is a genius. That I must accept his word.

From this book, he is murmuring, nibble, nibble at my ear, of Rita Nefertiti's drawings, all we have noted is the cumulo-nimbus.

I need to correct him but see something somehow reassuring nestled in the jumbled letters and the raised index finger tells me that I am not to interrupt. This, he resumes, sucking his whole face in taut around the gums, accounts for the *accumulation* of images (he marks out a bracket for me to recognize the pun) all amounting to one cloud which we have here resolved in a drop of ink.

Yes yes, my dear, she sews with ink. Sews with each line a scar on the living tissue she draws upon. And really, we need a bit of a break from all these dark romantic ladies, don't you think?

My laughter is laced with the visible harmonics of his as it echoes back to me. A feeling of treachery, but so remote, as I agree with him.

A bit of spunk. That's what we need. Not this turgid chorus of dark ladies bemoaning their origins in some viscous stream where they would have us applaud the vicissitudes of their hormonal variations. Spunk, spunk, that's what we need, old girl.

He claps me on the back and slips into the enormous cardboard coffin on the shelf: Just going to void this one. Be back with you in a moment.

In this library, I realize now, there are various exhibits. A voice coming through the P.A. announces:

And here we have, Ladies and Gentlemen, along with our many other attractions, the one and only SHRINE TO THE ANTI-ARTS: Expressionism, Fauvism, Dada, Pop and all their re-enactments!

Look around to check the other tourists I am with. There are none.

It is customary here to address each person as a plurality, each, *n'est-ce pas,* carrying within, in suspended discontinuum, past, present, and future selves, the female, the male, the hermaphrodite, the polymorphous perverse, the transvestite and what have you. You must acquiesce to your *potential fictif.* This exhibition has been arranged for your benefit by an inventive young immigrant from Algeria. To reward him for his contribution towards the proliferation of the French Cultural Heritage, the Government has issued him with multiple identity papers, a uniform to keep them in and unlimited computer time. Yes, you may smile, my dears, but dada, like all the movements staged by you petulant middle-class children, has long since had our blessing. You see, *les enfants,* we de-fuse your little bombs and then, you might say, diffuse the relics amongst you, to arrange as you see fit in your *musées imaginaires — pour la gloire de la République,* he laughs.

The voice has receded into the mesh of the loud speaker and I see now that his library — or is it a museum? — has expanded to enclose what seems to be the whole planet, but crowds have been reduced to their salient features, their resultant gestures, projected on the hemispherical wall: black gaping hole of hunger, the thrust of the clenched fist, the slumbering jowls of the replete. Towering above — why hadn't I seen it before? — are gigantic circular flies . . .

This is the city of the collective mind. Your good old global village — to stir some fond memories in the older amongst you. (Is that falsetto wheeze interference or some travesty of mirth?) We have you all on micro-cassettes, micro-video, electro-encephalograms and cat-scans: your very own *dada* becomes the data-ah-ah-ah here enshrined. And we invite you to include in your itinerary our library of rural and urban smells where you may experience, in the privacy of your individual, acclimatized booth: the rich, heady smell of the Judge performing his sacrificial duty! the faint smell of the Diplomat! and, for the adventurous, not for the faint of heart, the smell of the Urban Guerilla! the Black Panther! the Hunger Striker! You name it, Ladies and Gentlemen, we have it! Yes, yes, we can now envisage for you Happy Few the elimination of the distressing clutter of the globe. No, no, my dears, this is *not* genocide, this worthy practice is nothing more than abstraction which will, as we have advertised, enact for you the thrilling drama of Imagination as Resonant Abbreviator of the World.

Now I am inside a great perspex hemisphere within the other one. Huge flashing computer letters circulate: COMING HAPPENING: POP GOES THE DADA . . . SEE FEEL AND RIDE YOUR OLD-TIME FAVOURITES . . . COMING HAPPENING . . . As I draw near to the first display, the legend comes into focus: THINGS ARE REALLY HAPPENING IN ARLES. The head-set I am wearing whispers to me: You have just switched on Vincent. My fingers grope to readjust it, find that it is grafted there, onto my head, its wires continuing my nerves, it is pulsating, organic now and no no the high-pitched pain, the head-set a bandage, an excrescence of flesh rather, my ear, my ear . . . The stars are rolling around, can't focus on them, now fracturing, now fluid . . . Select from a glibly rotating stand Lolita's heart-shaped sun-glasses, and there they are, a myriad of them, trophied from the shiny dome around me: these conical cocky tongues. They are aimed at the hyperbolic ice-cream

57

erected in the centre as focal totem. It is clear now that the whole show is organized around this ice-cream.

In fact, we are flying now, yes, this must be the Ringmaster from Algeria the P.A. announced. My God, I am trying to ask him, what have they done to you? But no, it isn't him at all. This is the pure decadent. He must be myopic: his eyes bulge from the refraction through the thick lenses of his glasses. He is etiolated: *You have never seen the sun*, I am saying, or is it my voice? *You are all rickety. Drink the white milk of dawn*, the voice tells him.

But no, my dear, it is you who need a good draught. *Black* milk, black, wasn't it? We can give you Celan any day. We store him here, you know:

> Black milk of dawn we drink it evening
> we drink it noon and morning we drink it nights
> we drink it and drink it
> we're digging a grave in the sky there'll be no
> hemming in.

He fingers coquettishly the frozen locks of his horse's mane and his eyes blur . . . Around us, the ghost images begin to fuse, they are fusing into a white stream, now we are speeding and yet his voice follows the same languid pacing: I am a man of many tongues and I lap it up, lap it up, ride on, sister, ride on . . . This is the one and only galactic trip, this is the way, sister, this is the Milky Way, the cosmos is our cow . . .

But now the objects gather up their ghosts again and stand separate, remote from each other. The merry-go-round has stopped. Back with my cheek against the cold perspex. Now I see it and know that this is the exhibit which must have brought me in here in the first place: this immense white bed with its crocheted quilt in white too, and beyond, a *trompe-l'oeil* sky affixed somehow to the hexagonal facet of the dome cradling the great mattress. The interstitial armature ramifies, becomes a wind-tortured almond tree, bursts into shards of light. Splintering whiteness . . .

My child, so much light does disturb you after all, he is saying.

And now: devastating clarity, like an algebraic simplification. Eternal. Is she mummified? Lying in state? The hair: russet pools in the dark entanglement of locks against the pillow. It's as if . . .

No, but it can't be Laurence, they've got her all wrong. Why do I only see it now, this other head, hanging limp. The neck . . . But it's a travestied attempt at a connection: a broken hen's neck, loose, the head dangles loose. The head lacks consistence: the face is situated somewhere between the loose skin and the bones. Atrophied. The fleshy outcrops are undermined. Can't locate it, can't fix it and yet those lids, tucked in at the corners . . . and those straight, silken lashes. It is Laurence. Laurence on display and emptied of herself. My cry has been stifled; let the head fall back to press its nose against the perspex.

The broken hen has done its futile dash into history. Dry, monotone, it's that voice again, but the Ringmaster has disappeared. Next to her, the Mummy Queen sleeps on; see that this is Laurence too, but neutralized, almost beyond recognition, yet I have the knowledge that it's her and . . . *Air, air,* let me breathe! The dome has . . . How could I have made such a gross mistake: it is a pyramid. So . . . *Nefertiti,* that's why he called me that, to con me in . . . *Let me out let me out I'm not ready let me breathe* . . . Trying to shout it but I am gagged . . .

Saliva pooling around my mouth. Hold still. Still the boom of heart. Pivoted on the crest of its wave. *Et l'avare silence, et la massive nuit.*

Well, at least you seem to have found it now, your voice, he says.

II

LIGNES DE FUITE

No black milk of dawn. There is clarity in here. Levity. Am coiled like a famished cat. I can spring. I am not laid out for ever in this coffin of blankets and clothes. The Mistral has cleared the air, brought in the broken leaves, tattered remnants of autumn, now that it's nearly spring. With one simple gesture, I can throw back this weight. The chairs, the table and the desk will all redescend into places as I rise. They will sit aplomb with their normal volume, send their vertical images down into the tiles. It is simple. I can strip off these layers, whip back this weight. Night traffic. Trampled body. I am an *auto-route*. The crumbs casting long shadows across the table. The sun is still low. Macadam madam: the tonnage that passes over you. It was a mistake. You can be relieved of this pressure. The cold water will be good on this body, the skin will tighten over it. It will be lean. Who was that who equated leanness with intelligence?

I will leap out of this bed. I will be the ambulant armature of this room. I will be a knot of vectors. I will move along any one of them. No necessity in contiguity. Acquiesce to that *potential fictif. Pourquoi pas?* If Denise catches me talking aloud ... *Putain Rita, tu deviens fada ou quoi? Trop de pinard, Denise, m'suis un peu soûlée hier soir. Le gros rouge qui tâche.*
    Red Ned that goes to the head. The dregs of wine have evaporated from the Duralex glasses. They have left a rosy film. Gossamer projection of it on the marble, maintaining its veins through the overlay. Chardin could have painted that. *Nature morte,* not still life, but dead, possible nature. Trace the curve

of the painter's upward mobility through the series of *natures mortes*, objects more and more sumptuous, birds and fruits more and more exotic. Not for Vincent: a chair, a work boot, a humble flower, despised because available to anyone.

Easing now out of the tepid stream in the icy, soap curdling in the puddle at my feet. The little transfer, lamb, ribbons and flowers, is peeling off the baby's tub. The water breaks its veils over my breasts, nipples shrinking, hardened under the shock, the little rivulets scurry down. The colander collects the lentils. They have released their fog overnight into the water. Idiot images. They are all dispensible as the Ringmaster would say. No reason to harbour any souvenirs of it all. The slumped pouch of the camembert is continent now in its new yellow skin. No ugly farewells, Laurence. It lands obediently in the waste-paper basket. The crumbs are evacuated with one swipe of the sponge. This broom is expert: it veers around the legs of the chairs. The little door quakes around the toy bolt. That thunderous knock will be Denise.

O là là là . . . QUELLE *nuit! Ouff!* I'm famished. *Mademoiselle fait le ménage?*
   This room is too small to contain the choreography of those gestures swooping the sleeves around, the non-stop tap-tap flexion of the brown finger, bitten nail, on the Gauloise. A cylinder of ash on the clean surface of the desk. Another on the tiles. Polished blackness of those eyes. Their abstract focus. Her strange impersonal warmth. They scan the room too, do their inventory. Not like Antoine's though. Denise is simply alert to any innovation. Doesn't know drama, not one of her categories. Things happen, then more things happen. All meet with a democratically distributed: *ô là là, ouff, punaise, putain.* And then she feasts. For days on end she ignores the great demands of that body, its massive bulk and curves, resists sleep and then *ouff,* she says yes to hunger and the mountainous pile of oiled garlic spaghetti unravels as the fork plies its route from plate to mouth, the plate is bare: *ouff, j'ai trop bouffé.* She's looking in the cupboard now. *Tu n'aurais pas un bout de pain?* Just a crust, a *biscotte* or anything? Show her the knob in the waste-paper basket. But you can't throw all that out, Rita. What's come over you? Come into money or something?

Denise fishes it out. That and the camembert. Spread the wax cloth on the desk and put the steaming bowl of coffee before her. No problems with Denise. The stale end of the bread is shaven, the rest is broken, hers now a gesturing baton, just like the Gauloise. It dunks in and out of the bowl of coffee, loses its jam in there, the pools of butter glitter on the surface, the jam deposit is recovered. *Ouff, ça fait du bien!* Know who I ran into last night?

Gérard?

No. Guess again.

Antonine?

Close. Opposite sex.

Antoine?

Correct. So you kicked the poor man out, did you?

Did I? Is that what he said?

Umm. She tilts the bowl to her mouth drains it, crumbs and all. Seemed a bit dejected. Seemed to expect a dose of comfort from good old Mamma Denise.

Did he get it?

Ha ha. In a way haha. But not the way you're thinking. Just seemed to want to talk, that's all. You must have given him a hard time. Won't do him any harm.

If he's played some sort of misunderstood victim, that makes me sick. Needs to be congratulated all the time, reassured that he's floating free, and all the time pouring irony on the umbilical cord linking him to the home module. Had to do it *pour le gosse,* he keeps saying.

Ouais ... Mais enfin, Rita. You're being a bit heavy there aren't you? The way you put it makes him sound like some moral monster. He's *sympa,* really, just a bit young to have got himself domesticated. So ... Mademoiselle Laurence Santé ... or should I say Sainteté ha ha finally went back to Paris, did she?

Aïe Denise, that's a bit strong.

Who's talking now? Heard you wail through the litany of her saintly ways a few times, Rita. In any case, *c'est pas méchant.* She's got us all placed on her scale of moral excellence, me placed pretty low, you on a slightly higher rung, and she's not afraid of giving us the daily bulletin on our chances of salvation. Got to respect her for saying it, if that's where she is. No, that girl's got something I envy in a way. Hard core of self-belief. High density moral fibre ha ha hahaha.

Denise walks to the window, wedges her fingers into the back pockets of her jeans. Good solid mass of the buttocks pushing out the pockets. Another plume of smoke. The throaty chuckle is contagious. You betray me, you do, you do, Laurence said. I do. And then, the mummified saint and the broken hen? Won't tell Denise that.

Parc Jourdan. Sea of marble pebbles. Crisp. Crunching under foot. Crystalline. If Denise knew the scenario, she'd really laugh. The sausages confiscated, the lentils swelling in the still water, while the shoplifter plays Hérodiade. This pebble in my hand. The cold snaps around each step. Clean cold. There it is, the *gazon*. The carpet of lawn, the green component, must have its complementary opposite latent in the fallow beds. Euclidean rigour of it: the trimmed miniature hedges stencil out the arabesques, fleur-de-lys and diamonds that will flower in spring. The rigid cartoon of a garden seed sewn, bulb heavy now. Geometry germinates in France. The fertile Cartesian mind foresees the tilted rosace composition where the great steps divide. Further back, the Corsican pines and cypresses interlock their horizontals. A few verticals waver, pale off into the vague blue. Obedience to perspective. Obediently remote as a background in a Florentine Renaissance painting. Blued trees and rockscapes: signal of Mystery contained within the illusionist space. Never intruding on the action poised in the charmed foreground, the rhythm of those curves never threatening the evidence of the isosceles triangle, within whose security I place this step. Those other voices never butting in on the surface rhetoric. Man within the main triangle is there as master of landscape, purveyor of inscapes. God of perspective, and radiant with its visible lines, the *lignes de fuite* tapering to disappearance point, his keen eye keeps it all in tow. The cypresses are still held in check as I climb, he descends the stairs around the rosace. That body on the other side seems static, as if it will never complete its descent. As if it would arrest us forever at the base line of the triangle. Profile . . . three-quarter, frontal gaze now. As if he would freeze-frame me too. As if two profiles sliding past one another were impossible . . . As if he were challenging me to check the conventional non-encounter-in-park.

The smoothness of this particular pebble. That head of his is pure, still. As neat, as bald. Held perfectly immobile above the shoulders. Awful simplicity. As if it were irreducible to anything but its own inscrutable, unsayable dense mass. That gaze is directed here on me, unequivocally though. Tugging at mine. I can resist it but not by evasion. Resist it by meeting it with an equivalent strength. Its physical load pulls all the same. The face is an impersonal mask, and yet . . . those vivid eyes would . . . know me. The pebble rotates under my finger, in my palm. This man. Sixty perhaps, or seventy. There is no time. I will never move from here. My gaze is holding his now with an exactly equivalent thrust. My good eyes. There is no danger, after all. Could be locked forever in this balance, in this suspension. You are bald, you have no age, you have no name. You are stripped back to this nowness. You are simply there, in your gaze. Feel it making neural tracks back, back to the wall of my skull. But now . . . it's beginning to slip, feel myself slipping, viscous, need to break this concentration, distract myself from this. Of course you are an outsider. Only someone outside would offer this gratuitous . . . recognition. Do I look like a thief? Along whose lines am I drawn? No. No, I'm not out there where you are. I have an age. I paint you know. I might even paint this, Monsieur. I am on my way to see a friend who is normal enough. I have a *carte de séjour*. People send me letters sometimes. I get phone calls. My landlord smiles at me. Your face widens, sags below the jaw. Are you trying to impersonate Jean Genet or something? And yet your gaze is still rigid. It says: I am young, eternally, erect as Anubis, keeping watch within the pyramid. If that's what you want, no. I'm not Nefertiti yet, Mister. This is too much.

From the brow upwards, there are lines, knots, but somehow the perfection of that hemisphere is not marred. Those are mere surface accidents. Texture. How can you show such certitude in those grey eyes? You have too much faith in their message. Go away, dismiss me, pedagogue. I cannot, do not want to sustain it. This was a transparent moment, I was empty in my transit. How did this pebble get into my hand? I can drop it. And is that you saying: Know the moment's stone is egg is egg? I have heard you gurus before with your Be Here Now . . . The stillness of your face is going, there is a nascent smile. You have read it, you are thinking: Go back to your souvenirs then, go fondle your ambitions and sink in your guilt, Dutiful Daughter. You have seen the murky waters.

He gives me that profile again. Now he is completing his descent of the stairs. I have the railway line to cross.

That café is not the *Lapin Agile,* but something about its broken lines, the leaping rhythm of the hoop-back chairs under the desultory, staggered trellis . . . *L'Aiguillage,* must be a converted signalling post and maybe with the level-crossing close by, its sense of hypothetical or provisory departures suggested it to Gérard as a *rendez-vous.* Or would he be so precious? On the other side of the line, rearing up, but without the hint of a curve, from the protective flank of the embankment: the great rectangular planes of the Faculté des Lettres. Beige and the mildest of yellow ochres withdrawn into neutrality. Except for the remnant inscriptions from May '68. You can see from here the glinting jumble of mobylettes and bicycles. The students who still commute here have '68 as romantic refuge to keep them going. Perhaps why there has been no systematic attempt to restore the synthetic marble facing. The annual spring excursion into the promise of revolution LE PRINTEMPS SERA CHAUD is simply written off as mere juvenile exuberance. Underwritten rather. At your age, children, we all fondled thoughts of shooting daddy down; you'll get over it and be back for your diplomas soon enough. JOLI MUR BELLE FAÇADE: the red trail of spray paint gunned hastily over the back entrance. Graffiti palace. C'EST LUI LE CHIENLIT, it's De Gaulle, LA CULTURE PEDALE DANS SA PROPRE MERDE . . . LA CULTURE C'EST LA BARBE, RASONS LES MURS . . . not one fell though in sunny Aix. JOLI MUR JE TE BAISERAI . . . Lacy overlay of ejaculations, built up like a Pollock. Eventually they will elect, within the Ministry of

70

Culture, a *Conservateur des Graffiti et des Slogans Subversifs,* next to, say, POP GOES THE DADA HAPPENING PERMANENT; they will be shown in reverence, there will be *Les Archives des Palimpsests,* an army of clerks employed to catalogue them, a grammar, stylistics, semiotics of graffiti elaborated by the state linguists.

Perhaps why Gérard gives me his little stories to read rather than have them dismissed as psychotherapeutic exercises by that Raymond bloke or subjected to the refined torture of semiotic analysis by Sébastien. What does he want, apart from the knowledge that I have read it, recognize that he has 'been there'? These pages from his diary . . .

Ten o'clock. Fairly homogenized clientele in here, only the assiduous students come at this time. That one, all hennaed tendrils in the sailor's jumper with his *Histoire de la Folie* cocked before him, that could be Gérard's Sébastien. Or this one in the corner with his thighs royally stretched out, rather bored with his *Ni Marx ni Jésus.* Black concentrate in the eyes grazing the edge of the book; no particular modality in their assertion except *connect me with this title.* Studied dandyism in the négligé of the denim outfit; lambswool collar pulled up under the long black hair, plentiful non-functional zips at wrists and obliquely angled across the front panels, main zip undone on a golden skivvy, revealing the *trompe-l'oeil* chest. He greets the twitchy one in the Lennon glasses with an adenoidal *Salut mon vieux, ça va? Et le séminaire freudien, ç'avance? Ah oui, à propos* . . . says Twitch . . .

Vous consommez, Mademoiselle? The waitress smiles loosely. Learn the art of making an expresso last, ninety centimes for one, two hours of warmth. She yells it over her shoulder to the bar. *Traversal* Zips is saying, give you my dream travelogue, brother, see what you make of it . . . *Catachresis,* cata catapult you into my scene, see that catacomb in there, catastrophe of Laurence's hair, can't do a thing with it, *mnemo*something and *meto*blahblah, talking about those shifts, Finnerty to Nefertiti, not a bad one eh, self-glorification in that one and *metaphoric collapses,* whatever happened to the Siamese twins eh, what would Dr Freud say to that, the broken hen and her mummified companion, would I wish that on Mother Hen or was that me cluck-cluck no more,

genotext he is saying, not genocide and *archi pheno meta,* such
fervour, love bestowed on proliferation of prefixes . . .

GROCER'S WIDOW GROCER'S SON

Va-t'en dans ton cageot! She yelled into the pit . . .
Should've put him in an open crate, a lettuce crate, so that
everyone could see who the grocer really was . . . And
then her laughter started, cracked and high, as we walked
away from the grave. Suppose the relatives took it as a
sign of her grief: it's making her hysterical, making her
mind wander, can't quite connect with the loss, they must
have thought. But it wasn't that, wasn't that at all. I can
still feel the same crazy need to laugh and laugh, pushing,
contorting my throat, agony of the stomach
muscles . . .

Oui, Lacan aussi biensûr, Twitch is saying, the slippage of the
signifier . . .

But then it came over me, what it was like to be free as
we walked away. I thought cochon, cochon, *he was a red-*
faced pig, just kept muttering it like some magical
talisman and half-expected to be struck down by lightning
with every step. The sour smell he'd have when he was
angry with her, glistening with cold sweat, pushing her
off by the elbow, away from the counter until she was
staggering, tripping, pinned against the crates and the
hissed curses were frankly bellowed. Usually for having
dealt out too much change to a customer, or, on a caprice,
cut the price by half. The way she operated had nothing
to do with his kind of arithmetic which usually amounted
to topping up the kilo with doubtful tomatoes instead of
the prime: it was rather a measure of how she happened
to be feeling towards that person across the counter at
that particular moment. He'd yell: Get back to the
packing, woman, get back to the crates, vieille connasse,
you should stick to them, you with your fancy ideas about
education, thought you really came down in the world,
being a grocer's wife, didn't you and you can't even do a
goddam sum the kid could do in his sleep . . . The kid!
Only gave me credit for being able to do anything when it

*was a matter of putting her down. Normally it was: The
way you coddle him, he'll end up a pansy for sure, UNE
PETITE TANTOUZE, that's what your little darling's
going to end up. So, after the funeral, when they'd all left
us alone, she took my hand and said: My little prince,
you're going to make me young again, you'll see: we'll be
all right, we're going to have fun together, don't you
worry! And I didn't worry, for a while. She didn't
mention my going back to school and I didn't remind her,
of course. We spent the first weeks making puppets
together, writing little scripts for them, going to the
cinema, fairs ... She had sold the business for a song, I
was told later, but one day before the money had run out,
she said: We're going to do it in style, for once; Céleste
and her Little Prince are going to show them! She dressed
me up in these old velvet pants that finished half way up
the calf: Don't you think twice about it,* mon chéri, *we can
tell them a thing or two about fashion! The moment we
stepped into that restaurant, I felt mortified: the pants,
and then my socks gobbled up the backs of my shoes, an
old silk scarf of hers that she had insisted on knotting
around my neck as the 'final touch' ... It was one of those
quietly luxurious places,* style britannique: *lace and lamps
and silver and poker-faced waiters and it wasn't until we
were led to our table that I really noticed what she was
wearing: an old evening dress that had shed most of its
sequins, like a half-scaled fish and she had draped and
pinned bits of this and that all over herself: she was all
feathers and cloth flowers and brooches and beads ... and
her make-up: the* apache, *the look that was the rage
around the turn of the century, flare and smoulder of the
eyes and the rest was a mixture of clown and whore I
suppose. How CAN you? I thought. How can you do this?
She was so bright, so visible against all those people who
merged in discreetly with the place. Those stares and
nudges and muffled laughs all around us. Then after a
while, all the backs were turned as if it were simpler to
eliminate us from their range of vision, as if the waiter
had been dispatched with an aerosol pack to spray us
away like a pestilence and they needn't be troubled by us
any more. But* Maman *seemed oblivious: she ordered*

escargots, canard à l'orange, pâtisseries, *despite the slight sneer, the pinched nostrils of the waiter. She became more and more jovial with the wine, poured some for me too . . . I must have been about ten or eleven then. I began to feel the warmth mounting, swarming: people, voices, gestures swam, drowned in the blur and soon there were just the two of us. She was beautiful: I still have her photo from around that time in my wallet, a bit remote, faded through the little plastic window, but you can still see the delicacy of those features: the clear high forehead, the slightly cleft chin, the wide mouth with the distinctly etched lips and the eyes, refracting all the light, streaming with it. There's a radiant kind of harmony in that face under the floating cloud of hair, grey or chestnut, I can't remember how far it had gone then.*

Yes, but don't forget about counter-transference, Twitch is saying, take Freud's comments about Irma's oral cavity . . . and what particularly perplexes him are those 'remarkable curly structures' he sees in her throat! The zippered one is laughing, looks around to see if the joke is shared. Evidently it is not. Must try to get a peek at Gérard's wallet to see if he really carries a photo of her . . . All the gagged women . . .

And then the bill arrived, folded over on the little silver tray. Maman *opened it slowly and called the waiter back in the same dreamy posh voice she used to put on sometimes in our puppet shows: SURELY there has been some error in your calculations,* Monsieur? *I could see that it was two hundred and something francs. I can still feel the terror of the remote event which is going to impinge . . . She counted out the contents of her purse, note by note, until the table was littered with them. There were about seventy francs. Well, that is all right, she said, raising an eyebrow — she had powdered out her own eyebrows and pencilled new ones on, two great arches higher up. Her fingers scurried over the bank notes, snapped them together, conjured them away. She was suddenly as deft as a bank teller. She called the waiter back again:* Monsieur, I think I will have some more coffee, in any case. *She slipped one of her rings off into my hand and dispatched me to grab anything else I could find at home and take the lot to the pawnbroker . . . God, the daylight after the muted glow from the lamps in there, all that busy population elbowing its way along the streets, doing shopping, catching buses, hailing friends. But they were miniature insect people: this feeling of power, of weightlessness came over me, as if I could have stepped over the whole of Lyon, like wearing the Seven League Boots, and I started running as I'd never been able to run and I thought, Papa's bronchitic little pansy — not that I really knew what it meant — can he fly! A prince, I am the Little Prince, why not, and she is a queen above all of you with your dull commercial eyes and drab dreams of groceries. It was a miracle: I came back with three hundred francs from a radio, a watch, Papa's collection of stamps.* Maman *wasn't that slightest bit surprised that I'd managed it: she took the money casually and ordered a cognac for herself, another* patisserie *for me, tipped the waiter royally, swept her shawl around her — and there she was: like some fairy queen, draped in spiders' webs and all the vivid flowers. But after that, there were no more fiestas.*

First the neighbours. They must have seen me many a time crawling under the trestle tables at the markets for the odd carrot or potato that could be salvaged. They knew that I hadn't been to school for months either, so eventually the welfare people turned up and it was a string of psychiatric clinics for her and intermittent foster homes for me. Now when I go to see her, she often doesn't seem to recognize me at all or else she'll say: Oh yes, you too . . . and will start humming a little tune to show that she'd really rather be left alone.

Salut Seb! It's Gérard already. Exalted quaver in his voice. So the zippered one is Sébastien. Gérard blinks a few times through his lashes. Tosses his hair. His grace, the usual artistry in conjunction of texture and colour. Rusted ochre, pink ochre and chalky blue.

> *Talk about women objects, Rita. Wonder sometimes about you. Take that Gérard, for instance. Apart from being the latest in a line of beautiful boys, what has he really got to offer you? Idolatry? Idolatry. Yes, perhaps it's that.*

It can't be that. No, Laurence. Couldn't say at the time: *He touches me.* Touched at his expense? How do I deplete him? This is, as you say, only a boy. Never thought about him as desiring. Apart from desiring to be a poet. Is that a criminal reduction? Perhaps, perhaps. Never thought about him nude. Unthinkable: penis, testicles. His body always comes dressed, as mere armature for clothes. Florentine hermaphrodite for my collection? No, really, Laurence. Big Daddy in the Sky/Céleste Humming in the Dark? Do we meet there? Is that where we touch? Hold him? I could hold him close but it would be fraternal, maternal even. So, this Sébastien then. He doesn't break his posture: *décontracté,* the word for it, Super Joe Cool, thighs still stretched out, thumbs idling over his pockets.

Mais . . . J'suis désolé, I'm disturbing you, didn't realize you were working, Gérard says.

Oh . . . *On discutait Lacan . . .* We were discussing Lacan.

76

Sébastien gestures to his friend.

Jean-Louis . . . Gérard.

The *we* excludes Gérard. *We were discussing* . . . Gérard's sparkling, fragmentary chatter. He doesn't *discuss*. Gérard as neophyte in the sanctuary salons of Raymond d'Arlan, *Professeur à la Faculté*. Theorists of literature, semiotics, psychoanalysis, and Gérard says, an occasional musician and abstract painter. *Ah, Rita, mais ce mec est génial!* You've just got to meet him . . . Besides, he could help you with your painting, I mean, help get you known. Gérard's utopian fancies: that everyone he cares for should meet and appreciate.

Mais, te voilà Rita! I came early, didn't expect you yet! There is a swerve of the two Lacanian heads towards me. The drift of signifiers. Dimples indent, hands clasp, lips go *bisou bisou.* Sébastien gives a genial smile which somehow arrests and expresses the energy of the asymmetrical features: the strong swoop of blue-black hair over the eyebrow, the tilt from eye to eye, the big nose obliquing across from left to right. The smile gives a long exposure. Intensity of the gaze, almost megalomanic glare. Picasso. That's it. Handsome, but all the same . . . Face looks as if put together in a phase of analytical cubism. The gaze is the Master's inscribed signature. *Dear Laurence, just met this bloke with a head straight out of analytical cubism and a body . . . A body like Matisse's Faun? Don't you think he'd look nice next to my Florentine Hermaphrodite?*

Mais, j'm'en doutais, he says. Thought it was probably the fabled Rita at the next table. *Les vraies rousses, c'est bien rare dans ces parages.* He puts on a posh accent so that he can get away with the archaicism. We only get the hennaed *brunes* down here, he says. Jean-Louis' eyes bulge a moment under the lenses. A bit like the Curator in that dream. He gathers up his papers: Have to run, *ciaou* . . . Got a meeting with my supervisor.

Sébastien draws up a chair. *Alors, c'est vous le peintre-artiste,* you the artist-painter, he says. Little pedantic? In contradistinction to house-painter? And *vous,* he says. Since '68, it's a rare student who uses *vous* for a contemporary. *Tu n'aurais pas une clope* the cigarette beggars say to strangers in the Cours Mirabeau.

Oh . . . I can hardly call myself that yet.

And tell me, what is your *recherche plastique?* Again Sébastien disowns the pomposity of the term with the implied quotation marks.

Could quote Laurence, tell him that I want to paint beyond personality, that my work is, if it has to be formulated, a critique of the notion of expression? I mean, as if, in painting, writing or whatever, one expressed some essential lactation of the Self? Of course, that'd be rude, too obvious a send-up. Give him my little slogan: struggle of the rebel organic against the geometric ideal?

I say: Oh . . . Exploded organic forms mostly. At least, that's what I've been doing for a while. Trying to break out of that now. And you, you're The Semiotician aren't you?

Ah, well, yes. Working on representation in advertising. Amongst other things.

There is an uneasy lull. Sébastien's eyes are on Gérard's manuscript: *Grocer's Widow, Grocer's Son.* I'll have to respond sooner or later to it, without being intrusive. Hand it over, make an affirmative O with thumb and index. Cop-out. Gérard's face colours under the interrogative glance Sébastien gives, stuffs the papers dismissively into his satchel. Why should anyone have a monopoly over Gérard's embryonic productions? And anyhow, these oblique confidences we make to one another, that's our affair. Won't tell him about the Strasburgers though. He can do without the sordid peep-show.

Eh-dis, Gérard. It's only just clicked. How come you're free at this time? Shouldn't you be at work? Sébastien's gaze has just a touch of the inquisitorial.

I've er . . . Taken a little break, Gérard says.

Ah bon? Mais enfin . . . Qu'est-ce qui te prend? What's come over you?

Nothing. Nothing, I assure you. Even I'm entitled to a little break sometime, aren't I? What are you drinking Rita? *Seb, qu'est-ce que tu prends?*

C'est gentil, I say. Eleven forty-five by the clock. Not too early for a beer. *Un demi pression, s'il te plaît.*

But seriously, Sébastien says, watching Gérard's back retreat to the bar. *Un citron pressé pour moi, mon vieux,* he calls. Seriously, I would like to know what kind of work you do. In your painting.

Why not take up the whole personality bit? But that myth has long since been deconstructed, he would say with a so-what intonation. The self as social construct is practically a cliché. And I would say: Yes but it's harder to do without some imaginary self in practice and with fatigue in my voice, give him Mallarmé's line about literature consisting in the suppression of the Monsieur and add that about the same year, Einstein Adolescent got off on a beam of travelling light and holding up the mental mirror to himself, marvelled at the idea of his no-reflection, perceivable only from the immensity of space beyond, so in what, whose, time did that image form? And he would say: But yes, of course . . . We've got beyond those crises though: Freud, Marx, Saussure . . .

Mais, je vous assure, Sébastien (*vous,* better stick to the *vous*), I can't readily formulate what I am doing. It's precisely the instinctive type of stuff that I'm trying to break away from. And if you want a name for what I've done so far I suppose you'd say they were kind of sadistic readings, really. As I said: exploded organic forms. A kind of gastronomic obsession: the body as food? Struggle of identities to break out of their categories: body, bed, chair, orange . . . *Une recherche plutôt gastronomique.*

I make something like a cross between laughter and idiot spluttering through the foam of the draught beer Gérard has passed me.

Speaking of *gastronomie,* he laughs, wonder what's on for lunch at the Resto-U. His eyes hold still above his own beer. The hazel chinks within the amber irises. The curling lashes cast tiny shadows over the crease of the lower lid. Perhaps all he wants of me for the moment is to receive, without questioning, these little gestures of solidarity. His beer for my beer. His quick deflation of my rhetoric when he can see I've talked myself into a corner. The tooth that occasionally catches his lower lip: the only flaw in his beauty. Seize upon that as his resistant reality. I do not toy with him, am not toying with him. No. I don't dress him up to suit my mood. His hands are trembling. Is he speeding? Is it me? Is it the Rita-meet-Sébastien scene that is too much?

He says: Rita's preparing an exhibition, aren't you?

Oh . . . *Tu sais* . . . I'm a long way from that. You make the little I've done sound so important, Gérard. And anyhow, I'm going to have to get some sort of a job. I'm broke at the moment. Decided not to go through with the post-grad diploma at the Beaux Arts. Scholarship long since run out anyhow.

But Rita! I can help you there. Got piles at the moment.

No! Come on, Gérard. I mean, really. It's hardly been easy for you getting something together for yourself. I'm not going to be a parasite on your labour.

Well, as a loan then, Rita. At least you could let me give you some kind of advance. If I'm going to do that fucking job, I may as well get some kind of a charge out of the bread.

Could just borrow a bit for the rent. No. If I accept anything, I'm indebted. Might have all sorts of expectations then. The bike. Can sell the bike. Ask him for help there. Not like taking money from him . . .

Mais, tiens Gérard, there is something . . . You could help . . . If you could ask around, see if there's anyone wants to buy a racing bike. A real thoroughbred. *Un vélo de race.* You know my silver Peugeot, so light you can pick it up with your little finger?

Mais . . . Putain Rita! *T'en es là?* It's got as bad as that? Sure I can. I'll ask around at the Resto-U today. Of course I can. But that's chicken feed. All due respects to your bike. You'll need more than that to get you through. What about all those drawings? The gouaches and the conté crayon ones. I could . . . I could set up a stall for you. What about . . . Place des Prêcheurs at the Thursday and Saturday markets? Plenty of buyers there with spring coming. Tourists and that.

Yeah . . . Tourists would hardly . . .

Hey! Not all of them go for Montmartre urchins.

But, says Sébastien, would they buy exploded organisms?

He is laughing: his eyes affirm some kind of complicity.

But anyhow, how could you do it, Gérard? I mean . . . I don't want to put down your plan, but what about your job?

To be perfectly frank, Sébastien I've had it up to here. *J'en ai ras le bol.* I mean . . . What does it amount to? It's what they call upward mobility hahahah. Office boy by day, book-keeper by night. Grocer's son becomes accountant. Great. And I end up as a cash-register just the same. Figures are less dirty than spuds. Give me the real dirt any day.

Come off it, Gérard! Sébastien's mouth takes an ugly twist. He turns his head towards me and leaning forward, displays it more as a caricature of paternal frustration: You get used to it, Rita. Every couple of weeks, Gérard will have a little flirtation with nihilism. Just worried about becoming too respectable, aren't you, Gérard?

Oh! Sometimes you really give me the shits, Gérard murmurs almost perfunctorily to his feet. As if they were going through an old routine.

What figure does he cut anyhow in their lounge-rooms: a little picturesque to feed upon: the orphan, the vagabond child come good, chilblains gradually cured, verminous clothes stripped away but something vestigially Rimbaldian remaining in his febrile, almost over-refined beauty and the sudden bursts of rebellion they've come to expect. Quite a find, really. And just when they think he's sufficiently groomed, he begins to buck at the harness. Yet here he is, even now, punctuating his talk with the recently acquired vocabulary: I assure you, Sébastien, it depends on several contingencies . . . Ah, well, it's quite aleatory, *tout à fait aléatoire* . . . where, a few weeks ago it would have still been: Er . . . I don't know . . . *comment le dire* . . . well, anyhow, you get the picture . . . right? Anyway . . . it's cool, it's cool . . .

Gérard! I'm sorry. I don't want to come on heavy but you've practically got your diploma already. And you agreed yourself that you had to break this pattern of throwing everything in as soon as you start to get somewhere. Sébastien searches my face for some sign of support.
    I think I have neutralized it.
    Look, Gérards says. It's . . . about time I told you, I guess. I haven't been attending those classes for weeks. And, as for the office . . . Give me a labouring job any day. At least you meet real people.
    Sébastien's eyes are begging for some sort of intervention.
    It does sound a bit premature, Gérard. I mean, once you have the diploma, you can take a break then. And anyhow, what would a market stall for my stuff do to advance you? Where would it get you?
    Rita! You sound like Sébastien here, Raymond and all the rest of them. Look, I am grateful. I've always been grateful, but my way isn't necessarily what they *or* you imagine for me. I mean . . . I do have some idea about what I want. And I know I'd get quite a charge out of flogging your work at the markets. That at least would mean something to me . . . Anyhow . . . Speaking of money, don't suppose I could buy a Resto-U ticket off you, Sébastien?
    Sébastien extracts from his Moroccan leather wallet the

symmetrically folded booklet of tickets. Student restaurants must be a very occasional excursion into the other life for him. The booklet is complete, unfingered.

His silence instates something like a truce.

She is big — beyond the boundaries prescribed for the French woman's body. She has found a gait, a stillness, which creates an original value out of what they would normally denigrate. It is potency established, power to make the others move: one comes to her, she never comes, simply gives that slow laugh from a distance bearing you towards her, puzzled by its meaning — is it pleasure, is it *oh no, look who's coming?* — and her power is in the ambivalence of that laugh.

She is nestled there in an alcove of the restaurant foyer. Swarms of students emerging already, some drifting over to her. It is not a refuge, not a nest as she presents it: lines of perspective radiate out from her or converge upon her. Her own stylist. Seen from behind, the great rump could get comments like *Quel c'ul qu'elle se paie!* but she never gives them the opportunity. The shawls, the great fur jackets make the body a simple unified base, chestnut fur haloing the shoulders, shoulders maintaining the head in its immobile, hieratic assertion: high priestess or animal queen. The glistening fur and the subtly hennaed hair are a continuum. Antonine Vigier *la Militante.*

On the anarchist side *biensur:* apart from their conservatism, their ready cooption with the right wing power in '68, the systematic strategies of the communists are a bore. Her appearances at the head of demonstrations are capricious, intermittent, yet then her stature, her magnetism make their impact. Her mannerisms though are more those of the disinherited *pied noir* ruling class: she keeps them beguiled with that slow smile, slow gesture, the unpredictable censorial glance, the preserved mystery surrounding her own love life. *Une grande dame,* heard it said without irony. The Animal Queen colonializes quite effortlessly it seems these stray Greeks in exile from the Junta, the Tunisians, Algerian radicals and French Maoists: her presence so assertive that they dematerialize . . .

But here comes the painter all in black! she calls. Have you been recently widowed or something, Rita? At Antonine's cue to Mustapha, Telemachos, Maud, Dominique, the collective mirth wells up, relays back to me.

Oh, no. Made a bit of a split with the past though. Decided to drop Beaux Arts, make a go of it on my own.

About time too! Wondered when you were going to make the break from those academic conservatives. What are you going to do for bread though?

Won't say sell my little drawings. Hardly people's art. Antonine only respects the collective stuff. Would just earn me another sneer. Rita's bourgeois aestheticism . . .

Oh . . . I'll find something . . . *Femme de chambre,* English coaching . . . Something'll crop up.

But sit down, Rita. (I am welcome as a drop-out.)

Ah . . . Just came across to say hello. Got some friends waiting in the queue. Haven't eaten yet.

Aha . . . And who might that be . . . *Si ce n'est pas indiscret!*

No. It's not indiscreet but I don't think you'd know them: Friend from Marseille and his mate. Gérard Lagrange and Sébastien something-or-other.

Never heard of them.

There, interest ceases.

Oh Rita, been wanting to ask you . . . Would you like to take over my place in May? (She draws me to her side with a nod, lowers her voice.) Going to Greece to see *mon p'tit mari.* (The notion seems sumptuous, presented in such an attractive purr. The diminutive: my little husband, my homunculus.)

Antonine's apartment: the great canopied bed, miriad colours in cushions, hangings, the marble pebbled courtyard with its fountain, birds . . . and in May.

Ah . . . Antonine, I would love that.

You would LOVE that. Well it's a deal.

Echoes of sarcasm as buzzing interference. Still there is

84

warmth in her eyes.

Drop around soon anyhow.

I will, of course.

Of course I will come. Always come at a beckoning. And back I go to the mustering yard of Les Gazelles. Queue still ten metres long, two metres thick. Back to these boys. I reduce them like Antonine with her little Greek 'husband'. She also has her little Corsican. These private courses she plots to her various lovers . . . So easy to call them boys, or when they graduate, *'mon p'tit mari'.*

Gérard is an angel: his smile knows no malice. Rita! We thought you'd dematerialized, he says.

Hard to suppress a smile at that one. Sébastien too seems to have relaxed, gives the ebony glow of his eyes.

Eternity of this queue. At least shelter for a while from the Mistral, sunlight pooling amongst the meshed overlay of shadows from the metal fencing set up to canalize the queue. Locust plague polyphony, ratata laughter, sneezing, spluttering, gargantuan *brouhaha* of it. Caterpillar crawl: general tilt of all the shoulders, slouch of hips, all angling towards the great feeding benches inside, all the movements of its multiple arms, mouths, suckers, suckers, loop upon loop of its hydra humps straining . . .

The sluice gates go up: the compacted press of eaters releases its quota of saliva and gastric juices . . . C'EST LES TRIPES! someone bellows. Must have caught the whiff of a rumour from the platters on the tables. Offal and slush, guts and tripe, oh, the foamy texture disguised somewhat with parsley and complemented by the side dishes. The caterpillar has begun to break down already, segment after segment is being detached; that swelling moan of hunger from a moment ago has broken down into cacophony, shuffling, pushing and the old salient shout of protest. ON VA AUX ARTS ET MÉTIERS ALORS? someone yells. The tables of the technical school still hold the promise of the fantasized omelette and chips.

What about you Rita?

Oh . . . I think I'll just grab something at home — *tripes* are something I can't quite handle.

Got a little taboo on the organs after all, eh? Sébastien is grinning.

Yes! Well. If you put it like that, yes.

Well, it looks like *à bientôt* then. Sébastien clears his throat. Not quite as confident as before. Er . . . Rita, before you race off . . . Gérard must have told you about a mutual friend of ours, Raymond d'Arlan? I think you'd enjoy the cross-fire of *his* conversation and . . . Well I . . . We thought what about coming around sometime soon, having dinner with us?

Gérard's open eyes cue the response. Why not go? If I keep my distance, there's nothing to lose. Won't get drawn in to Raymond's circuit though.

Yes, I say. *Volontiers.* I would like that.

Troubled glimmer in Gérard's eyes as he gives me the triple *bisou.* As if he were watching the fade-out of a faltering image within. The wistful half-smile is only a tenuous connection, with me, with whatever he has lost in thought. Perhaps it is just an accident of light.

Arrested there anyhow behind me: the process of feeding fervent minds on *tripes.* Now back to this separation. Break out of it, be free to read any way, eyes to see inside-outside reversibly, at once, *I* is not fixed equation with me. *I* unboxed multiplying hydra-high on its own expansions, ambulant hunger as aptitude for receiving the world, sprung rhythm given to all of this, tumbling cubes and cones and cylinders of the jagged rocks, spines where plane meets plane are my vertebrae catching the light, all my molecules disparate busy with it, the pull, the pullulation of all the possibilities, streets sprouting out of me, all the meals are mine, the aromatic pines, old people basking on the benches like shish kebabs, this could be spring already, the man downing his pastis in that bar, take him in too, and Jacquie there, Jacquie hailing from the distance, his withered leg like a specially designed device to pogo-hop from moment to moment, that harlequin patchwork of the clown: Jacquie, give me a break from men, they say, give me a laugh, give me a souvenir for my bag of images, his gold tooth flashes, he laughs his foggy haschishin's laugh: Eh, Rita, he calls across Sextius, Denise is getting some lunch together, hoping you'll join her!

Tiens, Rita! *Tu as l'air épanouie!* You look radiant, she says. She is chopping up the garlic, now the parsley, the blade so deft, as if the steel itself were animate. You eaten? *Maman* left a carton of groceries. Convinced her little girl is starving! She cackles, slaps her thigh. It trembles slightly under the denim.

If it could always be like this, with the colours coming back, this is no still life, no *nature morte,* Denise's vivid spread of provisions. And now, this simple, unspoken communion, her rapt fork-to-mouth involvement with the mushrooms, brown pliant fingers returning to the croutons, serving the whole of Provence in the stuffed zucchinis, gleaming in their oil, pouring out the *vinaigrette,* its basil and citrus edge to cleanse the palate . . .

Face flooded golden as I open the door to him. Breathless again, he is laden. I cannot question him. He has come, that is all. He places the equipment, glances up at me from time to time: spreads out sheet upon sheet of mounting card, metal rulers, lino-knives, pencils. Hands me an envelope: that is for you. Sold the bike, no trouble.

It is six hundred francs in crisp, new notes.

But Gérard, it wasn't worth that!

Obviously it was. I got it without any haggling. Reckon you can survive for a couple of weeks on that until the money comes in from your drawings?

Oh. *Enfin . . . Tu parles.*

Now it's as if my body had shaken off all the nervy defences impeding it. New kind of energy in control. I can manage the limits of this room without the fear of chaos pushing in: the materialization of miscarried gestures. Pulse at my wrist my fulcrum, but maintaining the balance. No longer the panicked darting of the ant with each sully towards the crumb multiplying cancellations of the previous ones. This sudden ease in the simple signal, in grasping the object. The books keep their profiles aligned on the mantelpiece, the butts keep to the ash-tray, the floor tiles are the tilted base we manage to work upon. I measure the drawings, Gérard nods consent, marks out the dimensions on the mounting card. My hand closes around the lino-knife: its satisfactory contours, its good weight. The blade performs exactly, along the hair-line he has plotted for it.

Just look at the way you've made those flowers pulsate! The way the face echoes all the centrifugal lines!

An issue from the poppy buds, their secret darks trembling, unravel an umbilicus, unwither the spread of human flesh, expand it in the light.

Gérard's comment creates the drawing. This release: they are ours now, not mine. All of them. A draught disturbs the ash, scatters it from the tray, across the card: the door is opening. Denise.

PU-TAIN! What a day. Those *nanas,* those *minettes,* teetering around in their little ankle boots, parading their pert little bums in their perfectly pleated high-class jeans, don't know whether I can stand that job, *Oui Monsieur! Certainement Monsieur!* Practically curtsy to the boss, and the lies we're meant to serve out to the clients, they would sell a tutu to a rhino like me... She tugs dreamily at her cigarette. I'll probably get the sack before the week's out anyhow ...

Hey! What you doing there? Can I give you a hand?

Why not? That would be great, if you feel up to it after working all day. Gérard's smile is unequivocally welcoming.

Come on! That looks like fun, not work to me, she says. I'll put on some music, okay?

Sure, good idea.

Again Gérard has answered.

Clatter, click trump, trump, trump in her room, bang, click, electronic whizz, and now it comes: Ritchie Havens blaring out the monotonous rasping *No I ain't gonna work on Maggie's farm no more*... And now Denise is back. Of course it's the right song. If I could control this exasperation mounting, clenching me. Didn't need this as external expression, it has disorganized our calm, disrupted the fluid connection of gesture to gesture needing no statement. Yet Gérard's profile is unperturbed: straight line of his nose glows amber in the light, the etched lashes, the full lips still slightly parted in his concentration, neck gently bending where the locks of hair stray. No tension there. This resentment of Denise hateful, constricting, can't be jealousy surely; ease, must ease out of it. The knife has jerked: taken off a slither of card, now the edge is jagged. Slow down. Breathe deeply, evenly. Denise always so generous, welcoming to me. Learn from Gérard.

Let his quietness inhabit. This is a new moment. Denise has already set to work, anyhow. She is silent, quick, all accuracy when it comes to this measuring and cutting. Generosity . . .

Night already. We must have been at it for hours. At last we are standing, aware only now that our legs are cramped, backs aching.

Laughter dissolving boundaries again: a smile circulates — his, hers, mine, relieves the last knots of that tension, the pressure of my closed spaces. We are combined: this is our work. There, set against the wall: twenty drawings ready for the market place.

What would you say to a pizza and a drop of red?

Gérard, fey child of Céleste, your magical glow. Let the trance last.

Sounds pretty good to me! I'll make a salad.

Denise recognizes him with that hush in her voice and something in her eyes, a softening of their normally abstract sheen. Something celebrating Gérard. Sees more than that slight, almost etiolated body. Doesn't see him as a boy . . .

That suit you, Rita?

Of course!

It came out more like a strangled whisper. Gérard's eyes on mine while his fingers fumble for the knob.

The pizza has been eaten. It was just a pizza: pastry soggy, spiritless, ordinary olives, ordinary anchovies. Just one fatigued lettuce leaf left in the salad bowl. If Denise would go now . . . She is pouring another glass of wine. The delicate fluting of Gérard's lips in the candlelight, their lustre.

Did you see that Marx Brothers one where Chico and Groucho . . . she is saying. They are laughing together. Ahhhh . . . what a drag! Suppose I'll have to grab a few hours' sleep. Got to be at work seven thirty tomorrow . . .

Gérard has risen to say goodnight to her. Soundlessly closing the door now. I need a motive to move too. The salad bowl: empty the scraps. My chair screeching on the tiles. My hand has caught his dangling one. The rush of his face to mine, dissolving lines, planes fluctuating in the candle blur. His mouth . . . our teeth knocking together, inside his laughter now, as if I could drink it forever, in this same space, we have worked the same, eaten the same, our lips alive together, this strength of his, had not imagined that, against me, up, this climb, am, are, pivoted, both

. . . Our faces apart again.

The same querying in his eyes, again. A flicker of something almost like fear across his face . . . Does he think I was playing? Am I wrong to so impulsively . . . Can't be Denise watching, Denise that precipitated this . . . But this will not be an isolated moment in his mind: he will see sequels.

Bonne nuit, Rita . . . I'll be there Place des Prêcheurs, first thing, Thursday morning. You bring the drawings, okay?

This abrupt return to business. Does he prefer to leave it at that? That kiss: a fragile interrogation? Let it hover?

This is it: the beginning. In between the second-hand furs and the *brocanterie,* Gérard has already set it up: canvas sheet stretched out, screens erected, drawings pinned.

There you are Rita! Your first exhibition!

Gérard is laughing freely. Maybe that kiss . . .

From this café terrace, Denise and I are able to survey the scene beyond ear-range of the reactions to the drawings. They are not even giving them a glance, oh, she is going to stop, no, it was just a casual eye cast over them, a lazy lassoing of the whole scene, now she has said something to him next to her, they are both laughing. They think it is pretentious. They are right. This was premature. If only no one else would look . . . *Exposition,* the French word says it. Exposed, I am exposed. In this sun-lit space, what was vigour is vulgar, what was subtle has become hesitancy, cowardice, what was *dégradé,* a rhythmical stepping down of tones, looks like mechanical patterning. Easy solutions. Pancho and Peruvian hat stooping over them now. American student. He has returned to the first screen. Gesturing, seems to be talking to Gérard now. In front of the self-portrait with poppies. At least the drawings are real. Not begging for ready insertion into this or that tradition. They don't follow the easy path of good taste. Gérard's pride in them. Short toadish man, about fifty, coarse hair missed by the barber in the skinfolds over the collar, oh no, that would have to be Legouinec from the Beaux Arts, at least he usually liked my work, scrutinizing them now, of course, not necessarily admiration, just his short-sightedness, anyhow probably just a pedagogic reflex, see what his ex-student is up to. The symmetry: sheen on both buttocks as he bends. If only I could defend them, explain. That work doesn't bear such close inspection. He's squatting before the gouaches on the ground-sheet now. How did Gérard get all those screens here, did he hire them, make them himself, with what tools then? Did he have to apply for a licence at the *mairie* or somewhere to set up the stall? Didn't even think to ask him.

As if his efficiency, his resourcefulness were my due . . . Passivity, my passivity. *Power to make the others move . . .* as if Antonine were the only one who indulged in that game.

Denise has retrieved a crooked Gauloise from her pocket. Her eyes half closed with that feline contentment to be in the sun, bemused with the crowd, she sucks it in, avidly, with each pull on the cigarette. Her Thursday off. Time out. Rather her. To be like Denise. Draw her. Learn. Get involved with this new paper, these pens and ink, not watch the stall.

Her face must emerge along the lines of that connection: Denise and the crowd. Flesh alive with collective dreams: from the midnight prowls she takes in the Arab quarter to open commerce with the sunlit squares, it has dispensed with individuality. Seen childhood from the eleventh floor of an H.L.M. estate, but knows Marseille through the basements too, uneasily shadowed by ancient Moorish memories, that brooding Spanish blood, the smoulder and flare — *smoulder and flare,* who said that? — of what she loves in Bunuel. Beautiful, the miracle of the blue-black hair, like Sébastien's, but swinging its single mass, the constant signalling of the mobile eyes relayed to the eyebrows, radically plucked, emphatic, strong, animating in turn the clear space of the forehead; ugly in a way, too, a certain violence in the downward drag of the lower lip; man, woman at once, starkness of the shadow where the nose juts above the upper lip and then the fullness of the breasts thrusting an almost autonomous claim to existence; delicate, discreet rise and fall of the nostrils; coarse, the square jaws are flesh-bound, cylinder of the neck truncated where the fat creases it into segments; austere in her silence now, her patience is an ignorance of time but latently there's always the noisy agitation of the caricature concièrge, all scenes being hers, all entitled to her commentary. At least can offer her the drawing . . .

93

Mmmmm. I like it. Hahahahaha. You certainly haven't romanticized me have you? I like it.

It's yours if you . . .

Merci, Rita. *Merci.*

Straight focus of her eyes on mine. Reflected there, in miniature, in her black eyes: my face. Somehow, Denise always gives more . . .

The way the waiter is clearing the table, emptying the ashtray, if eloquent enough: we have overstayed our welcome on one *café-exprès.*

And Gérard over there, alone.

His face speeds its welcome towards us. With this soft light hovering over them, his features do have the gentle moulding of a Botticelli. His arms around us both. Laughter warbling: in each hand he's waving a fifty franc note: What did I tell you? It's going to work, it's going to work! Just wait till I tell Sébastien about this!

Creeping numbness, dullness intruding. Gérard is delighted but will refer to Sébastien for verification of his delight.

By the way, did he phone you?

But yes, Gérard . . . I thought . . . I thought he would have told you . . .

Gérard bites at the inside of his lip, frowns: Oh no . . . But I don't suppose he's had the chance. After all . . . I've hardly been home much lately. When did he make it for, the dinner?

He and err . . . Raymond suggested we meet at the Mondial around eight tomorrow night and then go to a restaurant from there.

Ah bon . . .

But you will be coming, of course?

Well . . . Yes, I expect so.

But it's only seven thirty. So why did I run run run Rue du Onze Novembre, Cours Sextius, even forgetting to cross before SUMA, down Victor Leydet, past the Cintra, and here, to fill in half an hour. What about the Mondial, I said, you know, at the bottom of the Cours Mirabeau? Silence at the other end of the line. They would probably have chosen the Cintra. More elegant. This café more *gauchiste*. Workers, students. More Algerians than French. *Quelqu'un vous poursuit, Mademoiselle?* You being chased or something? What is it then with me tonight? The waiter doesn't usually take this line. He is laughing quietly again as he comes up to take my order. Perhaps I've overdone it somehow . . . Kohl put on with extra care, this silk shirt?

A . . . A Campari please.

Surprise registering on his face: it's not the usual red. But Rita alone with a glass of plonk would hardly give them the right impression. But why should I modify anything for them. For Gérard I'm here, really. Too bad if they're offended by these paint-spotted boots with their gaping soles. Trouble is, they'll take it for some kind of affectation: the Artist on Parade. But the eucalyptus silk shirt Laurence tossed me that last night, that'll pass. Her cast-offs my most elegant items. And the ginger cords. Australian native I am. Bush colours. As long as they don't want to go through the chivalry routine and try to relieve me of the shawl, show the rip in the back. In any case, in a restaurant, the torso's the main thing: what shows over the table. Frontal or profile. Window glass with complex reflections gives back no

95

information. Nose probably red, hair wild from the run. And hands . . . purplish, calloused and chapped. Nails broken, bitten, still edged with the Prussian blue paint. They'll see it all in one glance. Light cruel in here. They'll take note of the freckles too. Although they have faded since.

As if children just existed for their use as conversation props, those benign aunts, they were all *Auntie,* whether or not they were related to us, used to console Mon, as if she needed consolation. Always Mon, never Mother, Mummy, Mum, she never minded. When she grows up, Mon, they'd say, bet she'll be quite stunning, you'll see. Ah that Celtic skin is a headache though, in this climate but plenty of zinc cream and later, with a touch of make-up, nothing a touch of make-up can't fix, and if she takes off a bit of that puppy fat . . . She's an affectionate little thing too, isn't she, such a smoodger, look at her on Harry's lap there, sunny little thing. That'll go a long way.

They wouldn't recognize me now of course. Somewhere along the line the sunniness has gone. The softness. Suddenly in the mirror tonight, there it was: bone and nerve, a hardness, almost a glare in the eyes, sending back the grey-green of the shirt. And the mouth, not mine, set like a clamp on the whole face. Still, under my palm now, the cheeks are there and the mouth, mole-soft, oyster-moist.

After the toothpaste, the Campari is medicinal. That was a Citroën streaking past — Gérard said he drives a Goddess, could be them already. Footsteps rounding the corner from the Bus Terminus, parking area just beyond there, must be them, footsteps sound determined. Must look nonchalant, not all angles riveting a defence on that gaping doorway. Be occupied, that's better than simple watching, use the paper, pen in my bag. Perhaps they're not coming anyhow, might have got the time wrong, why give a damn, doodle, scrawl, anything. Ice clinking in my glass, Campari wobbling, thighs pressed against my table. It's the waiter again.

C'est Rita Feenairtay *n'est-ce pas?* A telephone message for you: Le Professeur d'Arlan has been delayed. He'll be here within the half hour, if you can wait. He apologizes. Another Campari Mademoiselle?

Why not?

That tone in my voice, as if the cost were immaterial, as if I spent my life lounging in cafés. That waiter. Denise fancies him. Jose, said his name was Jose, something like that. High muscular buttocks, a certain arrogance in his gait. Spanish-Moroccan probably. No sycophant. The lines around his mouth, almost like scars. Despite all the cross-hatching of the laughter lines, there is something permanently unamused about the eyes.

He attends the social masquerade for what it is. If he notices me drawing him, he might take it the wrong way . . . An obstruction to my peripheral vision, man-sized, next to me. He'll take the sketch as some kind of invitation . . .

Not Jose. It's Sébastien. Classy, classy. Groomed like a diplomat tonight. The silk scarf brushes my hand with its fringe and there they are, the colours it combines in its interlocking chain motif: the dark red of the lips stretching to the out-sized smile, the blue-black of the blazer and the grey of the flannel trousers, and this . . . This next to him, is it Raymond? Pixie quality about that smile, surely not . . .

Rita, may I introduce you to Raymond?

The way Raymond side-steps around Sébastien looks like a send-up of Sébastien's ceremonious attitude. Hardly intimidating, physically at least: small-boned, dapper in his movements. He wears the biscuit kid jacket with disrespect, leaves it unstudded at the wrists and there is an ink stain at the pocket. The eyes behind the glasses alive with intelligence. Amber, hazel, hard to tell.

Enchanté, Mademoiselle. We hesitated to intrude — you looked so absorbed . . . Will you allow us to have a peep . . .

Should have whipped the drawing away.

Aha, says Raymond. Yes, he is a rather fine specimen.

Specimen: interesting sample of *homo sapiens* or what? Collector's item?

Mmmm. You have a nice hand. I see you are one of those irrepressibly compulsive artists!

That must be meant ironically. That slow retreat of the upper lip reveals a little of the pink gum. He's seen my busyness with pen and paper for what it was: a prop, an anxiety-masking device. But Gérard . . . Where is Gérard? It would be premature to ask, seem as if I weren't happy to make just Raymond's acquaintance for the moment. Gérard will be joining us later, at the restaurant, surely. The polished skull shows through the thinning hair, yet

97

it's not just that. There is a general baldness about the face, a softness in the little folds that gather under the chin as he studies the drawing. A delicate withering, the texture of onion skin paper, around the eyes.

Eagle's beak, verging on it, that nose and the lower lip groping upwards as he speaks, ladling out the words, as if to arrest the generally falling lines of the face. Spaniel droop about the eyes, too. The hand he just stretched out was refined, narrow, and yet he concentrated something demonstratively strong in its grip. There is a faint, exquisite perfume hovering about him. His eyes still flitting from the drawing to Jose: tracking me down along the exploratory lines, netting me where they cross and cross again, where I was searching the push and tug of all the vectors operating on that body. My hand has gone for the drawing — too brusquely, snatched it, crumpled it. Shock exposure: arctic light in here. Meanings frozen. Jose is still there, aloof, intact. His body has compacted its mystery, its cryptic calligraphy inviolate. He has escaped.

Really, it was only a doodle!

Thaw. Dissolve. Fade-out. They are the co-producers tonight. It's up to them to let me re-emerge; they can instigate another scene.

Wouldn't mind if I could toss off *doodles* like that! Sébastien laughs.

Sébastien is doing himself an injustice. He is *hardly* inartistic himself . . . Well, Rita, I hope your waiter at least passed on my message.

Thankyou, yes he did.

That's how he's directing me. Little girl, answering on cue. Pixie! This Raymond is no pixie.

I must apologize for being late. (He glances demonstratively at his watch.) Faculty meetings, you know. Tiresome things that go on and on.

I don't say I don't know.

The watch is hardly demonstrative. It is blank faced, or almost. The four lean strokes are a faint illusion to the vulgar passage of time. Must have cost a fortune. Cartier probably. The less display, the more you pay.

I have booked a table at the Grillade. Do you know it?

Er . . . No, afraid not.

Well, I hope it's up to its normal standard.

Since they are still standing, the car keys tinkling on Raymond's cocked finger, I am to understand that they will not take a drink here. Perhaps they would be more comfortable in the *Deux Garçons* . . . But that would be over-doing it, to drape them in languid poses in that shrine for society matrons and pouting gigolos, disabused *travelos* and cruising *minets,* unsuspecting English couples in search of a cup of *tay.*

Raymond has beckoned Jose.

Oh no, Raymond, really, I will deal with that, please!

No no, Rita. I insist. You are our guest.

Compared with his performance that day at the café, Sébastien is thick with silence. Since that initial volley of introductory noises, dumb. This distance between our bodies is alive with little lines. Raymond talks, Raymond pays the bill. Perhaps it is that. A wildness about Sébastien within that straight jacket. That swoop and swerve of the coarse black hair away from the jaw. His big thighs are there under the civilized column of the flannels. The thrust of the fists inside the pockets makes a mockery of the severe cut of the blazer. His eyes shift nervously, uncommitted to the scene. The whites flash. He is chewing at the inside of his lip. Gérard has the same tic. Picked up from Sébastien? Why doesn't he mention Gérard? Why can't I come at it?

Rita . . . The other day . . . Nothing . . . I'll tell you some other time.

Raymond is back with us.

Alors, en route les enfants, he says.

Jose is clearing the table already, looks up. Sardonic, that dilation of the nostrils? A quick expulsion of air: practically a snort. It says: So this is the kind of man you get around with!

Anyhow we're on the pavement already. Raymond's hand between my shoulder blades, its touch as light as air, directing me. I am abstractly encased in that space provided by the outstretched arms, the inclined head and torso, the retreat of the pelvic area, around the corner, towards where the car must be parked. Again, the deft side-stepping, suave curve of it, as we change pavements so that he can take his chivalrous place between me and the kerb. I do not protest. Sébastien flanking my other side. Dark: shadows fluttering like bats disturbed, headlights scanning, dark, light, dark, light and bracketed by these two strangers, me.

Wasn't quite like this when we came tumbling out of that Russian tavern that night, aching with laughter, arm-in-arm, drunk on *cameraderie* I thought, as much as the charge of vodka knocked back after vodka, Jean, that friend of his and I, ready to take in all the streets of Paris, when suddenly the friend was gone and I as sober and closed as a corpse in his bedroom. No. This is Raymond and this is Sébastien and there is no cause-and-effect linkage stapling this moment with all the others. I am free. Glad. Glad to be with these two men I do not know. Anything, nothing might happen. I can choose.

This is the Citroën D.S., not Jean's Deux Chevaux. I am to take my place in the front. Although . . . We must be two minutes' walk, if that, from the restaurant. Still, this evening is of their design and I am cushioned by the upholstery, buoyed by the hydraulic suspension, nestled in the palm of the hand of God. Sébastien has been relegated to the back seat. He asserts his involvement all the same by the hand on Raymond's head-rest . . . Place des Cardeurs.

Raymond has leapt around to open my door; my gaping boot is lowered to the cobble stones. The car has been slotted into an improbably narrow space, its sleek snout still rocking gently. The sky is huge here. The ultramarine persisting beyond the black, the faintest hint of coeruleum glazing in an endless transparency-upon-transparency, all the planes to infinity pulsating, stars . . .

Ah, c'est joli, Aix!
 Sébastien yawns voluptuously, like Adam awakening, stretches: this is an illumined hemisphere. He invests it with romantic glamour. Despite the slums. The tall narrow façades lean away in defiance of the stresses and strains Architecture has to deal with. More like anthills, pitted with orifices, releasing through them the spillage of their interiors: poles flapping their washing, angling at the sky, shreds of music, quarrels, yelps and moans, spicy smells snatched by the wind. *Couscous, mergez.* These buildings are dank and verminous, have no electricity, no running water; it's where the French bosses house their Arab workers, but under this great sky, tilting its inner life to the stars, yes, pretty, *parfaitement joli.* You can buy it as back-drop on a Carte Bleue.

La Grillade. Candles and open coal ovens and red cloths. Raymond gives the slight tilt of the torso, this time to the waitress. Tall, blond, Savoyarde by the accent: *Ah oui Monsieur le Professeur, par ici Monsieur, une table pour trois n'est-ce pas? Voilà! Ça vous convient Monsieur le Professeur?* Letting one's title slip over a telephone booking certainly works. A table for three, it is. Then Gérard isn't coming. Here it is, in its little alcove, discreetly tucked away.

Just yesterday, Place des Prêcheurs, Gérard nibbling away at the inside of his lip: Well yes, I expect so, he said.

Something wrong, Rita?

Raymond looks concerned. As a *maître d'hôtel* might be concerned.

Oh no. No. It's just that . . . I thought Gérard would be joining us.

Ah no. Gérard will not be with us tonight.

Will not be with us. Of his will, of their will? This man maintains ambiguity while assuming control: he possesses the future and the secret of its vectors. Fumble for a cigarette, fingers tangled in the shawl, have to retrieve the drawing now, bringing with it pencils, pens, paper-clips . . . finally the packet. A Dunhill lighter, slim, silver, has been produced, its flame sprung to attention.

No . . . (The *no* is more attenuated this time, gentler, begging sympathy, if not complicity.) We thought it better if Gérard didn't come tonight. (*We,* this exclusive bracketing device.) We

101

are rather worried about him at the moment. He has been behaving most erratically — self-destructively would be more like it — and since you are obviously very important to him, we thought you might be able to give us some idea of what's going on . . . We might have some chance of dealing more effectively . . . more sensitively with him.

In what way has he been self-destructive lately? I mean . . . I think he's quite aware of everything . . . both of you have done for him . . .
    Umm. Yes . . .
    Raymond's cocked eyebrow: cynicism, disbelief? But he is studying the wine-list. Mmmm. If I remember correctly, you have an excellent Chateau Neuf du Pape? . . . But what about an aperitif for the moment? Another Campari, Rita? (Does nothing escape this man?) A port for you, Sébastien, I presume? Yes and make it a dry martini for me. Well . . . Perhaps I should fill in a few gaps. When Gérard turned up about a year ago, he wasn't a very pretty sight — filthy, painfully thin, penniless, completely disoriented and virtually inarticulate. *But* . . . Since after all he is a nephew — by marriage — I do feel concern for the boy . . . I'm starting to wonder whether it's not to my misfortune. Er, yes, his mother, Louise, is the sister of my ex-wife, so you can see, it's all rather removed. *Nevertheless* . . .
    Louise? I thought it was Céleste.
    There you are Sébastien, what did I tell you? Sorry, Rita, but you can't afford to take the boy literally. Fantasies . . . It verges on mythomania . . . Anything to romanticize a very sordid childhood. Céleste eh? What will he invent next?
    Gérard's mother is an al . . . Sébastien catches Raymond's glance.
    Yes, I'll tell you about *her* later . . . When he turned up, as I said, he was a dead-beat. From sixteen on, he'd been chasing the drug scene. Amsterdam, Berlin — he'd seen it all. *But,* after a long battle, I persuaded him to undergo a disintoxication cure and then, with a bit of influence, *un peu de pistonnage,* I managed to cut through some red-tape and have him enrolled in the accountancy course. Despite his lack of qualifications — he didn't even have his Intermediate Certificate. And . . . then the job. All right, it was only conceived as a temporary solution, no one expects him to stick to that for life, but it was a job. And even in that, there was every possibility of advancement — he's not

without intelligence as you must know, quick to learn and, in fact, he turned out to be quite mathematical. Sébastien put him up in his apartment . . . and together we've tried to open his mind to a little culture. He began to devour books soon enough — not necessarily always the kind I might have recommended — but still, he was reading. And now: the bomb-shell. He drifted in last Saturday afternoon, when normally he should have been working and announced — defiantly, pretty pleased with himself — that he has thrown it all in: the job, the studies. It was difficult to extract much sense from him. He was certainly under the influence of some weed or other.

Hash, Sébastien says. Stoned out of his mind, Rita. *Il planait . . .*

So. I thought: well, so much for his reading. Now he fancies himself as some kind of Rimbaud. *Le grand voyant.* The instant visionary. Very convenient way of rationalizing a return to his old habits.

But . . . What adolescent with a bit of flair for language doesn't identify with some sort of Rimbaud figure?

That is all very well, Rita. But it doesn't stop with literary intoxication with Gérard. With his background . . .

What do you mean, with his background? (Does Sébastien's mutism mean he acquiesces to everything Raymond D'Arlan has to say? I have knocked back my Campari too quickly: they are both staring at it.)

What should I say? There is very little in Gérard's background which isn't negative. His father's grocery supported the family amply enough, I gather, until . . . Tch tch . . .

Raymond holds the ink-stained pocket of his jacket pinched between his fingers, the ladle-lip hangs as he examines the offensive spot . . .

Remind me to drop this off at the cleaners tomorrow, Sébastien. Damn biros! Yes, I was saying . . . Until his mother's drinking problem became too much for even the most faithful customers to handle . . . *Oui, hélas* . . . Louise Lagrange is a hopeless alcoholic, Rita.

Céleste: Sébastien laughs, tilts his glass of port, swills it.

Through the plastic window of his wallet: Louise the drunkard floats away from crates and till and vegetables, streams with other light, is Fairie Mother, is Céleste . . . How can they deny it?

> *Patrick Finnerty up-side-down.*
> *A clown. He was a clown.*
> *Ha. A clown. How can you know.*
> *We know. We know.*
> *Arlie Halliday Sébastien Raymond*
> *Give us a shoe-box, give us a crate . . .*

Perhaps though that's what she was for him. Why not? Céleste and not Louise . . . Perhaps she *was* a wonderful mother . . .

Raymond shakes his head imperatively: I have spoken out of turn. It is not appreciated.

Louise a wonderful mother to him! No, I'm sorry to say Rita, that was not the case. Time and time again I got phone calls in the middle of the night: Gilbert, Gérard's father begging for some kind of advice. But cures, therapy . . . The whole lot proved futile. She would be through a bottle of calvados by mid-morning, and try as he did to keep her away from the customers, she would reel into the shop, outrageously dressed, stage her private charades, slurring his name and making a mockery of everything the poor man stood for. It was Gilbert who had to see to everything: the business, the housework, Gérard . . . He dressed his son, fed him, got him off to school . . . And all that in between the buying at the markets, deliveries. No wonder the man's blood pressure caught up with him so early . . . Obviously she was in no state to care for Gérard and when the welfare people finally caught up with them, the place was squalid, the child filthy, half-starved and delirious with double pneumonia . . . Louise was quite oblivious to it all. So. You can imagine that after his father's death, Gérard had little chance of internalizing any image of authority . . .

Which you . . .

Better not to speak. The groper lip is hanging in expectancy. *Plaît-il?* Mmmm? You were going to say, Rita?

> *Birth register*
> *Cash register*
> *Death register*
> *don't know the words we coin*
> *the words we hoarded under the desk*
> cumulo-nimbus
> Zora
> Céleste

> *counterfeit identities*
> *words that have no currency*
> *with waiter shop-cop teacher shrink*

Oh . . . Which you hoped to provide . . .

Well, yes. I suppose you might say that. Obviously he came to me in search of something of the kind. You see . . . If I'd only realized sooner — I had no idea that the rest of the family in Lyon was doing nothing for him. Well . . . I thought we had succeeded in getting Gérard on his feet. And now he is throwing it all to the wind . . .

Raymond sighs, contemplates his martini. Is it the Pygmalion in him or is it the man who is hurt? An image of authority . . . was it merely that? . . . My *ex-wife,* he said.

But I thought that Gérard had saved quite a bit of money and that he was simply taking a bit of a break? I mean, he hasn't struck me as being ready to burn all his bridges . . .

But he loses all his chances of advancement this way! And what is more important, the discipline of regular work which has made more of a therapeutic effect than anything! He *is* burning his bridges. He was to sit for his finals in a couple of weeks. Rita, unless something is done quickly, he'll fall right back into his old ways — he was a *thieving little junkie* when he came to me! And he'll do it smugly this time, on the pretence that he is a new Villon, a new Rimbaud and that he can allow himself all sorts of aberrations.

I really thought that Gérard had more sense of direction than that . . . now.

Raymond ignores my comment. The wine has come. He sniffs, tastes, nods approval to the waitress, pours mine . . .

Yes? Please tell us anything that will enable us to help him.

Well . . . I've been very impressed with how practical Gérard can be when he wants to get something done, how efficient . . . He's given me a lot . . . The four interrogative eyebrows. That's what it is. They think I have led him astray, let him indulge in his fantasies. I can leave them curious. They're not going to practise their amateur psychotherapy on me. *Us, us,* Raymond says. Is Sébastien his apprentice elect or something? They would discuss nothing of the hungers, doubts, fears, wounds, all that sediment suspended in the dark slush of the unconscious to be repressed, compressed, aligned into the neat substratum of the MEN THEY

ARE so why should I be an open pit for the miner, uncover my murky waters and giddy for their descent or now this rush of words . . . I can let out one. One word, any one; they will not see the others banking up, constricting me in my throat, but I must tell something, I am going to tell, tongue is a trampoline, words will come to pelt their quiet wine, dissolve the rigidity in the aura of the red splash . . . No: a few words carefully released would be sufficient to maintain this connection between us, sympathetic really, look they are smiling warmly, they like me, but I will respect the etiquette of the table, this equilateral triangle we form, no need for me to admit to any weakness, no need to plummet to the baseline . . .

A while back . . . (My voice, that was my voice setting Gérard in a time-frame.) A while back . . . (The sentence once embarked upon must find its grammatical solution, that is all that's needed: nothing confided, no betrayal necessary.) Oh, I had a few problems . . . financial . . . and . . . (Of course, there is no need to say numb, I was numb, apathetic, catatonic almost, *Monsieur le Professeur,* I dropped out too, you see, and was ready to curl up foetal and let the tick and tick of days pass muffled in my pillow . . .) Well . . . Gérard was the very person who galvanized himself into action . . . He made things happen. He . . .

Yes, we are not unaware of that. Let's say . . . If you'll permit me to comment, Rita? . . . that you have interrupted your diploma rather than abandoned it, mmm? But suppose you were to opt out, to drop it completely . . .

But I *have.* I'm working on my own . . .

Suppose you were to — you would be better equipped for a more 'marginal' existence. You have your art, whatever your immediate material problems . . . Unfortunately, such is not the case with Gérard. Yes, yes, he has been helping you. What? One, two days a week? I gather you've been very generous with commission on what he's sold. But Rita, really, what kind of future is in it for him?

Look . . . I didn't know he'd thrown in his job too . . . And I begged him not to throw in his course. (Did I? Did I beg him?) But he didn't seem to want to listen. And I didn't really see it as my place anyhow . . . And then . . . He just took things on himself, he . . .

Mmmm. I know. When the boy becomes embarked on a

nihilistic course, he's quite recalcitrant to reason. And what is particularly . . . worrying . . . is the degree of self-importance he seems to derive from the little help he has given you. I might add, Rita, if you'll excuse me for saying so, that it's not without ulterior motives on his part. He has invested a great deal in you emotionally, you know. And I don't think that's all . . . Nothing he would like more, I fear, than to be some kind of prince consort for you . . .

Then this is where it happens/happened now here/then there/no place for Rita Aviator here either at this dinner table, I must eat of the listed items of the menu structuring tonight. These two men and I — of course Céleste is the crazy dream of a child... How could I have imagined? Broken images on the pawn-broker's counter: of course you can't simply fly away for another cognac, another patisserie with papa's old album of stamps... Of course I am the open one, a door at every pore and more and nag nag nag my many voices but here and now only one way out: Gérard is gone. Gérard must go from me. We must give up our games, he must learn to survive outside his fantasies. Only one cure proposed for here and now: Rita be with us, give up Gérard. Confront yourself here as he can only do elsewhere.

I have given him a certain confidence, an awareness of his gifts but to nurture his dependence on me beyond that would be ... Of course, thwarting to his growth. He is so small, so far away already, strange that I should be up here, so far above the Cours Mirabeau and yet, yes that is him a quarter of a centimetre tall drawn into the shadow of the book-shop awning. This is no mere scaffolding of rationalizations, no, of course not, this is simply seeing things from a rational perspective. The edifice is solid seventeenth century, perhaps one day he will see the beauty of this too, its austere harmony, these proportionate windows compass his perception no no it is not me teetering along the scaffold there where the boards are sagging, it is not my sentimentality warping things, I have not used Gérard, did not need his radiant flash to keep me going, I have my own light, have managed to dispense with all those fictions, all those gossamer emissions of the child, I have disrobed Rita Aviator long ago and can still keep my balance, you might have flown over the streets of Lyon that day, that perhaps was a necessary excursion for you, but now you must learn to walk simply along the pavement, you must understand that now, but Raymond, is that you, the boards are really sagging and this . . . façade you would have me paint is theatrical, *trompe-l'oeil* and this brush . . .

It is you, Raymond, who have put it in my hand, I can still drop it, but I turn, I am turning and as I turn, yes I watch myself falling as the brush is spiralling down down towards the insect activity on the street, Gérard, that is/was me and how the traffic still crawls, if I could break out of this, catch up with you, fall too in an upward falling as you once flew but I am still here help help oh I do need your help Monsieur le Professeur, I do not understand this space between me and it, the street and me, I mean, I beg you to maintain it, hold it until this vertigo is over *of course* I must abandon Gérard, for his own sake, naturally, we must have imagined the bonds that linked us, just give me the words that I might hold these lines of flight ha! these *lignes de fuite* yes and still be here, no no, I'm not afraid, it's simply a matter of perspective as they say, I admit that I was wrong to dismiss it all as illusionist, this representation, it's simply a matter of order, of harmony, of concentration and not of dispersion, of centrifugal lines, no, sorry, centripetal, a matter of respecting certain divisions, just give me time and I will point out its topology: There is the Imaginary/Here is the . . . but all the loci dance and dazzle down and up . . . Yes, I know, I must see reason, not yield to the lure of all the scattered foci where I might have, that is the field of fantasy and this is no sinister gang-plank you would have me walk — did I say that? — this is the fine construct of adulthood and my feet are on a firm terrain . . .

III

FRAMING

As if I were a celebrant of suicide, there is no glory in that . . . If Gérard thinks I would approve his return to dope, if he's cast me in that role, no, I agree, he's very sick, he's infected with the worst kind of romanticism . . . He must know, he must be shown that I won't applaud.

So good. So good to be inside this civilized interior and to be able to talk at last. I can talk. My mouth is oval, my pleated lips can tighten, I can pull that purse string, stretch them to a slit — it is elastic, can articulate me to you and you . . .

No, no. I'm afraid I wasn't aware of the extent to which he was . . .
     Projecting?
     Sébastien supplying the words now.
     Well . . . I suppose. I must say I've been uneasy for some time about the whole situation. I wondered . . . He's been very generous but that he should be content to get this er . . . vicarious sense of achievement through helping me. *Si l'on doit formuler les choses,* if we've got to hang some kind of label on it, then I suppose my feelings towards him have been ma . . . fraternal and nothing more . . .
     The rising flush in my cheeks again. They're alert to the slip, alert to the 'we' I used.

Exactly, Raymond says. (He means: good girl, you're learning?) Perhaps, Rita we can show him? Gently, of course. That your interest is simply that: fraternal. I mean after all, Gérard is barely nineteen and you are?

Twenty-five.

Yes. In any case Gérard has a long way to go to maturity. He has to learn not to throw everything away on a day-dream. But I think it will need some kind of word from you, mmm?

That interrogative, that weary drag in his voice as the waves and waves of his perorations recede . . . The mature commentator, a little sick at heart perhaps, going through the last motions of 'saving' Gérard. *Fraternal,* question mark. Knows my misnaming but knows also that he can use it. Reconstitution of Gérard-as-product-of-Raymond. Whatever I say, he can absorb us both. If I say, wait a minute, I might have given you the idea that his feelings were not reciprocated, that the dependence· wasn't mutual, we would both be Poor Children in Need of Help, each neurotically playing host to the other's fantasies, symbiotically bound as rival parasites, his suckers to mine drawing on nothing but illusion, oh yes, both terribly in need of the intervening wedge and the diet of reality, more robust, more nutritious, that Father might provide.

The mild irony behind the glitter glasses: he knows about that kiss. Knows I took it.

> *Chaste Hippolytus runs still blinking in his rosy confusion*
> *from Phaedra cradle-snatcher . . . to consult his mentor —*
> *Raymond.*

It's Gérard, it's he who's set me in a time-frame. He froze that moment, sealed its meaning, rushed it to Raymond. And that's when the emotions came — not with me, no — with the defrosting, the dissection. Psychodrama all right: Raymond had him stage it. No cool academic this. It's been something more like jealousy. Look at him now: his hands on the menu are not quite steady.

> *That woman is obviously playing with you, Gérard.*
> *Enjoying your subservience.*

And now he has come to intervene. Show me that he understands my psychology, doesn't need to ask many questions; he knows me through Gérard. He has come to show me that that kiss was a moment, in case I had further designs, and that this is another moment. Moments teach. Moments modify. I have been

114

modified. *Exactly,* I have learnt: I have answered on cue.

*Those finely boned hands with their tapered fingers, those
lids lowered, those glasses posed on the coffee table, hands
hovering, at a distance at first, then alighting on Gérard's
back, gathering up the folds of the shirt, moving along the
brown skin now, each finger-tip repeating* you are my ward,
this is my tenderness, *all along the knobbly backbone, the
whole rosary:* have trust in me, I will teach you, *making a
tentative excursion along that scar, reading its braille,
tracking down that weakness, a scar is always a potential
opening.* Rita, you've just got to meet this guy . . . things he
has shown me. *Of course Gérard schooled* à la grecque
ancienne.

Raymond smoothing out the bald skin there, under the chin,
where it has begun to sag. Would he have Gérard's youth by
osmosis? Gérard's sudden strength against me that day and then
his face jerking back: that flicker of fear. It was fear. Raymond has
won Gérard. I am not laying any claims.

Sébastien is here. The quickness of the black eyes as they dart under the straight lashes. Rich darkness: too much surly resistance in that body for Raymond to have groomed him. Of course, the Master of Ceremonies would enjoy intellectual fencing with him. Big Sébastien: deep voice with its strong meridional accent: *Eh bienG* . . . a contented sigh is released. From the menu selection or relief that the Gérard issue has been dealt with. He looks up.

He emerges. Vivid *bas-relief:* his features cohere now. His smile signals a solution to that shifting collage assembled, reshuffled that day in the café. This is another moment. Sequins of light play in his pupils. They soften, waver.

Céleste bedecked in sequins, like a half-scaled fish . . .

Two little flames beckon there now. The Dunhill lighter has been produced again. Its flame licks the tip of my cigarette.

Eh, Rita! It's not as serious as that. Gérard will be all right. He wouldn't have survived this far if he weren't resilient. If he can get back to his studies, recognize what he's been doing to himself. Sébastien's voice has a softer darkness too.

Raymond's glasses jiggle the flame briefly before he snaps the lighter shut. For a moment his eyes glowed red: So . . . tell us, Rita about your painting.

It's hard to get much out of her apart from *exploded organisms,* Sébastien laughs.

Aha, says Raymond.

116

Well, isn't it all a matter of the drift of signifiers? I say.

Haha. Oho: so you were listening to my rave that day in the café! I get a bit carried away.

Yes, Sébastien does go in for these virtuoso terminological displays. Should hear him when he really gets heated up. Quite impressive really, almost like concrete poetry.

Oh, well. It's a game as good as any other, don't you think?

There is a childish readiness in Sébastien's smile, a self-exposure. With that smile, he could get away with anything.

Yes, I wonder about Seb these days. Once he had good command of French. In the days when he was my student. But these days I'm a little left behind by all the jargon juggling. He tells me it's necessary for rigour, but all the same . . . Sounds like Americanese to me . . .

Seb?

Ah. Yes. Seb. Like the pressure cooker, Sébastien says. Raymond complains about my silences and then my bursts of hot air!

The Professor winks: Pressure cookers are also known to seize up sometimes . . . and to explode. With Sébastien here it can be quite a spectacle, which I hope, Rita you don't have the 'privilege' of experiencing.

Wine. Laughter. Boundaries dissolving. A warm recognition, a definitely focused glow in Sébastien's eyes. There are the candles of course. But it's a peeling off of the outer wax. A melting down of all the assumed forms. Throbbing contours, systole and diastole, as if he . . .

Well, *les enfants,* we had perhaps better choose . . . The waitress will wonder what we're here for!

The comment directed to me: the menu must have been here for some time, in front of me. The words are distinct enough: proceed systematically from one item to the next. I haven't taken in a single one. *Citron givré,* Laurence's favourite amongst the desserts. *Brochettes* brandishes its 't's: meaty chunks and vegetables and fats slip off the spikes, onto the tongue.

Well, what's the painter's choice to be?

Er . . . I think I'll go for the *brochettes.*

Come on. Surely you're going to be a little more adventurous than that. I would have no hesitation in recommending, for

instance, the *grive aux olives cassées,* a real Provençal speciality
— and they do it justice here. Mmmm? What about it?

> *You are my host, you know the restaurant, our table is*
> *marked by the waitress with your name, we are all d'Arlan*
> *tonight, of course, you own the evening, possess the future,*
> *you re-route it with your conditionals: if you were to opt out,*
> *you say, you slip yourself into my place, you will conduct a*
> *miniature fiesta on my palate, control its aftermath, my*
> *digestion, have me eat the songster, the* grive *is the thrush*
> *after all . . .*

Look, as boring as it seems, I really feel like a shish kebab.
    I couldn't entice you to try the *Pigeonneau?*

Pigeonneau à la crapaudière is there on the menu all right. If it's
not the songster, he'd have me eat the warbler or the cooer.
    And Sébastien, I suppose won't be able to resist the *Filet de
Lièvre?* That also is excellent here, Rita. Really, we can't have you
eating *brochettes;* you can have those any time.
    But of course, what do you think? Can never resist the hare.
How about you, Rita? Haven't changed your mind?
    Sébastien is grinning. Getting a bit drunk too.
    Okay. If you insist. I'll have the *Pigeonneau.* Since my banality
offends you both so much!

    The hare at bay. Sébastien's mouth is bloodied by the wine.
This . . . strong resistance at my knee. His knee is thrust on to
mine; for how long has he had it there?

What . . . What I'm aiming at is the risk in . . . er structure. To
make forms scatter in space, just maintaining a tenuous
connection, to the point where it almost but doesn't quite fall
apart . . . Like disparate voices that almost fail to harmonize. To
get the viewer's gaze in but make it fail to possess, make it the
desiring subject okay, but make it assume responsibility for its
intervention, make it aware of the loss it's trying to cover . . .

Their faces are swimming detached, their features displaced,
warping, this side, that . . . Must be the *Chateau Neuf du Pape* —
Raymond must have ordered another bottle, or else it's the gamey
taste of the *pigeonneau* . . . Surely I haven't been talking this long
and why, what did they say to trigger me off . . .

Ah. Yes. Some of us less endowed creatures have to content ourselves with more parasitic activities, alas. We critics . . .

Raymond's lip nuzzles the wine glass, presses its crenellations flat, rosy, paler where they stick.

You read *L'Anti-Oedipe? Machines désirantes* and all that? Sébastien says through a mouthful of hare. I am laughing in the shelter of their laughter, perhaps they're amused at my delirious rambling but they don't seem to mind, nobody does, nobody gives a damn as long as we imply what we cannot say, as long as nobody says it.

Delectable, says Sébastien.

You mean the *machines désirantes* or the hare? Raymond quips.

Both!

They are probably weary of being cast as Curators of Culture. There's an excess that can't be contained so easily. Perhaps what Raymond needs Gérard for, even someone like me, to enact for him what he denies himself . . .

The biro leaks all the same into the kid pocket of his jacket. Black haemorrhage. He will drop it off at the cleaners tomorrow.

119

Turn here!

This is my street. Gleaming snout of the Citroën penetrates its blackness. Heavy night now, uneasily cleft by the headlights scanning the façade for a moment as we turn. The grime-choked pores of the stone dance, dance. He might choose that texture in a lithograph. But not for his address. That *citron givré,* should've done without that. Its delicacy, its subtle tartness wafting, drifting irresolutely over the danker swamps. Bubbling, fermenting, this brew . . . from the bird which sang the woods. I ate the *pigeonneau,* ate the wood-pigeon. Its little corpse nested in my stomach. I will be sick. Get rid of it all. I did not want to. They made me eat it. If they will let me go now, without ceremony. There need be no sequel to tonight.

Raymond's upper lip curls away from the gums: a creeping, a shrugging of the skin towards the eyes. He is peering up at Sérisier's house. My place. He opens the door for me, once again. His eyes don't avoid my gaping boot this time. His gestures have quickened again. He wants a change of scene. This is Cinderella's return. Quick Raymond, oh Prince of Light, or the Citroën Goddess might metamorphose into a Deux Chevaux. He rubs palm against palm energetically. This sudden cold.

A bientôt, j'espère. We will certainly be in contact? *Allez, au revoir!*

Sébastien's outstretched hand grasps mine through the window of the car: mine like a little bird's claw, defeated in his heavy one.

The brown cushions of his strengthen around it. His finger briefly investigates my broken nails. He will not see the Prussian blue signature. This is simply banked up tension being released, this, surging up my arm, as if all my sex were concentrated there, relayed from my wrist. Shudder it off. Redrape my shawl to show that it was just the cold.

Merci! Au revoir!
Et bonne nuit!

The squeal of tyres on the macadam as they take off. Stomach yelping with its frequency. Dog, dog, lick the hand that flatters you. Someone has written LA FRANCE AUX FRANÇAIS on the wall of the *Ecole Maternelle.* The car has vanished, as if by vacuum extractor into some realm of light and open spaces. Raymond forgot his chivalry here. Could have waited until I found my key. This paper in my bag. The drawing. Jose. So long ago. Now it's hopelessly crushed. Lock-jaw, mute howl, for what, for Jose. For everything. Gérard, Gérard.

There is a shimmer of light on the little square window from the stairwell. They should see it open, animate. They might understand. See Denise drape her bulk there to take in her dose of street life, have a preview of the caller on the doorstep. Watch the dusky un-French children queuing up at the water-pump with their plastic bottles. FRANCE TO THE FRENCH. They should listen to the laughter of the woman in the basement.

All the lodgers have put their garbage bags out. Slouched, sleeping. Victims slumped against the wall at execution. What has happened? Did I say anything? A little quiet, a little sleep and things will simplify. My key finally, the big antique key. This is where I live. Tonight was an excursion into something else. Of no consequence. Ease on to my little bed, watch all the blurred contours of things settle, let night thicken around me, fill my space . . . The key-hole keeps jumping perversely away, playing chicken with the key and the steps tantalize my feet, propagating mirage-upon-mirage, looming up, giving way . . . If I can only make it to the door . . .

But it's open: light hits. Clattering, scraping. Denise with six eyes swimming, many hands stirring, spoons.

Salut, Rita. Hope you don't mind. Ran out of gas. Making a bit of *ratatouille.*

Her eyes are oiled orbits spinning off . . . This multiple exposure, if I concentrate, I can superimpose them, back there, in the sockets where they belong, but they separate again, if I could concertina together all those laughing mouths gleaming oil, the ghosted trail of teeth, like Francis Bacon's Pope, their successive positions fused in one long monstrous laugh . . .

Hope you at least got a good feed out of them. What did you eat?

Even the curve of her flexible thumb gyrates on the knife blades, prises, under my stomach and the image endures behind my lids . . .

I ate *pige* . . .

Furry thing. Warm, breathy. Teasing my ear. Voice soft with the effort of gentleness *Rita Rita Rita? Rita you awake Rita you all right?*

MMMM. Just a minute. Mmmm. Just . . . Oh Denise, it's you.

Yes it's me. You had me worried. You blacked out, you know.

Mobile leafy light on the walls.

Morning already?

Afternoon would be more like it, she chuckles. Here: letter for you.

Stamped *Château de Vincennes:* must be Laurence.

I camped here. Thought I might have to call a doctor. What on earth happened last night?

Denise rolls up the sleeping bag on the tiles. *What happened* . . . she can well ask.

Oh, I'm sorry, Denise. Suppose I just drank too much. Mouth feels disgusting . . . *gueule de bois.*

Here: I've made you some coffee.

Temples pounding as I raise my head. Denise's undemanding goodness.

Tell me about it, last night, she says.

Oh . . . Gérard wasn't there.

Well, what in the hell . . .

They wanted to talk about him. Say they're worried.

What? That shrink friend of his?

Ah... He's not exactly a shrink. *Prof de littérature,* seems to go in for a bit of amateur psychotherapy though.

Bloody cheek. I mean: worried about Gérard! What are they trying to get out of you?

I don't really know. They say ... at least Raymond says he's been behaving self-destructively. I quote: *Un comportement auto-destructif.*

AUTO-DESTRUCTIF MON CUL! If you ask me, sounds like that Raymond has problems. Gérard is one of the most together blokes I've met. And what did you tell them? You put them right, didn't you?

Yes. Well. I tried to. Don't know whether I convinced them though. (Leave me alone now. Don't make me say any more.) It's just that it seems Gérard has thrown everything in: the job, the night classes. That he's been projecting ... That he's hinged ... Well, they seem to think he has all his hopes pinned on a relationship with me and ...

Well, you could do far worse. If you don't mind my saying. Anyhow, that's something for you two to work out, surely. Who do they think they are, meddling like that?

Oh. I think they really are concerned about him. And Gérard's friend Sébastien turned out to be rather nice.

Did he? I wonder. Still, it's nothing to do with me, I suppose.

Denise is eyeing the envelope by my hand. By the way, she says. Old Sérisier's found himself a new tenant. For Laurence's rooms. *Une fille très sérieuse,* really straight. Already copped it from her for having the music on too loud. Oh well ... See you later on. They're showing *Le Charme Discret de la Bourgeoisie;* don't suppose you feel up to it?

Not quite ...

Ma chère Rita,

Now I've got some perspective on it, Aix gave me just the incubation period I needed. I think I gained a lot from your instinctive kind of energy. Claude Wahl certainly does. See photos of the new series. Would like your reaction.

There is busyness where there was effaced intricacy. Impasto slabs of pure hue. And within them, big forms roughly delineated, like the city become body, or the individual body throbbing with miniature street life: overlay of graffiti, blobs, spurts ... Dubuffet revisited by a colourist. By De Staël perhaps. But it's still Laurence. Breakthrough for her. She's broken out of that aestheticism.

Jean came round a couple of weeks back. Still the same charming Décadent. *He's looking very handsome: lost a few kilos. Plied me with questions about you. Greedy for everything I could report. Still very interested.*

Exhibition set for last week May. Can you make it? It would mean a lot if you could be there. Jean's coming to the opening, if I can use that as a bait! Am getting him and his mates to put on a little sequence: counterpoint to the paintings. Marcel and I have found an apartment (see above): we can put you up. He sends his love too. How's your work? And the beautiful boys?

Laurence. Jean. I shrivel and warp them. Rebel real yells from the mesh of easy lines. They are larger than that. Now. But it happens to them too. Generous, they can accommodate even me in my absence. Past presented as alternative future. *Jean revu et corrigé par Laurence,* revisited and amended by her. Again, I am summoned; to make manifest their corrected version of me. Jean will not be coming to Provence then. My familiarity with these streets, cafés, friends. That would not be so readily tractable. Have me return to Paris, his Paris. Again I would be *impenetrable: still the same little hedgehog, I see. All prickly defences is our Rita.* And again for Laurence, I would be an untidiness, an intrusive noisiness. She can better handle that on canvas: anarchy framed, held that way. *Now I've got some perspective on it,* she writes. Rita, her abundant *instinctive energy.* Look at me now, Laurence. Mid-afternoon and still unable to get out of bed. My potential energy, you can put that to use. I let them *cripple* me, you said that, that very first day, looking out over the sports field.

Shouting. Must have a soap opera on TV . . . But that's Madame Sérisier's voice. Really exercising her larynx. The old man's more economic, as usual. Just the few muffled grunts from him.

At your age, you should be ashamed of yourself! The way you were oggling her all evening — should've seen yourself, like poached eggs, they were, your eyes and pouring her drinks as quickly as she knocked them back, springing up and down like a jack-in-the-box every time she reached for one of those filthy cigarettes . . . No wonder your son turned out like that *BRAVO,* you say *OUI BRAVO MON FILS.* Ha! *C'est bien le cas de le dire!* When he leaves a perfectly fine woman for that brittle little flousy *OUI: BRAVO.* And what about the children? *Hein?* Thought about them? *T'as un peu pungsé auzungfung heing?* Ratty enough already with your example and his and if they think I'm going to babysit for them to carry on in those sordid dives they frequent, they can think again, Emile. *JE TE DIS QUE CE N'EST PAS CATHOLIQUE,* I'm so ashamed, I'm ashamed . . . It's our son, our son, Emile. There's like a siren wail, then a great gulping of air . . .

But *she* cleared out. Marceline left him with the children, didn't she?

Of course, Marceline left him with the children, she's got to find a job, hasn't she? And she's trying to get something into that thick skull of his, show him for once what it's like trying to look after children without any support. Oh, you can be sure, he'll come snivelling back to her, but it'll be too late . . .

More sobs.

Allez, allez, Viviane, they'll sort it out, you'll see.

SORT IT OUT! (Viviane Sérisier is resilient in her grief.) Sort it out . . . and what about Marceline!

There, there, Viviane. Calm yourself down a bit . . . Marceline was always cold. Ambitious and cold. Hasn't so much as given him a smile in years, squatted on him, she did, squatted on his soul, never anything but nag nag nag . . . I tell you, once you get over the upset, you'll see, this is no flousy. She's a gentle, warm little thing who appreciates him as he is. Can you blame Pierre for that?

Blame him! Of course I blame him. He'll always go for anything that flatters him, takes himself for Casanova, he does! Marceline is a good solid honest woman: saw him for what he was, that's all. No secrets under *her* carpets. I tell you Emile: your son is a bad potato . . . Ah, but you'll never be able to see that. In your heart, you envy him, don't you.

Emile Sérisier must have drifted off into the courtyard: a plume of smoke rising, torn. He's going to let the tirade exhaust itself.

Still shouting after him: Go on Emile, have another cigarette! You know what the doctor said . . . And as if I get any sleep anyhow, with that filthy cough of yours hack hack hack all night . . .

The bankruptcy of virile song leaves a space in which perhaps . . .

Have woken drunk on it, the heady smell of turpentine and the fat oils. But the canvas in this light! Too much of the Indian Yellow, shouldn't paint under that weak bulb. Overdid the *terre verte* too and the pink ochres, too abrupt against the blue. Those lines carved out into the belly and the thighs, energizing the pelvis . . . No it's all too much. Has to be more equivocation . . . But then, perhaps Denise is right: There's a little of Laurence coming through these days, don't you think, Rita? she teased.

Oh, but that expressionist stuff I was doing . . . There was too much emotional display. Too much crude aggression.

But Rita! Since when have you been afraid of a bit of aggression?

Okay. You mightn't have sold much, but you're surviving aren't you? You're taming things down, refining so much . . . As if . . .

She meant: as if I'm trying to appeal to Good Taste.

The brush is working away, pliant with the canvas; the canvas is compliant, yields tentatively to the bristles, replies with its tension. That's right: those jags were too flagrant, like violence celebrated, make them tend towards the vestigial, the pleats holding their reserve . . . prod prod prod into the granular drumskin, the Sérisiers are silent at last: so good to be able to let silence work it out, to be able to roll out of bed, pick up a brush and resume the work of the night before, drunk with it, this silence, this truce. Strange hiatus accommodating me. Antonine the other day surprised I've made so little effort to find real work. The Hôtel du Centre needs a domestic, she says with a hint that I should come out of this hiding, learn about the real world for once, other people' struggles . . . The great knocker outside banging: if it's for me, pretend not to be here . . .

I'll take it! Sérisier calls. *Ah oui, Monsieur, Mademoiselle Rita est là.* But you are laden!

Of course you can count on him to know where his lady lodgers are. Different when it's a matter of collecting rent from them? If he cared so much about his own daughters, Viviane snorts.

Ah là là là là. Sérisier will be shrugging his shoulders, winking at . . . Gérard? complicity of two males. *Oui Monsieur,* go straight up, he says.

Eh, Rita? It is Gérard. There is a thud of something heavy on the landing. Can hear his fast shallow breathing at the door. Have to tell him, *gently of course* that my concern for him . . . But he can't see me like this, my eyes, this burning, something wrong — maybe that was the turps rag I wiped them with . . .

Gérard, *salut!* Can you wait just a minute? Just woken up . . . *J'arrive* . . .

Eyes . . . No wonder so many mistakes in the painting. They're all seamed up, the lashes stuck together, pus . . . Can't face him like this, can't look at him through these little red pig pricks, what is it anyhow, can't control this trembling, I'm usually so expert with the kohl . . . That's right, *Mademoiselle le Peintre,* draw them on if they lack, fumble for your magic wand . . .

Coming, Gérard! . . .

Must be conjunctivitus, free them first in the cold water but they still sprout their little pains, like porcupine quills, *all prickly defences*... These eyes, that's all there is now, my eyes: I see well and far, I see strongly, I feel their muscles working, pupils constricting, dilating, feel that change of focus, that shift as gear change, and now they're gone, eyeless face all lip, and these lips, they have learnt to part too readily, disclose the secret space of mouth, blind withered cushions they are with their blistered fluting, pressed now with a prim seal, but they shrink against intrusions . . . Like the blind squirming mole in the D.H. Lawrence, its tiny toe-fringed feet curling around the cruel umbrella spike ... Impotent against a real intrusion. Can't keep him waiting; why defend this face against his realistic assessment, why not let him see. At your door, keep the patient puppy waiting for the get-together scene ... Quick ... Grab the dark glasses anyhow.

Gérard tilting in the architrave. He is gasping. He has carried that huge package. Careful. After that swim last summer, his bony back stooped for the shelter of the towel, and there it was: the sun flashing a cruel sheen on the scar tissue where one lung had been removed. Only then, he admitted that the 'bronchitis' had been a little more serious than that ... But now: his skin is smooth, fresh, the line of the jaw, the slightly cleft chin so precise. The general gloss: eyelashes, hair, teeth making up the Picture of Health but still the sight is ruptured by that scar. His laughter has a touch of embarrassment, as if his emotions were too nude.

Rita? Going to let me in? Got a little something to show you! He leans the package against the desk. Slow ceremony.

Look!

Numbness taking possession. It's good to have these dark glasses on. He won't see dismay. He's spent his money on framing, that's what it is. He's easing off the masking tape from the brown paper. Hold it, don't let him see. He's gone and paid for a double mount. The darker line of the inner mount throws such relief that the drawing seems set like an obsession, far below, with the phantom rhythms from the recumbent body coming through all the shattered planes: the bitter whites of the crumpled sheets connecting the sleeper to the early morning window.

But Gérard, I don't remember giving you this one to mount, let alone to frame ...

Er ... I must admit, Rita, I sneaked it out. Wanted to show you just how good your work can look when it's professionally framed. Actually . . . No, no don't protest Rita, please . . . Actually it was Raymond who convinced me. He was so intrigued by you — as I predicted — and he wanted to see some of your work. I showed him some of the conté crayon drawings I'd mounted, some of the gouaches too . . . He said it was criminal to put them on the market like that — and, no, Rita: he's right — he said my mounts were fine for a student's folio but they didn't do justice to your drawings . . .

Oh. Gérard. I thought your mounts were very impressive. And in any case, that's what I am. I am still a student. I mean these are little more than doodles . . .

I know you don't take much notice of my opinions . . . You should listen to Raymond though . . .

Raymond, Raymond . . .

Raymond does know a bit about art, Rita . . . He's been making enquiries for you in Marseille . . . He has connections.

Connections, Mmm. Strings. *Des coups de piston.* I don't know whether I want any of that, Gérard.

Wait a minute. WAIT a minute. There's a guy, a Maurice Galant, runs a place in the Panier quarter — you know, near the Old Port — who's . . . already interested. Umm. We took the liberty, Rita, of showing him a sampling of your work. Rita? (*We,* Gérard still using *we.* Couples himself with Raymond. Raymond's *we* excludes Gérard.) Rita? You could have a show by June . . . Rita?

Ah oui, oui c'est chouette. Great. It's great. It's just that . . . (Voice came out atonal.)

It's just what, then, Rita? Why do you seem so depressed about it all then?

His face, luminous as he came through the door, is darkening. I am clouding his joy, can't do this to him . . . And yet, this take-over bid by Raymond . . .

I'm sorry, Gérard. You are a darling. It's just that it worries me. I know how much this kind of framing costs. How much this must have set you in debt and then . . . They mightn't even sell . . . And now, Raymond is putting himself out too . . .

So what? Are you going to deny us that pleasure? Take it from me, Rita, as far as Raymond is concerned, it's just a matter of not seeing talent go to waste on idle browsers in the Aix markets. *Il va te lancer,* Rita. *IL VA TE LANCER.*

(Launch, me, launch me. Raymond will turn Gérard's risky attempts at pulling me through into a winning ride . . .)

You would have critics, a real public . . . The chance to communicate with other artists.

Gérard's lips are poised, eyes focused elsewhere. He is setting out the gouaches now, in their expensive frames. Those little experiments claiming the status of works of art and somehow glittering through that pretension. As if it were not enough to have Gérard love me, have him serve me as Artist, but also, in denying the definition, have him see me as some kind of living monument to modesty . . . Won't say anything. In any case, it would be a lie to mask this pleasure. The colours through the glass . . . Take the dark glasses off: he might wonder if I'm becoming a junkie too. *La poudre,* they call it here.

But Rita! *Bon sang! Qu'est-ce que tu as?*

Oh, nothing. Touch of conjunctivitis, I think. Not very pretty is it?

Oh . . . You should get it treated!

The gentle amber of those eyes querying me, my eyeless face, endlessly open, cannot sustain it. Perhaps that's what it is, perhaps all I use them for, my eyes, to keep the world at a distance, keep it in tow. Perhaps that's all it is, this panic, something like loss of mastery, or even crude vanity. *This is your ugliness, Rita.* Would not give Gérard false hopes but would not have him see this: this wandering flesh, my face undone by the red rims, one pink continuum for his sad scrutiny. Close them, keep this redness, this rawness to myself, but cheek is coming alive under this touch, his lithe fingers stroking it.

Oh Gérard . . .

How to repel him: this is a perfectly acceptable *fraternal* gesture and if it's not? My arguments? What are they really? His youth? His insecurity? Something about Sébastien the other night, his dark power. *Sébastien is a Lawrentian cliché,* Laurence would say. His mute power. I would crush Gérard's fragile body. Maybe it's simply that. Would be heavy, graceless in comparison. Crudely dominant. Don't want dominance. Cannot tell him that though. In any case, it is simply fraternal, this light caressing. *You are a darling,* I said that. Diminished him that way.

I don't know what to say. Thankyou. Thankyou for everything.

What about . . . Feel like grabbing some breakfast at the *Mondial?*

Why not? He says, biting the inside of his lower lip, working nervously away at it.

Could you just give me a moment to wash and change? Been in these clothes non-stop for a couple of days.

Rita, I'd give you every moment, you must know that.

He has said it. I cannot say it to him. All I can do is send back this smile: is it sifted tenderness he receives, sex being retained?

Yet now we both have this jaunty pace on the street, freedom in his laughter, in this attunement of our strides. It's I who have proposed breakfast as medium, I who would take him out into the public space. I have dismantled the Intimate Scene. Egotism of it. I need breakfast, therefore you shall accompany me to the Cours Mirabeau. But the light is kind. The day is new, magically held on the edge of spring. High clarity of the sky, cheeky slithers of travelling light on the tubular metal of the chair legs, tender haze hovering between yellow and green on the plane trees. There are birds.

Why didn't I see this: haven't looked at Gérard properly. Out here, his eyes are huge, cheeks more cavernous, bones thrown into sharper relief by that shadow of a beard.

Have you slept at all, Gérard? You look desperately tired.

Why say that? Deny that I perceive his real mood: he has the nervous energy of one who has paced through the night, come to a decision high on adrenalin and who is wonderfully glad to be still awake.

No no, I'm not tired. Must admit I spent the night controlling the urge to rush around with the drawings . . .

And what's it to be, *Monsieur 'dame?* Jose's face holds no comment.

Gérard doesn't raise his eyes; fingers the buttons on his jacket sleeve. He is not here for breakfast. A narcotic voice somewhere beyond him orders *pain au chocolat* and *un chocolate chaud.* The little boy lost dreaming of comfort. I have ordered *croissants* and *un grand crème.* Now the *pain au chocolat* is before him, his fingers idle over it. There is a tremor in them as they hover, then pluck at the crust.

I need all this busy sipping, this *croissant* breaking, clinking of the cup against the saucer to fill our silence. It is silence, despite the rush of cars around the Rotonde — reflections of trees, cafés, hurtling along their windows — the brisk concentrated pace of people heading for work, bank, market, students emptying out of buses. Strangely out of these circuits, this little round table: a still and awesome island. My hunger, my pleasure in this hot coffee, the warm, light layers of pastry, must be offensive to him. Delicate Jack Spratt watching the Big Wife engorge her spiritless spaces, gagging the voices that might have spoken to him. Could he have listened? Still it was about the labour of conjugal consumption: *together they licked . . .*

Rita . . .

Oui?, I manage, scooping up the last crumbs now.

Rita, I . . .

What is it, Gérard?

(Please don't let him embark on declarations.)

132

SSSS. Something I've been wanting to ask for so long. That day I met up with you and Sébastien at the Aiguillage. I watched you, you know. You seemed so engrossed in what he had to say. I expected that, anyhow. I knew . . . I know I could never measure up. Well . . . But since then, I don't know. Sometimes I think, well, I could offer you something. Well that day I'd wanted to ask him what he thought . . . I'd talked to him a lot about you . . . I wanted to ask him what . . . whether . . . what he thought about my . . .

Your what, Gérard?

These crumbs on my plate. There are seven. Exactly. If only he would never complete the sentence. Postpone it.

My . . . Our . . . My proposing to you. I mean Rita. I mean would you marry me?

Still seven crumbs casting their precise shadows. This column of air squeezed tight and tighter in my throat. Never, I will never be able to raise my head.

Oh, Gérard.

It's all right, it's all right. Don't say it, I beg you. I beg you to say nothing, Rita. I know — I knew — it would be too much to hope for.

No. I *must* say. It . . . it comes as such a surprise that's all. I mean, I just don't think in those terms. I mean, I don't feel I'm ready even to think about marriage with anyone . . .

He has not looked up. There are tears beading on his lashes. *Pain au chocolat* still untouched.

So that's how I rank is it? *Anyone?*

Oh, Gérard, of *course* not. Quite the . . .

It's okay. It's okay. *Ça va ça va ça va.*

(The sudden *mitraillette* of his voice.)

Forget I said anything. I didn't sleep last night. Put it down to that. Raymond thinks I'm a bit crazy. Out of touch with reality. Maybe he's right.

Of course he's not. Of course you're not.

(Reach for his hand — he snatches it away. Tightly sprung: virginal reflex now. Raymond said that night: *Verging on mythomania . . . You can't afford to take someone like Gérard literally, Rita . . . Céleste, eh? . . .* Again he is betrayed.)

You know . . . You know how close to you I feel . . .

Don't say it. Please please don't say anymore.

That dry hacking cough shaking him. He is standing up.

133

You'll understand if I don't come round for a while. Raymond will be contacting you again soon, in any case. Wants to see your oils. He's right: he'll be able to help you much more effectively than I can. *Salut.*

No *bise* this time. He threads the falling lock of hair between his fingers. His angelic beauty smarting with this sudden bitterness. *Androgynous,* who said that? The chestnut waves, *châtain-roux,* of his hair still responding to the sun. That is why I can't say yes, more gentle than I have ever been ... *You know how close to you I feel, Gérard* ... but oh no, no, not like that, in bed, I would feel mountainous, too powerful ... Gérard, no no, I would feel trapped in your total worship, you have mistaken me, you will see when you are older ...

Now he is a quarter of a centimetre tall, already engulfed in the shade of the bookshop awning, lost. This pressure behind my eyes, sprouting their pains again, this clenched heart trapped in its cage. Lost, he will not come back this very dearest one, but still I could pursue him, catch up, we were striding together a moment ago, I was still innocent then, I can still find him in the crowd, say yes, YES I WILL Gérard, you took my breath away, that's all, I was overwhelmed, I was being absurd, it is absurd to worry about a few years' difference, we could live together, take an apartment in a little fishing village outside Marseille, we could both work part-time and I would live in wonder at your beauty, your stories and you would reflect in my paintings and I would give you strength, belief in yourself and you would teach me gentleness and your children would be exquisite in their gentleness too . . . But no . . . The mechanics of it. I cannot move from here. This obscene plump presence of the *croissant* so insensitively devoured, weighing me down. Here are the black trouser legs again: Jose.

Monsieur est parti, Mademoiselle?
   Oui, Monsieur est parti.

He is gone, gone and the milky coffee gives a constant feedback to my palate. *Can't you see that he's gone?* The sting in my eyes means that he is gone. How will Raymond save him from dope now? Jose takes the chocolate, sealed in its skin now. The skin wrinkles as the cup is buoyed away on the tilting tray.

135

Sea of bleached ochre tiles parts its waves and now we are plummeting through down down into the gaping jaws: it's the Gare St Charles.

How did I manage to leave Aix so easily? But what does it matter — this feeling of elation anyhow. Sérisier is there on the platform. Isn't that sweet of him! *Mademoiselle Rita,* he calls. *I've found the perfect studio for you in Marseille. And you'll look out on Notre Dame de La Garde! You see: It's not so difficult to move after all.* I am stepping out, he is right: it's all so easy. But the platform is streaming away under my foot, this carriage is moving off again, it's taking me with it, I've lost sight of him, but his voice still, hoarse from shouting, frayed: *Mademoi...* We are simply gliding away. It's normal, this slight squeezing of the heart, farewells are always like this: Denise, even Antonine has made the effort to see me off and there is ... Jacquie, hobbling along on his withered leg, the only one able to keep up with the train ... On the end of the platform: there he is, his hair a golden stream behind him, his mouth poised in an oval ADIEU ...

No, no. Not the son of SUMA OUR LADY OF THE HEIGHTS not the son of CÉLESTE, this is simply GÉRARD LAGRANGE, forgot that, didn't you, and yes, of course you have left him behind, but my dear, aren't you going to give him a little wave at least?

Who is speaking? That man opposite? Hadn't seen him before. It's the one who was in Laurence's carriage. This is the observation car I'm in then . . . But it's moving off of its own accord: the other carriages have been shunted off on to another line. Passengers disembarking from them. *If they get off, that is their decision. Marvellous, isn't it? Our modern public transport: one moment in Marseille, the next, half-way to Paris?*

Why doesn't he lower the newspaper when he speaks? Perhaps it isn't him, perhaps there are others behind me. But it's quite impossible to turn around. Too much weight in my body. *A matter of will-power you know, quite simple really,* he clicks his tongue, turns the huge newspaper. Astonishingly expert gesture. A colossal headline facing me: so, it's not the *Figaro* after all he's reading, the format is more like *The News of the World. Sensationalism,* he mutters, *Listen to this for instance: BIG BROTHER IS WATCHING YOU! Fantasies, verging on paranoia . . . Well I never . . . What will they invent next?* He suddenly slaps the newspaper down on his knee. His face! It's Raymond but . . . He has a monocle. The lens flashes white, I can't see the eye there. He is leaning forward now, to fill my glass, this wine glass in my hand. Now I see it: the eye is huge, a crystal ball swelling and far below the surface, there it is, the amber fossil of the iris . . . My hand is on the emergency brake, there is a squealing as if, as if . . . The wheels themselves were flesh and screaming . . .

There is still screaming, it . . . was me all the time, here, still here: the jaundiced wallpaper, its tired bouquets. My cold sweat. And outside, it's nearly spring. Antonine there, on the platform.

Antonine's place, in May. I can go there.

Be walking again. Toes brown clenching, lifting, clenching the leather of my sandals, hand on the hot rough denim of my jeans, on the muscled potential of the stride. Walking towards the big canvas in the courtyard. Working through it. Away from these toy streets, the glamour faces of the Cours Mirabeau, the banks with their shining brass letters, away from the cafés with their catch-cries and slogans, away from the bookshop and the alphabet of culture, past the Roi René with his cold bronze gaze, out out out through all the frames of reference, springing steps jolting and felling the successive horizons, stripping away all the anchylosed sheaths from nerves alive and ramifying out out as frames fall away to bristle, bud, earth-clod, lit and shadowed, engulfing, swallowed, violets and reds dancing out the anarchy of all the morphologies undone: bird, rat, vine, tree.

Earth heaves plump with death now pulse prod push the webbings out out and up its sexes course from head to hand. Brain sprouts fingers through the canvas. The chair is a journey. The wall is its mirror. The slaughter of poppies: the total fiesta. The riotous tendrils, the dark roots snaking, squiggle and spurt, the cancelled notations affirming it all the same.

Be needle and loop of the swallow's career, unravel the seam of that space, be silk blood of resin, be lance of the pine, the body of sky expanding expanding and cluster my suns on the spikes of the broom, be random, be theorem, be victor be victim, be dance of the cripple, be voice of the gagged, be penthouse nymph and basement hag, be vice be versa, be miner be flyer through widows and windows . . .

Shatter forever that monocled eye: that mannikin watching, that crippling spy.

That fossil: his iris. Explode it in paint.

Antonine Vigier's courtyard through the wrought-iron gate. The sun is lower now. Each pebble sends across its tooth of shadow. The concentric green darks ripple the fountain bowl. The cloistered quiet in here. The militant's retreat. That must be her in the deck-chair, her long hands hanging limp, knuckles to the pebbles. The canvas weighted with the cleft sphere of the buttocks within the intersecting rectangles of the frame. Again the organic struggling within the rectilinear. Sébastien's body *farouche,* wild, disrupting the cut of his clothes. If I could get him here, to pose... The hinges of the gate groan. The arms, the feet, fly up from the deck-chair; there is a scattering of pebbles.

Arrrgh! *AH RITA MAIS C'EST TOI!*

Antonine without the golden aura of her hair. She has it darkly plastered to the scalp: henna mud on it. Her focus is slightly beyond me, the skin is stained around the eyes and elsewhere, there is a pallor. Antonine without her usual *mise-en-scène,* without her animal lustre.

My God, you gave me a fright! She laughs. Her hand goes up to defend her mouth.

Oh, Rita... I thought it was... I thought it was Sun... But, of course, you don't know...

What's wrong? Who Antonine? Who?

Oh Rita. Sun Diatti . . . When I think about it I want to SCRRREAM. *J'ai envie de CRRRIER!*

The 'R's have a rasping gargling sound, not the usual uvular purr of the North African French.

140

Sun Diatti?

Sun Diatti, yes, you know. The Malian guy I told you I was crazy about. You KNOW: I pointed him out to you at the Resto-U one day.

Ah. Yes. Well, wouldn't you have liked it to be him instead? I mean . . .

If that was him . . . He didn't need to be pointed out: that white robed figure, remote, so erect: the vertical axis from head to hip undisturbed by his gait. The physical pride and the carriage of Jose, giving from a distance the illusion of exceptional height. As he walked up to Antonine, he gave a minimal nod, a sardonic smile, as if to cut short her stuttering efforts to introduce me. His eyes never left her, in any case. Seemed fascinated by his own effortless power to disable her; by her sudden loss of composure. Does she want him for his emblematic value, though: black flame of her own liberation? SUN DIATTI, the heat and diamonds of his name. Perhaps she's not the actress I thought: she plants her hands palm to palm in a wedge, between her thighs. She is rocking slightly, like a small child in trauma.

If he saw me like this, I'd die. After . . .

After what? What did he do to you Antonine?

He did nothing, I suppose. He just taught me a few things about myself . . . *A là là là là* . . . You saw the effect he has on me. Until that day I introduced you, he'd always looked at me as one looks at an object, to ascertain its solidity. He'd always scared the hell out of me. I attended the same seminars on politics for a while. Finally I plucked up the courage to — I wanted to get to know him, to show him I wasn't the fake he seemed to take me for. So I asked him if I could borrow his copy of *Black Masks, White Faces,* of all things. Yes, Rita, you can laugh, but it's not quite as ridiculous as it sounds. After all, he was always quoting Fanon. Anyhow, he looked at me quizzically and smiled one of those slow smiles that make me collapse at the knees . . .

But Antonine, aren't you aware of the effect *you* have on people? You could make or break them with that smile of yours too . . .

Come on!

She winces. The self-stylist I had her as is irritably dismissed.

Anyhow . . . Of course, once I borrowed it, I had to return it. I needn't have taken it to his room at the Cité Universitaire. He

141

knew that. Anyhow ... When I came in, he was eating. Rita! You wouldn't believe it! Not the way you or I would snatch a hunk of cheese and a bite of bread when we are alone ...

Antonine's sudden assumption of identity between us ...

No. He was eating in ceremony. A little clearing amongst the books on his desk: a place mat, cutlery set out, spicy rice and ginger chicken in a serving dish, a crystal wine glass, napkin on his lap ...

What was it? A parody of the French way?

No. No, I don't think so. I mean, he always says that play can't be sustained without ultimately contaminating. *We blacks know something about the Age of Enwhitenment,* he says. No ... He said that he was glad I'd come, that he wanted to know what I was on about. *You'll excuse me,* he said, *I believe in eating properly, not that pallid rubbish they serve in your canteens.* For ·what seemed an eternity, he continued eating, sipping the wine he had poured, saying nothing. Suppose he expected me to speak. Offered me a glass of wine. Look, I said, I only wanted to return your book. That seemed to irritate him. He gestured for me to sit down. On the bed: that was really the only place to sit, anyhow. *Of course you haven't come for that,* he said. *And by the way, are you sure you don't want to display the Fanon for a while longer on your coffee table?*

Oh. The bastard!

Yes. That made me really wild. Told him I wasn't necessarily the middle-class white bitch he liked to caricature me as. He just laughed: *Well, I'm sorry but you're hardly black. No need to get up-tight about that though. SIT DOWN, Antonine: I told you I'd like to get to know you. I'm always interested in exceptions to the rule. Show me how you've managed to break away from your colonial upbringing, ma GRANDE PIED NOIR ...* All the time, his voice was very quiet. He keeps his cool all right. Then he put on Beethoven. *The Emperor,* of all things! *Western Culture!* He laughed. *Your armchair revolutionaries. The Individual of Talent laments his disabusement with RRREVOLUTION and centuries later other Sensitive Individuals will still be weeping over it in their concert seats. Still, it's interesting. I'm learning, I'm learning,* he said.

What's he learning? It's a bit too easy to frame you like that as Europe.

142

Oh. I don't know, Rita. Anyhow, I don't know how it happened but we were laughing, chatting. I thought, well, he's probably quite sincere, he does want to get to know me, that sarcasm was just a way of disarming me. And then, I don't know, his arms were around me and I could feel myself stiffening. I mean: I really hadn't expected *that*. But I was losing all sense of what I wanted, how to say what I wanted. I didn't know anymore . . .

But, Antonine . . . You've always said you were attracted to him . . .

Yes. Of course. But I hardly know him. And that's what I told him. That brought on the sarcasm again. *So, the physical world isn't enough for you, what's happened to your dialectical materialism, Antonine? You've got to get to know me metaphysically first, do you? You and your sexual politics! I've seen a look in your eyes — you're not going to pretend now that that was metaphysical yearning are you?* So, I told him, yes, of course I was attracted to him but that didn't mean that I wanted to leap into bed with him straight away. Oh I don't know. I ran out of arguments. That's what it had become, Rita: a debate. I couldn't mention Dmitri, that I was going to Greece to see Dmitri — I would have copped a speech on sexual possession . . .

Yes. Of course. Antoine served me that one not long ago when I reminded him that he had a wife . . .

Yes. Yes, but he wasn't quite taking that line anyhow. He said he at least was serious, not as casual as I might imagine. Oh, and then he came out with things like: *Look, maybe you're afraid of black men anyhow, maybe you believe the myths, think we're all rapists. Maybe that's what Black Power is to you: Rape. Don't worry, Antonine*, he said. *There are plenty of girls who would let me into their rooms any time. They're willing to play for a while, see just how NAUGHTY they can be, how LIBERATED. A casual fuck with a black ô là là là là. Exchange notes with their friends. And then they'll get engaged soon enough to a nice white medical student to make their mummies and daddies happy. But I don't happen to want that with you*, he said. *I don't want a casual fuck, I want to make love to you.* He said he thought I might just be different from all the rest of them. And then, that I didn't mince around, make every man think he was automatically the master.

But effectively the master, just the same?

Antonine ignores it.

I didn't have any words left. Anyhow, I couldn't speak — he was kissing me and my whole life swooned away. Dmitri. Everything. I suppose that's when I started to panic: I knew that once I became involved with Sun Diatti, that would be the end of everything else . . . And yet . . .

And yet what? Would that . . . Would it matter, if that's what you want?

Rita, I know, I know . . . But I wasn't sure enough. And I still wasn't certain he wasn't playing with me. Or perhaps he was right. Perhaps I was afraid. Of the consequences. You know my father, Rita. He still hasn't forgiven me for going out with an Algerian. He kicked me out of home for that. Had me followed by a private eye too. It's only lately that I've been back on some reasonable terms with him. For my mother's sake. He's an old sick man, now . . . But . . . Oh well, there we were: suddenly nude together. Beethoven was played out. The record was still spinning round and round. And I just felt this overwhelming inertia. I was stunned by the suddenness of it all: my body and his like an apparition. *Antonine, Antonine,* he kept on saying, *just relax, relax, where is all your laughter, you always seemed so full of laughter. I want you to be joyful with me, I want this to be a good moment for you.*

I want, I want . . .

Yes, she says. And then the light was on me: brutal. I reached to switch it off. *No, why?* he said. *I want to see this beautiful big body of yours moving, I want to see it dancing . . .*

A shiver runs through her: It's getting cold out here in the garden. She draws her knees up, under her chin. Her eyes are still focused beyond: on Sun Diatti. Rita! (It's practically a shriek, through the whisper.) It was a disaster! There was my body and I didn't want to see it. I couldn't 'make it dance'. He slipped away for a moment. Put on another record. *The Music of Mali!* he laughed.

Oh no. But really, that's too much!

Yes. Frenzied drums and joyful choral singing. And I realized what I'd become. At least to myself: pale pink Europe, spreading out its soft fats to be ransacked.

Oh no. Antonine. Since when have you been pink? Or soft!

I was: pale pink Europe asking to be *fucked,* unable to *make*

love. I couldn't say of course. That I wanted to be active, free . . .
Oh, and then he was saying: I want to hear it from you, Antonine,
I want you to say it, tell me BAISE-MOI, say it out loud BAISE-
MOI SUN DIATTI, I want you to shout it, that you want to make
it with me.

But that's . . . ridiculous to expect that of you. What does he
want? The total broadcast, to screw in an auditorium?

Well, I don't know. He wanted me to be ready to risk having it
heard. You know how thin those partitions are between the
rooms, Rita. In any case I was unable to say a word, let alone
protest against the absurdity of it. In the end, he said it: *Get up,
Antonine. Get up, you're a corpse. I'm not interested in
necrophilia. And despite your expectations, I'm not a rapist. I
would like you to go now. I've got better things to do . . .* Antonine
has buried her head in her arms.

Antonine, it's being racist not to protest. Of course he was just
engaged in crude sexual warfare. Wanting you to shout his
victory, that he's finally got Antonine under his control,
Antonine whom they're all after.

No, Rita. I knew that if I sought him out, he'd only interpret
one way. I must have known. The thing is, he's shown that I am
no exception. That I'm a . . .

That you're a what?

That I'm just like all the rest of them: the ones he sneers at.
Like all the rest of the Dutiful Daughters flirting with rebellion
and deep-down, riddled with hang-ups. And now, I suppose I'll go
off to Greece and play wifey to Dmitri. I don't know if I can
anymore. I'm involved, somehow I'm involved now in his anger,
in Sun Diatti. He is probably right: he's been just a mascot for the
French girls around here, wanting to display how far out they can
go . . .

But why should you be his mascot either? Look . . . if he cares,
he'll be around to see you. Or else why don't you go to him and
explain where you are?

· I can't I can't! Urrrgh! Rita! My hair! My God: it's been in
nearly an hour — I'll be even redder than you!

Redder than Rita.

You could carry it off.

What will Dmitri say! His family take me for a whore as it is.

They want him to stop the relationship. At least to keep me away from the village.

Why, why tell me? Just for the cathartic effect of telling? Determined to present it as her failure: a problem with no issue. Now she has rushed in to wash out the henna. No words of her own so she accepts herself as product of his words: *pale pink Europe spreading out its soft fats.* Hard to put that in a painting. Would look like a celebration of rape. Antonine frenetically rubbing, agitating the gravelly medusa locks under the stream of water, releasing the dark flood: the brightness prized by Arab women goes with the mud. To be subtly hennaed, not to overdo it. She almost forgot though, in her involvement in the night with Sun Diatti. Quick quick: the subdued image for Dmitri, if that's what he wants. The alternative future: *play wifey to him.*

Oh look, it's not so bad after all! Antonine is purring again. The jade of her eyes is limpid now as she takes placid account of the tangled hair in the mirror. She takes my shoulders, brings my head into alignment with hers: Look, she says, we could be taken for sisters!

It's absurd. In a way though, she's right. Despite my smaller bones, my paler skin, her bigger show of teeth when she laughs, her more sumptuous body, there is an identity. We both exhibit a surface vividness in our hair, our green eyes, the words we fling about. But when the crunch comes, we're both drained of colour, both inert. Struck dumb, stricken with paralysis. We let the others move. We could be taken for sisters, seen from the inside.

By the way, so you still want to stay here Rita?
    Yes, I do . . . but are you sure? Are you really going?
    Of course I'll go. Dmitri is probably not the phallocrat I made him out to be. And I know he loves me. I need that . . .
    She dreamily towels her hair.
    I'll leave the key with the woman upstairs — make yourself completely at home, won't you. Use up the food, play the records. I like the thought of you living here!

Of course. We are the same. We have not progressed far. We uphold our right to our own space but then, so did the princess in the tower with her menagerie of dragons below: this is my space, come frame it for me, modify me by your framing, make the monsters that haunt me docile pets, charm them into art by your song or slay them with your sword. Power to make the others move. My solitude, my immobility were just an artifice to lure you, come sweet lord, deliver me, the tower I inhabit is nothing but my father's space.

Antonine spreads out her soft fats to be ransacked.

The ventriloquist's doll unlocks its jaws, releases a no to Gérard.

What would they think if I said yes to you now? I must be consequent to the adult words across the restaurant table. Marry you? Oh, I know that it was just a way of putting it. Perhaps I was your chance of breaking free from Raymond. I told him I would say no to the son of Céleste. You framed my pictures, thankyou Gérard, but as Raymond said, the help you have given me was not unmotivated. The identity you would have gained that way would be so fragile, Gérard. You must face solitude without me, without Raymond. For your own sake?

Le Professeur d'Arlan on the line for you, Mademoiselle!

So I am not alone for long. The future precipitated by a phone call. Need not be. Sérisier is positively glowing from the reflected prestige. Raymond would have said in his cultivated voice: *Would it be inconveniencing you too much, Monsieur, if I were to speak to Mademoiselle Finnerty for a moment?*

Ah, Rita, Raymond says, as if we were old acquaintances. I gather that you have spoken to Gérard. Mmm. Yes. Oh, he is in quite a state of disarray at the moment. Natural enough but give him time — he'll reorient himself. This was to be expected. But let me say how grateful I am to you for letting him know where he stands. It can only be positive for him in the long run . . . Not at all, not at all. I'm glad you enjoyed it. You must have dinner again with us soon. Since we met you, we have also had the pleasure of seeing some of your work. And . . . I think that it is essential that an alternative outlet for your paintings be found. I took the liberty of showing some of your work to a friend of mine — a Maurice Galant who . . . Gérard told you? Well, yes, he has a small upstairs gallery which he reserves specifically for new artists and . . . From what he has seen he is very enthusiastic about giving you a show, possibly as early as June? Mmm? Believe me, Rita, this is not a case of 'pulling strings'. Maurice Galant knows his work well enough and besides, I think you show little trust in my aesthetic judgement. I do recognize talent when I see it and I consider that I was doing as much a service to Maurice as to you by showing him something of what you can do. I was gratified to see that he thoroughly endorsed my opinion. From the little I have seen, your work is quite original, daring in fact. And also very attractive.

It's a translator's error. It's cultural difference that he's perceiving as originality. They don't know Arthur Boyd, Fred Williams. *Attractive,* he just said. These paintings of mine please too readily. Therefore they fit into their value systems. Therefore they rank as saleable beauty objects. Therefore they simply reiterate the status quo. Of course there is desire in my paintings, female desire, but it's not received as anything that might disrupt the impeccable surfaces of their world. They can see it as the lyrical expression of my own conflicting drives. The viewer can seize upon that surface lyricism and modify beforehand his latent perception of those other, more disturbing aspects. Of course they are unanalysable anyhow through the frames of reference they impose. Certainly not seen as any subversive allusion to the social ideas Raymond and Company would perpetrate. And if certain jarring elements are too strong to dismiss, they can be received as the *necessary contradiction,* that note of ugliness upon which Beauty depends. Therefore, yes: I can be safely backed as *daring, original,* therefore I can be promoted as a painter.

Rita? . . . Rita, I was saying . . . All the string-pulling in the world wouldn't make a painter of you. You have done that by yourself. But it would also be naïve to pretend that any activity is possible in a social vacuum. *N'est-ce pas? Hein?* Carmelite nuns . . . Yes even Carmelite nuns depend on those who work in the world outside for their spiritual pursuits. Hippies . . . And you are not begging, I know, nor would I want to place you in a situation in which you felt in the least dependent.

But in any case, Raymond, I'll have to find a job. I know I can't live in a vacuum. There's some domestic work I can get in a hotel. I'll have to work. I have enough debts as it is. There's the money I owe Gérard for the framing, for instance.

Ah. You can forget about that. Since he was out of pocket, I took it on myself to reimburse him. No, no, Rita, we can talk about that later. You talk about taking a job now when there's the possibility of an exhibition in a few weeks' time? You would be

149

doing yourself much more justice by devoting every moment to your work. And what I would propose is that you accept a little advance to tide you over in the meantime.

By paying Gérard, he's already binding me to accept this offer. And now: this advance. He's taking over completely.

No, no, Raymond. I couldn't possibly accept that.

Rita, as you know, I am a single man. As you might have gathered from Gérard's prattle, I'm rather too often inclined to spend my money on frivolities. I might be a cynic, but I do happen to believe in a few things. And art is one of them. Are you going to deny me what amounts to a purely egotistical pleasure? It's not as if I'm offering you a gift. It's simply a matter of a loan. You will make ample money from the exhibition to pay me back then. I'm sorry but I just can't see you as a chambermaid.

I've done that work many a time.

Mmmm.

Look, I'm very grateful . . . very flattered by the interest you have taken. But . . .

But?

I don't want to get caught up in the whole machinery of gallery politics. All those middle people . . . The opinion makers . . .

Really, Rita. Perhaps you are deluding yourself a little there? You were hardly avoiding the middle-man with Gérard, if you'll excuse me for saying so. And the marketplace gave you exactly the same sort of situation in disguise as a gallery, *except* that you were employing a self-styled dropout as marketer-promoter and I hardly think you could have counted on the flower-people to keep on buying your work. Please, Rita, think it over. Believe me, if Maurice Galant is willing to give you a show, it is not as a personal favour. He is a businessman. There will be no moral obligation imposed on you whatsoever.

He means: as there was in accepting Gérard's help.

Lulled and soothed by the rock-a-bye of his demonstrations, here I am emitting more positive signals . . . Yes, I am saying, yes, I'll be in on Saturday. Yes until then. *A samedi alors. Et merci, Raymond.*

TRIPTYCH

Voici la chanson du pigeonneau. This is the song of the wood-pigeon.

I.

Caught in the strokes of the barbed wire thicket — foetus? carcass — a form is struggling. Bird or human. From the contours of its struggles, a tenuous line unravels — memory? mirage? — loops upwards, once, twice. Falls again. Its freedom was postulated coquettishly. The sky remains a painted space. Whatever you do: paint it in, paint it out, it is the space that culture appropriates. Oppose a field of pure hue to a dense overlay of staccato strokes, oppose a suave parabola to the mass of broken lines, a nest of possibilities to the spaces it articulates — the very contradictions will be read as *her* silence, *his* horizon: *Oh, yes, it's a figure in a landscape.* The painting only *is* when *they* say it; it's becoming-voice is theirs.

II.

Let the thicket invade the whole pictorial space with its fiddle-sticks and thorns, the sky will be spoken all the same, in its absence:

    i. *Prince Charming will come, cut through the barriers she propagates in her hundred-year nubility — the sky is the limit from his castle-of-light-ever-after.*

    ii. *It is the prison of one awaiting grace, dark cry of*

someone seeking God.

iii. *Good grief! Rita Finnerty is still trapped in the influence of Jackson Pollock.*

III.

A body dancing on its bed of twigs; the contact points between the jags and the bland are the loci of its moment. It *is* at the junctures between the self and the rest: where the twigs prick, the nerve-ends sprout a voice. The thicket is the armature which says the body of the sky: *Here I sing, am, might be. Not pleasure not pain both am am am. Vertical horizontal moving immobile. I precipitate these strokes and blobs, they sing me where I am.* Excrutiating buoyancy and density, the bulk of it relayed through space contracting back, from them to me, from me to them, reversibly, at once . . .

Whatever they say, the three panels are emerging, now. They will be arriving soon. Should clear up, prepare myself. But there should be more of it to meet their eyes, recalcitrant, whatever they choose to see. Sébastien and I are in the thicket? His silences incubate a passionate volley — there they are, his silences, in the neutral greys, interlocking with the dense dark strokes, black-reds, black-greens. We knot and knit a cryptic script which could be sung.

But before the thicket finds it voices, Raymond has come and laced the air with his precious intonations. Painting the thicket, denied the upward curve of that song, the brush is nervy, febrile. No exit from this entanglement. I ate the wood-pigeon, my body did not reject it. It does not sing in my flesh. The mirage of it there, in the unpainted space could be the voice of the lark, the black-bird, why not the nightingale? Denied, it is the perfect rendering of any transcendent cry. If it were painted though, that line would be sleek, all style. Resist it like the mellifluous voice of a treacherous faith. Every thorn painted is tongue potent from that refusal. We are not dumb bodies, nobody can *say* us, we can embody our own texts. And yet . . . this silent wood, its hieroglyphs asserting their presence through the absent sky . . . the brush performs the paradox I live through them . . .

This soft padding, bare feet across the tiles. Denise exudes her sleep. The smock sends its undulations from the breasts to the top of her thighs. Her presence is at one with her mass. Denise is exactly incorporated within herself. The word fatness cannot be used. Or else she is fat as a Maillol bronze woman is fat. She watches the brush: it is a busy little animal involved in its inscrutable tasks, commanding some sort of respect all the same in its autonomy. Only the slight metallic pulse of the crickets outside and the brush performing in the space of her drowsiness, am am am, it sings, amamam, the noise of the brush against the fat paint, amamamamamam, like the rapid plucking and slapping of lip on lip . . .

Here they are, on the landing already. Smiles. But the imperious way Raymond raises his chin says: *What is going on here?* They look from the three panels back to Denise, as if my nudity were somehow located there between the painted surfaces and her bare legs. *Denise je te presente* . . . But she barely raises her lip from the rim of her coffee bowl as she edges past them. Raymond flattens himself against the jamb of the door as the smock and bare thighs pass. Her eyebrow pushes up a ripple into the blank space of the forehead. *EX-cusez MOI MESSIEURS,* she says. There is laughter in the slurping noise the words make. Raymond's crisp elegance: the linen jacket, the bone canvas slacks, defenceless against her nudity.

Sébastien seems amused.

Please excuse us, says Raymond, twisting his neck in the direction of Denise's disappearance. I thought . . . I didn't realize you had company.

He wants an explanation. I needn't give it.

But that is perfectly all right, I say. Denise has the room next door. Err . . . I lost track of the time, I'm afraid.

Raymond is interrogating the dishevelled bed.

Of course, he says. His glance at the unfinished triptych locates a more satisfactory explanation.

But now the chamber music has begun.

Raymond moves with the economy of a mime. He glides along fluid lines from one suspended gesture to the next. Even in tights, his body would be abstract rather than sexually assertive. It mediates. His pelvis is the pliant fulcrum from which the room is tilted. As the canvasses are tilted towards the light. The room is disconnected through the planes he makes with the painted surfaces he examines. He has come here to do just that: to sum up the moveable planes, those that can be concerted, in another context, into Art. Galleries Maurice Galant. He turns the painting, examines the stretcher, sets it against the mantel. A finger rises to his lips, as if to silence the almost audible hum that lubricates his movements.

Sébastien turns slowly from the triptych: *Mais c'est toute la violence feminine qui s'élabore,* he says, his gaze black, heavy. The words repeat, repeat and the smile takes them up now: *I have situated you and now your violence preoccupies me.* Something like that.

Do you . . . Is that how you receive it? I mean . . . why?

You must be aware of it. I mean that panel for instance . . .

He's pointing to the third panel, laughs, installs himself in the bunched folds of the bedcover. The black eyes maintain that *violence, violence* unequivocally. They still persist, wherever I focus.

On Raymond's back as he resumes the dance, stepping, one, two, three, feet together on the down-beat. Two black holes bore in there the dual stigmata: *violence violence.* But the pursing of Raymond's lips promises a different verdict; the lids squeeze, narrowing the eyes to a slit through which the irises send their concentrate. As if he would set a different kind of pact between us. As if he acquiesced to something there. I let the gold light from his eyes into mine.

May I? *Vous permettez?*

He accepts my nod too, as if it meant something more and leafs through the folio of drawings on the floor. He sees me there, in the precarious juxtaposition of oranges and violets in the *Spring Rhythm* pastel, in the scar the charcoal gives to the shadow of a slumped breast.

Oui Rita, he says.

Some pastel dust has alighted on the canvas of his trouser leg. He aims a precise cone of breath at it. *Art, but not too close to sully me.* You must get yourself some fixative, he says. His hand poised lightly on my shoulder. As if I had been absolved, as if it had been already said: *Go forth my child, now that you have unburdened yourself.*

And I am slipping, the slope is a subtle but sure glide, the chute gleams through the velvet curtains, I go, through the space of a cremation: through that charcoal dust I have been absolved.

Well. Yes, certainly, these Maurice must see. Now . . . about that advance . . . Raymond's hand slides into his jacket. The light catching his glasses obliterates his eyes. The verdict will be expressed in francs.

No, really, Raymond, thankyou very much but I cannot . . .

Rita, will you do me a favour and accept it as a loan? I mean, I ask you, what is money for? Look, if you prefer, you can treat it as an advance buy, say I've put some money down on . . . say this painting and a couple of drawings. Mmm I rather fancy the pastel in my study. That suit your morality better, *ma p'tite puritaine, eh?* The biro hesitates, the ball of the palm rests a moment on the crisp cheque book. Date? *On est le vingt-huit avril,* says Sébastien. The handwriting is fluent but extravagant, baroque. And, a more suitable place must be found for you to work in . . . Raymond's eyes zig-zag cursorily amongst the jars and saucers and tormented tubes littering the floor, I am thinking . . . I'm sure your friend Valda knows about the studio situation in Marseille, eh Sébastien?

Eh eh eh Raymond, wait a minute! Don't bulldoze Rita like that. Sébastien laughs all the same as a show of sympathy for Raymond's enthusiasm.

Hardly a question of bulldozing, my dear boy. Artists are a notoriously apragmatic bunch when it comes to organizing the practical aspect of their affairs and I suspect that our Rita here is no exception . . . Anyhow, first things first, I suppose. We'll get these to Maurice to start with — with your permission of course, Rita. What about coming with us, though. I'm sure he'll want to talk to the artist herself.

Err . . . If you don't mind, I'd rather leave it, just for the moment.

Well, as you like. You'll be hearing from us very soon, in any case.

It's settled. After all, why should I feel bad. I've accepted payment for work I wanted to do. Raymond has the *Self-Portrait with Pomegranate, Spring Rhythm.* It's hardly prostitution, *ma p'tite puritaine.* The cheque on the desk provides its signature. The room is stripped except for Laurence's *Inscape* and the *Triptych.* At least those resisted. Laurence's refusal of rhetoric. That frayed cloud with its painfully delicate gold edging is shown as an aesthetic vanity. Its skeins so insubstantial, they are barely held within the frame. Only the calloused, scarred underpainting asserts itself: the fossilized permanent enigma untouched by art.

And Sébastien only saw female violence in the *Triptych*. Raymond refused it even that attention. It is unfinished and besides, *not* my *normal style, surely*. One must be consistent. Maurice Galant looks for homogeneity, a continuity of style, a uniformity of framing, especially in a first show.

I will not be at Laurence's opening.
   I will be having my own.
   The equation is fixed.
   Rita Finnerty struggles with her paradox=tension between the rebel real and the geometric ideal.

I am a style to be marketed.

Laurence says: So you'll be having your own exhibition, will you?

There she is, in a silver lamé sheath, giving a Hollywood ankle slide against the inner thigh of the other leg, exhibited in the fissure of that wall. HIATUS, apt name don't you think, is what I'm calling this little demonstration. You may operate, dear Rita, in the gap between this disclosure and our collective exposure. *Strange hiatus accommodating you,* you thought. Wrong, Rita. Wrong. There never is any real hiatus. Oh, there seem to be gaps, spurts, vertical departures, breaks for the better, gaps where you give total attention to your authentic potential, lulls. But now it seems the very lulls were active. Mmmm? Those idle words spoken, even to yourself, to fill the gaps, to justify the break, to placate those who came to interview you, to stay their curiosity — it's those words that have busied themselves for you, *n'est-ce pas?* entrapping in a mock determinate mesh the very *hiatus* you claimed to renovate your life. In any case, even if there seemed to be this luxurious possibility at the time, this lull somehow allowed for your rebirth, your *auto-genesis* — eh Rita? — it wasn't *strange.*

It was Gérard, your beautiful boy, who guaranteed it for you. Just as Raymond's intervention allows you to take this time at Antonine's. To recompose yourself, put together a picture of it away from them and their words. You claim this as the next renovative space and yet look at you, still arranging your portrait just like your eyeless face for Gérard that morning. And what about the living gaps between the frames?

158

Jean and his troupe emerge from other fissures, niches that must have been concealed in the gallery walls. Dumb show. Jean mimes to Laurence's voice. The gestures you made, Rita. Subtly perhaps, ambivalently, but of course they were taken as tokens of this or that. Gestures of Gérard's you silently accepted. Silence taken as meaning. Gestures and silences heaped up, compacted, generated his stammered proposal. You knew it. You were able to complete the sentence for him as he sat tortured by the grammar of it, fingering his *pain au chocolat*. (Jean turns his head slowly from his red-headed partner across the table from him. He has a mask on now: it's the face of Botticelli's Mars but the open mobile eyes give a terrible contrast to the relaxed slumbering features, the loose open mouth. He rises, retreats. The red-headed woman also rises, fondling a small male figurine. Her eyes are glazed, expressionless. Laurence's profile moves into alignment with her head, static, hieratic as an Egyptian wall-painting.) *This boy, this waif, this androgyne straight out of Botticelli, now he is a quarter of a centimetre tall,* remember Rita? Who reduced him, who pre-shrank him? He made you grow did he, you feasted on his beauty, no longer Jean's little *bébé* but Amazon? Eh? His naked face, you took it in. His tremulous voice, the urgency of his word-spurts, images springing, legends emerging. Wouldn't put it past you to make them yours, *Céleste* and the rest. You're all right, you can afford Céleste as a story; you still have a mother working away in the world, always ready to send you a cheque if necessary. You didn't tell Gérard that, did you? You were too busy managing his image of you as some sort of eternal *déracinée*.

So you see Gérard as the victim marked from the beginning. (Through a sutured fissure in the wall, the puppet reappears, the whole body caught inside the loosened wound.) The scar ruptures him, as if the damage incurred, the bitterness smarting his features, were preordained. Cheap tricks, lies, *n'est-ce pas?* And by the way, you did not simply lay the hand of fraternal gratitude on Gérard's shoulder. So many times your hand sought out the nape of his neck, under the chestnut hair, sought responses. And yes, that one-lunged chest of his, what about the times you drooped your head to find shelter there? A mother to Gérard, a sister to him!

And all the time, behind the dark glasses, refusing the courtier your reality. And what is that word, anyhow. A courtier! You made of him a courier, a vibrant link between yourself and the world. While you luxuriated in that timeless suspension away from such ugly concerns as money and marketplace, even casting the landlord and lady to play out the conjugal drama so that you could preserve yourself uncoupled.

(Laurence has turned her back. The walls once again have formed a seamless space. She attends a wall socket: a sculpture has been plugged in. Like a vacuum cleaner-bag within a tubular steel rectangular prism. It inflates, deflates. Crumpled collapse. On the catalogue I have in my hand, it reads: *Finnerty's Trophy: One Lung* . . . 600 F.)

All very well to claim me for your sound-track. Go on, I'm not your tutelary angel. I never wanted that, she says.

IV

TRIPTYCH

It's true in a way: it's the gaps I have to work in. It's what I tried to do in the *Isis* series, what I tried in *Vice Versa:* to link now with then: Sydney-Marseille. It's Rachel of course, the living hyphen. I work in the space of her sleep — I who was unable to share my space with her father. Whose story does she belong to? Theirs or mine? That spring at Antonine's, I did try to compose myself some kind of picture of it all, some kind of story, rather. After all, I couldn't paint. The *Triptych* had been rejected . . . That was my violence, my violation. *Toute la violence feminine qui s'élabore . . .* I began indulging in those private scrawlings: Rita Aviator and why she pinched the sausages — all that.

At least the *Triptych* remains as backdrop for new moments, new departures. It at least resisted the voice-over. And now the *Inflatables* with their aleatory movements in disobedience to the voiced instructions they receive from the tape. Looking through the notebooks, it's not hard to see where they come from. Whose bag of images is it, anyhow? Who owns the story anyway? I'll always inhabit other people's stories. Never a landlord, always a tenant.

I think that's what Rita prefers, says Mon to those who suggest that, you know, maybe, I should think about putting a deposit on a house. They say *now, Elsie, she's got the right idea: a nice quiet cul-de-sac, room for the kids to play safely. Something like that'd be nice for Rita. One of the northern suburbs, Pymble, say, or Turramurra.* They think I'd be better off in a quiet vegetable niche: willy wagtails and great gums. *What's she trying to do in*

163

*this new stuff, Mon? Oh, I'm sure it's all very clever, but it beats
me. Oh ... Well, Rita calls them 'narrative sculptures',* Mon says.
Narrative! You could've fooled me, they say. *Now, those
paintings she showed when she first came back, they weren't
exactly figurative, but at least you could tell what she was on
about.* And then, in those consoling looks and sighs they say: *Just
to think, you send your kids away to do fine arts in France and this
is what they come up with! S'pose it's hard for her, though, you
know, with the child, all on her own. Does she hear from him, the
father? Oh yes, I think so,* Mon lies. *They keep in touch. Still,
must be a bit of a battle for her, bringing up a child all on her own
... She manages,* Mon says. *She has friends. Mmmm.*

For the moment, there is only this neutral, far-away morning
voice, modulating as closely as possible the harmonics of the
universal airport announcement: *Is this you, my dear Rita,
mmm? Who would have believed it? In Coogee, east Sydney,
1976.* The voice cannot so easily be identified. It is not Raymond
anymore saying my situation. Perhaps that's why there is a calm
in this, this lack of sense in what I see. That bicycle over there, for
instance, refuses to supply any anecdote. It leans casually against
the litter-bin. Chained there, in fact, under the street light,
sending the oval shadows from its wheels diffusely across the
pavement. It has been frozen with the front wheel at a right-
angle to the frame. Throw away gesture of the unknown rider, a
crippled mechanism with a semblance of permanence. A
complex of strokes constituting its mystery. The shadow spokes
cross-hatch the stained pavement. But the bike is not a future
drawing, cannot provide me with a motif. It quietly mocks the
theme *Art as Alchemy*. The bike articulates its own space, not
mine. The metal resists that kind of easy transmutation. Still, the
liver-brown facades opposite, with their central stairs thrust out
like flying buttresses, ASIANS OUT scrawled on the bus-stop
there ...

There is the Mediterranean and here is the Pacific. The few
salt-thwarted shrubs are fidgety all the same with that pre-dawn
agitation. This lull in which to work: suturing, suturing. This *Sky
Surgeon after Nietzsche*. It's good to watch the big apartment
blocks steeped up behind the shops for that moment when the
windows pale before glowing with the real light. Gradations of

the spectrum tentatively there in the sky: the yolk-yellow, the translucent aquamarine, coming through to the violet, the emergent blue. Good to watch the redness of the bricks begging for the first smack of heat. Pulse racing against fatigue, diminishing time. Tensing myself for the first cries from Rachel, the sudden eruption of traffic on the bitumen.

The sun pops red: there will be just a hint, a ruffled reflection in the sea.

The gossamer sheen connecting me-to-me stretches and breaks on the searing pinnacle: I am there, arbitrarily pin-pointed in a moment (pleasure unspeakable, why not? who could dispute it?) . . .

but there she is, the Rita of that moment, her pulse still quick with the receding throb of sex, as the light of his smile breaks the seal of anticipation for the release in their common space, even as that space is spermed, as he ebbs and seeps his full weight into her, her mind arches away, claims its solitude; wanting to see her pleasure, find an analogy, seeks out the golden Lady of the Harbour, NOTRE DAME DE LA GARDE rears up as a souvenir to be plucked from the heat-haze and she is not Rita-with-Sébastien but molten from that searing pinnacle, she flows out into the Marseille sky *aaaah pleasure unspeakable,* she might think it but not specifically for the lover sleeping next to her, she rocks and guides, buoys and loses all sailors, falls asleep . . .

Could have been any one of their times together that last summer, but probably not. More likely one that slipped its frame that produced Rachel. *Space, their common space,* did Rita ever give access to Sébastien? Why couldn't she say it? Uneasily tenanted even in her own space, she let her landlord tell her.

She is flushed from a little self-indulgence. Tossing into the supermarket trolley the cheese, dried figs, a bottle of *Côtes de Provence*. She has cashed Raymond's cheque, after all. Returning now with the crisp paper bag to pay the arrears in the rent. As if she were a mere visitor to the house, she fondles the knocker for a moment. Lets it drop back. It is a gloved hand in cast iron: to ward off the caller with evil intentions. She retrieves her key. She has the money ready in crisp, folded banknotes. Business to be dealt with expediently before leaving for Antonine's: a quick knock on Sérisier's door.

It is answered by a strangled croak. His spent, sagging flesh, the pinked rims of the eyes, their faded blue already welling with tears show her that business will not be dealt with as quickly as anticipated. Perhaps her sharp intake of breath is simply a reflection on that. His *gravel voice,* is dulled, atonal. *Mademoiselle ... Ma femme ... Elle est morte ... Une crise de foie l'a emportée.* She hears, as if it were a caption in a foreign film, that, yes, Madame Sérisier has died from something-or-other of the liver. Briefly reviews images of the landlady to check the accuracy of what she's heard. She was in fact looking puffy, oedematous, yellow. She can identify now, in retrospect, what she hadn't bothered interpreting: the commotion and cries, the sobs — all the business of mustering the relatives around the dying woman. And now Viviane Sérisier is dead. Sérisier takes Rita by the hand.

He leads her. It strikes her that his body is a bony abstraction beneath the baggy clothes. He has hitched his trousers at mid-chest and yet they still blouse, voluminous. The parquet and the heavy oak furnishings give her no clues, no words for this. He unfastens the shutters and then the double glass door. She has never seen the courtyard garden from ground level before. From here the roof and walls of the morgue are invisible. Is that where they have taken Madame Sérisier? Here the horizon is leaf, bud and twiggy profusion. Bird-call and twitter enclose their silence. He leads her gently, as if in a trance, to a corner where . . . There they are, drooping their precious green-white heads, the *muguet*, the lily-of-the-valley to celebrate the first of May. He opens his hand towards them, trembling: Let me pick some for you, Mademoiselle. This is the last spring I will be here . . . You will understand that I cannot stay here now. This . . . without Viviane. Mademoiselle, she was a fine woman, *une bien brave femme . . .* Oh, she had her temperament, as they say, but . . . do you know, she held us all together with her fighting spirit. And the way she died, Mademoiselle . . . She had fought it, she refused it, but when it came, do you know what she said? She said: *cette putain de mort elle ne m'aura pas . . .* Death is an old whore and if she thinks she can take me lying down, she's wrong. And she laughed, Mademoiselle Rita. She looked death in the face and she laughed.

Sérisier closes Rita's hand around the little bunch of lilies. Then, he says, our son Pierre arrived with his lady friend. You know, Viviane had sworn that she would never open the door to him again until he had gone back to his wife. But when they came, she smiled. She said: I know I've been an old battle-axe. But I do want you to be happy, both of you. Ah, I know I said some things: I was worried about Pierre. I was wrong. Life is too short to go without love. Go on, she said, don't look so tragic all of you. I want you to do one thing though, go and pick some *muguet* for one another.

Sérisier guides Rita back to the terrace. Mademoiselle Rita, he says. You are young. *Vous êtes artiste-peintre n'est-ce pas?* Yes, yes you are a painter. Good, that is all very good. But I would like you to remember what Viviane Sérisier said: *life is too short to go without love.* It's not bad, is it, to say that at seventy-four? *Soyez joyeuse dans la vie,* Mademoiselle. *Allez . . .* Let's sit down for a moment . . . if you have the time? Just look at that spring coming into the garden!

His hand with its papery sun-spotted skin alights gently on hers. Nestled in this double clasp, the lilies. Like a miracle: they need no metaphor. Silent, on the little wrought iron bench, they are fiancés, beyond it all. You know what? he whispers. My wife is dead . . . Tears, yes, of course I cry, but I am glad, I am happy, Mademoiselle. Because she died well. *Elle est morte bien . . . oui, elle est morte bien,* he murmurs like a prayer of thanks.

That's how Viviane Sérisier escaped her caricature, slipped her frame: the woman Rita had seen as a pecking hen, a harridan, squatting on her husband's soul.

Through May and June the trance is prolonged, on the rise and fall of Raymond's voice, by the topography of the excursions conceived by him, Provence in the palm of his hand, the roads radiating from his wrist as it rises, falls and slides into the breast pocket, drops the hundred-franc bills into the restaurant saucer: Toulon, Rousillon, Meyrargues, St Paul de Vance — the villages are tasted at the table, do their pointillistic dance on the retina, swoon and dissolve as the big wash of organ music takes them in . . . Places lose their names as Raymond Rita Sébastien exchange theirs, for as long as Raymond combines them with the *we*.

July fifth: the date set for the exhibition makes of this time another hiatus. Rita Finnerty, the artist, is to emerge, but the metamorphosis is no longer hers. Her hand hovers over the white canvas in Antonine's courtyard, panics, abandons the brush. She could only have painted in the perspective opened up by the Wood-pigeon *Triptych* which was not to be shown. Raymond's voice fills her inner ear: *Oh no, Rita, that painting was an . . . explosion, if you'll excuse me for saying so, one you perhaps had to make, but you who have such finely developed critical faculties, Rita, you must admit that is not resolved, it doesn't have the beauty of your other work . . .*

So now, in the few moments she has to herself in Antonine's place, she tries to prepare another emergence. And in writing, she finds Raymond has replaced Laurence; he has become the new censor against whom she might find a voice. She tells

169

herself: I can only paint against what I have already done. But you, Maurice and the rest of them would have me consistent: you would lull me in to calm production of what you have already sanctioned.

She still believes that the words left unspoken in Raymond's apartment, in Raymond's restaurants, in Raymond's water-front café terraces, offer an authentic way out. So she writes:

Raymond binds me to Sébastien by the common need he thinks he has found and defined: the need for the father. He makes us meet in the space of that confessional. Show me your fears, show me your twists and knots, children, no, no you need feel no shame, and I will define them for you . . . Sébastien needs Raymond. He needs Raymond as an ersatz father. It's as if Raymond had convinced Sébastien of the symbolic necessity of his name. Sébastien was martyrized by his own father's tortured notion of virility. Sébastien's father was a MONSTER, Raymond tells me. And the son does not demur, hearing his father so described. A monster, says Raymond, because he so obviously suppressed all traces of the feminine in himself . . . He fashioned for himself, as he would have for his son, a brutish parody of masculinity. If his son challenged him he would score a thrashing in reply. Not hard to understand . . . I mean (Raymond tilts his chin in Sébastien's direction) if Sébastien is inclined at times to violence . . . But what he has to learn, I think, is to look at these impulses dispassionately . . . I think that I can claim in all modesty that I have been helping him in that . . .

Sébastien is ensconced in Raymond's armchair. It moulds him tight as a womb. He laughs, almost complacently, tugs on his ritual after-coffee Upman cigar. Back in '68, he says, I nearly got launched on a career as an anarcho-terrorist. (He squashes and screws the butt into the dregs in his coffee cup.) It wasn't really political, although I prided myself on being Bachunin at the time. Raymond is right, you know. It was probably more a matter of striking out against my own angoisse. Raymond's taken a whole load of shit from me, Rita. But without him, I swear it, I would have ended up . . . Well, doing myself in.

Je me s'rais flingué . . .

The recitation by rote is familiar. Raymond has spoken about it often enough: In certain situations, you feel inadequate — for whatever reasons — and to punish yourself, you smash the very object in which you have the most invested . . . And does Sébastien bring Raymond the recitation of his misdemeanors as tribute to the Master's readings, to ensure the continuation of the 'talking cure'?

Sébastien's big hand makes a gyrating movement as another cigar stub is crushed in the fragile little cup. That big hand could smash this salon full of glass and light and precious paintings.

But Raymond keeps on speaking . . . And Rita, I suspect, from the little you have said, that your problem isn't dissimilar . . . Your very ambivalent attitude to . . . authority, for instance . . .

There the diary entry finishes. Besides, she has caricatured them both beyond recognition. Besides, neither of them has said any such thing. In any case, Raymond has gradually eased the anecdotes out of her. It's finally a relief to give freely of them, in gratitude.

Raymond's face softens in the alcoholic blur.

Her hand is on the big crystal globe, it is *armagnac*, it is *armagnac* she is drinking, she swills the clear distillate around, nurses the luxurious warmth expanding from the puddle on her tongue, lets it descend, pervade. They are both waiting to hear it: they are so physically close now. This is a new intimacy, her sense of hierarchy fluctuates with it: the sight of Raymond propped on his elbows waiting to hear it, just as Sébastien is, across the wool-shag carpet. Is she so easily flattered by such relaxed attentiveness? In any case, she tells herself that, after all, they have a right to know her. Yet she balks. She has emptied her glass. They both stare into it as if it had become an intriguing, mythical space. Of course Raymond has already extruded from her — no, the word is too strong, she opposed so little resistance — he has drawn out of her, as a silken thread is drawn out, the odd introductory phrases already: Er, Rita, who *is* this artist friend of yours . . . this . . . Laurence, was it? who seems to have been so important?

And so she donated the little-girl-left-out scenes, took them down the green lawns of the school where it all began. And now there is a still life to prompt her: the left-over *charcuterie* on the table. It has been something like a high tea for tasteful bachelors, she thinks: no culinary expertise necessary but champagne duck paté, Corsican sausages of the vintage type, prized, it seems, because of their curious archaeological-specimen look — pungently earthy, weathered and wrinkled — and of course, the usual *proscuitto. Jambon corse.* In fact they have just about exhausted the topic and she has performed wittily enough, she hopes, having come up with the term *edible history* for such phenomena so distinctly French, or rather, Corsican. Sébastien then follows suit with a more sophisticated analysis of those *signifiers* of European culture so envied by Americans, and, he hastens to add, I suspect Australians? His lips stretch into such a transatlantic smile, that she lets him get away with it. Bordeaux, he laughs, is exported to the U.S. with sprayed on fake dust to convince buyers of its authenticity . . . They all chuckle quietly, relax into a bemused silence.

Speaking of sausages . . . she has begun. But in any case, it's a while since they have been speaking of sausages. Their attention is on her.

Yes? Speaking of sausages? You were going to say?

Raymond's right eyebrow shoots up in a sudden, acutely tyrannical apex. She could simply say that, speaking of sausages, the first she had heard of Raymond was from Gérard, in connection with cocktail Strasburgers and leave it at that. But somehow her tongue slips and slides around one word after another and she sacrifices the Suma episode to the tune of their fingers caressing the crystal rims of their *armagnac* glasses.

So: you participated in it unawares, she tells Raymond, making him an accomplice to the theft.

We-ell, Raymond laughs, since you seem to be trying to provoke some sort of comment from me, shall I give you the obvious? No, perhaps I should leave it to Sébastien.

Go on! Sébastien says. Go on! Raymond has a secret love for crude Freudian explanations!

Well, what do you want me to say now? That your petty theft

Rita was a timorous attempt at appropriating the phallus?

Herrurrurrahaha! Sébastien is enjoying this: he has collapsed into the woolly loops of the carpet and is rocking with mirth. Hamming it, Rita thinks. They're making a conscientious effort to defuse my self-involvement with their laughter. They can't fool me. They've planned this, to get me so relaxed, so secure, that I would feel free to stage my own little psychodrama, just as they must have done with Gérard. And where is Gérard now? Why do they never mention him? Her finger threads the loop of wool.

No, but it might have been an attempt on your part — ironically enough — to integrate yourself into a society from which you felt excluded? . . . Well, fancy that, eh!

Raymond's voice is soft, reflective. The pause invites her to raise her eyes, to determine its nature, perhaps re-establish some kind of complicity with him. Fancy, he says, making one's first appearance in your life as a pack of mini-strasburgers! Look at Rita laughing along with him as the gentle hand, but it's Raymond's this time, tentatively strokes her cheek, teasing the tiny hairs there, whispering at the nerve ends. That Raymond should take the anecdote as cue to this kind of intimacy was not foreseen. Ah, Rita . . . (He is addressing the face which ignores his hand) if you don't mind me saying so, you have one little fault. You take yourself just a little bit too seriously!

You are WRONG WRONG WRONG she wants to tell him, it was simply the vulgarity of the sausages, their pretension at plump immediacy against all the idealism, all that bland abstraction, Laurence's lentils and the rest, that somehow I wanted to make mine . . . But then, he is right in a way. She chooses not to interpret the impulse that brought the hand to her cheek a moment ago.

Funny thing is, he resumes, I never could stand those little sausages — party food for children, I've always thought — but Gérard! Gérard had an improbable weakness for them which I suppose I pandered to when he was around. Must have been some sort of Proustian epiphany he got out of them — those and the Meaux mustard together . . .

Easier for her to ignore this other Raymond, his face nude-for-her, the amber eyes searching out hers in a confession of weakness-for-her. No, get back into your caricature, Mr Groper-Lip, Mr Glitter-Glasses, Mr Bird-of-Prey, stay within your polished skull, keep that carapace bolted down as you do in your daily academic routine. Impeccable speaker, maintain the distance with the slick formulae and the easy ironies of the Master-and-Mentor: *one must assume one's will to power, n'est-ce pas?* you say as you begin to relinquish yours. No, go ahead and quote Nietzsche if you must, be the corrupt, manipulative cynic, not this wistful man who now withdraws to his bean-bag, who takes refuge in a hummed refrain, who bites his nails, too aware of what Sébastien's silences might incubate.

Have you heard from Gérard lately? she asks. Raymond's frown suggests that the question is not innocuous: Gérard is a person whom I would rather forget, to be perfectly frank, Rita.

It's Sébastien who speaks now, a hiss and whistle through the teeth: Gérard, Gérard, Gérard . . . I'm sorry to destroy your illusions, but Gérard is a little prick who has finally shown himself in his true colours. He's a little prick, not worth worrying about. And a bum.

Come, come, Sébastien! (Raymond has selected the melodic voice he uses for cajoling and placating.) I think that such a passionate outburst warrants an explanation. (It occurs to Rita that Raymond may well use Sébastien as his safety valve — to vent a violence of feeling which he can't afford to allow himself.)

174

Let us explain a little, Rita, he says. I'm afraid we were both a little deluded as far as Gérard was concerned. Sébastien, especially, spent a lot of emotional energy in trying to solve some of Gérard's problems. As you know, he gave him the use of his apartment, but not only that — endless time, listening to his raves, his fantasies . . . I had him believing — that was my mistake — that he could be a poet.

Where's the mistake in that? Rita says, but a glance at Sébastien silences her.

For the first time, Rita is forced to confront what she has chosen to ignore: Sébastien wanted to do a Raymond on Gérard? He probably romanticized Gérard as pure rebel and then sought to harness it, and, unconsciously, to strangle it. What he had lost in himself. *Can you imagine,* he said, *back in '68 I was an anarcho-terrorist.* To justify his own cooption, he would have done the same to Gérard. But Gérard asserted a certain autonomy: something escaped. Rita was someone Gérard had found for himself. That was scandalous. But Gérard was not the shuttlecock they imagined.

Sébastien says: Gérard had the cheek to accuse me of trying to poison your mind against him, Rita. One night he came into my apartment ab-sol-ute-ly stoned — his whole body looked disarticulated — a crazy look in his eye, and made the wildest accusations. He said that I'd pinched you from him. Of course it was impossible to appeal to his reason. He took no notice whatsoever. I said an accusation like that amounted to a complete put-down as far as you were concerned. That you were hardly an object that could be passed on, borrowed or *pinched.* That surely you had your own free will . . . (Rita looks down.) And in any case, I assured him that our relationship was primarily intellectual. JE TE DIS MERDE he said, you are all fakes — all three of you. At least you've given me the jolt that leaves me free to say it.

Sébastien seeks out her eyes, to absorb the impact of their hurt.

Well, he says, I'm afraid I ended up laying one or two into him for that. At least I didn't need to throw him out: he was already flinging his things pêle-mêle into his pack and he was gone.

This smug elimination of Gérard. How could she have become close to such people? She will ask Raymond to drive her home. She will not open the door to them again. Damn the exhibition. She will manage alone. But Sébastien is launched . . .

And what is more, Rita, Gérard has . . .

Look, Sébastien, says Raymond, I don't think there is any point in reopening old wounds. *En tout cas, les enfants . . .* (He gives a cursory glance at his watch.) It's already past my bed-time. Rita, would you mind very much dossing down here? I don't feel in a fit state to drive you back to Aix. Besides, I'd like to see you at breakfast. Give me a change from that surly face! No, no, I assure you, you must consider yourself completely at home here. Sébastien will see to some sheets, won't you? See, he is only too ready to oblige! But I'd watch him, if I were you, Rita! *Allez, bonne nuit!*

Sébastien's smile is too glaringly exuberant.

I wish I could feel as pleased about it as you obviously do.

Rita addresses the mouth rather than the eyes.

Ah *Bon sang,* Rita, you've got me wrong. Raymond didn't give me a chance to explain why I feel like this about Gérard. It would be . . . too . . . revealing . . . about Raymond, I mean.

I *don't* understand. All I can see now is that you *do* want to poison my mind against Gérard. And in any case, I do think his reactions were understandable. He was rash, struck out wildly. Okay, he was hurt. He believed . . .

You loved him, didn't you, Rita! Didn't you!

Yes yes. If that's how you want me to put it, I suppose I did. There's no crime in that, is there?

Well, why in the hell . . .

Sébastien falls back, clutches at his mouth, as if it were some kind of uncontrollable beast.

Oh, I'm sorry. I'm sorry. Of course there's no crime in it. It's just that Gérard betrayed us both . . . I mean he pimp . . . I mean he betrayed Raymond. And to his students, of all people.

But what do you . . . What does he have to fear?

Come on, Rita, surely you picked that up. But if I have to spell it out — I know you at least can be trusted — Raymond is not exactly your run-of-the mill heterosexual.

That's to his credit, surely?

Yes, yes, of course. He . . . married very young, when he was still a student. It was a disaster, left him feeling totally inadequate. Well, for a while, I gather, he experimented in what I suppose you could call a gay life-style. He made the mistake of talking freely about all that to Gérard since he was going through a similar kind of crisis. And now he gets the knife in his back for his trouble. Gérard has gone out of his way, it seems, to spread stories around that Raymond is some kind of debauched pederast. Which is an outrageous lie, and obviously, it could ruin him completely. I mean, if his colleagues get hold of such stories . . . You know the kind of rivalry that goes on in universities: it's pretty savage.

But how do you know it was Gérard, in the first place?

It couldn't have been anyone else. Listen, Rita, I was there. It happened in a lecture he was giving on Gide. On *L'Immoraliste*. One guy gets up — a militant gay — and says: What is bothering me, Monsieur D'Arlan, is why you, *a known homosexual*, should so conscientiously avoid the central issue of this story! He was addressing the whole amphitheatre rather than Raymond. *I* collected a few amused looks, I can tell you. And . . . Well, Rita, the only way such a rumour could have been spread would be through Gérard. I've never admired Raymond so much as I did at that moment. He really kept his cool, peered over his glasses and said: With all due respect, Monsieur, I consider that my sexuality is my own affair, however it might please you to fantasize it — and I'm afraid that you would be disappointed (this got Raymond a round of laughs) — but I would like to point out to you that I do not find Gide worthy of study *because* of his homosexuality . . . Here it's the issue of hypocrisy we are dealing with . . . And so on . . . I forget the rest.

But Sébastien, don't you think that guy had a point in a way — look, I don't mean for bringing Raymond's sexuality into it — but don't you think that Gide's concealment of his own homosexuality, even from himself for a long time, was behind the obsession with . . . you know . . . hypocrisy that runs through his work? I mean, it does help . . .

Of course. But that's not the point. The point is that it can only have been Gérard who spread the rumour.

I'm sorry, but I can't see that that's any proof. Students do fantasize — Raymond's right. And he hardly comes across as a super-butch machismo . . .

Why in the hell . . . Just because he is gentle, elegant.

And how did you . . . Do you mind me asking, Sébastien? How did you come to hang out at Raymond's place?

Hang out! Thanks *very* much. Much the same way as you have, Rita! No . . . I'm sorry. But you make it sound as if I'm some kind of gigolo. I'm sorry, this whole business has put me a bit too much on the defensive, that's all. Some more *armagnac?* No, well I'm going to . . . It was in my first year of studies. I had problems, to put it mildly. Couldn't face social situations at all. I'd spent the whole summer on the balcony of my mother's place, just lying there, making smoke rings from my cigarillos. The only thing I accomplished in those three months was the perfect coil. Oh and I read all of Le Clezio. That corresponded nicely with my despair. I caressed the idea of suicide in a narcissistic kind of a way. But I couldn't even stir myself to do something about that. Oh, I was knotted up about a sexual failure I had had. Well . . . Classes resumed at Aix and there was this prof. It was Raymond. I followed his lectures, sensed something special about the guy. Not that everybody didn't. They were superbly constructed lectures but there was an uneasiness about them. That struck me in particular. He called the series *Language as Mask.* I went to see him ostensibly about a reading list . . .

When I turned up, he simply nodded, as if he had expected it sooner or later. I must admit that it disturbed me a bit. I became impassioned for linguistics and he . . . nourished that interest in me.

Rita? Rita . . . You just feel contempt for me, don't you? You find it laughable . . .

The tears jump into this eyes, over the brim, cling to the long lashes. His eyes appear big and stupid, as those of any begging creature appear stupid.

What the tears beg, he doesn't say. Is it just that he's had too much *armagnac?* She has stiffened and yet would soften, repelled at this maudlin indulgence when it comes to himself. Yet she is equally repelled by his hardness, sharpening its blades within herself. She has not asked for the suppliant victim. He will not say what kind of grace she is meant to bestow. Now he is kneeling next to her, his face contorted. Sobbing: Rita, don't turn me away. I . . . I know I'm screwed up. But maybe not as much as you think. Rita? You despise me, don't you, for my dependence on Raymond but . . . My God, Rita, I couldn't have survived without him . . .

Of course, of course I don't despise you. What makes you think I despise you for your attachment to Raymond? I . . .

She doesn't quite know what to do with this head that has happened into her lap. Her fingers work upon this proffered head as if they were dealing out a baptism. Placating now, the fingers take on a new suppleness, stroke the beautiful heavy hair.

I can't help liking you, you bastard, she laughs, fondling the idea . . .

He raises his head: heated glow of the child coaxed out of a tantrum, she thinks but fights the image. Superimposes instead the wan radiance of Emile Sérisier, through the trembling green-whites of the lilies. She moves into this new kiss, water-veils part, satin cushions give way, she can sleep on it . . .

This, my dear Rita, IS the *Côte D'Azur!*

Raymond strings together the glittering gems of the sea with a heroic swoop of the arm. Rita's perception is wedded to his equation. The blues and greens thus rock their crystals, scattering the light, the light attacks, with the fall of Raymond's hand, the sea-pocked rocks of the *callanque,* fills, as he turns his amber eyes, the aromatic pockets of air in this pine glade and there is Sébastien, un-martyrized, simply radiant child of the Mediter-ranean as all the arrows of light diverge from him . . . And then the Master's Voice comes on again, embodying itself in the curvature of Sébastien's arched back, caressing the strong musculature of the Latin child *ah oui ah oui,* it says . . .

> *La mer la mer toujours recommencé*
> *O récompense après une pensée*
> *Qu'un long regard sur le calme des dieux*

How silly, really, Rita thinks. *Une pensée, a* thought. O reward after *a* thought, how can anyone have *a* thought and claim a reward. Valéry must have resorted to *'une'* for the sake of the meter, surely, or else to represent some classical idea of unity and harmony. With Raymond mouthing them so possessively, she finds the lines pompous and only curbs the impulse to say so when she sees that his capillaries stand out purplish, that his skin has a vague mulberry blotching from the shadows of the pines. Yet her silence does a violence to the moment all the same: Did you carry on like this, Master of Ceremonies, in your literary circles in Algiers, yes, see it quite well now, Raymond, you would be light-giver, perpetrator of Greco-roman aesthetics, oh, honeyed voice of *France Culture,* modulating your harmonic variations, stringing out the prestigious jewels of your Port-Royal grammar, your imperfect subjunctives wearing almost visibly that coquettish circumflex, this is the real artillery of you colonizers, this is the way you would have annihilated the voice of *Algérie Liberée,* did you laugh when all the freedom fighters received on their transistors was the static interference of His Master's voice? . . . *C'est beau n'est-ce pas?* you are saying, but there is a quaver in your voice, I was wrong, I have caricatured you again — it's as if you do feel some immediacy after all, despite your need to borrow Valéry as mediator and your smile is no longer the cultivated grimace I saw, it has opened wide, almost unbearably, showing the vulnerable pink of the gums and the secret of the long irregular teeth . . .

Rita smiles in turn, acquiesces: *Oui, c'est beau!*

Did you enjoy that, Rita?

Again, Raymond wants some verbal show of pleasure. There is a limit to the range of expressions of gratitude, and the frequency of the gifts bestowed upon these *children* devalues them all. What can she say? *Oh, thankyou, thankyou, Raymond* but he has taken her so far away from the stuffed zucchinis she shared with Denise . . . That seems irretrievable now, the simplicity of sharing in their bedsitters.

Rita begins to understand that sullen resentment, that spoilt boy look about Sébastien. His supply of expressions of gratitude has long since been exhausted. Of course Raymond has supplied the whole sweeping curve of the bay, those algae strung rocks, this fruity *Blanc de Blanc de Cassis* following the wet kiss of the oysters down their throats . . . Oh, Raymond, she says. I don't quite know what to say anymore . . . It all seems such a dream . . . Perhaps she means that it's improbable that she should find herself constantly in his company together with her male counterpart, as his Companion Elect, for reasons she doesn't care to admit. Still her eyes are troubled with the fear that she is becoming addicted to all of this: the idle life, the flow of luxuries, Raymond's Culture and Cuisine . . . But more than that. As the water-light ripples over it, Raymond's face shivers with melancholy . . .

181

Ah no. Surely not. How can you devalue it like that? *Mon Dieu,* Rita. This is life, not a dream . . . that you have given us.

There is a hush in his voice that she has not heard before.

Rita, you have given me a taste of happiness and I don't feel like dismissing it as a dream.

His fingers creep tentatively over hers: their touch is a dream of satin. She had not attributed him with an inner life, especially not as far as she was concerned. Heartbreaks, he might have known, but that was conveniently tagged as his Mysterious Past. No, no, not this . . . This was not in her scenario either. This *was* to be a dream, in parenthesis. But his eyes make her responsible. She must respond.

Oyster slide and swallow. It is too late. *Even in tights, his body would be abstract . . .* She thought that. She has tried to keep them both in their place, type-cast. Denise has teased her: *So you're having another love-affair with the establishment, are you?* Or another time, with her gurgling laugh, observing Rita's preparatory toilette: *Off for another round of pleasures with those culture-freaks?* No, no, You've got it wrong, Rita laughed, It's *France Culture* and her Body-Guard!

It was a lie already, a betrayal and she had winced afterwards. She knew already that she had been affected. And soon enough, she began to avoid Denise. She was relieved to get away to Antonine's place.

Now Sébastien's stare shows that Raymond's gesture was a transgression. The whites flash. His fingers torture the broken bread, roll the plump dough into little balls. In that stare, there is a demand for information, for the response which she has not yet given. It says imperatively: *For how long are you going to perpetrate this charade, Rita?* As if, in that moment, he would annihilate Raymond and weld Rita to his own brooding body. She seeks out a refuge in the lavatory.

If only this anaesthetic numbness could be prolonged forever. She has folded the paper with such perfection. It is not a dream, she tells herself. It is my life, my life still waiting out there at the table, my still life: my glass with its wine, my napkin which fell to my seat. I am still out there with them. There is no such thing as a parenthesis, a hiatus. I cannot stay forever in this freeze-frame. In any case, the uncoiling trickle of urine is petering out, the foot-

182

grips of the Turkish toilet might be two little islands left behind, but the water is flushing bounteously around them, the room is awash and she will have to weave her way between the tables, dodging their eyes, the view of Cassis which Raymond has afforded them and now . . . Somebody is trying the door.

It is Sébastien. No, no, I haven't come for that, he says as she theatrically shows him the lavatory. It's something like mutiny congesting his face. His hands hang heavy. They could throw punches. They *laid one or two* into Gérard. They could fling things. She would take him out into the open spaces, make it public, but then, that's what she did to Gérard that day. She'll have to confront it, this time, whatever it is she has generated. He has her by the arm. Rita, he growls. I can't take much more of this.

Mais . . . Quoi . . . de quoi? Of what?

His mouth makes an awful snarl: Oh . . . As if you don't know! The way you and Raymond carry on . . . As if you didn't give a damn what happened to the two of us — what *we* have. Or maybe I dreamt that, eh? Maybe that was *my* dream, Rita? Look, I'm sorry. But I've got to spend some more time with you. I suppose I'd be very lucky to get a booking eh?

But, Sébastien, we've been seeing one another all the time — you could hardly say that I've been avoiding you . . .

Without *him*. When? WHEN? When can I see you alone?

He has cornered her against the empty oyster crates.

Well, yes, of course. Yes, I'd like that too. Er. Not tonight, that would be cutting it a bit fine with . . . with Raymond. Tomorrow night? But Sébastien . . . You seem so . . . tortured by it all. Oh. Don't worry, I think I know.

This fear which she cannot name. As if, without Raymond, there will be no real words between them. This fear telling her that if Sébastien is screwed up, then, yes, so is she. Yes, yes, they will have to break out of this, this dependence on Raymond's presence. They will have to break free of this spell he has over them: his Linguist with no words of his own, his Painter who can no longer put brush to canvas. Yes, Sébastien, come around. *Chez Antonine. On fera un petit diner ensemble.*

As if he knew what has been going on, Raymond cocks one of those sparse eyebrows from over the menu and resumes with his normal stylistics: And what shall it be for dessert, *les enfants?*

The female child formulates her revolt as she surveys the menu: *Titillate our palates with your sugars as you like, you cannot keep us in this infantile dependence forever. I'll be seeing him without your close readings, without your magical cheque book to conjure up the settings for our encounters, the Bach in romanesque churches, the Mozart in perched villages, the* coq-au-vin *in sun-lit squares, without the creams and bronze greens and tarnished golds of your living-room, the suave contours of your bauhaus furniture . . . We cannot remain captive forever, collector's items . . .*

Oh, now, come on, Sébastien! Be a bit imaginative for once! You and your eternal *crème caramels!* The *crémet,* for instance, would be a little more adventurous, that with the *frambroises des bois.*

Raymond will be content with a *café exprès.*

Rita watches in fascination as Sébastien dutifully eats his *crémet* and the wild raspberries. She notes with what ease he converts his new verve to a fitting expression: a grunt of gastronomic pleasure.

The Citroën D.S. laps up the road as glibly as Raymond's tongue divides the world around them. But Rita purrs inwardly as he takes her coursing through his nervous system. It seems as if he would have his sexuality told by this virtuoso driving and anyhow why should she destroy this moment by dissonant thoughts — he is happy, all he asks for is affection, she can give that, and now he is humming Charles Trenet's *La Mer* in a slightly nasal falsetto. It's almost like a self-parody but a glance at the falling lines of Raymond's profile, the vagueness of the eyes mechanically on the road but misted with other thoughts, makes Rita wonder. Listen, he says, I am obliged to take a . . . er . . . little excursion into Spain this weekend, Barcelona, more precisely — what promises to be a rather tiring conference on baroque poetry and . . . Well, I'm counting on you two to make it less tiring, shall we say? Your presence would make all the difference. Mmm? What do you say? You don't have to burst with enthusiasm, you know! Or was I wrong in hoping that I might have your company?

Sébastien, in the back seat, has his hand at the nape of Rita's neck.

Raymond's eyes switch to Rita, then scan the rear-vision mirror. Is he trying to gauge what kind of mute pact they have formed? Raymond glances again in Rita's direction. He expects the answer to come from her. There is the insistent pressure of Sébastien's hand under her hair.

Oh, Raymond, that would have been wonderful but really, I just can't afford the time. I have to get back into some work and besides . . .

Ah no, Rita. Look, you mustn't become neurotic about your work, you know. And you said yourself that you were blocked as far as painting is concerned at the moment. This would probably give you just the impetus you need. In any case, you already have enough work for the exhibition, whether or not you paint this weekend. And *surely,* you the artist are not going to deliberately deprive yourself of the opportunity of viewing some of the treasures of Barcelona? Mmm? Think about it, Rita. And what about our *Grand Taciturne* at the back?

You know, Raymond, sometimes you really are impossible. It doesn't seem to occur to you that we have any other commitments. Rita said she wants to work — can't you take her word for it? And . . . Look, *of course* I'd like to go, but I've already told you . . . My thesis . . .

Well, I'm glad there is so much solidarity between you as far as your work goes. It augurs well, *les enfants.* But I must say, with all due respect, Sébastien, that I haven't exactly observed a fanatical devotion to your work these last few weeks! Oh, well, it was just an idea. I'll just have to cancel the room I'd booked for you . . .

In any case, Raymond, I don't think it would put an end to the rumours if we accompanied you. It would hardly be discreet . . .

Damn discretion! I've had enough of discretion. In any case, you would be quite entitled to be there in your own right, Sébastien. Just happened to bring your girlfriend, that's all. Oh, let them think what they like. But if you don't want to come, you don't want to come. Let's leave it at that, eh?

Slowly, at the base of their silence, melancholy builds up its deposit. If she could only divide herself, send one off to Barcelona and have the other waiting for Sébastien in Aix . . .

She twists the lamp around to create an Intimate Space. But now the cushions look too composed. She retosses them, this time with the crushed velvet kitsch one to the bottom. He might not understand Antonine's little joke. The luminous palms and the tropical moon might provoke some jarring commentary. Now with the Moroccan brocade cushion with its complex design of interlocking arcs, the Persian one providing a touch of the figurative with the warrior motif and the patchwork ones combining their myriad patterns on muted velvet, she could stretch out like an *odalisque à la Matisse*. She tries herself in that composition. No, really, this is too much, Rita suddenly sumptuous *gonzesse*. Might be Antonine's style: she could carry anything off. But it is not hers. But then it is all too studied, too prepared. For instance, the veal with its white wine, champignons and cream which she is checking for the twentieth time. Sébastien will probably be mildly irritated to see her trying for an approximation of Raymond's hospitality.

And then, the vintage port which she has bought especially. Its seal still inviolate. He will see at once that she has pandered to his special taste: he knows that she never drinks the stuff.

She must lower the level, pour one for herself. She feels the strong syrupy warmth mounting, examines the glass, the reflection she has been tasting in the gilt oval mirror, accusing both. This is a winter drink in any case, and how can he bear it as an *apéritif*. She will make out that it was just here and that Antonine had said she should just help herself. *Antonine doesn't drink, you know,* she rehearses to the mirror. Anyhow, another glass of the port and glowing with its sweet astringence, she can ring like a gong for him, ring like a gong, russet hair and bronze shirt. Fingers plying their way erratically, backwards and forwards through the record rack. Theodorakis? Jazz? But Charlie Parker might be too . . .

Blues? Muddy Waters will do. He needn't think the choice is for him — she just happened to have it on. Guitar wail, insistent thud of the bass and weaving through, the alto swoon . . .

> *Ya said ya loved me baby*
> *pl-EEA-se call me on the phone some time*
> *ya said ya loved me baby*
> *pl-EEA-se call me on the phone some time*
> *ah know when ah hear ya voice*
> *s'gonna EEA-se ma worried min'*

More like it, with the blues combining the objects, the darks aflame, the lights flitting with shadows and all she need do is lie down with a book, belly flat to the bed, an occasional sip of the port as if she's expecting nothing. But being here in this canopied shrine issues too much of a welcome. It's quite ridiculous really: he'd never be very flattered if he knew . . . The oven: she can concern herself with that. Maybe he won't come anyhow, the bastard. The veal is already getting singed . . . But there's crunching on the pebbles outside, the blurred dark shape behind the glass . . .

She has run towards him. Too bad. Why not be welcoming. To a friend. No harm in that. Yet with the words stripped away, they are still gagged with the equivocal. Does he want this night with her now because it seems Raymond might have wanted something like it himself? Is that all he's trying to do: *shoot daddy down, let his own manhood advance?* Yet she says, with her head on his shoulder, her hand exploring his cheek, contouring the jaw: *Mais tu es tout frais!* As if even his coolness were a gift. She lets her hand drop, thinks she sees a glittering hardness in his gaze. Or is it an accident of the indirect light? Something treacherous in this man as she shows him in, takes his jacket, breathes a mixture of lambswool and sweat. To keep her distance she lets the treacherous imagery incubate:

Fresh though it may be, your body has the dangerous hormonal perfume of the seasonal tom-cat . . .

You might be radiant, but it is the radiance of a Greek statue, its gaze anonymous, the colour long since stripped from the marble. You have the cynical gaze of youth, fully aware that whatever its failings, it will win the prize again and again. Because of your innate beauty. You are a naïve, childish Achilles.

Ultimately cruel, the way you're summing up the scene prepared for you; cruel with the cruelty of the loping cat, needlessly testing its power and accuracy of aim on some miniature marsupial.

Tu as l'air si rêveur . . . A quoi tu penses? What is *la belle rousse* thinking about to make her look so severe? Would you rather I hadn't come after all?

Oh, tu parles . . . I . . . I wasn't sure you were going to turn up. I'm glad you've come, that's all.

His eyes alight on the scrawled notes she has been amassing: Ah! So this is what you've been up to then!

Oh. Trying to work out some images, find some pattern in things . . .

She puts a falsely modest *ennui* into her voice and the hand she throws limply in the general direction of the desk is meant to discourage. But he selects a page at random before she can redirect his attention:

Ze mouse eez surft, clurzez slurlee eets cush-ee-on on cush-ee-on . . .

Mais c'est ta bouche, je te jure, c'est ta bouche que tu décris là!

He laughs as she snatches the sheet of paper away from him. It's your mouth, I swear, that you're writing about!

As a matter of fact, it's not! It's not my mouth at all!

But his touch parts her lips, dislodging any words. He doesn't want her explanation. He probably sees this writing as a way of furnishing the hours marked with the same lack, the signature of the male whose presence she would summon up. The written mouth ready to open for him. His bemused smile is an ironical reflection on those lips, an emblem of her own narcissism.

Put down your brush, shut your book, stub out your cigarette, now that I have come to complete you ... You are echoing with the voices of your lack: paint them, write them, it's the coquettish toilette we allow you ... Can tell by the way you paint, you are a violent girl, makes one wonder ... So much passion caught in those barb-wire strokes, let me unravel it freely for you, let me release that pressure with the flow of juices, leave your inks and paints, yes: lips, you write, but here are those lips not closing but ready to open ...

and now his tongue with hers mute, plunging, she rocks slightly in her clogs as his big hand works rhythmically on her buttock, his mouth gropes under the mass of hair as she shifts under the pressure of that hand, her ear is too fragile a conch, pearly intricacy filled, too full, with the warm insistence of his breath, the sonorous whisper: Rita, you are stunning tonight ... But why are you so tense? I can feel it in your body, every single muscle, BON DIEU . . . Are you afraid of me suddenly?

Afraid of you! She tosses her head, teeters a little, pivots around and breaks free, laughing. Surprised somewhat at the deep seasoned voice that wells out of her, like some depersonalized and wilfully belittling manifestation of maturity: What about a port anyhow? Afraid that's all there is . . .

The attempt at casualness didn't quite come off, though. He is examining the label, gives it the connoisseur's *aahaa* of approval: But Rita! I hope you didn't go buying this on my account!

N-no. I had some already.

He purses his lips, widens his eyes in surprise.

That was a lie, she says. I took two swipes at it so that you wouldn't think I bought it especially. But still you did, you egotistical bastard!

They both laugh. On. Off. Stand there with their hands dangling at their sides like two gauche adolescents. There is only Muddy Waters filling the room. Sébastien adjusts the knob of the stereo: Sorry Rita, I've got a low threshold for noise at the moment . . . Hope you don't mind?

No. Go ahead.

Look, I'm sorry. It's just that I've got a migraine. A migraine, she thinks — he wouldn't be able to open his eyes if he had a migraine. Still, allow for Gallic hyperbole. He takes her by the shoulders: Been working all day. COMME UNE BRUTE. If you could have seen me. I've actually finished the chapter on Lacan!

Really? This mild irritation that a man with a migraine and such a low threshold for noise could show this exuberance when it comes to relating his own accomplishments.

And for the next chapter, I got some fascinating material from Valda!

Valda?

Valda Schleiermacher, fascinating woman. Runs the publicity agency . . . I thought I told you about her. Publikon.

Mmm. I wonder. Giving her business a name like that. I mean, really . . .

Sébastien tosses up his hands in mock exasperation: What do you want, he laughs. That's the whole principle of publicity: the ultimate signified has to be sex, and . . . Well it's always there at a subliminal level, anyhow. Pub-li-con. Haha. I think it's very good. Urrhahaha. *Pub-l'icon.*

Surely those aren't his real views, but if he's joking, it's not very funny. She reaches for the cushions, throws one down on either side of the table. The kitsch one she concealed a moment ago is now perfectly visible.

Hey!

What?

That! That cushion. A-mazing! What sort of woman is this Antonine? A bit histrionic? I mean . . . The canopied bed, the Moroccan spread, oh, you know, all the tastefully trendy exotica she has around . . . But then to juxtapose it with this mass-produced *rêverie!* He dreamily caresses the cushion.

No, not really. Oh, she passes for a militant *gauchiste* but really I think she'd resist any political straight-jacket. She's more emotionally inclined to anarchism.

You trying to tell me something about myself?

No, Sébastien. I'm not! Antonine is quite different. She is quite effortlessly dominating: she exerts a charismatic pull on people . . . Well . . . I haven't observed you in enough situations to see if you do that! She is beautiful. But beneath it all, despite the impression of strength and self-assurance she gives, I think there's quite a bit of insecurity. Sometimes you can catch glimpses of a paralytic little middle-class daddy's girl.

Ri-ta. Tut-tut. That's the way you talk about your friend?

What's wrong with that? She would admit the same herself. I

could say the same about myself . . . She *is* my friend. You asked me, I answered you.

Anyhow, she thinks. The way he speaks about Gérard. She sees Antonine as a giant 2-D image on that bed and the black athletic body of Sun Diatti going through all the motions of love-making to that inert form.

But the way you represented her, you surprise me, Rita. I didn't think you were capable of that kind of cliché. I mean it's not far from the 'sad clown', that kind of easy paradox: the powerful, charismatic anarchist who *deep down* is a crippled little *bourgeoise*.

Rita chooses to explain this present irritation by the ineptitude of Sébastien's analogy, or at least by her inability to pin-point its illogic, its injustice. He at least is loosening up, anyhow. He pours himself another drink. *Tu me permets?* he asks. *Et pour toi, ma belle Rita?*

He dilates his nostrils demonstratively towards the oven: *Mmmm tu vas me régaler ce soir!* You've turned on a feast.

Oh, nothing much.

She balks on the rehearsed line.

Just a little veal thing I threw together.

She plants the *asperges sauce hollondaise* before him on the little table. Napkins, wine. He has put on the Brandenberg Concertos. Neglecting to play the other side of the Muddy Waters.

They eat silently for a while. He toys with the rejected woody parts of the asparagus, systematically raking them to the side of his plate.

Rita watches him from over the table; his navy and white striped top with its slit yoke make a bit of a sailor of him. They are rocked by the greens and blues of the mat and with their legs tucked under them Japanese style, they could be at sea. She smiles to her sailor, pours the wine — to the brim of his glass. His hand makes a cutting movement through the air, clamps down on the glass: *At-ten-tion!* I can't knock them back as quickly as that!

Rita feels herself reddening, attends to the oven. The veal is definitely singed now. Sorry to rush things, she says, but this can't stand much longer.

But Rita, please! I'm ravenous!

She watches the animal fury of his eating.

Mmmm, by the way, he says, his voice thick with the mushroom sauce, Raymond sends his love, *il t'embrasse.*

But . . . I thought he'd gone to Barcelona.

No no. He cancelled that. On the grounds of flu. Well, he does have a slight cold. He's getting someone else to read his paper for him. He said it was meaningless, such an excursion, if we didn't accompany him.

Sébastien's hand reaches across to hers: I know, I know, it's awful, he says, but what can we do?

All the same, it does sound a bit like emotional blackmail, Rita says.

Oh, that's hardly fair! He has become very attached, you know.

I know. I know he's attached to you.

Rita, you know that's not what I meant. Actually, he only seems to be able to tolerate my company these days if you are present. As distasteful as it may be to you my little *femme fatale,* it seems Raymond has quite fallen for you. When I phoned him tonight and somehow let it slip that I would be seeing you, there was a long silence on the end of the line. But then he was *so* protective of you. He said: Well, Mr Body Beautiful, she's no ordinary young woman, so you damn well had better offer her a bit more than your surly presence. Then he apologized and wished us both a good time. He even expressed surprise that we hadn't got together before this. The most I can ask, he said, is for you both to be happy.

Rita's turn now to toy with the crumbs.

Come on Rita! Things aren't as bad as that. It's life, I'm afraid; it's not your fault that you've got us both hooked.

Sébastien reaches out to raise Rita's head. There is a discreet shudder in her acquiescence.

Anyhow, she says.

Anyhow, what?

Anyhow, why should he presume . . .

Oh? Of course, he can't presume anything, Sébastien laughs. Come on. Don't let it spoil our time together.

Rita smiles wanly. Drinks.

You're not a bad cook after all; I must admit I'm quite surprised.

Well, I *like* that!

No ... I just thought you were too absent-minded, too intent on your artistic pursuits to put a meal together. And it's really quite a triumph, you know. Err ... He is mopping up the last vestige of sauce slowly, studiously, reflects on this final taste.

What?

Just one little thing ...

Well? She smiles quickly to attenuate the sharpness of her tone.

You could have done with a little less ... oregano is it? It dominates the sauce, don't you think? Which otherwise is ... quite exquisite.

Well, I'm afraid all I do is heavy-handed. I pour too much wine, overdo the oregano ... Any more complaints? Oh yes, and I put on the music too loud. And Muddy Waters at that.

O là là là Rita. VINGT DIEUX. I was just being objective. You have an artistic approach to everything ... I imagined you'd be able to take an objective observation, since obviously you *can* cook.

I really don't give a damn. Of course I tried with the dinner. I can't really cook. I just didn't count on such a close culinary analysis, Mr Semiotician, that's all.

Sébastien laughs, she supposes, to cover his inability to retort. Instead he puts on some jazz. Hot Club.

Hey, your migraine went away quickly.

Of course! His frank laughter this time invites her to drop it.

I was tense, damn it! he laughs. Now I can see that I wasn't the only one, it makes me feel better.

He sketches out a dance pattern, its syncopated jerkiness rather inept for the heaviness of his body. Rita rises from her cushion, taking the soiled plates, hesitates, rocking slightly. He comes from behind, relieves her of them, placing them on the bed-side table. They are now irrelevant. He has her in his arms. Her fingers part as his hair streams through them. She swallows, is swallowed, kisses confuse, limbs knit, un-knot, re-ravel, in amongst the cushions now, blind and furious, the alto sax pipes it all out, Grapelli's violin whining giddily as he rears out of his jeans, her own body slithers out of hers, he liberates her blundering feet with one deft gesture, she struggles ineffectually at the buttons at her shoulder, her eyes close, again she is that submissive freckled little girl struggling on some uncle's lap, *such a smoodger, little Rita, so-oh affectionate,* again Sébastien's more expert hands put an end to her fumbling efforts and the golden Afghan shirt is off, *ring like a gong for him,* and ringing, tremulous, Raymond's face appears. Even when she closes her eyes, it persists, as her fingers search out the firm young jaw, the chisel-blade of the chin, they find the softer contours of Raymond's flesh. She opens her eyes fully again, wanting Sébastien to course through all her neural tracks, to fill the total field of her perception. His hands define the exact limits of her body; yet as she watches their lingering fascination for the jutting bone of her hip, where the skin stretches bluish, and her own hands make their stuttering way to his shoulders, redescend his neck, bring his face down towards the fluctuating dappled light on her breasts, again she is Hérodiade, and that head sacrificing intellect to her body, breasts swell, nipples harden with the analogy, is this pornography she vaguely worries, this need for other imagery? but still . . .

Et ma tête surgie
Solitaire vigie
Dans les vols triomphaux
    De cette faux

Comme rupture franche
Plûtot refoule ou tranche
Les anciens désaccords
    Avec le corps

her lips murmur the Mallarmé in a tranced monotone that could be taken for the caressive nothings of love enumerating the splendours that lurch and roll before her eyes.

Hein? Tu disais chérie? he whispers. You were saying, darling? She closes her eyes and gives in to a feline purr: *Que tu es beau.*

Et que tu es belle, Rita, et que t'as un p'tit sexe adorable! He nuzzles her neck. Irritation jars her for a brief moment. *What an adorable little sex you have,* worse than *Little Red Riding Hood,* how could anyone say that, but then, perhaps she's just reacting to the French language . . . This machination of his hips over her so far away, she tightens the clasp of her hands around his neck and struggles to raise her face to his, already straining towards its separate orgasm, clouds rip, the palette rains a confetti of colours, the sea dissolves the sailor's portrait, she moans and buries her head in the shelter of Sébastien's flesh where, trembling again, a faltering dream through the rear-vision mirror, those amber eyes . . .

He takes her moan for anticipated pleasure and crashes down towards her as if to clench its centrifugal pulse, he comes . . . And Rita, still, pinned, pulsating with the signals that hers was yet to come, through the white heat of it, the reds, the pinks, the violets, oh the waters in the pool rippling with its radiance but his body shuts her horizon as his sobs come thick and hard, there is nothing, nothing but the concentric ripples, no reference but yes, this dark heat closing in, this Africa and oh yes *baise-moi Sun Diatti* if only I could dance for you, she mouths the invitation, is silent, still.

Sébastien rolls over, props himself on one elbow; his fingers explore her face as if in wonder but then they halt their advance over the cheek. Her eyes must appear glazed. She shuts them: this troubled querying is too much. Excruciatingly acute.
Rita?
Oui.
Rita? Are you . . . Was it . . . Rita?

Her hand glides down his hair. Through an interminable silence, the ripples radiate, it's Van Gogh's drawing of the fountain at the asylum, she realizes now but then above, it's the spikes of her own thicket jiggling the flesh of the sky, her tongue in it . . .

His hand descends, cursorily explores the torso, makes its way in a lazy, desultory fashion, from the collar-bone, over the breast, traces out the canal between the rib-cages, down over her belly. Rita retrieves it, smiles — bleakly, she realizes: *Mais non, je t'assure . . . Ça va! Laisse, laisse, je t'en prie, c'est bien comme ça.* Really . . .

The softer glow in his eyes now, muffled tenderness in his voice. Delicacy in the kiss he gives her this time. He rolls over, on to his back. He has drawn one of his thighs over her leg. His breathing becomes slower, more regular. Its rhythm against the dull boom of Rita's heart fills the sound track.

Rita's eyes are open now. In a rage of wakefulness, they devour objects. Their scrutiny is so intense that visibility increases, as if in day-light.

It is in fact morning already. Birds, the plash-splash of the fountain. The darks of the real concentric ripples are alive with colour. Her brow knots as her gaze encounters their entangled clothes strewn haphazardly across the floor as they were flung in the first fury of their love-making. The dishes where the beige sauce glitters with its buttery sparkles, gelled over the remaining lumps of veal. *Too much oregano, it dominates.* The soiled napkins. Her face lurches upwards from the pillow as if through a sudden urge to deal aggressively with this chaotic evidence: the *pêle-mêle* of kitchen and bedroom things. The weight of his thigh defeats the impulse to move brusquely, however. She has to ease herself from under it.

The way she assesses the sleeping body is ambivalent ... As if she were summing him up for a drawing, tentative lines make their way across her field of vision, charcoal lines, analysing the planes of his back, the distorted purse of flesh where the weight of the head, turned on its side, presses the lips into a collapsed oval. The benign loll of the penis on the recumbent thigh. Or perhaps it is simply: *What shall we do with this?* rather than the artist's speculation. She does in fact have the exasperated look of the nurse, frustrated in her desire for efficiency. As if she would deal deftly with that bed, those sheets, and eliminate every vestige of that organic disarray . . . This . . . sleeping partner.

But it mocks her solipsism. It is not an emanation from the artistic matrix, that sleeping body. Not a mere flickering on her inner screen. It seems to have its own life. It groans, makes a vague attempt at scratching its flank, gropes for her absent form on the bed. Perhaps she loves it. Because it resists her efforts to accommodate it, because of its indisputable physical presence.

He has rolled onto his stomach. The black fuzz emphasizes the power there, in the cleavage between the muscular buttocks. Perhaps his childish abandon to sleep, his naïve presumption that he has found security here, endear him to her. The way he has drawn across one leg to occupy her side of the bed, the almost reptilian sheen of the blue-black hair against the pillow . . . This is not a phantom of the past, not a mere resonance that drains back into the holes of the telephone receiver. It is Sébastien. His sleep functioning in her still life. The rest: the basket spilling its round fruits, the crumpled cloth, the screwed napkins, nursing their green-whites and blue-whites in the crevices of their folds — that could be Cézanne. But this body does not belong. It is too dramatic. Look better in some kind of allegorical representation, say, by Caravaggio.

No, but it has weight, volume, integrity, that body and its presence has dislocated the rest of the room. It has re-allocated the roles that were to be played out by the cushions and canopy, the college of motifs shuffled and reshuffled by the tossing of the cushions, the orchestration of tone and hue from the Berber spread to the carpet: that was the setting for her dream-haunted odalisque. His body is heavy with the slumber of the satiated. *Ahhh*, it says as it rolls again. The thick penis lounges there — oblique shadow of it cast across the thigh. He is so dark that his body is clothed in its nudity. The vigour of his black black pubic hair, that rebukes her too. She had not really expected such uncompromised beauty from his body. If it had been flawed, she would have already levered herself out of this trance that binds her to its harmony. Despite the power of the thighs, they have elegance in their length. The calves and ankles, too, are unexpectedly fine. She glances down at her own as if to compare, take stock.

That self-image in bronze and gold tones she composed last night in the oval mirror, that ringing gong — lost. She has not designed this set. This *débâcle* strewn with organic refuse. Now there is a play of bluish light on her flesh where it was white and of green where it was golden. Her flesh quivers, is gelatinous in its nudity. It is suddenly as un-muscular as that broken hen; it has done its futile dash into history. There have been too many departures, too many farewells. She must come to terms with this . . . Sébastien or she is lost.

If she moved now, to restore the order of last night — gather up the dishes, that bowl with its limp lettuce gleaming, speckled with the pitiful touch of tarragon — she would be only too aware of the faint tremble of her flesh as vulnerability. He might awaken to that sight: the junkety tremor of her femaleness. She would hide this from him. This is no water-sprite, no Arcadian lover, no nymph. This mottled flesh is Renoiresque at best — its blue-veined filigree might look good as painterly fiction, but not in this real life polychrome. Oh the pink and ginger tints. She sees her mother Monica and the whole red lineage informing this auburn mass and its more timorous pubic echo. The pinky brown of her own dilated nipple. It is a softness she would rather not see in herself. And not only is she dilated but dilute, dissolved in this here . . . tepid trickle down her thigh . . .

oozing morning's milk oh lord and so I am the soft receptacle . . . His time still welling in her gives her the urgent need to find some kind of carapace, a shelter for her spilling softness. She whips the drapery from its hook. Indeed, it is a kimona and, presumably, Antonine's. It had been hung there to fulfil a purely decorative need.

She finds a further refuge in the shower.

Watching from above, I do not find myself. Already Rachel fills that space with the first full vowels of her cry. But there is a further retreat from that intrusion below the great oval of Rita's frizzed hair splaying the water-curtain downwards. Her vision rippled within that fluid niche, she finds the lines of her body as reassuring in their flow, in their confidence that they *are* style, as the body of Ingres' *Source*.

In that water-world, there need be no unsettling cries, nor any black eyes challenging her perception of self, unsettling the firm intention of her flesh. Sébastien can be recomposed as he sleeps, that intrusion accommodated. Watch her appropriate the recumbent body she has escaped: As the water uncoils and spreads, retightens its spirals and splays its sheaths from arm to breast to belly to thigh, a new version unfolds. Modified through the falling waters, Sébastien's body undoes its planes and loses in the wash the recalcitrant identity which had her transfixed a moment ago. The conté crayon explores its maleness through the liquid folds, connects its somnolent rhythms to the bleaker chalks of morning light upon the sheets. It's the counterpart to the *Solitary Sleeper* which Gérard had framed. She shows his forms as the disruptive principle of what might have been Euclidian harmony. He is the nexus from which the crumples radiate . . .

You fill me with your growing moan then fall so hard your crisis stilling me my horizon hesitates then oh you shut it with your last release but even now it teases with its sweetness piercingly mirage upon mirage still welling here would make me simply that a poignant oval and O you ebbed and left me echoing could have taken in the world through so slow . . . These piping signals, only the expectancy enduring. Oh yes. You sleep. Spent your time in me. You make me remain.

But none of this can quite dispel the dull marginal presence nudging at her consciousness, getting more insistent now as the water is sucked towards the growling drain, performs its vortex and is funnelled through the floor, some voice saying that she was elsewhere all the time and so cannot share his sleep. As the greedy suction snatches at the shimmering planes of her projected Sébastien, withdraws that version, the voice is quite distinct: *Shunted to another room,* was that your line?

While in his sleep, he is coursing through to another time. The Sébastien she saw — liquidated, down the drain.

False time anyhow. Waterbells of time past. Can't take refuge there for long. This is no sealed space, no cork-lined room. Doors and floors and ceiling emit receive tremble rattle honk. Even the routine itinerary of padding feet will infuriate a trained ear in the flat below. Then there are Rachel's cries. Wayne below will come in from his night-shift at the *Herald*. Then the broom will do its tap-dance on the ceiling through to my floor before I manage to reach the convulsion of pain and rage in the cot. The more I tense myself against her, to will her silence, the more she'll strain against my gritted teeth and amplify her screams. No, *her* is wrong. It will amplify *its* screams. Because the *she* or *he* is lost. The scream intransitive breaks identity.

Look: the mouth, tell myself *Rachel's* mouth, but it doesn't help, the ravenous O of it has me disabled. Its vacuum draught distorts and sucks the contours of the little face takes in my flesh and all its memories objects warp and swarm together into this spiralling demand the room the flat and all of Coogee with its rectangle of sea buckling give way to the omnivorous scream. The eyelids cheeks and neck collaborate to put the focus on that pure demand, the uvula trembling and beyond the crenellated dome, there is the throat and am funnelled through and spiralling down. Tell myself: let her emerge from this terrible anonymity. Of course, she is victim of a metaphor — her mouth is not a drain. Tell myself: break out of this false eternity, the refuge I took in the shower, help help me reach out to her, give her face some human precision, make it say: *I am Rachel, I have a right,* let me convert this vertigo to tenderness, mothers lose themselves in that, not in fascination for the enraged oval of a mouth, remember, even Laurence, impeccable artist, most of them have to cope with this, they don't tense themselves against the high artillery of the cries, they pat the rounded back of the little impotence they care for, support the wobbly head, they sling it across their chest and calmly, casually, bring out the breast, they make sweet coo and fuse themselves and *O my little Rachel, my darling dark one, I'll save you from your awful solitude, I'll reabsorb the howl* and the milk flows our connection and warmth ebbs back from her little body and the padded fists released from the rage of hunger open out and make their fumbling exploration over this face, my face, her lids are flickering and at last it emerges from the dark indeterminate blue not Rita not Sébastien not any element in my story but suffused with a certain splendour, that look says *am am am* and these hands, prehensile extenders of the eyes, blunder, jerk and tug at this otherness encountered and I become the moving shine, the tingling pricks, the blobs of open, mounds of shut her fingers learn, her mirth warbles it to me.

V

RAMSHACKLE RETROSPECTIVE

From here Rachel looks like a disabled frog. The contraption she is strapped in to minimizes the human. It is a cross between a deck-chair and a trampoline; its netting cups the rounded back, the tubular steel frame compliant with the rhythm of the jerky scissor-kicks. I try to look and withhold interpretation, pan in closer where the onyx marble eyes resist metamorphosis. Forget that picture I've learnt to use when she's a red-faced howl, staccato agitation of arms and legs . . .

She self-ejects out of the bouncinette, and with the slow ease of the pole-vaulter, loops over the railing and beyond and then, when she is above the traffic, she is suddenly snatched up on the whim of some cosmic draught, reaches her beautific altitude and hovers forever with her puckered smile: a cupid against the benign blue sky.

Right now the tilt of the bouncinette gives her the world like a mistake on warped graph paper. Tapestry caught in the grid made by the balcony railing and the sagging overhead wires, world unlabelled, liver-brown beige and taupe, the odd pure primary piping out irreverently and then engulfed in the shadowy mix, but mainly she has sky. The freewheeling gulls, looping their flight from blue to brown region, defy the dictates of the matrix and make her laugh. The gulls give me a few minutes.

The growing gap between that Rita and myself is the space I can invent in. If I could loop from space to space like the gulls, trace new trajectories . . . Ones I haven't been able to follow.

At this very moment the striding pace taking her out of the walled garden into the Traverse de St Jean gives other possibilities. There is no inevitability in the purpose of this excursion. Nothing to stop her walking right off her story-line.

There are practical objections of course, but they are easily dealt with. There is the sleeping Adonis she has left behind in Antonine's apartment and its projected resolution in a drawing. There is the mess from last night's meal, which is certainly irritating. An implied solution can be squeezed in between frames. Or, perhaps preferably, a metamorphosed Sébastien could cope with that. Why shouldn't he also buck the trappings of his caricature? He could awaken to the soft gilding light and find something mellow, warm, like gratitude for her acceptance of him coursing from cell to cell, through his body, filling him. He could don the kimona she has left draped over the chair and set about, like the perfectly good humoured domestic pet he might have sometimes been at Raymond's, whistling as he pads around bare-footed, shaking place-mats, scraping plates, finding something that looks like detergent and leaving the dishes there on the sink to dry, in a staggered sprawl. A rather succinct job, as he would say, but still, not a bad effort.

And here he is now, coming back into view with a broom, sweeping the crumbs out through the *porte-fenêtres* into the garden where the birds will find them. But then, perhaps he should not overdo it: Rita has shown her hesitations after all. He

205

leaves the broom leaning there, against the glass. Let Rita come rather in pursuit of him, decide for him. She mightn't come straight back, in any case, wherever she's gone. When she does return, she will find nothing as evidence of Sébastien except the absence of mess and a note:

Rita, what do you really want? Come and see me if/when you feel like it.

Or there might be no note. Simply an absence. Sébastien, looking for clues as to Rita's departure, finds himself sifting through her papers — notes, most of them, for paintings. His eyes alight on her description of him. The violence she sees, the narcissism, the spoilt child in him. There is disbelief: the eyes track, retrack the same phrase. He rocks his loose fist on the little pile of papers.

But she thinks as she walks along: what about Raymond, what about his hurt? This spring morning can take her right on past the *boulangerie,* all the way to the coach terminus at Aix, all along the Route d'Aubagne to the Old Port in Marseille. Here she is negotiating the traffic on the Prado. The voice through the intercom registers pleasure and surprise: Ah! My dear Rita. Sébastien is not with you? I hope I don't owe this visit to some tantrum he has thrown. But come up.

The glass doors click open, obedient to his remote-control.

Here is Raymond in his wheat-gold peignoir at the pop-up toaster. Something like a reminiscence of Le Douanier Rousseau's *Snake Charmer* hovers between Raymond and the back-drop of potted palms in this bronze kitchen with its black lacquer trimmings. As he kisses her, she notes that here is one balding man who doesn't go in for the careful raking of a few treasured strands over the dome. Likes him for it. The sliced bread, *à l'américaine,* as they say, pops as he reaches for the MacRobertson's marmalade. The fragrance of the Eau Sauvage aftershave (which Sébastien must pinch from him) gives her a somewhat Proustian mnemonic twinge. Somewhere in the apartment, a door is being slid open. Then there is a shuffling of scuff-style slippers into the bedroom.

So, Raymond says, are we to have the pleasure of your company for breakfast?

The approaching shuffle, together with the blast of a

forcefully blown nose promise an explanation of the *we*.

Ah, Rita, I would like you to meet Dah-veed.

Les messieurs prennent un déjeuner à l'anglaise, she thinks.

On inspection, Dahveed is decidely Dayvid: the sleep crushed skin on this grave oblong face takes on a pink hue perhaps through juxtaposition with the mushroom corduroy shirt. This is also crushed.

The eyes, that tender watery blue you forget about in the south of France, are quickly averted as he tends his hand.

Rita Finnerty — David MacAlister. Young David is doing a season at the *Conservatoire* and picking up a bit of literary culture at the Faculté while he is here . . . and Rita is the painter I told you about.

There is a slight tremor in the musician's hand as it fumbles for a Royale cigarette and now the index finger is tapping away before the ash warrants it. It has probably just dawned on him: *My God how on earth did I get into this? What happened last night is already made into social currency. And he is displaying me as Good Value.*

Raymond says: What's wrong with you both? Sit down, please — the toast will be inedible.

Downing his orange juice, pith and crushed ice, David gulps, makes his Adam's apple jump, mumbles something about an early rehearsal at the Conservatory, no time for breakfast *malheurEUSement mais merci beauCOUP pour votre hospitALitay,* gets up, offers that cold cod of a hand once again, bumps into his chair, pushes a strand of pale hair away from his eyes, goes frankly red this time and is gone. Raymond follows him: there are lowered voices in the lobby.

Raymond's mind will be on David's precipitous departure. Here he is, gentle, concerned. *Alors ma belle,* he says, what brings you here? Mmm? He fingers her bracelets.

I . . . ah. I don't really know. Just wanted to see you. Came here like an automaton. I just . . . Sébastien . . .

Yes?

Sébastien shot through.

Mmm. There seems to be an epidemic this morning. Raymond tugs at his ear-lobe.

Oh . . . I'm sorry if my coming . . .

207

Ttt, ttt. Not at all. I rather think he seized upon the opportunity. Oh these young men have their curious *volte-faces.* But I wouldn't worry about Sébastien. He's an old hand at dramatic disappearances. Especially when everything is going well. Just a childish need to be missed, that's all.

Here the projection blurs as they ruminate on either side of the table. No, Rita cannot reclaim Raymond's intimacy. Last night has happened.

She should fill her mind with one talismanic line: *j'ai un amant.* Her tongue tries it out. Got a lover in my borrowed bed. This will unlock all kinds of gestures. She can come back with the croissants and grind the coffee. The pores of things are definitely open. Lizards positively flicker-lick out of the crevices across the lit walls. She should fix herself an address closer to Sébastien to receive this new life. Borrowings have been but a rite of passage. There need be no solitude like after Jean. That glove of darkness has been eluded. Each tree withdraws its fingers of shadow. The glass need not send back a victim face. The train that takes her need not say THANATOS THANATOS with its wheels.

The deep pores in the swarthy neck of the man at the bar. His profile shifts slowly, three-quarter, full gaze. His fingers negligently curled around the glass of pastis. That must be his lorry outside. He says: *C'est ben jolie, vot' ville,* fine place, your town.

Ah oui, she says. He's from Lyon maybe, driven through the night. The warmth of his eyes affirms things. She practically sings her request for a packet of Gauloises Filtre across the counter. She takes a copy of the *Marseillaise.* She can look for an apartment there where Sébastien can come, where she can see him on her own terms.

More space to paint in, too. Before Raymond organizes her studio situation. She feels a sudden protective tenderness for the teeming life she carries. No more dwelling in the lapses. Who was that? — *She Dwelt Among Untrodden Ways.* Rita's pulse will dictate the rhythm, not some poet's remote metronome. *And oh the difference to me . . .*

This is a sure gestation of the future she has willed, linking this to all the rest: *we will have breakfast in the courtyard.* The first person plural need not be a trap. Her hand asserts it over the glass counter of the boulangerie pointing out the *croissants,* avoiding the *pains au chocolat.*

He will grope half-blind from the morning light and pull her towards him. He will have a kind of blundering tenderness. She will ask him if he'd like some *croissants* and he will answer that she is *vraiment une chérie.* She will give the quiet smile of the *Gioconda* knowing that his reward is prepared, that her decision has been made: to find a place where she can maintain the separation he surely respects but where they can both meet free from the patina of old loves. She will eject herself out of the Aix identikit, out of the cloisters of other people's stories. Into the real city. Aix with its water cures, its Transatlantic students, its transported workers, inbred lawyers, doctors, shopkeepers and landlords.

Marseille: the postcard ripples and the raucous port wakes up untidily, its gutters awash with yesterday's refuse. Obscenity does easy commerce with seduction as the fish and vegetable sellers shout their wares across the marketplace. Marseille contrives its labyrinth of gestures and glances, every emission from windows and doors reads and is read by pimps, spying concierges, cops and brothel manageresses, its stenches and perfumes in easy dialogue. The city snorts and honks, flaunts bad taste like the carnival counterpart of continence. Marseille incontinent, indiscriminate in its centripetal drive, is bombed out mediaeval, baroque, flamboyant rococo, sober neo-classical, nineteenth century vulgar, twentieth century functionalist, the ancient sinuous streets of the Arab Quarter release their spillage on to the Haussmannesque grand perspectives, rationalized boulevards with uniform façades, engulfing fishing villages, sprouting high-rise apartment blocks, giving way to the luxury swoop of the Corniche, threading the pink marble cliffs of the *callanques,* flattening out into the main drag along the sea-front cafés, pausing for an exclamation mark with the vulgar giant copy of Michelangelo's David . . .

This calorific excess that has to be spent beyond Sébastien. Here, in the *petites annonces* is an advertisement for an apartment *centre ville* with two rooms and kitchen. Here is a phone number, a *jeton* for the telephone and here is the agoraphobe with her finger in the dial, her voice an easy fluid answer to the crackling bass at the other end of the line. These are the noises of the Marseille connection: bar noises, a chaos of voices overlaid with clashing dishes, clinking of glasses and a tinny Mireille Mathieu on some juke box.

Deux cents cinquante le mois, Mademoiselle. Yes, yes it's furnished all right, a little primitively I must admit. But it is clean enough . . .

And later . . . Would it be all right to share it with a friend? *Un ami?* It's not a convent I keep, you know! (A deep guffaw tagged with a musical *râle* and a coughing spasm.) Yes, you have a balcony and Notre Dame de la Garde to watch over you hurrhurrheughheugh. Of course — come around say at eleven o'clock. Ask for Alphonse at the bar. Oui, le Bar Cannetti. *A onze heures alors, Mademoiselle.*

Alphonse, Bar Cannetti, Rue Fongate scrawled on the newspaper. The sudden future.

But Sébastien disobeys the stage directions: there is no slow-motion stretch-and-yawn of the infant voluptuous, no groggy mumbling of her name. She sees the falling mass of black hair, the hanging hands between the knees. As she rattles ineffectually at the door handle, rustles the paper bag, he raises his head, but slowly. He shows nothing on his face as he moves slowly towards the door. The voice that comes is thick and nasal, cracks a little like an adolescent's: Ah, Rita. I thought you'd shot through on me.

But ... As if ...

No listen ...

He tries to grab her hand as she walks purposely to the sink.

Rita, I don't feel ... How to put it? I get the feeling I don't ... I know last night I behaved like a clumsy adolescent. Or at least that's how I must have come across to you.

But ... Oh, hey! What do you take me for? Some monstrously clinical ...

No, of course not. But you, I mean ... How could you help seeing it in that way? And then, at times you seemed so distant, Rita.

Now the panic sets in. Is he trying to project whatever reason he has for not continuing on to her? And she has already planned him into her life. She is touched by the poignancy of what she might easily lose. It is there in his voice, still raw from last night's drinking. Whatever he is trying to say comes out this time as a broken bleat. It's her turn now, he's asking for her to assume control. His finger-tips blanch from the pressure they apply to her shoulder.

Look . . . If I seemed distant . . . Well, I was tense, you know, found it hard to be myself, here, in this place. And then . . .

And then?

Oh there were other things interfering.

Like what? You mean like Raymond.

His voice is flat, bleak.

Rita, we'll go and see him. I think we've probably both underrated his generosity. Eh?

His smile is not glaring this time.

Now she has him in the deckchair. But this moment holds her too in its grid: the light metallic percussion, like the tinkling of triangles, cymbals sliding, timpani, even the timorous harpsichord coming in, this busyness of insects and birds inseparable from the throb of optical pleasure. As if each marble pebble in this courtyard were concerting itself to ring with the total brightness. He is stretching his thighs as he did that first day at *L'Aiguillage* but this time the bareness of the chest is not a *trompe-l'oeil* effect. She will not be a mere dream consorted through the flesh of this voluptuous faun. Here all the clichés about animal simplicity are so adequate, it is marvellous. He does laugh like a child, he tears recklessly at the crust of a croissant to expose the tender fat flesh and plunges his hard white teeth in. He eats in earnest, as if to consummate the unspoken possibility of domesticating what they have found together. He dunks the rest of the croissant into his bowl of coffee. The eyelets of grease swarm and eddy each time his hand returns to his mouth. She accepts the fountain whose ripples still hold the morse code of her desire. Lounging back, gesticulating with his new croissant, he has the heavy insolent grace of one of Picasso's young minotaurs.

It can only get better, you'll see, he says.

Yes.

But, he yawns, reaching for his watch, better get moving all the same. Got to attack the next chapter, Rita. You know? I feel charged now.

She registers a slight disappointment, a dullness. This day should have been a slow, quasi-ecstatic ceremony, a release from the ordinary pursuits.

212

If you're heading back to Marseille, I might come with you, she says.

Pleasure in buying the ticket with him. Now the warm insistent contact of his thigh next to hers in the train. The train races their pulse. People stare at them. Perhaps it is their physical contrast. But then, he is extraordinary. The asymmetry of his face makes its lines dynamically alive, its areas of perfection all the more astounding: the pure moulding of the jaw, the straight wedge of the chin. His vivid beauty. They are snaking through the marble hills, the villages straggling at first, fusing more and more now, the monolithic towers of the H.L.M. state housing blocks rear up and now the wide shock as Marseille opens up to the swooping train, tumbling towards them from horizon to here, its sprawled descents rising up again to hyperbolic pinnacles, arching and plunging, its animate entrails below the level of the track as they approach the station. Workers: she wants to plunge too and stride with them, be part of the swarm. Be part of this city, pay for the apartment with her own work, check out that Publikon, why not? Sébastien said they were looking for artists. They are hurtled out of the light into its guts: the huge boisterous Gare St Charles under the great vaulted roof.

Sébastien diverges punctiliously at the St Charles steps. He will be heading for the Bibliotèque Municipale. Strange that he hasn't asked her where she is going. But it might simply be discretion. And he kissed her well just then.

The Bar Cannetti is triangular, thrusting an acute elbow into the intersection of the Rue Fongate and the Rue D'Aubagne. Something topologically puzzling in these dislocated planes and their seams of fusion: the street level on one side of the triangle is several metres below the other. The Rue D'Aubagne plummets towards the markets and on this side drops away precipitously to the Rue D'Estelle: dense traffic coming up with second gear roaring. But the bar is hardly animate. The woman behind the counter has skin the colour and texture of chamois leather. As Rita's eyes adjust to the darkness, she can make out the line where the gingery foundation cream stops, the emerald green eye-shadow, the blonded hair trained back in little spikes showing the dark roots. Something latently witty in the reptilian stare she keeps on Rita as she polishes and repolishes the same glass and yells over her shoulder: *Al-PHON-seugh, une demois-ELL-eugh à te voir!*

There is a man in the shadows against the wall: the gleam of the round opossum's eyes refers to Rita and then to the woman at the bar. He begins whistling, drums his fingers. There is a trundling vibration down the stairs. Through the moth-eaten velveteen drape, a towering cork platform-sole appears, gold toe-nails, then a polished knee. Conical breasts and a huge smile present like savories on toothpicks. But the smile was apparently abstract or retrospective; she looks dully at the seated man. She gives a slight nod and sits down at the table next to him. Now a little compact man emerges from behind the drape. He goes to the bar

214

and gives Rita his rounded back in shiny navy, flicks a speck of dandruff from the padded shoulder. *Une anisette,* he says. The woman at the bar doesn't reply but pours him one.

AlPHON-seugh une demoiSELL-eugh pour l'apparteMUNG!
Ma OUI pu-TAING j'arrIV-eugh!

It's the same crackling bass she heard over the phone. It is a lurching Blue Beard who appears. Smile creases extend like radical scars from the nostril bulbs, disappear into the whiskers. He has the same big flattened out lower lip as the girl on the cork stilts. Father perhaps? As he walks, he bends to manipulate the stiff leg, clapping it on the back of the knee with the flat of his palm. The steady dark eyes seem affable enough.

You the one who phoned ugh?

He unhooks a massive bunch of keys from the wall.

Show you right away. Come this way, Mademoiselle.

He weaves amongst the traffic, managing the stiff leg skilfully, virtually thrusting the cars out of the way. He stops at a great wooden door, its curling flakes of paint an indeterminate colour under the soot. It gives way with a shoulder lunge. He stabs at a time controlled switch and edges Rita in front of him. You're a student ugh?

Er no. I paint, she says.

The sudden easy social currency: *I paint.* But it won't be a hit with a landlord.

Oh, I've got some regular work as well. In an advertising agency.

The lie came out just as easily.

Artiste peintre, hein?

His hand lingers a moment on her waist as they move over the diamond shaped tiles in the hall.

You go on ahead. I'm afraid it's a bit of a climb. I've got to deal with this leg of mine.

After the first open swoop of stairs in what might be marble, they become narrow, reverting to the normal provençal terra-cotta hexagonal tiles. Doors crack open as if by some telepathic impulse received behind them. The stairwell is alive with eyes. At the fourth floor, it's a tousled hennaed head. The red-brown eyes, set in this grey collapsed flesh are shockingly vivid. Vermillion lipstick has been slashed across, obliterating what shape there might have been in the lips. Rita tries for the category of 'aging prostitute' by Rouault but can't sustain the tenacious gaze of the woman.

Eh! You've found yourself another red-head, Alphonse! she calls over the landing. She takes in quick little sucks of air, amplifying the harmonics of an asthmatic wheeze and underneath the black and silver shawl, the chest seems to be doing some kind of laugh routine.

A final toy spiral flight gives way to a narrow landing. The dosage of light from the meter-controlled switch has given out but up here, a skylight gives a tender chiaroscuro to things. Alphonse emerges from the pit of darkness below. These would have been the maids' rooms back in the times when the building housed a handful of bourgeois families. Eighteenth century, judging by the vestiges of *rocaille* shell ornamentation in the plasterwork.

Well, here we are. It's not in the best of repair. I must get round to giving it a lick of paint one of these days.

Alphonse jiggles the key in the lock: This is the kitchen. Not exactly every modern convenience but . . .

There is a diffuse glow in here, the green shutters at the window sifting the light in long shafts. It is redispersed by the heavy texturing of the walls, applies a cream curve around the massive hooding over the stove, throws amber where it reflects from the floor tiles. Alphonse flings back the shutters, opens the small door onto the balcony. The window panes, turned out to the light, are a silver flash.

Voilà! He opens his hand to the sea of roofs, the dance of bleached ochres, their mobile grey, yellow and pink overtones. The balcony slopes too; like the room back in Aix, everything seems to give way to a general subsidence. The light in the main room is also fluid, eddying in and out of alcoves, projecting diaphanous patterns on the furniture. The leaning gilt mirror over the mantelpiece takes in the sagging double bed, canopy and crucifix, the Belle Epoque hat-stand, the reproduction Louis XV desk. Beyond, there is a tiny second room: dark, windowless, at best a foetal retreat.

Too much raw enthusiasm might give him the wrong idea. Rita bites her lip: Mmm. It should do. I was hoping for a *cabinet de toilette* but still . . . What are you asking for the bond?

Ah. Mademoiselle, there is no bond. But I would ask you to be

216

discreet. Let's say, don't let the whole world know who you are renting it from. Because . . . er . . . It doesn't have quite the facilities stipulated, it is not *quite* legal, he laughs. That's why I'm asking so little rent. As long as you can pay me each month in cash, I won't bother you.

Rita hands over the two hundred and fifty francs, leaving only a hundred from Raymond's advance. Alphonse gives a slight bow, hands her the key.

There you are, it's all yours, Mademoiselle er . . .?
Finnerty. Rita Finnerty.
Aha. You're not French?
No. I'm Australian.
Australienne hein? Oh ahahahaha les kangourous!
His voice booms down the stairwell and he is gone.

Sébastien will be astonished, delighted at this quick move. And she can entertain Raymond here. He can be her guest for once. Laurence can come to stay. No, but she won't crowd this new space. For once she can set up a decent studio. And she will be autonomous. Check out that Valda Schleiermacher at Publikon, bring in her own money. Branch out into new work whether or not it is sanctioned by gallery owners. Street paintings: the kinetics of crowd and traffic, flattened out by the bird's-eye view. And then a series called, maybe, *Dislocations,* working out the clash of realities here, Notre Dame de la Garde, the Golden Madonna, watching over Cannetti's family business, bar, mini-brothel and who knows what drug transactions. The space and time warps here, this humped street, its basements and its vertical life, the light randomizing the boundaries of things, shifting the planes.

Maybe at Publikon they have some freelance work to offer. That way she needn't be contaminated by it, won't have to drape semi-nudes with orgasmic smiles over the latest Motto Guzzi. Plenty of artists, writers, do advertising copy, sign-writing. Gauguin, for instance.

It is at 25 Rue Paradis. Street of the golden fruit. Just near that respectable little square, Place du Général de Gaulle. So Sébastien said. But there is no sign, no indication at street level. Up the ancient stone steps, around and around a capricious vortex, past snatches of invective *Fais gaffe ou je te casse les couilles ... Eh eh eh va te faire enculer,* up to the fourth landing, still no sign of any Publikon — Sébastien must have been having her on. Now at the sixth landing, there is an open door: the buzzing of phones, rattle of typewriters and a voluble luscious female voice dominating quieter interrogative ones. Every surface in here — the screens dividing the place up into units, the windows, walls and ceiling — is plastered with advertisements: a million slogans, brand-names, entwined limbs and ecstatic smiles. The name must have been one of Sébastien's inventions. Or perhaps this is an illegal business, not registered. Rita will say that she is looking for the solicitor's office she saw on the second floor — the brass plate there was discreet enough to be feasibly missed. She stares at the bald light bulb rocking slightly in the draught from the door. No, it would be prostitution, worse than accepting Raymond's help. Raymond at least is a friend now, it would be just less honest, that's all, than the girls at Cannetti's bar. And this might be Valda walking towards her now, picking up a beeping telephone *en route — ah oui alors, mais tout de suite* — her round monkey eyes set on Rita now as she weaves her way amongst the desks, greeting Rita with emphatic *ahs* and *biensûrs* ... So you are a friend of that charming and SO talented young Sébastien

Coustou?

Before Rita has asked, she formulates the question for her, as simple as that light bulb, as neat as an egg: You are looking for work? Of course you are, what artist can make it on painting alone, and I hope it's not simply in distribution, we have plenty of students who will do that, no we need people like you to design some video sequences, or at least supply our technicians and production staff with a few ideas . . .

Her fine dark hair swings its unified mass; the bang above the eyebrows and the side bangs frame the eyes which bind Rita to her total spectacle: as she gesticulates and ripples up and down the scale of exclamations, perches on a desk, circumambulates it, stubs her cigarette, it becomes more and more astonishing that she keeps her ample flesh together while she appropriates the whole volume of the place, astonishing that the inflection and resonance of her voice, so obviously studied, can still be efficiently seductive. She wears perfume which says something like mellow voluptuousness. She has a plethora of fine gold chains directing the eye down to the deep scoop of her neck-line to the heavy load of her breasts. She has that animal perfume, the muskiness that lingers in fur. She would bewitch a little child like the infant Baudelaire but reserve the full organ chords of her laugh for more lusty conquests. Like Baudelaire's mother, she would then totally withdraw from the little boy's intimacy, waltz off on the arms of a chance general, sensing that he would grow up, that sensual little one, to desecrate every female fleece for the trace of her betrayal, his maddened senses still hungering for her, that slow, insistent pendulum of her displaced passion in his brain. Valda is a mobile *bric-à-brac* store of images. She sells them obliquely, she says. OF COURSE we do not want direct representation of the commodity . . . What we are looking for is that teasing enigma that will tick-le the retina, make the consumer chafe a lit-tle, you see, and then lead him or her — we always have one sex or the other as primary target — to scrutinize the slogan itself, as a kind of promise that he or she will be released from that irritation by buying the commodity. That lit-tle germ of irritation has to work in the pit of the viewer's mind.

She laughs and sends a jabbing gesture with her lacquered nails to the back of Rita's cranium. Look, she says, perhaps we could try you out on a little scenario for video and if we like the kind of things you come up with, we can give you some work. It's a matter of . . . say, let's see . . . Let's say launching a new polish. *Une cire.*

The hiss of the sibilants, the sharp vowel, seem to delight Valda as if she were sucking Rita's mind, most delicately, through the finest of straws. *Oui, une cire.* A polish as yet nameless. Well, as you know, the market is already flooded with them. In any case, the company I am thinking of already has several with the same basic formula. What I would like you to do is to try to capture a section of the market which has so far eluded it with the other products, those that are geared to appeal to the penny pinching petit bourgeois easily seduced by words like silicon and hydrophobe. You could aim, say, at those with pretensions to more traditional culture, the more deeply snobbish consumer, eh? *Qu'en dites-vous,* she sings. *Hein? Mademoiselle?*

To sell a polish no different from all the others, of course, you have to tamper with language a bit, it's what Sébastien says, what those linguists and semioticians he quotes say, what Valda Schleiermacher is saying now, she must have taken the Schleiermacher Veilmaker as a joke on the art of selling, you've got to use that verbal veil, the onomatopoeia, the chiasma, the porte-manteau, the paronomasia, Sébastien says, that seem to buoy the essence of the product in the sweet bowels of its name, like, as he said, from something he'd read, *I like Ike.* Every time an American in the sway of the slogan said *I like,* the General-President's name was also spoken, he was the verbal agent of that affinity: I like the President. I like hamburger, like nuclear family, like nuclear fall-out, like Cadillac, like Elvis, the white gyrator, like nuke, like bald-headed small-nosed newts like Ike, like the baby boom, preferably of bald and blue-eyed future blonds to be bald old men like him, bald as the bigger bomb, like the Cold War, like to stockpile my deep-freeze . . . Every time they sent out a sleek missile of their liking, the spikey little syllable of Eisenhower's nickname travelled along. *Une cire.* A polish. Why not the English name to encode the snob, get that kind of consumer in, *le cocktail, le bâtiment de grand standing, le grog, les Quakers Oats,* they say *Kwahkairzote* here and porridge is magical, exotic, why not *polish, peuhleesh, le peuhleesh. Peau lisse,* rather, smooth skin. The hand caressing skin as smooth, as impeccable as celluloid CUT to gossamer surfaces everywhere, as the exquisitely manicured fingers trail their caress, *peau lisse,* smooth silk skin over everything, could take out a copyright or patent or whatever they call it on the adjective *lisse**, spreading its aura like glad* wrap over all the shunted planes of light, *peau lisse,* a veil of opalescent luminosity singing love in on your very own vinyl floors CUT to the apartment of Raymond, the Light-giver and we will show you how we make all our surfaces chime, how you can be Penelope and Siren all at once, watch the one who *knows* weaving the fabric of light, her translucent finger-nails trailing the silky warp and weft of it, just like the trajectory of a fairy wand to enrapture forever the homing Ulysses, you too can call your sire in, serene you are although it's been a decade, no, no decay, the teeth of this Penelope say it too through their Hollywood orthodontal perfection, siren you are and no need for him to be gagged and mast-tided, this is the foyer, the pulsating focus, and as he sails euphorically towards it CUT to the loosened fingers of our *femme fatale,* and you too can be in the crafty sailor's arms and fainting slowly, but watch how the pearly index nail points to the source of this beguilement: CUT to the secret, the centripetal pulsing of this light around one innocent cylinder bearing the label SIRÈNE and below, in more modest cursive script: *la reine des sires,* queen of polishes and queen of sires and now the video gives you the chance to sing your sire in, in one long enchanting celestial hum, the transfigured harmonics of the polishing machine fill your sound-track and *heureux qui comme Ulysse retrouve la peau lisse de Sirène la Reine des Cires . . .*

I will give it a go, Rita says.

What are you doing?

Denise sucking on her Gauloise.

Packing. Found a place in Marseille. Ideal studio. And maybe even some work in an advertising studio.

Jesus! When you move, you certainly go fast. You're not moving in with Sébastien are you? I mean, taking a place in Marseille sounds a bit close for comfort.

No no. I'm not that masochistic. I like him but he's got no chance of making a take-over bid. Too addicted to my own space.

Yeah. Well, sounds okay. This town's getting a bit small for me too. Might follow you one of these days. Did you know old Emile's got the place up for sale? Here, let me give you a hand.

Raymond arrives in the Goddess, loads the last of Rita's canvasses onto the roof-rack. Puffs a little with the effort of tightening and reknotting the ropes, securing the work against the freeway winds. Denise stands with Sérisier in the doorway. Her black eyes welling, his rheumy eyes veiled. This landlord has returned the bond with interest without inspecting the room. I have trust in you, Mademoiselle Rita, he said. Rita gives way and hugs them both. Denise whispers: Can understand now why you're attracted to the Body Guard!

Heart tightening like a fist, Rita watches it file past: the morgue, the sugar almond factory, the Théâtre du Centre, Suma, the Office du Tourisme . . .

In the back of the car Sébastien is whistling.

So Rita stakes her claim to a living working space. A job, only partially disabling, which perhaps by the ironies it generates, will feed her work. The big chance to explore the space in which perhaps... Why then does she arouse the sleeping reasons from the margins to give causal links to casual scenes.

Here she is already, entertaining Sébastien for the third time in a week. *Receiving* him, as they say in France. The artifice of his visitor status is starting to get to her. As they lounge on cushions, idling over their biographies, linking their reciprocal signposts, vivisecting the immediate past, offering prognoses for the future, she beings to agitate over the present. There is the trial scenario to refine for Publikon, there are the tubes of paint aligned on the bench, the jars of clean brushes graded to thickness, her *Vice Versa* notebook open ready and she is drugged by his voluptuous presence.

Silly little verses come to silly little tunes as she returns once again with the breakfast food:

> *Sébastien*
> *ce n'est qu'un nom*
> *c'est mon amant*
> *tout simplement*
> *mais faudrait voir*
> *dormir ce gars*
> *et les beaux plis*
> *que font les draps*

autour de lui
autour de lui

Sébastien
ce n'est qu'un nom
que je fredonne
en ramenant
les bons croissants
et le pain blanc
mais faut goûter
faut faire une vie
autour de lui
autour de lui

But still she agitates. She grinds her teeth in her sleep, he says, somewhat offended. Why, despite their increasing sexual understanding? Why? She hasn't the immediate courage to formulate it. Of course, it's all too petty: she actively resents departures of this constant guest which leave her with unshared deposits. The broken crusts under the table, the water to boil for the pile of dishes, the dirty sheets which must be taken to the laundromat, the *Municipalité de Marseille* bags of garbage to haul down the ten flights of stairs. He is always around — his absences only brief lulls in which to prepare for his presence. Her revved up inactivity. If he lived here with her, at least they could both get on with their working lives instead of this endless retrospection and projection. They could withdraw from one another because latently, they would be constantly together.

At last she says it to the empty wine bottle: Why don't you move in properly, Seb? His joy is intoxicating. He smiles, takes her in his arms, her feet leave the floor.

He slams the door forever on his student pad, hands in the keys. This must have liberated some bond money at least, but he doesn't mention participating in the rent. That will come, she supposes. He arrives in a hired removal van full of his trappings: covers, lamps, hangings — more readily a coherent decor than hers. He asks her if she intends using the imitation Louis XV desk and if not, where he might set it up for himself. Ah . . .

Aren't you . . . But don't you work at the library?

Ttt ttt. No. Here it'll be perfect. Besides, I've got to type things up now, can't do that at the Biblio Munic.

At her suggestion, he sets the desk up in the big room where the lighting is good since, as he's often said, he has bad eye strain these days. Also, in the main room, he will have more insulation from noise; he'll be further away from the neighbours along the landing.

I can work with noise, she says. I'll be fine in the kitchen. Anyhow, need to be near water, doing a lot of gouache at the moment.

There he is, anyhow, at it already, the jumping typewriter throttling the fragile desk, bringing down its metallic hail, the chair screeching on the tiles as he leans back to study the sentence already completed, his feet entangled in a spaghetti maze of wires, his face irradiated from a multitude of improvised sources of light, despite the *porte-fenêtres* giving ample illumination at this time of summer. When he pauses between the machine-gun assaults on the keyboard, she feels she must guarantee the established hush.

Voluptuous faun? Indolent young minotaur? No this is the pure frottage of cerebrum against the register of academe. He never seems to relax now. At least never with her.

Thérèse, for instance, she could teach him a few things. Living in the *chambre obscure* next door. Diminutive, fragile. Forty, fifty? She is beyond that kind of reckoning with her swimming grey eyes, her hands that rise and fall like birds, Piaf-like hands, in fact, that float on the air and then open like flowers as she talks, shuffling images like a conjuror. Never attempts explanations, up to the listener to perform the arabesques, the sinuous lines that might connect them all. Presumes you are there in the scene she inhabits, past or fantasy, and she talks from there. At first Sébastien is tolerant, even amused, but just today he has declared that she's tiresome: It isn't my business, of course, Rita, if you want to waste your time on such a self-indulgent wretch, but I'm damned if I'm going to any longer. Anyhow, sympathy doesn't help her, she just becomes more and more sorry for herself. I wouldn't mind doing something practical to help but she rejects any suggestion like that. She'd rather cling to her fantasies and imaginary sorrows.

It is true that Thérèse claims to have an ex-lover hanging around somewhere: a Corsican, who will come back to her when he can.

He hasn't had time to visit me, he's working so hard, you know, to save the money to get me away from all this. Ah, but you can trust a Corsican, Rachel, you should get yourself one, they're grimly faithful.

For some reason, Thérèse ignores corrections, Rita *is* Rachel. Rahshell, Thérèse says. They're tenacious, those Corsicans, hold on like the ponk of a goat's cheese!

She gives a wild laugh. Pours Rita a pastis from the little flask she has brought in. Is she aware? Sébastien is quite demonstratively securing the door, quite noticeably stuffing the anti-draught sausage along the crack at the bottom. Let his semiotics incubate, if that's all he wants to hatch. What has happened these last weeks? Their conversations have become so sparse with real connections — because they are choked on her mutinous undertones?

Rita wonders about it long hours at night. This vigilant inertia, her body next to his. One night there is a soft *ooh-hoo?* at the front door.

Ooh hoo? Rachel?

A glance at Sébastien's watch in the flare of the cigarette lighter: four am. Rita slides out, attends to the door. Thérèse is there, smiling widely, innocently. She is tottering under a steaming pot of tortellini. She has a squashy looking package tucked under her arm. Pastis and Eau de Cologne are battling it out on her breath.

Tenez, Rachel, je vous ai apporté du mou pour le p'tit chat.
Lung for my cat? Surely she didn't say that.
But I don't have a cat.

That is exactly what I am saying. I suggest that you do have a cat. You have him there, *un pauv' p'tit minou* curled up in your brain. You need to deny him, you want to deny his power. But sometimes he gets out without your knowing. He leaves tracks in your paintings. I have seen them. I have brought him some lung so that he can breathe, you see. Yes, you think it's a joke. It's no joke, at night I hear him yowling. It's a suffocated yowl. You have to let him breathe. *Hein? N'est-ce pas ma p'tite?* And then, before we have the pasta, you must take this. Some garlic gargle from the apothecary of Thérèse! For your cough.

But . . . Thérèse! You know I don't cough!

Mais si, puisque je vous le dis! she insists.

Rita takes the cure then and there. Perhaps she does cough, anyhow.

You know, I hear my Corsican coughing every time you hack hack hack.

Thérèse is sobbing into the tortellini now. *Mon pauv' p'tit Bruno qui s'esquinte pour moi.* He doesn't want me to worry, that's why he hasn't contacted me yet. Denies himself all the pleasures, ruining his health for me. But when I hear you coughing Rachel, I know it's him, all the same.

Rita looks up: Thérèse is gone.

It's nearly daybreak. Becoming cold. Mistral outside loosening the shutters, rolling the empty pots around the balcony. Thérèse back again, this time with a tureen: soup made from scraps, on the fringe of non-existence. As if the veins of lettuce were left to pulse immaterially in a mist of garlic, parsley, fennel, leek. In fact, it's hardly a hint of garlic, there seem to be at least ten cloves in the pot. Thérèse fishes one out, then another: *mes précieux oignons!* she calls them, as she pops the translucent husks into her mouth.

Here is Sébastien's face through the gaping door, sleep-puffy, scowling against the light: *Mes CHÈRES dames,* he says, are you both absolutely crazy? Do you have *any* idea what time it is?

Of course we do, Monsieur, it is soup-eating time in the kitchen, Thérèse says. Won't you try some? There is plenty left.

Thérèse ladles it out in anticipation, humming faintly. Rita can't decide whether in defence against his hostility or simply in ignorance of it.

He shuts the door with a sigh and makes emphatic steps back to bed. Thérèse is singing in earnest now: it's a wrecked voice, in a way, but she can exploit it. It wafts idly for a while and then it begins to soar, hovers, comes to a ragged halt, is fretted away in a desultory hum, gathers up its energies once more, takes off as she grabs Rita for a dance amongst the chairs and pots of paint and dishes in the kitchen.

227

She is trying to develop a looser gestural style in these urban graffiti drawings, working along to free jazz on the little cassette player, letting it work through her and counter-acting it. He leaves his final draft and pokes a wincing, loose-lipped face through the kitchen door. *Mais Rita, enfin! Figure-toi un peu!* Just imagine trying to do academic work against that! It might be all right with that libidinous stuff you are doing. *Ce genre d'expression pulsionnelle,* he said.

She turns the Miles Davis off immediately. Lips pressed grimly. Almost a pleasure in the austerity of martyrdom, the undercurrent of the rhetoric she denies herself simply playing at her speech organs: You bastard, here I am involved in the most Vicious Games of Capitalism at Publikon to get some degree of autonomy — for us both — let you forget your Material Situation so you can do your Intellectual Work; who found this place anyhow on her own initiative and who pays the rent, you seem to think that topping up the kitty every now and again with a few francs scrounged from your parents is enough to share the load and set the rules of the place and play Master when visitors come and all the time I say nothing. You say to them: Yeah, we had quite a find, must admit I've always been lucky in that way. And you make all the decisions on the decoration, decide which of my paintings are *convenable* and which are too disquieting and I say nothing. And now the aggressive rattle of the typewriter has resumed, charging and recharging and even if I found time to work (what about my deadline for Julienne towels?) I'd have to fight for a half-hour slot because, after all, your Discourse Analysis is more important but only yesterday you expressed surprise that I hadn't taken on more work this month.

Of course this is all petty and unreasonable: it's only because she's clenched against him that she can't think against his noise. He is oblivious to these little concerns and look who is thinking now that lunchtime is coming up and that she'd better do something about it, make maybe a *salade niçoise* and a mushroom omelette and that she'd better pack up her *gouaches*. He shuts the door on her in the kitchen so that if anyone comes, she's the one who is disturbed. Even if it's one of his own friends, he hisses through the crack of the door: Rita, tell him that I'm on the last lap and that I can't spare a moment and so she ends up trapped there, chatting desultorily to some stranger who has no particular place to go and who offers her a capricious analysis of her work in progress. Here is Sébastien now asking whether she has thought about lunch.

She says: Yes, that's why I'm packing up my paints, what do you think?

You're crazy to worry, we could go to the Resto-U. I feel like a break anyhow.

But the long walk there or waiting for buses would make just one more hole in her time: Really, it's no trouble, she says. I've already chopped the mushrooms.

Then she goes down for bread and cheese and ends up washing up because, after all, she was the one who insisted on eating in the flat. Now, at three in the afternoon, when she has managed to resume painting, he wants to wash. She has his gaze from the sink where he is splashing jugsful of water over his noble body, interfering with her brush, her painted space. Or when it's her in the tub, he'll burst into the kitchen from the landing; this was a quick, mechanically executed wash she was having, but now it's being assessed as peformance and sexual invitation. *Oh que c'est délicieux,* he says and cups her soapy buttocks in his hands, tries the consistency of the flesh and says: Oh-oh, Rita, you'd better watch out! You're actually starting to get some cellulite!

Once again, she is exposure of junkety flesh for his teasing analysis.

She tightens her muscles, tightens her throat, eats less, even

229

though she would defy him by becoming fat. Even her painting arranges itself against his premature scrutiny. It is becoming cramped now. Or else too full of nervy attempts made too late to loosen it. Over-painted. She hears him whistling up the stairs and a mad heart jumps within her, her pulse races and she defends the painting with one annihilating swipe of the turps rag. The paintings gelled in the foetal folds of that rag, the weight of them. And then, at night, his day having been uninterrupted by idle visits and petty domestic concerns, he will stretch in the frame of the kitchen door, grunt and give that prolonged yawn of satisfaction. Just as she is setting herself up again after the washing up and taking down the garbage for the morning collection: Ah, Rita, not bad going today, got ten pages done. I'm really starting to think I'll make it!

His heavy hand works the tense muscles of her neck, *Ah ma chérie,* he says. Of course, she thinks, of course he is innocent of the prisons she secretes around herself. The smell of his salty dark skin dilates her, her hand releases the brush. They are rolling together on the bed; laughter in the tumble of canopy and cushions.

At midnight she slips from under the weight of his thigh, sheltering, not possessive, she thinks this time, but there is a groan, as if in sleep he knew her abandonment as she creeps back for some criminal activity in the kitchen. Maybe this is just perversity. Maybe she can only work through a sense of transgression. He recognizes that aspect of her painting, coverts the energies he berates only half-jokingly as onanistic, developing and exploiting an excess not released in their sex together. There it is, developing a tenuous line, multiplying its knots and folds now into a billowing colour field, as if some atavistic repository had been tapped, unfolding within her and at last she feels something more collective, something beyond the accidents of her specific womanhood. She will snarl and hiss if necessary to defend this chance, this space.

Against him, the too enthusiastic carnivore, she buys the bloodless meat, the meatless meat. She will adhere to the outer form but cancel the contents.

In the kosher butcher's shop today, there is something about that knobbly back and the wild tumble of red-brown curls that gives her a slight pang. As she asks for her four hundred grams of veal, the head turns: it is Gérard. Shock of it. He is bronzed, even fleshed out a little. This is not the victim she created that day on the Cours Mirabeau in Aix. She registers a mild offence even that he can treat her with such easy warmth.

He is in a violet withered cotton shirt and has a tie-dyed scarf with little spangles. For once, Sébastien is not at home. Big day for him, offering a chapter of his thesis to a seminar on the reproduction of gender in advertising — she could tell him a few things about that if he'd bothered to ask. What has happened to them, she didn't even wish him good luck as he went off, she was so relieved to get some time on her own. And now she has shown this disarray seeing Gérard. Even the butcher seems amused as he calls her back: she has walked out without her veal.

She picks up a bottle of Côtes du Luberon, some *charcuterie,* cheese: Roquefort and Reblochon, and for bread, a *fougace,* its irregular holes make it a perfect grid for the *imprévu.* Lunch with Gérard. She has blown a few more francs than usual.

Rita, he laughs, you'd better be careful, you're developing a taste for the luxuries. You'll soon need a budget like Raymond's.

231

She has been staring at him. He knows it: he tracks her eyes to his biceps showing through the light cotton.

That's what you get for being on the end of a jack-hammer, he says. Working on a site on the Plaine. But what's . . . Hey, it's only just dawned on me. Since when the big move eh? Hey, you made a real strike, right in the middle of it all! It's crazy Rita, crazy, this is my favourite street: la Rue d'Aubagne. What kind of neighbours have you got? he asks as the light expires on the third landing.

His voice leaps and swings from one pliant twig to another, all nervous monkey exuberance, without ever waiting for a reply, it seems. Thérèse lives behind that door — tell Gérard? Later, later, there is time. Perhaps he is just biding his time for the real leap. He will want to know what her feelings towards him are now. He gives a slight wheeze and coughs to clear it as they reach the door, its label centred in the middle panel giving the evidence in Indian ink: Rita Finnerty/Sébastien Coustou. He's taken it in or has he? The silence as she searches for the key must be filled somehow:

There's a woman next door, you know, who reminds me of your mother . . . I mean what you wrote about your mother. She . . .

Gérard seems to be sneering in anticipation: What do you mean? You think she's crazy?

No. Come on, no. She's . . . beautiful. She makes me realize how much I've already eradicated from myself . . . Amputated. Sébastien though doesn't quite share . . .

She shouldn't have introduced Sébastien so quickly, brutally. Yet Gérard doesn't seem particularly perturbed or even surprised.

You know, Rita, he says, a lot of things have happened to me too. You don't need to worry about Sébastien. I guessed that. Bet he's loosened up since living with you. Certainly needed to. Not the coolest guy I've met.

She won't betray Sébastien to Gérard, though. Oh, *tu sais* . . . I can't say I've been exactly good for him. He's racing against a deadline for his thesis. Everything I do seems to make him tense these days. With that woman Cé . . . Thérèse, for instance . . . Oh, he found her quite intriguing at first: she fitted his sense of himself in bohemia.

Wow, what a place, Gérard says. Far cry from the hotel bedroom sort of digs you had in Aix. Sorry, go on. What about this

. . . Thérèse?

Why isn't Gérard listening? He used to savour every syllable. Now he is dosing Rita with uncommitted *ahs* and *vraiments* and *pas vrais* . . .

Oh, Rita says, she brought me some lung for the cat I have curled up in my brain, to let him breathe, she said. Some garlic gargle . . . Yes, go ahead Gérard, the cork-screw is in the top drawer on the left. Well yeah, at first Sébastien was tolerant, even amused but just lately he's been saying he can't understand why I want to waste my time on such a self-indulgent wretch. Oh, I make him sound . . . I make it sound crueller than it was because . . . She is a wretch, if you like, in the real sense. She lives behind that door I pointed out. Some people have bigger walk-in robes than that. Raymond does. No direct source of natural light. She'll arrive in the early hours of the morning with a tureen of soup . . . mainly lettuce and garlic, a mirage of a memory of something . . . Pastis and Eau de Cologne on her breath . . . She says that what my husband doesn't like . . .

Hey, how do you react when she calls Sébastien your husband? Oh, you know, coming from Céleste . . .

Mais enfin . . . Rita! From Thérèse!

Yes yes. From Thérèse I mean. Sorry.

If the slip has made him angry, he doesn't show it.

No, it doesn't bother me coming from her. Because of a certain delicacy, I suppose. Doesn't want to offend me by the inference that it's *concubinage* — that's probably all it is. In the midst of all she'll take me off for a dance amongst the paints and jars of brushes in the kitchen . . .

But Rita, I don't get it. I don't get you at all. Honestly, if you are painting in the kitchen when it's obviously in here . . . I mean this room's the obvious place for a studio . . .

There is a strange querying light in Gérard's eyes. But, Rita thinks, Gérard does care. He wouldn't burst in on her and Thérèse with my DEAR ladies, do you have ANY idea . . . I for one would like some sleep, *I* have a heavy day ahead of me . . .

But perhaps he is simply disgusted that she should indulge in this dishonest kind of masochism.

Oh, Sébastien's been having trouble with his eyes. When he's finished the thesis, perhaps we can swap over again.

Yes. Perhaps, perhaps, Gérard says. Show me some of your

work. No, really, I'd like to see where you're at.

Rita rummages in her folios for longer than is necessary. Cheeks ablaze. This is it: the drawing she calls *Céleste*. Perhaps she shouldn't show it. Gérard believed in her when she wasn't looking for style. But it's . . . Well, an effort of tenderness. She should offer it. But she balks, tries to defend it with words before the exposure.

Drawing Thérèse, you know, taught me more than anything. She talked, talked all the time. Your husband, she said, he has heavy things in his head, the poor man. But you and me . . . We are lighter. We can get through the cracks of their thinking, those big lumpy boulders, wiggle our way through. Slip through the gaps and breaches like the shadows of cats. As she talked, I let it take over and found I was dealing with faces and more and more faces below the outer face and somehow . . . I think I managed to avoid the easy habits, you know, the pet gestures of my usual stuff . . .

So easy, such a trap, isn't it, becoming routine? Gérard says.

It is, it is . . .

Rita fingers his arm. No, she musn't do this; he'll think she's trying to restore old possibilities . . . For want of direction, her hand explores her own cheek, pretends to find an itch there. She clamps the drawing onto her board: suddenly now, there it is. Like something she once saw and rejected in Laurence. The cloud face, glimpse of another kind of sensibility that refuses easy affirmations. Translucent network of veiny branches and behind that, shifting screens, differently featured, more and more opaque, the outer features undone by the multiple nimbus.

Umm, Gérard says, umm. Rita, I'd forgotten, or maybe I never realized just how . . .

What?

How . . . Well, how romantic you are.

Rita startled. Anyhow, who's romantic? Wasn't *Céleste* Gérard's story once.

You are 'sincere', I know, he says, softening his mouth, moistening it. But . . . You're still, I don't know . . . Taking refuge in . . . the picturesque? Don't you think? Look, I don't want to put it down. It's quite beautiful, 'beautiful', he says, stressing the quotation marks, pinching the air. Trick he got from Sébastien, she thinks. No, I mean. You should take it out in real life. It's not all that easy.

What do you mean?

Hey, Rita. I don't want to get agro with you. I didn't want to offend you. It's just that . . . I mean, just as an exercise, why don't you let your images take a walk in real life. I mean . . . Say, what would happen if you took this Thérèse of yours somewhere like . . . Raymond's for dinner, say. Just the very night when he has people there he wants to impress. With his mastery, you know, the way he likes to be the perfect host. But this sort of thing is very easy for you. You keep her to your kitchen. Maybe you even get some sense of rebellion out of it because Sébastien doesn't approve. No, sorry, that's a bit hard. But still . . . This woman has real material circumstances. Okay. You say pastis and Eau de Cologne and lettuce soup and garlic gargle. But no doubt she's had a past. She's probably had an occasional job. Pension problems. Seen something of a sex life. Eh? But what do you do with all that? You celebrate some sort of fairy spirit. It's not that pretty. She's . . . Okay. She's alienated. But she's a woman who has been alienated. Your drawing suppresses all that. And just a moment ago, you romanticized her soup. But what about the thousands like her, here in Marseille alone, who wake up with the hunger still there and who try to trick their bellies with some watery concoction. Your drawing promotes the . . .

What are you trying to say, Gérard? The Eternal Feminine?

No, no, he laughs. I wouldn't go that far. But you could have suggested the stinking reality of what she's been through. You've made a dreamy creature for the living-rooms of your bourgeois aesthetes like Raymond and all those other professors of yours.

They're not my professors, Gérard!

Oh, but you've still got that whole trip to reckon with, haven't you? The Maurice Galants who spend their time bootlicking high society bitches to get sales for their pet artists so they can make their fat commission.

I didn't give a damn if I sold nothing!

But I gather the exhibition was quite a success. One of Maurice's mates gave it quite a rave in the *Provençal*.

Gérard. I didn't work to sell. The direction was already there when you were helping me. And I didn't paint for the critics. That was really a bit much . . . That was . . .

No, I didn't mean to be cruel. I just figured that this new kind of . . . spirituality might be some sort of compensation. I mean you can't like that gallery scene. It must be getting to you, anyhow. Otherwise you wouldn't react like that. Hell, I'm sorry. I always respected you as someone who wouldn't delude herself and . . . Well, you seem to have, like, areas of blindness about where you are at the moment.

All the same, what you're accusing me of amounts to bad faith.

Bad faith! Come on! I don't get my kicks any more hanging that kind of label on people. No . . . It's just maybe . . . You could take a cue from that Thérèse there. That 'yowling cat' she talks about. You seem to be stifling the very thing that was great in your work. Like that over there. The one with the three panels. Bet you did that a while back.

What are you suggesting then? Social realism?

What do you take me for? The sort of thing I'm talking about is what *you* showed me. The way you played with contradictions. Like you'd have a pretty bland surface and underneath, all these other things that wouldn't be so easily slicked over. But this drawing . . . It's sort of . . . over-achieved. Resolved. The problems are solved from the beginning. No, that's not it. They're not there at all: they're deleted from the beginning.

Mmm. You're right in a way. It's true. But you're not right about Raymond. I mean, his criticism only got to me because that's where I was at the time. In any case, he's making himself pretty scarce these days. When I first moved in here, I asked him for dinner. It was pretty obvious I had it just about ready: chicken in its flour, chopped vegetables all over the place. But there was no way he was going to stay. He rushed in rattling his keys, saying he had better things in mind than watching me over a hot stove — he'd booked a table at a restaurant. Well, you know, at first I just saw it as his reclaiming the right to be Master of Ceremonies.

You wouldn't be far wrong there. I mean, it's an aspect of his generosity we've all . . .

No, anyhow. I also thought he couldn't stand the slumminess of the place. And being a visitor to a *ménage* that didn't immediately rely on him. But he said he really thought it was better if he left it to us for the time being. Since we were trying to make it together.

What a cheek! *Trying!*

Oh . . . you know . . . He's not far wrong there. Anyhow, since then, he seems to have taken stock. But there's an awful kind of sadness about him these days. And if he catches you watching him, he summons up this sort of high frivolity. Which is even worse. The most he reproaches me with is having taken on Sébastien when . . . Well so quickly. Impulsively. Just when . . .

When?

Oh, in the past, I suppose I often talked about my need for space. You know, space to myself.

Was he right?

Who?

Was Raymond right in saying it was all too quick? Really, it's pretty obvious, Rita. *Ça saute aux yeux enfin.*

What?

That you're not happy: it's obvious.

Oh. I might complain. I suppose there are always conflicts at the beginning. I do love him. But . . . I don't know whether . . . Maybe I just can't live with anyone. I find it hard to contain myself when he . . . censors me. He censors me. All the time. He oppresses me . . .

Maybe this is simply his sympathy making her talk like this. Perhaps just the wine. To be happy. *Make happiness a value . . .* That was Laurence. Way back, she said that.

No, Rita says. It's just that he's so big and the place is pretty small, really. He takes up all my space. I can't think, I can't paint, I can't breathe . . . I know I'm betraying him right now because, I mean, if I explained it all to him, he'd probably be the first to understand. And it's all petty, really. I just build up resentment at the way he takes over. But I don't want to bust it. I know it's wrong, dishonest of me. I asked him if he'd like to move in. Let him have this room. But somehow I didn't expect him to move in so . . . totally!

He is laughing. She has him laughing.

You know, she says, I thought he'd be absent some of the time.

Well, he is now, he says. Seems pretty absent to me.

But look at it: his piles of books, his desk in the middle of the room, all those machines, record player motors and things he reckons he can fix up when he gets the right parts, you know, he says he's always been a good *bricoleur,* just look at it, all dismantled on the floor and then the clothes he steps out of, that he leaves in heaps all over the place hoping some benign fairy will come along . . . And then he sends me up for being *une petite femme d'interieur bourgeoise.* Oh, he tells me that I have better things to do than his laundry. Seems astonished that I should bother . . .

Well, Rita. It does sound to me as if *you've* got a problem there. It's just a matter of being a bit more frank, isn't it?

Oh yes, I know. I've got to stifle the impulse to peck in his wake like Mother Hen. I never thought I could be like that . . . Oh Gérard. I shouldn't be carrying on like this to you . . .

Stop being so bloody . . . Of course you've got to talk about it. Jesus, this cheese is pretty strong! Look, what I'm trying to say is what you recognize yourself. You can't go on storing it up. It doesn't give him a chance either. Something's going to bust and I bet it's you if you don't have it out with him.

Yes, I know. But . . . What about you, anyhow? You haven't told me what you've been up to. Or . . .

Ah. Well it took me a while to get over *you,* if that's what you mean. No, it's okay. I realize it was a ridiculous thing to ask of you anyhow. Marriage is the last thing anyone should ask of you. Obviously . . .

Obviously . . . So he has come to conclusions, sees her as unfit. And in any case, I've grown up a little bit over the past year . . . Work?

Mmmm? What? Oh, sure, work's got something to do with it, I suppose. Mainly North Africans I work with. Algerians, a few Tunisians. Learning a few things through them. The way a French guy like me has to play it . . . Not to get the bosses' hackles up against me, I mean, without becoming his ally. Give you an example. I'm there for a week, right? I already get entrusted with the most expensive machinery. And with promises of a quick rise to foreman if I keep it up. I mean, I could point to a dozen Arab blokes who've been on the job for two years or more and who've probably been much more competent than me from the beginning. Arabs and machines don't mix too good, the boss says. He laughs and slaps me on the back. Filthy bastards they are too, he says, take in a bottle of water with them when they go to the bog, clean their bums with that, never heard of paper. Use my toilet, he tells me. And by the way, sonny boy, I'd watch your wallet. Can't trust these bastards an inch.

Oh, surely, Rita says. It can't be as flagrant as that!

Oh *surely* it can! That's tame compared to some of the obscenities I've had to listen to. Anyhow, that's the least of their problems. Every time there's a police check, you know, a sort of routine ceremony they carry out on all the work sites, the Arabs who don't have work permits have to scatter. Everyone knows they're here without papers — Pompidou and his lackeys know it, they rely on it for the economy. Lots of cheap muscle. No social security costs with these guys. And there's a virtual curfew on them after work. They have to stay in the hovels the boss designates for them when they're first recruited and arrive in Marseille . . . Things are very slowly starting to happen, though. Very slowly, because a lot of them are pretty hard to stir up, they're so scared. And they find it hard to see that anything much will come out of political struggle. I mean, these guys have always ended up at the bottom of the heap. They're still colonized really. And the problem is, as far as the bosses are concerned, these men are always replaceable. There'd have to be a big chain of strikes to make any impression. Strikes, I mean involving French workers and migrants *with* papers. Anyhow, that's what we're aiming at . . . Plus rallies, street theatre, hunger strikes if necessary . . .

We. The *we* of solidarity. He has cut short. Vague unfocused shine in his eyes.

Putain, Rita. I haven't even noticed. You've got me a bit drunk. You must've kept filling my glass. And I've been raving on. Must sound like a load of hot air to you.

No. No, of course it doesn't. *I* do nothing. Nothing.

But you could, you *can* do something. I mean, you already have. Look, I was harsh about that drawing. Might also have something to do with my anger about . . . Oh, forget it. There's so much you can show them in your work. Things they don't want to know . . . About . . . female power.

Her work for Publikon. If he knew about that. The towel advertisement. Slip into a Julienne. *Caressez-la, enfilez-la.*

You could insist that Galant hang that for instance, now that you've established yourself.

The triptych? Oh sure, that's got a lot of revolutionary potential, that does a fat lot for oppressed workers!

He shrugs his shoulders. *O là là,* he laughs. Everything is swimming. He tries to prop himself up, misjudges the position of the cushion. I got a bit shaken, I guess, he says, bumping into you like that.

You hid it well. I felt a bit offended really. I mean, you seemed pretty casual. But I know I had no right . . .

Pas vrai, pas vrai . . . Not true at all . . .

There is a heavy clomping getting closer with a metallic click in it, *pas vrai*, Gérard is still murmuring, you know that's not right, Rita. But he must have heard it too — it has to be Sébastien — past the fourth landing now, must be getting to the spiral stairs, it's him all right, he has a loose metal protector on his boot heel.

Who's that?

Gérard's amplified whisper won't allay Sébastien's suspicions, if he has any. But why should he, anyhow? Gérard clutches at her arm: *C'est lui? C'est Sébastien?*

Act innocent. Must act innocent. They are innocent. Yes, yes, Gérard? she says.

But they haven't been warned early enough and the kitchen door is being opened . . . Their knees are too close for it to be a fraternal reunion. Oh . . . too bad, he'll have to accept her fondness for Gérard. It's not as if he's a rival. The metal crescent of the boot is scraping against the kitchen tiles. What evidence have they left in there? The pink and white waxed paper from the *charcuterie*, the wine cork still in the screw . . . The shadow across her peripheral vision already. And this arrangement here: their too sudden readjustment on the cushions . . .

Sébastien has stiffened with that martial look. Unshelled mollusc with the first shock, now withdrawn under that horny shield. He'd come in wanting to tell her about the seminar. He's flinching a little, trying to summon up something of a welcome to Gérard, long time no see kind of thing, cool, it's cool finding you both together here drinking in the middle of the afternoon, I'm sure you're aware of the effrontery of it, no need for me to make any allusion to that, but don't think, Gérard, that I'm so sexually insecure with Rita that there's any problem for me in her spending time with another bloke. The pupils dart around. Finally, finally he is going to speak.

Mais Gérard, mon vieux . . .

The left hand still holding the briefcase which he might have put down in the kitchen as the right hand stretches out for the greeting. Sébastien leans slightly forward from the hips but the knees remain stiff so that Gérard has to rise. He brings himself to a partial crouch on one heel. Welcome him, they must welcome him. Not sustain this incriminating freeze.

Salut Seb. *Tu prends à boire?* There's some other wine in the kitchen.`

Why not? I can see I've got a bit of catching up to do! Been at it for a while, you two?

His laughter is a quick nasal burst. By the time she comes back with his drink, this tension will have been dissolved. But all they seem to manage while she is away is a bit of throat clearing and a couple of *ça va's*. And now she and Gérard come out with it like two kids caught playing truant: We ran into one another in the butcher's shop, they say. Poor duo performance, judging by the way Sébastien is working away at his jaw muscles.

Not the most inspiring setting eh? he says.

Well, no. But it's pretty nice here! At least Gérard can manage something like a relaxed smile.

How did it go? Rita tries for a soft earnest tone but it doesn't quite achieve conjugal sympathy. Ah, she says to Gérard. Sébastien was giving a seminar today.

Do you really want to know?

But . . . Of course I do . . . *Enfin!*

Oh, they gave me a pretty hard time. But I guess it was well enough received.

He's not going to play that game. Not going to let her little ruse work its effect. She can't rely on infantile appeals to his ego. He has read the scene. His constant blinking: like a nictitator cutting frame after frame through the fixed stare. This silence. Bones creaking.

Alors Gérard, he says. *Qu'est-ce que tu deviens?* Formal patriarchal tone he has assumed. It says: *How do you account for yourself? As you can see by my briefcase which I have placed at my foot, my relative sobriety and the mention of the seminar, I have come from serious pursuits. I think more than the mention of a butcher's shop meeting might be necessary to justify your presence here.*

Must say, he says, I thought you would have shot through to Morocco by now.

Gérard has relaxed again into the cushions on the floor. No attempt to cancel the first impression his pose would have given.

Ah yes, I was tempted for a while. But a few things happened to make it worth my while hanging around here a while longer. I'll give Marseille a bit of a go. Reckon I should congratulate you though . . .

Why? What on? I can't see what warrants that.

Sébastien practically hissed it. Hostile. No humour. Pompous bastard. Just as Thérèse says: heavy, heavy presence. *Trouble-fête.* Wet blanket.

Oh . . . (Red ellipse of Gérard's wine sloping dangerously towards the rim of his glass.) You two have got yourselves a good set-up.

Gérard flutters his fingers about to summarize the decor,

glances up at the bulbous sags of the hessian ceiling Sébastien strung up to catch the falling plaster.

You've got an ideal little spot for your work there too.

He nods towards the desk with the litter of wires around it. Was that a wink in Rita's direction?

Hmm, says Sébastien. Yes. We had a stroke of luck in finding this place.

We, we. That line again, he's out to show the inviolable solidarity of the union. Symbiotically entwined *we* are. We have been coordinated for some time, let that be known, Gérard. We are the fused subject and agent of our destiny.

You certainly did! Gérard sings.

Sébastien is too smart a linguist not to recognize that intonation as a send-up of his own. He lurches away from the desk, makes towards the kitchen. Rita throws a panicked look at Gérard, *help, help*.

There's still some Reblochon left, it's a beauty, a real ponger, she says to Sébastien. She gets a growl from him:

Rita, cut the frivolity. Surely you're not so insensitive that you can't see that this might just need some sort of explanation. I want to know what that little turd is doing here!

How dare you call him that!

I want to know what this is all about!

Ssshht!

I don't care whether that little prick hears or not!

Ssshhh! Please, I beg you, Sébastien. You know he's got much more cause to be resentful than you. Gérard was your friend once, wasn't he? Surely I'm allowed to be fond of him? Or... Maybe I've read you all wrong! Maybe it's a monopoly you wanted all along...

Stop spitting and calm down. You might care to reflect a little on your own behaviour . . . when you sober up. For someone constantly invoking her *own* sensitivity, you've got a sublime disregard of my feelings.

I don't see why you have to react like this, that's all. Just because you come in here uptight from a seminar, your academic ego slightly bruised by your hair-splitting colleagues, doesn't mean you have to take his being here as a personal affront, something that threatens your so ELEVATED mode of being!

Thanks very VERY much. You've taken things a little too far this time, Rita Finnerty. If that's really how you think of me, all I can say is that you must have been hypocritical all this time!

SALUT!

The last syllable came out like a yelp. He is gone. The door has slammed so hard that it is still trembling, reopens slightly. A little piece of plaster crumbles away, falls at her feet. She is clutching the edge of the sink when Gérard's hands take her shoulders, pull her around.

My God. I had no idea he ... I'm sorry. I should have left ages ago.

Don't you be sorry!

She has shouted it, finds herself glowering at him. She tries to annul the violent effect; her voice is softer this time: Don't you be sorry. You have nothing to be sorry for. If he's so perverse to see things that way, too bad for him. *Tant pis pour lui.* Come on, let's go back in and sit down. Have another glass of wine. Just because he's so ... pathologically jealous. He can't stand anyone else being present the moment he thinks he needs me. That's what I've become for him, an environment, that he wants to walk in and out of at his own leisure, fill with flattering-mirrors-all-bespeaking-his-Beauty-and-Brilliance ... Any other presence brings on a tantrum. Or else a bout of petulance. That's really what he objects to with Thérèse. Just because I like her. He can't stand the thought of my spending my time or emotional energy on anyone but himself. And even Raymond ... He's jealous of Raymond. That's why Raymond is so uncomfortable with us these days ...

Gérard studies his fingers. *Ecoute,* Rita ... Listen, he says. I should be going. He'll be coming back. I think you should ... Well, give yourself a chance to confront him calmly.

No, no. Gérard. That's how he got rid of Denise, when she came here. Remember Denise? I hadn't seen her in ages. We drank, ate, listened to some rock I can't have on when he's around. I laughed for the first time in ages. Sébastien comes in, takes one look and the first thing he thinks is how to dismantle the scene. Denise makes a crack at his ministerial demeanour, you know, with the briefcase and his grey trousers and she's had it. Sébastien tells me that if I want to get those drawings to the framers on time, that I'd better grab the opportunity. That he has a mate waiting in a van below. If Denise wants a lift, then they can drop her off on the way. Well, it becomes obvious that there's been no such arrangement with his friend. He was genuinely astonished

244

to see me coming out with my drawings and canvasses. It had just been an on-the-spot inspiration to break up a little party that seemed to exclude him.

Oh-oh Rita! Sounds as if you're being just a little bit paranoid there! Calm down. Calm down a bit. It can't be as bad as that. But really, I'd better be going.

She has become ugly in his eyes. That's what it is. Her tirade. Her spiteful betrayal. He's leaving. Their fingers come together for a moment in an apex. They kiss briefly. She feels this aching restraint that she knows she will wonder about later.

I really *must* go, he says. I'm sorry all this has happened. But you'll sort it out. You will, I'm sure. He's a passionate guy. It's hard to find that in anyone, you know . . . Without the possessiveness as well. I really must go . . . I'll catch up with you again soon . . . I should . . . Ah . . . There's also someone I don't want to hurt. This girl . . . Solange . . . We've been together for a while now. She'll be wondering where in the hell I've got to. And anyhow, I don't want to do any more damage here . . .

Gérard. Gérard in control. He can afford to listen charitably. He's immune now. The scandal of her own presumptions comes to her like an iron slug in the lung. Her little victim! The outrage of that reduction doesn't prevent the staggering voluptuousness of the shock. Now there is the whine and creak of the door hinges. Sébastien again? He has or hasn't seen that kiss. How long has he been there? She can hear his breathing as he pauses in the kitchen. It doesn't matter now. She has gone too far. That's Gérard's voice, discreet, muffled: I was just going. Sorry about all this. You've got nothing to worry about . . . Really. But I'm sure you don't want my version right now.

Allez. Ciao.

Now this terrible silence. Sébastien must have sat down in the kitchen. He makes the chair screech on the tiles. He must be breaking a crust she has left there in her rapid preparation of lunch for Gérard. He has probably eaten nothing. They have eaten most of it too: the *jambon de Corse,* the *pâté en croûte.* Only the Reblochon in a stinking slouch in here. Now, in a few minutes' time they will be going through it all again. Tedium, fatigue of it. This past they have accumulated in a year. All the resentments will be laid out on the table once again. Better nothing than this noxious density. Better a void. This claustrophobia they have created. Try to think it through. He is silent in the kitchen. Sick too at the thought of another confrontation. The look she gave him when he first came in, that must have been it. She can still reproduce the sharpness in the retina when she gave it. She really cut him out from the beginning. Even Gérard said she was paranoid. The way she has struck off the good times, the moments of real euphoria they have had. This room is more than his imposition on her. The hatstand there with all the cloaks and shawls, even a top hat and a boater they found in the street. It's not so long ago that he joined her and Thérèse in a silly music hall routine with those. The coloured sea-glass bottles on the mantelpiece. The wild tendrils caught in the gilt grid in his Islamic hanging over the bed. The dialogue he accepts between her *Woodpigeon Triptych* and Laurence's *Inscape.*

Her rebellious mutism, Laurence's quiescent music. The

billowing hessian ceiling he rigged up. That was quite an inspiration. It all looks a bit desolated now, in the late afternoon light. But they were gestures they made towards one another. Gestures of optimism. Pseudo-bohemian perhaps. But at least they believed then.

Maybe it's a mistake coming to him so soon like this. He is still sitting facing the kitchen wall. Dark, sad, clenched. He doesn't look up.

Alors, he says. The voice is adenoidal and blurred. Has he been crying?

Alors, je ne sais pas . . . she says. I just don't know why you have to react like that.

Don't you? Don't you really. You . . . *la grande intuitive,* you wouldn't have the faintest why I might get a bit upset. I rush home, longing to see you and I get greeted with a glaring look . . . Medusa has nothing on you! A look that froze me in my tracks. It was quite obvious that you both resented me coming home when I did. But you . . . No, I really think you weren't aware. I refuse to believe that you're as monstrous as that. And then you take to me like a wildcat, you're so carried away with that little fop, that lay-about, you probably wanted to stir things up with me, provoke a fight to show him I was quite dispensable. To let him see you were readily available. No, no, don't protest, just listen for a minute. Your problem is that you're so attentive to the . . . to the *seismograph of your own sensitivity* that you never listen to anyone else. And drinking doesn't help, you know. You should take a look at yourself. *Tu deviens fripée.* You're showing it. You're starting to show it. You're drying up and your skin is red. The way you're going you won't even be able to seduce little pansies like Gérard pretty soon.

SÉBASTIEN! How dare you! How can you be so . . . Piling abuse on me is one thing. You know damn well Gérard is no pansy, as you put it, and even if he were . . . I never thought you would stoop to that macho thug stuff. Someone you once professed to be your friend! Maybe you just feel a little insecure because he's not as worshipful of your GREATNESS as you would have liked . . .

That is *so* vicious that I'm not going to stoop to comment.

(The great Sébastien is not going to stoop to comment. *No comments,* he says as he pushes past the reporters with his

247

defence lawyer . . .)

Oh, the great Sébastien is not . . .

What? Say it. Say it!

His fist comes down on the table. The salt jumps out of the eggcup, an olive rolls off the greaseproof paper. It makes a scuttling movement across the floor. For a moment she wants to laugh. She must cool down. Not provoke him. That's a form of violence too. There's a conté crayon here, a scrap of paper. Draw, doodle, anything. That there could have been such recesses of hatred festering. The folds within the coils of the brain . . . Her hand is not completely in control and the conté crayon skids — the paper is greasy from the butter left there. How can he expect her to work in the kitchen? Keep at it though, she should keep at it, it makes her less available for whatever charge he's going to lay on her now . . .

Go on. Plunge into your obsessional doodles! I suppose all that visceral stuff is dedicated to your little Gérard too . . .

Thanks. Thanks a lot. This visceral stuff as you put it is not dedicated to anyone.

Ah no. I don't suppose it is. It's just a little wank you're having. But as far as wank goes, it looks pretty violent to me. Rita, I really wish you'd lay off the wine. Look around, look at it. Look at the stuff you've been producing lately: it's . . . out of control.

He is enjoying this. He knows, he really knows where to attack so that it hurts. The doodle is now a blurred entanglement through the tears.

She keeps her head down so that he won't get that satisfaction.

You might say it's out of control, she says. Maybe what you mean is that it's out of your control. And you're jealous of any expression . . . any action of mine that doesn't ask for your sanction. What I'm trying to explore . . . Well, it's my need for a space. Space that you deny me. You can call it violence if you like. What I've tried to show in these paintings is a potential . . . A potential for movement outside the boundary, outside the frame. And what there is inside is only a mark. An impulse that might look violent because of its concentration. That's why I have small centres of activity and then these . . . sketched in . . . ways out. And in any case, if the quality of the work is suffering, it's not because of alcohol, as you'd like to prove. Okay. I might have had too much today . . . But I don't have the best circumstances. Look at this: a fantastic studio! And you take over my space, you invade it, you fill it, you fill it, YOU FILL IT . . . You oppress me. You burst in with your comments all the time before I've really got into something . . . You're judging it before I've even stained the canvas . . .

You . . . do . . . me . . . an injustice there . . .

Sébastien's slow-motion solemnity. Even now, he has to bloat himself up with rhetoric.

You, he is saying. You saw me jumping about more excited than anyone when you had that exhibition. And when the reviews came in, I was the one who wanted to celebrate. You couldn't have had anyone more supportive . . .

Yeah? And so why do you write off all this as *wank,* as you so delicately put it?

But Rita, come on. I was only trying to appeal to your objectivity. I don't think this work you've been doing lately is up to your normal standard. All I was pleading with you for is to try and cut down on the wine a bit . . . It's . . . You're becoming self-indulgent . . .

(Look who's in control. How nicely he articulates the problem. The distance he can take . . .)

You're painting out of the same little obsession . . . The SAME . . . LITTLE . . . OBSESSION over and over again. I mean, look at what you've just been drawing, it's the same thing again. What do you want? Yourself? Perpetuated, non-stop? Your female interiors. All those *vagina dentata* . . . all those kilometres of . . . well, it's like Michelin tyre tread. Over the past couple of months, I don't know, you seem to have been chain-producing the same . . . Amazonian fantasy is what you'd call it, I suppose . . .

Go on. Call it that. Call it what you want.

Her voice is drugged and slow. Can't, she can't struggle anymore. Get . . . crawl away from him . . .

Anyhow, why not? Why shouldn't I be producing Amazonian fantasies? Why shouldn't I? After centuries and centuries of male-dominated art, with all its nudes laid out: acres and acres of fleshy fields for your voyeuristic pleasure . . .

What you're saying is borrowed anyhow. Don't think I can't recognize that. That's the John Berger I gave you to read. Funny how you feminists have to resort to male intellectuals to support your claims. And you can't even quote them right.

Okay, okay, I don't care whether it's a man or a woman. I'm not as crudely polemical as you'd like me to be. At least he's a bit more sensitive about . . . It's all right. Let's leave it at that. I'm a set of plagiarisms, I paint decadent, repetitive wank, thus spake the Great Semiotician . . .

It seems *in vino veritas* has got something going for it! Go on, go on, have some more wine!

He marches over to the bench, returns with bottle and glass. Slams the glass down in front of her, pours, keeps pouring, it's going right over the rim now, onto her drawing, now it's trickling down, uncoiling onto her lap, onto the canvas jeans that Raymond bought her for the opening, let it flow, let him go to the limits of his viciousness, it's pooling around her feet, soaking into the leather of her sandals, between her toes . . .

Drink it! Drink! The painter must drink! Any more home truths! *In vino veritas, n'est-ce pas!*

Get out. GET OUT!

The horror of the hoarse whisper that just came out.

Ah no. There you've got it wrong *Miss* Finnerty. You get out.

You get out Sébastien! I'm asking you. This is my flat, anyhow. Who pays the rent? Eh? Who has paid it all along?

Oh. No! I don't believe that you'd stoop to that. You know damn well how much money I've put in, if you want to resort to cheap material arguments . . .

I know how little you've put in . . . And I never cared until . . . Until you began strutting about as Maestro, bossing me, pushing my visitors out, imprisoning me here in the kitchen so that you don't get disturbed by your own callers . . . Okay. I will get out. You've made it your flat. There's no room for me here any longer. I wish you luck with the rent — it's gone up you know. It's three hundred francs and not fifty as you seem to imagine.

She must get to the door: the room is lurching, maybe it's just this awful pressure behind her eyes, she must get away from him, maybe Raymond will help, she can come back later for her things, her paints, her work, no, he wouldn't be quite so vicious as to slash her paintings. Get out first, onto the street, away from him . . . Blast shock and weight of it, this coming down on her shoulders, no it can't be, this tugging at the roots of her hair, he is really doing it, could laugh, could laugh but can't, this is caveman stuff, her skull will pull off, he would look odd, if a caller caught him like that, a red-haired skull in his hand, and now the blows, leaden weight of his fists, is that her screaming, and what's this, he's sobbing while he's dealing them out, sobbing her name, he's gone mad, *Raymond, Raymond, your* enfant terrible, *look at him, he's going to kill me,* the walls, her inner cheeks clapping around her, her teeth hitting the tiles, pink, red, pink, red, black, red and all these sparks, thud, thud, thud, no that can't be her head surely, up and down again, the tiles lurching up and down, her brain is being pushed out, it's going to haemorrhage soon, she won't be able to see anymore, won't be able to paint, this is not her, he's not doing this to her, it's a bad dream, she will get out of this, she is hovering above it all, no, but it's outrageously painful, it's all swarming now, stretching light, concertina'd into dark again, where are her muscles though, frightened animals have an adrenalin rush, why can't she run, no strength, he will end soon, surely, the blows are starting to flag, slowing down, his sobs are louder, separate with these ridiculous hiccups in between, why is he sobbing HELP ME HELP ME RIIITAHAHA, but still the skull is cracking, was that it splitting then and thud, another time, but that's not her now, it's him, on the floor too, he's stupid, why is he on the floor too and this is his bloated face in the blur, that howl, it can't be the *sapeurs pompiers* coming, who would have phoned them, it's coming from him, it's not a siren, it's subsiding now and he is trying to say something, make some sort of noises begging forgiveness, too much hurting to twist or raise her head . . .

Sébastien, I'm asking you to go now. Go now. Please . . .

Did she say that?

The bird's beak is gagged, caught in the inner pockets of the thicket. Snagged claws curl. Compost generating its own kind of heat. Drops of blood congeal like perfect berries on the twigs. Thicket festering: it's all the dropped bodies of the little birds. In the inner pockets, the heat builds up, explosive. The ginger cat prowls; careful poise of its front paw. The movement of skin over rib-cage. See the amber eyes, the pure cognac of them through the cross-hatching of the thicket. The cat goes deeper in: feather flutter, snapping twigs and a long high shriek.

Thérèse walks past, maintaining a steady profile. The violet glow from her eyes lights up the thicket. Her cloudy hair invades it like a mist. It is her singing: alpine, crystalline, as poignant as a song from Auvergne. The marmalade cat is on her shoulder now. It turns its head slowly towards Rita, slowly, slowly as it finishes the song. It's the sound of the wood-pigeon in the last glissando of its purr. Its breath condenses in the air. A toy puff detaches itself and floats Rita's way. Rich luxuriant stench of it. The cat winks slowly.

It says: A small slaughter. Just enough to convert them to music, poor strangled things. Doing no one any good as they were, were they?

But how did you learn?

Oh, she's taught me a few things! says the cat. Far better to risk offence than to fence it in and let it fester, don't you think?

Prrahourrahrou! Prah! Prrrah!

There is a slither across the balcony: straight vertical tail and arched back. It darts the cutting glare of its eyes towards Rita. It nuzzles the glass. Elongated Burmese head. It ambles off. Grinding gears, trumpeting horns coming up the Rue d'Estelle, hard climb, that one, into the Rue d'Aubagne, one blaring out the *Marseillaise*. Now there is a massive crescendo and a prolonged finale. Must be a traffic jam. What time? What day? There are soft arching things below her. She must have somehow made it here after he . . . She's on the cushions now. They chose the fabric and stuffed and sewed these together. The imprint of the weave, it must be that on her cheek. Corrugations there. How long has it been? How did he get away? Did he go?

What if . . . Head too heavy and tongue filling mouth. Furry. Terrible. *Gueule de bois?* No, not simply hang-over. Something else. Her fingers explore her face for torn flesh, odd protuberances. No ragged meat? Bulbous swelling will come, perhaps. And earlier, was that in a dream too: her strung up and rotting on a hook and there was Soutine, wild, red urgency of his face, pluck-prodding at his palette, puncturing the dobs of paint sealed in their overnight skin, she noticed, *untidy worker,* she thought, and then he was saying: Love this shredded flesh with cellulite when it's gone to the dogs, it says it all. Then he picked his teeth, dark and heavily textured.

Bits of blood there on her cheek all the same. His knuckles, or perhaps his ring caught her there. And then, the cracking against the tiles? Her brain? Brain not split at least, no blood from there. No flakes dried on matted hair or bone splinters. But that smell like a ripe open carcass. Something has died, something killed after all. Gérard, it was Gérard she was with when he came . . . Over there, on the oak plank in an unctuous spread, the Reblochon. The black briefcase, still against the jamb of the door, its pores shut tight. Inscrutable leather. Sébastien. This silence. Normally he's a noisy breather, so he can't be here. He's gone, all the same. Got efficiently away. Or maybe outside, collapsed on the stairs? Thérèse would find him there. Administer some potion, drag him in. Where would he run? Not to his parents, no. Wouldn't show them the bloated tear-stained face. No, he's made it: first tertiary educated bloke in the family. Wouldn't show them that he's been thrown out by *une petite australienne.* He's got mates, that Thierry with the van, for instance. No, too proud to blunder into their place. Raymond? Raymond would always open to him.

Help me! Help me! Sébastien would say through the intercom. The glass doors would open, the lift would take him up. Get some sleep now, we'll talk about it tomorrow, Raymond would say. He would throw him some sheets, blankets for the sofa. A brief hug. Enough for Sébastien to say: Look what I've done to her! Can't believe I've busted it like this! And Raymond, soothing, but struggling against tiredness all the same: Well it won't be the first melodrama you've staged. We'll talk about it tomorrow, all right? And Sébastien will get his story in over breakfast. Tell Raymond how she provoked him, tortured him, built up impossible pressure, hysterically, bit by bit. *Gonzesse hystérique.* It takes two, as they say.

Why worry anyhow? This slow dance of things, objects parading, fusing in the milkness. She is surprised to find this doped irresponsibility. And no one around. Let the crumbs and smelly cheese wait.

Sébastien's anger-dark face, the inhuman growl coming from him, the terrible hands rattling her skeleton, teeth and skull in its rag-doll pulp, was that her creation then?

Her scenarios: *Sirène la reine des cires,* polish, *peau lisse,* a stretching of the gossamer skin over everything, the infinite graft . . . But these metastases multiplying under the surface, this hatred. It can no longer be contained.

Gérard was right. The cat was right. Better risk offence than fence it in . . . Her images, the clouds she would contain in their neat frames, the multiple nimbus of Thérèse's face, the pockets of thermal disturbance what about those then? What kind of giddy piloting will it need?

Cumulo-nimbus Zora Céleste . . .

It's time she brought them out, into the light.

CÉLESTE

The paint is blistered along the wood-grain; curling flakes
like a security under the finger-tips, alive and vivid under
the palm. Will I go back there with the intercom open-
sesame to the electro-magnetic doors, the glossy acreage
of vinyl tiles, the plants, oh the plants casting their
studied shadows on the walls, quietly textured and all
discreetly beige. I can give the practised shoulder thrust to
the great bulk of this door. It does not give way. He
completes my efforts with an extra lunge, shouldering me
away. Careful Pascal. He also makes an accurate stab at
the push-in button of the light. Something shuffling
there, in the gloom. Slumped shape shifting under the
stairs. Circling slow, enslaved to its axis, as if . . . That
face emerging from the blur. Waxen. The little woman
from our floor, Céleste. The light streaming from the
eyes, precision of the nose, strange clarity of the brow and
the slightly cleft chin. Her hair has an independent cloud
life tonight; is it chestnut, is it grey?
    Alone and palely

MIAOWOWOW

                         plaintive, prolonged.
It must have issued from her. She seems to have
forgotten what she was searching for. Pascal is searching

255

too, as if to interrogate the loosened tiles for traces of the lost object. But no; his hand encounters her arched back. He gives it a cursory pat.

Monsieur, I am not a cat.

The musical protest frustrates his gesture at hip level. His hand is rather stupidly suspended there. Ah, but Pascal is in form tonight. He flourishes a metaphorical hat:

Can we help you at all, Madame? You seem to have lost something?

Madame, you are amusing, Monsieur. You know me: Céleste. Céleste de Filou-le-Pin. *En tout cas, c'est Mademoiselle.* And anyhow, it is too late: we have all forgotten what we are searching for. What is the sense in my maintaining this vigil?

The grey eyes set on me and well with tears: And you are so young . . .

She is traversed again by that strange miaow. Like the weak siren wail recalled when news of the calamity is already out.

But . . . err . . . Céleste, you are hardly old yourself . . . Pascal is back to cultivating *courtoisie* again. The choreographed routine will now unfold. You have misjudged the moment this time.

Eh bien, Céleste, what can I do for you?

Go on, Pascal, do an Anatole on her, launch her on a therapeutic monologue, but try at least for some of his finesse. Be careful to structure it with your questions. Questions only, or else there will be a shift of power.

I do not know you so well, Monsieur Pascal. I know your friend. I have seen her many times.

Look, we're in a bit of a rush at the moment. A friend waiting to take us off to dinner . . .

Ah, les enfants, allez. Allez manger. Eat, eat and forget me.

You know Pascal, I'd really rather not come anyhow. Don't think I can cope with the sort of frivolity that will be *de rigueur* tonight. Pâté, cheese, Chivas and repartee . . . Don't feel up to it at all.

Ah, non. Non ma chérie. It's quite unthinkable that you

do not come. Nuncle Totole has arranged the whole thing for us.

Yes. For . . .

Well if you don't find it worth celebrating . . . Or is it . . .?

He whispers, points to Céleste. His eyes widen, the lids flicker. He flashes a beggar's smile.

If it upsets you . . . I mean, leaving her alone like this . . . Perhaps we could bring her along. Why not? Come to think of it, give Anatole something to distract him. Pretty depressed these days.

Nnn-o. No, Pascal, that would seem like pure chari . . .

It's too late. He is already over there, crouching next to the sob-shaken body on the first step. Dispense your bounty. Be Anatole's apprentice. Trophy her, your first find. A bit of vaudeville, Boulevard Prado tonight. Anatole will be biting his nails by now.

The street is blocked with the rush-hour crawl. The logic of Marseille. The immobile procession is unanimously leaning on its horns. In protest at the nail-biter who is, in fact, blocking the traffic with his Citroën D.S. Alone in his slinky Goddess, the diminutive, balding nail-biter.

Anatole my strange brother, it seems I will be eating your *pâté de canard aux truffes* once again, tonight.

Pascal is gesturing for me to come away from the door. It seems he wants to get Céleste up the ten flights of stairs to the fifth landing. It is an operation that will take a lot of skill. The dosage of light from the meter-controlled switch is calculated to give out before even the most conscientious climber can reach the maids' rooms at the final landing. Céleste takes my elbow. Her hand is as crushable as a tremulous bird dropped from the nest. And yet, now he's literally hauling her up. His savage bursts of adrenalin.

Céleste wants to collect a few things . . . and give herself a cat-wash, he laughs. You stay with her, will you, while I grab a change of clothes and a shave?

So much for my wash-and-brush-up then.

You look perfect as it is, he laughs as our apartment door closes behind him.

C'est la chambre Céleste, she chuckles as she reveals her little room. The door bumps against a stretcher-bed piled high with linen, folded to perfection as if by a professional laundress. The shelves at the foot of the bed are stacked with canned food, arranged in little columns, equidistant from each other.

One must have one's stores, you never know . . . Céleste pats the small clearing beside her on the bed.

I am intruding, there is so little space. But the hand insistently pats the bed next to her tiny lap. She is laughing gaily now. I must accept. She reaches to the basin, at arm's length from the bed (a cripple could manage in such a cupboard) and opens the powder compact. She dabs her cheeks where the rivulets of a moment ago have eroded the mask, unhooks a basket from the back of the door.

Just a few artefacts! She chants the inventory as each object falls into the little Red Riding Hood basket:

* Two candles, Mademoiselle, in case of power failure, one never knows these days.
* A collective portrait of my mother and my seven sisters, two of whom — *les pauvres* — were left out by that careless photographer.
* Some sachets of linden tea.
* Some fennel, rosemary and garlic, because these are always appreciated, *n'est-ce pas?*
* My rosary beads . . . Ah my dear little seeds that split and germinate under my fingers!

She tries on a beige shawl, a burgundy shawl, four silk scarves, a little beaded cardigan, abandons them all . . . I'll come JUST as I am, don't you think, because that is how I was invited. She pats her stomach into place (does she imagine it bulges?) and recites in the same liturgical chant:

Classical black jersey:
Optionally belted and
Correct or unbelted and free;
So suitable for all those occasions
When in doubt.

Do NOT dry-clean,
Hand-wash only and do not wring,
Dry out of direct sunlight

I will come just as I am, *n'est-ce pas,* as I am, as I am.
Footwear? . . .
    She crouches at the bedside, out slides a little shoe-rack
from which she selects:

Jiffies shot with silver thread,
And each is crowned with a pleated flower
In the same, in the very same jiffie weave . . .

Ce sont mes chaussures de fée, she whispers
conspiratorially and the tripping of the slippered feet on
the floor has us both laughing. But now Céleste is
unpacking the artefacts, the candles are lit to the family
portrait and she is plying her way tearfully through a
rosary. The little door quakes: You ready you two?

Pascal is resplendent. Hair gleaming blue-black, brushed
in a perfectly sculpted swoop away from the jaw. He has
squandered *Eau Sauvage* all over himself.
    Well, are you two coming or . . .?
    He extinguishes the scene with two exact puffs at the
candles.
    All the same, enough is enough, he mutters between
his teeth at me.
    But Pascal, *enfin* . . . As if it were my idea anyway . . .
But he is chaperoning her down the stairs without
waiting to hear any protests from me.
    Close the door on the miniature altar with the smoking
candles, the basket still rocking on the floor. There is one
tiny square window high in the wall facing the stairwell:
the sole source of light.

The profile of the Goddess is quite isolated now. Anatole
must have yielded to the pressure of the horns: he has
reparked it on the footpath.
    Anatole . . . (Pascal breaks away from Céleste and me.)
Allow me to introduce to you Mademoiselle de . . . Filou-
le-Pin . . . or is it Minou-le-Fin? (he is trying to elicit a
laugh from me) . . . er . . . Céleste, whom I have taken the

liberty of inviting along to our little celebration tonight.

There is a quick exchange of what seem to be highly irritable whispers. It culminates in an *Enchanté, Madame,* left uncorrected this time by Céleste, which Anatole begins over his shoulder, completes with a swivel of the heels and punctuates with a military click bringing him face to face with her. Not exactly informal either, the mechanical *bisou* administered to my cheeks. He rotates once more on his heels to open the back door to her. Anatole's exaggerated *panache* when he is annoyed.

He gives a flurried gesture that I should climb in beside Céleste and the car lunges, nudges its way over the curb, around the corner of the Rue Jean Roque, takes off up the Cours Lieutaud.

Céleste is laughing: But Monsieur, we are afloat, this is no car.

We can glimpse the amber eyes with their very slight spaniel droop every two or three seconds in the rear-vision mirror. Céleste grips the head-rest of his seat to secure the audience: You buoy us along in the palm of your hand, ha ha haha *n'est-ce pas Monsieur?* No no . . . it's no use denying it, you are a leader, *un chef, Monsieur, et attention,* I have an instinct for these things, the nose for them, as they say. You give me a crowd, I can smell the leader out.

She ignores his silence. Perhaps she can detect a glint in his eye that acquiesces to the definition; she resumes. The tone is heightened now:

Monsieur le Colonel, you are of the pedigree, that goes without saying, *vous êtes de la race des chefs.*

He clears his throat, raises an eyebrow, sends ripples from its apex up his forehead, deftly negotiates a lane change in top speed, breaks at the lights and we rock gently on the fluid suspension.

Non, non Monsieur, you are too modest, you must not protest, take it from the daughter of a Resistance fighter . . . (she executes a summary cross on her chest; the eyes well with tears) who was, believe me, a leader of men, gunned down . . . But . . .I am alert to the presence of the invader, don't you worry, I note the signs . . .

Of course . . . It was Céleste, that night on the stairs, in
bikinis, underneath the umbrella, singing along to the
strains of the *Marseillaise* from the pocket transistor,
tapping out the beat with the jiffies. Moonlight streaming
in from the skylight above. Daughter of a Resistance
fighter and still fighting, in all weathers.

Monsieur le Colonel, I do not know why you should show
such kindness as to invite a poor old woman like me
along . . .
    Anatole throws a fierce glance in Pascal's direction.
Pascal whispers too audibly: Come on Anatole, stop being
so bloody rigid.
    He leans back, gives us a reassuring grin: Anatole
doesn't like being kept waiting, that's all.
    Like all leaders, like all leaders, she adds.
    And what, my dear Céleste, tells you that I am a leader?
    It seems Anatole might be being drawn in all the same
. . .
    Ahhh, little things . . . How should I say? You do not
waste . . . yourself. You move sharp . . . precise. Your
silence too, Monsieur, I have seen it before, don't you
worry, that kind of silence . . . Tell me, can I give you a
little song perhaps, while we are still in transit ha ha
hahaha?
    Well, why not, Anatole says . . . Why not a song for the
Colonel?
    The voice filling the car is frayed, throaty, but beautiful
all the same:

> *J'ai dansé avec l'amour*
> *J'ai fait des tours et des tours . . .*
> *Lui et moi contre lui*
> *Pendant toute la nuit*
> *La . . . la dada da . . . da*

For how long has she been singing? Glitter and flash of
cars fusing in their circuit around the Place Castellane.
Anatole, thoroughbred driver, slips us into the luxury
sheath of night, as glibly as a tapered hand into a glove:

261

he's taking the *contre-allée* now. For residents. We are
siphoned towards the inevitable address. A *pipeuse* there.
She breaks her pose from the niche of the wall, the
variegated shadows lift, the face is nude, quivers in the
headlights. The siphoness. The heavy jowls negotiating
now from the Renault 18. *La pipeuse te fera chanter,*
quips Pascal. She services the bourgeois family man from
around here with discreet dispatch; in five minutes' time
he will tuck into his entrée with the most fluent ease,
take his napkin from the habitual place and between
napkin dabs and mouthfuls, benignly elicit a résumé of
the day's doings from, say, Jacques and Marie-Laure across
the table.

Anatole's residence at last. The concrete catacombs where
they park their cars. Now the lift bearing us silently
upwards.
    But of course, you are a *resident de grand standing . . .
C'est un monsieur très distingué . . .* she sings as we are
brought to the level. The Master unfurls another display
of virtuoso gestures. The supermarket, *charcuterie* and
fromagerie bags nestle under the armpit, closely moulded
by the silk sleeve, the door unlocks, the anti-intruder
chain unhooks, the aluminium tubes, flush with the wall,
cross their cones of light, catch the surface incidents of
the glamour blacks: the matt and the gloss black
panelling.
    Mais . . . c'est tapisse de ténèbres chez vous, Monsieur,
hung with night . . .
    The tone is coquettish now, cajoling even. You ARE an
o-rrr-i-gi-nal, Monsieur, I know, you are keeping us in the
dark! To what crystal kingdom, *à quelle royaume de
cristal* is he going to lead us?
    Her warm breath lifts the hair from my ear. It is
almost fear now in her eyes.

Retrenched from the first plane are the sliding doors,
only marked out by the denser shadows cast from the
architraves. The one on the right glides in obedience to
the index finger he inserts there. A blast of light, a wave
of electronic guitar music breaks over us. Pascal takes

refuge under the noise, says half to her, half to me: Don't
let it worry you too much, Céleste, it's just a stage effect,
pinched from an American actually, what's his name
again, Rachel . . . No don't tell me, Reinhart, that's it, Ad
Reinhart's the name. You see, if he keeps you waiting
long enough, you will find your just reward. Gradually,
there will be light: the colours will begin to emerge from
the black, it will yield its hidden primaries, eh? It's your
fantasy waiting room, *n'est-ce pas* Totole?

Ah bon? Monsieur has aspirations then? Céleste
assuming now wide-eyed innocence.

Aspirations. The strays who gravitate into your circuit
Anatole, and yet you tremble at the nucleus.

Nah, he says. Leave aspirations for the neurotics; I am
happy to exert the occasional influence . . . horizontally.
(The Master and the Disciple share a laugh.)

But no, that is wrong anyhow. I have seen waiting
rooms, *Monsieur le Colonel.* I have sat in their waiting
rooms under their neon strips; I know their waiting
rooms and their ante-chambers. And their two-way
mirrors. I've seen myself doubled in their two-way
mirrors. Ha. I can tell you, this is no waiting room.

But my dear Céleste, you are not with them now. You
are with friends . . .

Machine-gunned me they did ratatatata with their
questions. Just as they did to my father. Sixteen. I was
sixteen and they dragged me in just to watch them line
him up. Ratatata. Because he hid a family from them.
And that's what he got for it: RATATATATA . . .
Anatole wipes a spray of saliva from his face.

Allez, Céleste, *vaut mieux n'pas penser à tout ça,* better
not think of the bad times . . . Come.

Anatole attempts to guide her by the shoulder but she
dodges sharply away at his repeated *venez.* As if averting
a stream of bullets. He is calm at the moment though,
ushering us into the lounge room while transferring his
armful of packages to Pascal: You will be good enough,
my dear boy, to set out the *hors d'oeuvres* for us?

Oh the crystal platter? *Oui, certainement, mon Colonel.*

Pascal is doing his bit to establish frivolity as the mood
for the evening.

It is a celebration, therefore one must celebrate.

Ah, mais comme c'est beau chez vous, Monsieur!
Céleste's hand makes a swooping gesture taking in all the
shunting planes of light as the door opens: the sliding
glass onto the balcony, the glass table on its tubular steel
stalk, the Rachel Deschamps *Self-Portrait with
Pomegranate* with its triple mirrors multiplying
reflections, the glass doors of the wall-to-wall
bookshelves and their reflected reflections. But we are *not*
misled, she exclaims, this *is* a palace of light. She laughs
in a pure easy mirth this time, a musical gurgle.

Torso tilted forward, Anatole steers Céleste around the
massive bulk of the armchairs. He keeps her at arm's
length ahead of him. But then, he always adopts a
distance opening a letter or a can of asparagus. I am to
take the place next to Céleste in the nest of cushions on
the sofa.

So he has company already then. They are set in the
shafts of light from the chrome plated spheres in here.
They have the mock permanence of polychrome polyvinyl
resin sculptures draped, as if for a joke, just to introduce a
little kitsch into the decor. Simply draped there, for want
of something better, in their identical beige velvet bean-
bags. Anatole makes a rousing gesture that the polyvinyl
figures should break their poses and recognize our
presence. There is a barely perceptible movement of the
two torsos towards us, a relaxation of the grip of the two
right hands on the Orefors glasses. Anatole glances
eloquently from the glasses to the Chivas Regal bottle
nestling in the spaghetti loops of the woolshag carpet:
Hrrrhmmmmmm. Dany, since you are proving such an
enthusiastic barman, perhaps you might care to fix a
drink for *mesdames.*

But they drink to his amber eyes, Céleste hums, reabsorbs
her words. Anatole's polished skull sets in a solid pact
with the jaw. *Oiseau rapace,* Pascal has said. Bird of prey?
The light grazes the great curve of the nose ridge. He
fingers the volume knob of the stereo. The electronic *râle*
he has reduced it to accompanies him out. As he exits, he

adjusts the frame of the Estève. Céleste is brimming with
mirth again: The Colonel is a geometrician too! she
laughs. But she is studying the asymmetrically arranged
bodies in the bean-bags: one is the negative image of the
other. Silvio is liquid amber poured into the mould the
bean-bag has set beside Dany's indolent sprawled shadow.
Silvio tosses back the drape of chestnut hair: One might
say that Anatole does go in for a certain kind of err . . .
ow do you say eet, Rachel? *Topographie différentielle?*
Breathy unvoiced laughter from Dany. He uses Silvio's
thigh as a grip, it is improbably lean, it will snap; but he
leaves his ghost shape lounging in the bean bag. Then
what is it to be Ma-DAME? The bow is executed with
rococo flourish. Bad parody of Anatole. Dany is heavy:
the cannon ball buttocks push at the shiny serge of the
pants throwing them out of alignment at the pockets.
Silvio gives me an angelic smile. The wistful gaze could
be just an effect acquired to illuminate the Botticelli
moulding of the features. But it breaks the repose of the
perfect lines as if he would establish some kind of
solidarity between Céleste and me? And Silvio is uneasy
here, as usual these days. The lithe fingers pluck at the
folds in the white jeans, comb and comb the hair.

Ah, *peu importe Monsieur,* you are too kind, a pernod, a
pastis, an anisette.
   Céleste is perched on the edge of the sofa. How she
watches with those shining eyes. *Un vermouth pour toi?
Un campari?* Silvio puts it to me but follows Dany with
his eyes, stressing his neglect. *Le chef n'est pas chez lui
chez lui.* The chief is not at home in his own home, not at
all at home . . . Céleste seems unaware of the volume of
her voice. Silvio winces over his shoulder as he follows
Dany into the kitchen.

They must be holding the door open: It's already voluble
with the noise of plates and cutlery but as you focus your
attention, Anatole's voice rises above the percussion. It's
becoming falsetto, exasperated, no more clashing of
cutlery now, just the blurred bass of sullen protests from
Pascal. As if I don't have enough dealing with cases like
her at the clinic all day . . . Tonight of all nights.

Sometimes I really wonder about you, Pascal. It's not as if it's going to do that poor woman any good. Just when we were going to celebrate your reunion intimately!

Intimately. Ha ha HA. You've got to be joking with your household pets sprawled all over the place . . .

Anatole must have become aware of Dany and Silvio. Just the concentrated aggression of the cutlery now. Don't let it worry you, Pascal is just having one of his little tantrums . . . And don't forget the *pâté de grive.* Yes, and the Greek olives can go in a separate bowl . . . And then the pasta, that goes on at the last minute of course. Ah good, the basil and pine nuts for the *pesto.* Three minutes maximum for the pasta since it's fresh, *n'est-ce pas,* Pascal.

Yessir. Before the veal. *Al dente. A votre service!* Pascal adenoidally dulled, but sarcastic all the same.

It's as if Céleste has not heard a word. Her hand is on my knees: And you *ma chère* Rachel. Are you at home here? You too are so silent. You let them talk. You lean back, like a queen. Like a queen. They tip-toe around you but . . . *hein?* If you speak?

Mais, je vous assure, Céleste. I do have my say, when I want to.

But you and Monsieur Anatole. There is . . . It is Monsieur Anatole who wants you to be with that young man, no?

No, not at all. I mean he cares for both of us. He understands that I've had problems with Pascal. If we've come together again, it's because we both want it.

Ah bon, she says. There is no conviction in it. She has made up her mind.

It's Anatole again. A simple Eau Perrier for himself. Ah, Céleste. Feeling more relaxed now, are we? Daniel is attending to you, I hope? Hmmmm. I don't know if they have told you but tonight is rather special. Pascal and Rachel have settled their differences and are together again.

And you bring them together, Monsieur? Céleste's words gurgle through the pernod she has just been given. She is frankly knocking it back.

Anatole sips his water.

But not at all, Céleste, he says. These children are made for one another.

Oui oui, if you say so, Monsieur. Amen . . . *Excusez-moi* hahahaha. One little burst of laughter induces another.

Anatole leaps to his feet. He is glad to break the moment. Here come more props: the *hors d'oeuvres* arriving with a flourish on Pascal's arm.

But . . . My dear boy, you must be feeling more exuberant than . . . Hrrrhmmm. What a perfect organic rosace!

Orgiastic, I would say, says Silvio.

C'est le partouze à la parterre, says Anatole.

C'est la vie en rose . . . La la la la lalala . . . Céleste gives her hand to Dany and sweeps him off for a foxtrot. He blushes darkly, searching out Silvio's eyes to join him in mockery of Céleste. She gives up anyhow: he has trodden all over her fairy slippers.

The scrolled corollas of Corsican raw ham are the armature of the composition, radiating from the centre piece, each offering its pistil slither of gherkin; laced through these is the spiral of overlapping salami slices ending, as if in homage, at the base of the bulbous decapitated capsicum with its dark gleaming load of Greek olives, where it is joined by a circle of fetching, innocent, fluted scrolls of butter. One gherkin pistil slithers from its sheath. Céleste holds it pinched between her finger-tips. The nails are clear and pearly. Not bitten. She has it poised before her mouth: *Vous permettez, Monsieur?* It slides away without her waiting for a reply. Anatole frowns irritably at the hilarity Céleste has provoked from the bean-bags. She is right. They will get you. Differential topographer indeed.

Céleste plucks another olive from the capsicum chalice: Tell me what *is* your kingdom . . . Is it animal, vegetable or mineral, Monsieur?

Well, Pascal, he says, it seems to me that you have found yourself a worthy colleague in semiotic analysis . . . And what would you say to a slice of Corsican ham, my dear Céleste?

Du jambon corse, Monsieur? Ah les Corses . . . I can
tell you something about Corsicans. You should have seen
him then, *mon corse.* It was a picnic on the banks of the
Marne when I met him. The lads and the other girls from
the office. From the beginning those eyes on me. Black
like these olives or, yes, like those eyes of Monsieur
Pascal. Oh, I fooled around with the rest of them. I tried
to ignore him. But still those eyes bored into my back.
Pierced me, they did. He was a strangely sad man. As if
he knew already that they would win out in the end . . .
that they would drive us apart . . .

But why always *they*, Céleste. *They* are not all against
you, surely.

Oh but they were. His cousins . . . You know the family
had a nice Corsican girl picked out for him. His cousins
span stories about me . . . Until . . . but he will come back
one day, I know I am still in his heart. *Ah, Monsieur, les
réunions,* you speak of reunions, reconciliations, yes, of
course, we must drink to the duo. *Mais, hélas, les couples,*
they do not stay together so easily, *Monsieur.*

I would be the first to agree with you, my dear Céleste.
But let us drink to the future, and to the future of this
couple in particular . . . If we all lingered in the past,
there would be no hope for any of us . . .

Anatole's voice is fatigued, drags on the last words. He
is watching Dany and Dany's hand is draped around
Silvio's bean-bag.

Did I say something wrong, Monsieur? I am very sorry
if that is so . . .

Don't let it worry you, Céleste . . . Anatole likes to
share his wisdom around, *c'est vrai, hein,* Rachel? Silvio
says.

No, you go too far. It is the job of leaders, *n'est-ce pas,*
to get people talking and to stop them talking. They
fiddle with their fingers, they look away but all the time
they are using their silence. Take it from me, I have seen
some things.

Ah, but Pascal! You have forgotten the *pâté de grive!*
Rachel, I *insist* you taste that at least. From a little
charcutier, hidden away in the back streets of the *quartier.*

Quite a discovery really. And while you are at it, Pascal, could you put on some decent music and spare us from your electronic cacophony?

A little Boccerini to restore your nerves? *Mais certainment, mon cher Colonel!*

Eh, dites, barman, would you be kind enough? Céleste holds up her glass, to no one in particular. It is Anatole this time who serves her. He mutters something to Silvio on the way back with the bottle.

Céleste goes to meet him, swaying slightly, rocking on her heels.

I think you are really wrong, Silvio, Anatole says, with all due respect, to try to stir your Arab friends into strike action. You are over estimating the solidarity of our unions. Instant extradition, that's what you'll get them for your troubles . . .

But that's what they get in any case, as soon as their bodies are fucked . . .

Really Silvio, what has come over you, your language!

Come on, Anatole, you know as well as I do that Pompidou is quite content to exploit a few million slaves for less than the basic wage as long as the supply isn't exhausted. But he also knows they are doing all the shit jobs no Frenchman will do.

Silvio! *Enfin* . . . Can't we discuss something more . . . It's better we don't discuss politics. Nothing I say is likely to cure you of your romanticism anyhow. Ah, here is the *tagliatelle al pesto.* Perhaps, rather than treating us to your repertoire of expletives you might care to serve us with the pasta? This is no ordinary pasta, *n'est-ce pas,* Giovanni made it especially for us. This *is* pasta . . .

Ah . . . *Excusez-moi, Monsieur* . . . Céleste's elbow has sent her glass flying as the tagliatelle piles onto her plate. Her tongue is caught between the glistening teeth as she concentrates. All eyes focused on her as she coils the long flat pasta around her fork, draws out a continuous conveyor belt from plate to mouth, and through the glass plate and then the glass table top, refracting, grotesquely enlarging them, the beige loops of the deeply piled carpet . . . *Ah là là, quel vertige,* she laughs. It is like I am unwinding the carpet. Ahahhahah I am unravelling your world Monsieur!

Anatole is watching Silvio who has left the table. He is opening the sliding door, on the balcony now.

Ah, mais Monsieur, you have even arranged the plates in diamond formation! It *is* the kingdom of light you have brought to us!

Céleste is radiant.

Come on Céleste. I assure you that if that is a diamond you see, it is there quite by chance.

Ah oui, biensûr que c'est tout à fait aléatoire, les combinaisons du Colonel . . . *Of course* there is no strategic planning here . . .

Pascal is hoarse with sarcasm. Never has quite achieved a light touch. No real humour. Céleste ignores him anyhow:

No, you of all people Monsieur le Colonel, you would leave nothing to chance. Of course you are joking, you would leave nothing to chance . . .

Adamantine. She is right. Adam far from the original fires, fragile, suspended in a world of mirror facets. When does he receive any real warmth?

And if I have ended up in a *chambre obscure* it is not by chance either. *Ça c'est certain aussi.* Ah it is nice the play of light, *n'est-ce pas,* Monsieur, bouncing, bouncing?

Saves one's vital energies, eh Céleste, if one runs on borrowed light? Pascal's gaze swivels from Céleste to Anatole and back.

So. I understand. It's 'get Nuncle Totole' you are playing tonight. I think, *les enfants,* if you have to resort to that kind of past-time, you must be sadly lacking in resources yourselves. Anatole has not touched his *tagliatelle.*
Pascal's face is congested, dark. Céleste is watching him. Her fork is improbably loaded; if it completes its rotation, the whole pile of *tagliatelle* will be unravelled. The tears are rolling now: *Ah mon pauvre corse, lui ne pouvait faire de mal à personne.* His eyes were dark too but soft, soft. Diamonds, diamonds, ha. We had our *fiançailles* without diamonds. We were happy, happy, you can't

imagine . . .

The sobs will shake the little body asunder.

Look. Céleste, if we live in the past, what chance have we? Eh? You are not alone here. Now please. Eat up.

Dany's hand is on Silvio's shoulder, as if alighted there by chance. Céleste staring at the hand now. She is about to question Anatole, say something like: *And where do these boys live, in the future, then? Eh Monsieur le Colonel?* She lurches towards him, her foot catching in the shag of the carpet. Anatole, catches her, his torso tilted, pelvis held back to avoid the wine wobbling in her glass; deft as a matador.

Céleste, I think you need some coffee perhaps? And a good sleep? I think it is about time I drove you home, or perhaps young Daniel here, who is in such good form this evening?

But of course Monsieur, if you want. It is too kind of you to have had me here in the first place.

Come come . . . But I do think a little sleep might do the job.

I understand how you feel, Monsieur. You are a man . .

I should certainly hope so, Céleste.

. . . who is afraid.

That is . . . Céleste, I think you are definitely out of sorts this evening.

Anatole stands, rattling the car keys already.

Rachel, are you coming? Really, I am sorry but I assure you I have reached my limits of tolerance. We have to get this woman home.

I would have liked to try the veal but still . . .

Yes yes. Of course. But this is a case beyond . . . *Ma pauvre p'tite Rachel,* we'll celebrate some other time.

Celebrate!

Anatole clicks his tongue, draws my face towards his.

I AM sorry . . . But at least you two are happy, *n'est-ce pas?* You and Pascal.

It is a request, a supplication rather than a question. He wants no answer.

Allez, en route alors, Madame.

He gives Céleste his arm. He will finish with panache.

Lui et moi contre lui pendant toute la nuit la la lala la la . . .

Oui oui Céleste, the good old songs.

We have somehow been organized into the back seat of the car again. Her voice has altered. Business-like. Precise delivery. Low:

Of course he is a psychiatrist. I have not been through it all for nothing. They all usher you out, oh so politely, when the time is up, when their time is up.

One last display of gallantry up the steps. But Céleste keeps sitting down:

But Monsieur, you are in a hurry to pack me away, she jokes.

Not at all, my dear Céleste, not at all. But it is getting late.

But sit down for just a moment. You are out of breath, Monsieur. Let's talk things over a little . . .

Céleste be reasonable, please. This is really quite impossible.

He turns to me; the whisper is a stream of hissing sibilants: Why on earth can't you and Pascal find another place to live . . . This is a ruddy rabbit warren . . . My *dear* Céleste, come on now. A little courage. We must get you to your apartment.

To my cell, Monsieur, to my cell! She plucks a key from the niche in the wall where the plaster has crumbled and the door gives way.

My God!

It escapes through his teeth as Céleste turns on the light.

Good night, Céleste!

He has put the cat back in the bag.

And you, my dear Rachel? Are you coming back with me so that we might salvage something from this abortive 'celebration'?

Anatole . . . I am exhausted myself I . . . I just don't feel up to it. No, I'm sorry.

Pascal will feel so let down. But . . . if you must. Here . . . For Christ's sake buy her some decent blankets . . .

It is a cheque. The perfect calligraphy flows.

No no Anatole. You can't do that. Besides, she is so proud.

Proud, really Rachel.

The Colonel trips lightly down the stairs.

Yet still there was this gagged self she wrote, call it Rachel as she may. Still this partition willed between herself and Céleste. She has returned them to their respective spaces, their silences. Rita/Thérèse, Rachel/Céleste. Take her imagery for a walk in real life. Ha.

But it did that in a way, by default?

She must have known that Sébastien might find the excuse of a forgotten file to return. That he had a key to use in her absence.

The Colonel tripped lightly down the stairs, his signature left on a cheque. The semiotician also left his post-script, scrawled on the last page of her little story:

> *Thank you Rita, now I know.*
> *The sign-posts are flagrant enough.*
> *You're not very good at covering your traces.*
> *In narrative at least.*
> *Pascal-Sébastien*
> *Silvio-your precious Gérard, I suppose . . .*
>
> *Adieu, Rita. Or should I say Rachel?*

At the Marigny airport, Raymond swivels his bar-stool towards her, takes her hand: Rita, you know I'd help you through financially with the baby, if in fact you are . . . even Sébastien might change, too . . . He has been under a lot of pressure lately with the thesis. And I think he's learnt that you must have your own space . . .

There he is, depressively slumped between Denise and Antonine. Denise is laughing, attempting to distract him. Perhaps she and he will get together? No, she wouldn't wish that on her.

No, Raymond. After that night, I would always be afraid. I'm sorry, I can't go back there.

And there they are, shrunken to doll-size now as she escalates down to the tarmac. These new lines of flight opened up by the mobile stairs, warping through the blur.

Rachel drags me back: she wants another look. It must be the way that kelpie is twisting on a flea. Below the window of the delicatessen. Behind the greased up window slowly, a rotisserie turns a shrunken chicken. Something in that conjunction holds me too.

There is a remote terror in it, hard to say. Whose bag of images is it?

Whose shoes once fitted in that box? The red-cloud kelpie. *Zozo, kelpie, good sheep-dog,* I said that day to Arlie. I turned to that against my father's photos, then shuffled it away. I must go back there to that farm, where was it? where Monica first took us, testing something to do with salt. Where Elsie and I went later for a holiday. *You were bitten alive by mosquitoes under those peppermints.* Those words didn't unlock it. Turning, turning red rotisserie, little carcass on its impaling axis. Why does it hurt so much, that together with the face of the dog, the intense querying of its yellow eyes, one ear cocked, the head on a slant.

Why can't we have a dog, Mummy?

Oh, I say, it'd be cruel in a flat.

Keys turn in locks. There is the accident and suddenly with the same violence of dog-to-Dodge-bumper, the images begin to bump, red, the Dodge was red, the sounds, cicadas and the squealing of the twenty-eight parrots, Cedric's ears suddenly aglow also and then the dark-room where the gagging must have happened at the same time as all the images. Like tongue tongue curled back in its mute terror dome and then the terror in the acquiescence to other people's words, anyone else's but mine forming in the space of my mouth where he had been. The thicket in the *Triptych,* tried to say it there, but still didn't know. Expression of the gagging gagged itself. *Triptych* never shown outside.

Finally I'll have to show it, the origin that they seem to want anyhow. My Australian story. Give it back to them, give the ventriloquist's doll on daddylap her own voice at last. Say it in English.

Really? Narrative sculptures, well you could have fooled me! they say. I will tell it this time, let Rachel see I didn't turn artist to remain mute, multiplying frames from the terror of the gaps.

If the other voices take over, let me at least have a brief disruptive tenancy in them . . .

RAMSHACKLE
Some notes on an instance of auto-iconoclasm

Sarah Doogue reviews Rita Finnerty's happening currently at Woolshed 33.

After the show, the dog did not turn in my *mental rotisserie* nor, let me warn those seduced by the rumours, was any retrospective light cast on a hitherto elusive message in Rita Finnerty's art.

I recall earlier reviews, with their pertinent warnings:

> The best of these canvasses achieve an interesting calligraphic play between knotted impasto clusters and areas of tenuous stain. (Where the line risks becoming confidently cursive, it is denied, broken and scattered; where the surface is most beguilingly sumptuous, it is cancelled as mirage, or its status devalued by the blind, unpainted periphery defining it.) They would indeed seem to plot the failure of the Eurocentric gaze to find any comforting resonance in the Australian landscape. But that this failure should be allegorically disguised as Isis in search of her scattered Osiris seems to be an unnecessary literary loading. If Rita Finnerty disentangles herself from the clutter of a fatigued mythological corpus, her work might well yet attain the wry, cryptic elegance it flirts with.
>
> Nancy Pickett on ISIS[1]

1. *Sign and Sight,* Vol. IX. No I., pp 73-4

This use of heterogeneous materials is hardly novel . . .
Surely we have moved on since Kurt Schwitters'
innovations in Merz . . . Lace, chicken wire, rather nasty
drippings of plastic paint are the 'grids' here. These
superimposures (or impostures) of grid upon grid articulate
nothing but a spiritual void paraded here as international-
ism. Finnerty appears to be locked into a '50's brand of
nostalgia for dada.

Ralph Hoffman on GRIDS[1]

In this series of 'inflatables', we are apparently meant to be
mesmerized by the slowness, the silence, the systole and
diastole of these strange soft vinyl sculptures with their
corollas and vegetable hearts. (. . .) There is an all too
fashionable nihilism behind the surface excesses of this
baroque.

Nancy Pickett on INFLATABLES[2]

Need one continue . . . The negative turn of this artistic
itinerary became evident to most with the exhibition
entitled VICE VERSA in which the artist explored
antithesis apparently for its own sake: this play on the
flip-side, the wild-side, the double, corruption underpinning
virtue, squalor erupting in glamour, metastases multiplying
in health etc, etc, was clearly a turning point to which the
current RAMSHACKLE refers. The manifesto clarified the
pseudo-dialectical intent here, in case one missed the point
of the all too flagrant images. To give some idea: *Be Needle
and Loop of the Pilot's Career* was offered as 'explanatory
note' on the 'sculpture' entitled *Sky Surgeon after
Nietzsche.*

This was a double-sided, free-standing canvas of huge
dimensions (6x5m) uniformly stained silver-blue. A
monstrous tubular steel needle 'sutured' the sky space and
inter-face, looping the 'thread' of steel piping in and out, the
parabolas thus described being complicated by the shadow-
play from indirect lighting. Here, it must be conceded, there
was an austerity of conception, if mystified by the
pretentious title, and certainly an admirable degree of
professionalism in craftmanship.

1. *Artfacts,* Vol. II. No 3, pp 61-2.
2. *Interface* Vol VII, nos 2-3, Special Issue on Feminist Art, pp 7-9.

Another notable exhibit was *Penthouse Nymph meets Basement Hag*. The left and centre panels presented a centrefold nude laid out before a 180° city-and-harbour view while the right panel was dominated by the huge convex mirror she held. This was like a detail of a Francis Bacon (to whose influence we shall return) erupting like a hideous melanoma on the sumptuous skin of a Lavender Bay Brett Whitely. In the space of the mirror, the giottoesque hues (notably ochres, blues) and the arabesques of bay, cushion, breast and belly were broken down and contorted as if sucked by a vortex. The oblivious confidence of the pin-up cliché was converted to the rictus of geriatric oblivion. Although blatant in its borrowings (extending back to the mediaeval allegory Young Girl and Death) this was undeniably a powerful piece.

Pilot's Widow's Window was a virtually three-dimensional work, consisting of a canvas curtain painted with a Magritte-style sky: a monotony of woolly white clouds. But they were mocked by a plethora of falling heads, torsos, legs, arms, feet, repeated in serial fashion, as if some doll factory in the sky were emptying itself of its sub-assemblies. Apparently caught in an eternal draught, the folds of the curtains were snatched to one side, revealing the space of another sky: this one was cloudless, an invariant azure blossoming parachutes and their pendant figurines. Here again, the motif was serialized, as if applied by the monotonous stamp of obsession.

The worst joke though was perhaps the *Self-Portrait-as-Shish kebab*. A chromium plated skewer-pen of outlandish proportions (some two metres long, I recall) was slowly rotating its meat and vegetable load by virtue of a discreet motor. Each item, from the still 'innocent' (R.F.'s term) if already singed onion, to the more aging, heat-withered meats, bore the artist's features in varying degrees of time-warp and, as she amiably informed me, critic-mediated distortion.

RAMSHACKLE, then, ostensibly mounted by the artist's friends, according to instructions 'left behind'[1], gives

---

1. One suspects that the alleged 'disappearance' of R.F. last year is yet

further insights into the mechanisms of a pathological imagination trapped in its own ironies and, perhaps by default, into the relation of aesthetics and ethics.

The first assault on the retina — and, I warn, an enduring one — was the word RAMSHACKLE itself: etched in dry-point (frame after frame of these evidently self-titled 'concrete poems'), RAMSHACKLE travelling like the World News at Picadilly Circus on a dozen computer terminals, RAMSHACKLE slumped in cushioned letters at the base of the far wall of the foyer, as if from the machine-guns of a summary execution. One is induced by the diffuse drone of machine-gunning and certainly by the monotony of repetition, to investigate what appears to be a series of cordoned pits on the left. (The mind boggles at the cost involved in such installations, this one partly subsidized by taxpayers' money having attracted a grant from the Visual Arts Board.) In each pit there is a typist, this one in miner's dress, the next in aviator's[1], typing over and over again the same message: RAMSHACKLE UNDERWRITES THE DETOURS R.F. HAS TAKEN RAMSHACKLE UNDER-WRITES THE DETOURS YOU HAVE TAKEN ... The base of each 'typist's pit' is strewn with reams bearing the same inscription. There is perhaps some relief from what has been aptly called the 'aesthetics of boredom' afforded by the aperture (it is hardly a door) at the far end of the foyer ... As one insinuates oneself between the softly ballooning 'architraves' of this orifice, a concealed electronic device triggers off a languid voice: RAMSHACKLE *is your running exposure.* One would run indeed, and in the other direction, were it not for a crowd, seduced presumably by Rita Finnerty's reputation as *artiste maudite,* subsequent to her alleged 'censorship' by Austrikon. I realize at this juncture that I have entered the fantasized interior of one of her earlier 'inflatables'. From one or more of the wagging protusions of this hyperbolic anemone in which I am, comes

another performance and that she may well have re-emerged elsewhere as the lyrical abstract expressionist ...

1. Reference to the VICE-VERSA MANIFESTO: 'Be miner, be flyer'? Unfortunately, narcissism isn't limited to this kind of self-reference ...

another voice, apparently meant to be hypnotic: *labio labio dental I am the sea flower that eats and wags that eats and wags . . .*

From yet another hidden speaker comes the following proliferation of slogans rendered in hybrid style somewhere between Oz racing commentary and liturgical chant:

I am the word re-embodied new locus of your logos I hiss the sibilants of all gagged sibyls I am the implosion of your plosives I am the introplasm you expectorate I hum the nasals out of numbness I am the lapsus of your relapses the an-enemy your mental kitchen fears I am the sea-dog that tracks the steps you take to avoid me I am (here the 'singer's' voice breaks into another octave, evidently jubilant) *your hidden itinerary I am the something you chased from your null and void . . .*

Now there is barking, fluctuating at the will of the wind, it seems, coming closer now all the same — one must concede that the quadraphonic tracking is effective — a whining and scraping of claws (?) on wood. Against this background, a voice has imperceptibly taken relief:

In the next gallery, you will see before you a rectangular perspex prism whose emptiness you will supply with the image of a dog, according to instructions. You will notice that there is a choice: you will be asked to rotate which image you supply through your mental rotisserie: If it is a mere skeleton of a canine you choose to rattle abstractly around the spit, ask yourself why . . .

The 'voice' accompanying our exit from the labyrinthine anemone-scape is revealed as a choral composite, ill-synthesized at that, of male, female and a lagging falsetto echo . . . But here we are already at the promised destination. The gallery has an awesome 'dream-kitchen gloss' (to quote R.F. once more) on all the surfaces. In the centre is the rectangular perspex prism all right, and of the hyperbolic dimensions one has come to expect, surrounded by fifty odd relaxachairs (foot and head-rest), all in ivory vinyl mock-hide. As we dutifully install ourselves (some twittering), the lights grow dim, abating to a diffuse infra-red glow. Yet another voice, this time blandly soporific, female, reminiscent of the airport announcer's:

Before the dog rotates in your mental rotisserie, you are relaxing. You may supply one or more of the following . . . Remember, the choice is yours . . .

I watch the tubular steel spit, watch the handle which appears to be quite functional. I feel satisfied that I can manage it. That the perspex prism remain empty. That I can keep it clean.

This is the dog's moment before the Dodge Ute flung her through the air. As the handle turns, you will become aware of the farm boy's heat. Don't be disturbed: we can give him names later. You might care to note how the lip of the muzzle shrugs as the head is twisted to the rump, watch the scissoring of the incisors at the flea they cannot catch

(I, for one, refer to this as image of perpetuated frustration or eternalized desire, the circular pursuit of satyr after nymph around that Grecian Urn . . .)
The spit is effectively turning now, although for some reason the handle-grip remains at the same angle relative to the horizontal. It is a dingo-cross, a bitch, a bit of kelpie, bit of blue-heeler in her. As she is turned, and as she turns on the flea, shifting negative spaces are revealed. Her little legs are pathetically attendant upon her involvement with the flea: the right front one, in particular, sticks stiffly out. Here again, I have to note the derivative nature of most of Rita Finnerty's productions. In this case, Francis Bacon's *Study of a Dog* springs readily to mind. It is not unlikely either that the artist has seized upon an expression coined by this critic to sum up her earlier and happier work: an exploration of the relation between the rebel organic and the geometric ideal. I grow uncomfortably aware of the heat in here, of the clammy contact of the vinyl mock-hide.
One imagines a slouching travesty of a curtsey to accompany the introductory words, rattled off carelessly by the artist herself:

Auto-iconoclasm is the only form of narcissism worth dying for! Take RAMSHACKLE *for instance. You don't need to have read Freud to see the* Schadenfreude *in that. You might remember when I was working on the horn series, the series referred to by some as my 'vorticist' period, by others as some sort of 'meditation on the Holy Grail'. I was the putative investigator of topological puzzles, my 'convolutions (I quote) espousing the principle but never attaining the reality of verticality'. Here again, there is a play, if you like, upon your need to immunize yourselves against random conjunctions with that nifty serum called logic. Okay. So this is a random construct. In a woolshed, of all things. Some amongst you might well have seen ram-shackled in it: the female by the male, the male impeded by his own phallocracy, compressed into a black hole of gravity by the sheer force of phallocentricity. The shackle might be the bind to meaning you say I assault at every turn. Might be my own nasty 'Version of the Pastoral': 'at last', you might say, 'Rita Finnerty speaks to Australia of something Australian': ozified again. You might think that in the ram's horn series, there was a hint of this return from 'luxurious exile'. Might be a petty revenge on the Austrikon indictment against my un-Australian practice, a reply to 'oztracism' (the joke made off-the-cuff in an interview at the time long since stored up my sleeve).*

Listen, all of you, you have come for images, you are in the dark. I will give you the anecdote — up to you to farm the pictures; nibble and graze as you like.

Somewhere above the perspex dog chamber, the sphere of red light contracts: perspex planes and tubular steel glow incandescent.

There is a long silence.

R.F.'s voice intrudes again: this time drugged and drugging, it fondles syllables, lingers on vowels, expels plosives, chops out dentals with a precision close to violence at times.

More precisely you are in the dark room now. It is one

of a ramshackle series of weatherboard outgrowths staggered around the brick kernel. At the moment, its darkness offers a cool retreat from the lit world. It will grow hotter in here though. Remember what happened to the mother of the boy you are with. While you finger the negative of the giant anemone he took last summer off Point Peron.

She had come in on some vague twinge of curiosity when a dugite had the same idea. A whopper, a six-footer — no, more — its length keeps coming, watch the slow push of its muscles to the left of the architrave where the door gapes. She clenches her heart, contains its beat, makes a lunge out of that terrible fascination. To the right of the door. She slams it, jamming the last three feet or so. The other three feet are the exact radius of the lethal sphere it makes as it arches its defence at her. For three hours she has it caught there, blocking her own escape. Then she hears the throaty drone of the Dodge: the men come in for lunch. Then she uses her voice: the mezzo that makes her son wince. It was contralto before Training.

The snake is no more a symbol than René Magritte's pipe is not a pipe. It really happened to her. Gwendolen Huebsch. And now what is her son doing as he presses up to you against the old school desk with the basins of chemicals, presses you against the enlarger, amongst the entanglement of junk that you can't understand under the mean glow of this little red bulb. Why is he breathing like that? He wanted to show you something in here he said. The Developing. The Enlarging. Will you ever tell? Anyone?

The sound track gives only this: the quick tinny TSS TSS TSS of a cicada. A distant rooster crows.

No no the rooster crows.
Listen to the mezzo voice of Cedric's mother coming from the kitchen:
Ze-hed! Riii-tah! You-hou! Lunch is ready!
In your muddled way, you wonder how they ever got a cock-a-doodle-do from that rooster's crow. Cedric's father, Ernst, says it's kikeriki.

285

Listen to the little girl's voice: No, no, Zed,
pleeease! What if you pee . . .
  Listen to Gwendolen Huebsch: Ceh-dric! Riii-tah!
  Now listen to the way the voice of the adolescent
breaks out of the grainy growl into a falsetto: Rida
Rida, come ON, it WONE hurdya, LOOK I just wanya
t'HOLD ut in yer mouth com'ON . . .

There is now a rough padding, as if on dry boards,
becoming amplified in the sound-track. Just that and the
vibration communicated along the creaking ones in here. A
little cry. Or a gasp rather. As if muffled by a hand. Now
there is Cedric's voice: an incomprehensible curse through
the teeth. The spectator, or the listener rather, is then
subjected to the amplified rewinding of the tape, this time
with the dual heart-beats: that of the child doing its
syncopated dance around the heavy, more regular thud of
the male's. Another rewinding. A further replay. This time,
it doesn't seem to be a curse at all: it is a suppliant, almost
tender cry. It could almost be: *awe Rida mmm love!* Now
there is the sound of claws scraping against the door. Now:
Rit-AH! Ced-RIC! Gwendolen Huebsch's voice is decidedly
angry this time and closer. The whine of the dog dominates
now, and you realize that it has been going on for some
time. Rita Finnerty resumes:

As you feel his heat, his urgency, notice the bulbous
crenellations of his lip, the strange little fossils in his
irises. You have admired his ears: you believed the
rosy transluscence meant he was an angel and when
you pray, you give Jesus something of Cedric's face.

There is a noise of fumbled gestures, ruffled cotton.

It is over now. (I notice at this point, that R.F.'s
commentary has taken on the neutrality you get as
signature in an A.B.C. news report.) *Listen . . . That is*
Cedric shoving the dog away from the door. (The
hoarse whisper now must be Cedric again.) *Stay there*
until I throw the pebble, right!

There is a protracted silence. Then quarrelling voices
from the distance. From the kitchen, one supposes, since

they are accompanied by the clattering of dishes, cutlery. Then it erupts, at an unbearable volume:

Geeze Mum! Carnya bloody ledme be for a minute. I was developing the shots right!
Watch your language, my boy, or you'll be right out on your ear. (This must be a ritual gesture at discipline, since the voice is kept low, sounds calm enough.) *What I'd like to know is* where *is Rita. I suppose you haven't got the faintest. And you promised to see to it that she had some company, that you'd take her around, give her a decent holiday. But it seems you can't think past yourself. All you seem to have time for is that sacred photography. She could be drowning in the dam for instance.*
Come ORF it Mum. She can look after herself. Sure as eggs she'll be angin round the fencers with that boong's dog.
Cedric! I won't have that language in my house. Now would you kindly go and find her please.

There is a shower of pebbles against wood. From the distance, Cedric's voice shouting:

Carn see er roun ere Mum, I'll take the ute okay?

Silence in the wake of grinding gears, the rumbling motor. R.F.'s voice becomes audible again:

The door opens onto a shriek of light. The broken stubble and weed is beige. It's blonder than beige. Aunty Gwen uses that: Beiger than Beige. *You see her laying it on over the delicately withered lids, into the cracks around the nose and some sticks onto the little nostril hairs. She lets you try her foundation* Beiger than Beige. *She gives you jellied tongue and tripe, your running says that now* tongue and tripe, tongue and tripe, *you are running away, away from Cedric, away from the snoring Dodge, away from the dunny, away from the shadowless peppermint tree, he took your photo there with Zozo, there is the washing line with its two wiggly wires silver, the pegs are bleached too, they make awkward little marks on the sky, only one rag hangs there, plastered permanent, must have been badly rinsed,* you will remember it that rag, the inscrutable is forever equated with your fear, *you are running through a patch of double-G's now, they look like devils, you have thought that, he is not Jesus, you can still smell his perspiration, did you open your nostrils to it, he calls Zozo the boong's dog, Ernst is pink, he is a* Lutheran *and has pale watery eyes, he calls them boongs too but not when Aunty Gwen is there, they have them come for shearing and fencing and sheep dipping and things and then they go, they say they muck up the tennis courts at Wagin, they leave tinea in the showers, trachoma in the pool at Narrogin, what does Aunty Gwen think, she has a picture of this running population, but it's called something else, she says it's a* limited edition, *she calls them* Aborigines *sometimes* Aboriginals, *the ones in the picture are different, they are thin and make jerky leaps, a little girl looks over her shoulder at you as she runs, they can run forever, Uncle Ernst told a joke once about a gin on the rocks, you heard Cedric say it to his friend Wayne and Wayne made one up about Narrowgin, Aunty Gwen is different, she says it's a shame, but she says they spend their money on grog, she wears peekaboo toes and stacked heels, she only believes in shopping at Aherns when she goes to the city she says thank goodness she never joined the Country Women's, they have meetings and cake stalls, she has funny rhymes for things your mummy never gave you:*

Codliver
Lifegiver

Molasses molasses icky gicky goo
Molasses molasses it's all over you

he thinks you will tell, it has no name, how can you tell, it has no name, you can't say he put his ... in my ... *you will run till you reach the scrub over there and get your breath back and maybe hide till night and then you will get far far away, Zozo is ahead, they might see her, you'll never catch up, she is too fast, her tongue is wobbling out, she is chasing some 28's, they do say it* twennyoit twennyoit, *they wheel in and out of the gums, Cedric shoots them with a rifle, Cedric says they are a bloody pest, Zozo is running back to you, that is the Dodge, the Dodge is coming, you can crouch here in the mallee, he is accelerating, he has seen you, there is the squeal of brakes, the dust rises and it showers you, you have heard a thud, it was a heavy thud, he has hit something, there is a hoarse screeching, mad whining, it is Zozo, he has hit Zozo, you are rushing at him now, he is standing there, and Zozo is going round and round, she is dragging her hind leg, he has grabbed his rifle from the Dodge, his face is red, his hair is bristling white on his neck, his shorts are all caught up in curved creases, you are throwing your fists on him now, you hear your voice, it is a pitch from somewhere else, your fists don't dent his back, it doesn't move, the T-shirt is plastered to it, the knobbles of his spine poke through, he pushes you away:*

> *Cud it out Rida!*
> *There is a cry, you have heard it in his voice.*
> *After, you will hear him say in the kitchen:*
> *Christ Mum, it wasn't my fault. I had to do it. I'll . . .*
> *I'll get them another one. Anyway, the boongs don't have 'pets'. They've got about ten anging roun em. They don't get bloody emotional aboud em.*
> *When will you stop using that vile language. And in Rita's presence too. Stop moping, Rita. Eat up. It's a real treat today. Or it would have been if you'd both come when I called you. See, it's crumbed brain. Cedric's favourite, isn't it Zed?*

In the gallery, there is a stunned silence, becoming fidgety after a while. Then a spotlight tracks a female figure carrying something. The figure seats itself on a small stool someone must have placed there. Gradually, as the light intensifies, you see that she is wearing a mask. It is modelled, as far as I can see, after Rita Finnerty's features. The head is topped with Finnerty's auburn afro frizz. What this woman has on her lap turns out to be a ventriloquist's doll, also bearing, distastefully caricatured, the artist's features. The voice animating the doll is however other than what I recall as Rita Finnerty's and of course, grotesquely high and nasal, coming from the doll.

With one voiced anecdote, I have spared you a whole series of exhibitions or avoidances. For that, I am sure you will be grateful. You won't have to speculate on my Variations on Plastered Rag *or my* Distortions of Dodge Bumper. *But the anecdote I have given could have been reworked in an infinity of figural postures: I ask you if you really wanted it. Should you share my prodigal doubts, I ask you to ruminate on this small parable. It dates from a time when I took another kind of retreat:* Bush Notations on the Great White Australian Nude.

> *we like the way, they said,*
> *her nudes set up, in their impasto*
> *and their stains, an ambush*
> *to easy speech, a mute discourse*
> *articulate of paradox*
> *in land not meant for pink and white*
> *but as they spoke, she hoped to flaw*
> *their ear with memories of flesh-*
> *embedded other things*
> *a metal whirr which bullet-quick*
> *would seed the field of salon sound*
> *when the dark blade of a shadow*
> *mixes images not far from here*
> *not oedipal not anecdotal*
> *(big daddy dropped from sky)*
> *but helio-blasted icono-*
> *clast come off some foreign ship*
> *her hovering craft would drop*
> *its egg of meaning*
> *then beat it to a vortex*
> *whose potent spray would mock*
> *the glaze of light on thigh*
> *and lend those nudes a gruesome diction*
> *meaning (mutant) more than those*
> *could ever mean*

through the loosening yolk
of austriconic
metafiction

The spotlight tracked the ventriloquist's retreat and then showed us the door. In this further corridor, we were affronted by one last garish gimmick: a dozen Rita Finnertys as side-show alley clowns, each slowly turning its ceramic head through a 90° arc. No ping-pong balls were available for these gaping mouths. This ventriloquized, ill-synchronized chorus of clowns was calling another game:

To find the exit, follow the lines

But in this white passage, there were no markers. Once again it seemed, one was required to plot one's own,